all that charm

LIZ TALLEY

All That Charm
Copyright ©2017 Liz Talley
ISBN-13: 978-0-9985187-1-8

All Rights Reserved
No part of this book may be reproduced or transmitted in any form by any means, including photocopying, recording, or by information storage and retrieval system, without the written permission of the author, except for the use of brief quotations in a book review.

This book is a work of fiction. Names, characters, places, and incidents are products of the author's imagination or are used fictitiously. The use of locations and products throughout this book is done so for storytelling purposes and should in no way been seen as advertisement. Trademark names are used in an editorial fashion, with no intention of infringement of the respective owner's trademark.
This e-book is licensed for your personal enjoyment. This e-book may not be resold or given away to other people. If you would like to share this book with another person, please purchase an additional copy for each recipient. If you're reading this book and did not purchase it, please purchase your own copy. Thank you for respecting the hard work of these authors.

Edited and formatted by Victory Editing.
Cover design by the Killion Group.

dedication

"*As iron sharpens iron, so one person sharpens another.*"
Proverbs 27:17

For my "Wine Posse"
who lets me bask in their fire,
with a special thanks to Wallace Rakoczy
for her help with the theatre bits.

also by Liz Talley

Morning Glory:
Charmingly Yours
Perfectly Charming
Prince Not Quite Charming

Home in Magnolia Bend:
The Sweetest September
Sweet Talking Man
Sweet Southern Nights

New Orleans Ladies:
The Spirit of Christmas
His Uptown Girl
His Brown-Eyed Girl
His Forever Girl

also by Liz Talley

Bayou Bridge:
Waters Run Deep
Under the Autumn Sky
The Road to Bayou Bridge

Oak Stand:
Vegas Two-Step
The Way to Texas
A Little Texas
A Taste of Texas
A Touch of Scarlett

Novellas:
Hotter in Atlanta
A Wrong Bed Christmas
Cowboys for Christmas

For something spicier:
Cowboy Crush

chapter one

EVERY TOWN HAS *that* family, and Morning Glory, Mississippi, was no exception. The Voorhees began their infamous run back in 1909 when Bailey "Dutch" Voorhees built the still that produced the best white lightning this side of the Mississippi River. For twenty years Dutch sold his hooch to sinners and saints alike, bribing the local deputies and running an operation that made plenty of money for the backwoods Voorhees. But then the outlaw patriarch got too fancy and lost his shirt in the stock market crash of '29. And everything went downhill for the Voorhees after that.

Which was why Eden Voorhees wanted to get the hell out of Morning Glory.

Like yesterday.

But that didn't mean she didn't have qualms about packing up her best boots and one nice sweater and moving to an apartment, sight unseen, in New Orleans.

"I'm nervous," Eden admitted to her good friend Rosemary Reynolds Genovese. Rosemary was perched on an aqua Adirondack chair on the patio of the new house she and her husband had moved into a month ago. January peeked around the corner at them, blowing a cold north wind down Eden's back like a prankster, making her shift closer to the crackling fire. Rosemary had raved about the slate patio her husband Sal had put in and had been ecstatic over the patio furniture her parents had gifted her for Christmas. Eden couldn't imagine receiving anything so expensive beneath her tree, but she didn't begrudge her friend the spectacular present. She just wished Rosemary had debuted it when it was warmer than thirty-eight degrees. Fire pits only put out so much heat.

"Don't be nervous. This is your chance to do more than community theatre, to get out of Morning Glory for a while," Rosemary said, picking up the fireplace tool and stirring around the bits of log in the flames. Above, the stars vibrated against the cold, clear sky and the large holly berry bushes lining the wooden fence lent unintentional holiday cheer to the backyard.

"I know, and I'm excited about going to college. Finally," Eden said, repressing her chattering teeth and snuggling into the down depths of her secondhand coat. The new scarf her friend Jess had given her for Christmas was cashmere and mocked the worn material she burrowed into. "But I feel guilty about leaving Mama. She's not the easiest of people to deal with, and I'm used to her."

"You're not abandoning her. Your sister's taking your place."

"Still, Sunny just lost her husband. Maybe the timing isn't right." *And what if I'm not smart enough? Or talented enough? What if I can't hack it in the real world?* But Eden didn't want to admit to those fears even though they slithered back and forth in her gut, turning her stomach into a Tilt-A-Whirl platform.

Rosemary made a sympathetic noise. "What happened to Sunny is sad, but you've taken care of your mother for a long time. It's your turn to have a life, Eden. Besides, where else would Sunny go besides here?"

Anywhere else.

Eden started to say exactly that but held back. Rosemary loved Morning Glory. Not to mention her husband Sal had moved here from Brooklyn so he could live the small-town life.

They were still caught up in a rosy newlywed haze and thought everything about the small town sitting forty miles east of Jackson, Mississippi, grand. Except the heat. No one really appreciated the viscous heat of the Deep South.

But that wasn't a problem in the last days of December.

Eden shrugged. "I don't know. The funeral was just last month. Things have been so hard for my sister and I feel . . . selfish." And petrified of failing.

"Are you joking? You're the least selfish person I know." Rosemary tossed another log on the fire and gave Eden a stern look. "You gave up everything to do the right thing, and it stranded you here. You're not being a bad daughter or sister merely because you're claiming a life for yourself. Sunny would tell you that."

Eden nodded and swallowed the sudden burning in her throat. She didn't know why she felt so wishy-washy . . . so terrified about changing her life. Maybe it was the time of year. With New Year's Eve a few days away, people started evaluating, thinking about regrets and forming plans to change their futures. For the past eleven years, Eden hadn't had to worry about goals. Her life was about existing. But last spring everything had changed.

For one thing, she'd lost Lacy Guthrie.

From the beginning of junior high, Eden, Rosemary, Jess, and Lacy had been the best of friends. They'd weathered breakups, deaths, getting boobs, and cutting bangs for prom. They'd laughed, fretted, danced, and cried their way through high school. And though they'd all taken different paths, the four girls had remained ever dear to one another. But then Lacy got cancer for a second time.

And she died.

Shortly after, Eden's brother-in-law had gone missing in Afghanistan. His chopper went down in enemy territory, and he'd been declared MIA. Eden's older sister Sunny had been stuck in limbo, not knowing if Alan was alive or dead. Over Thanksgiving they'd learned his body had been identified. Alan

Stewart David had been killed in action, leaving Sunny a widow. Finally, after thirteen years, Sunny was coming home to fulfill the promise she'd made to Eden all those years ago—taking her turn as caregiver to their wheelchair-bound mother.

"I know. Sunny said much the same thing. We had a deal, and she's coming home," Eden said to Rosemary, not knowing how she could explain the excitement and dread wrestling inside her. What she'd always wanted had finally come to fruition. She was getting her chance to bust out of Morning Glory and go to college. A bit late, but better late than stuck forever working as the manager of Penny Pinchers or doling out medications to her fractious mother. Not that she begrudged taking care of her mother. Okay, well maybe a little. When her mother had overdosed on cocaine and then had a stroke Eden's senior year of high school, Sunny was already married and living in Virginia. And since Eden's brother had died three years before and her stepfather was in prison, her mother's care had been left to Eden. She'd been forced to turn down a scholarship to the University of New Orleans in order to go full-time at Penny Pinchers, a discount chain store. Complaining wasn't in Eden's nature, but she could acknowledge feeling just a teeny bit sorry for herself upon occasion. Hey, she wasn't a saint.

"Are you scared of living in New Orleans?" Rosemary asked, inching toward the fire. "I mean, I would be. Just the other day I read an article about the rise in New Orleans's murder rate. Did you know—"

"Cripes, you sound like your mother," Eden said, rubbing her frozen hands together.

Rosemary's eyes widened and she snapped her mouth closed, looking horrified. Finally she said, "Oh God. It's happening."

"What?"

"I'm turning into her."

Eden laughed. "No, you're not. It's not as if I hadn't thought about how different it will be living in the middle of a city. By myself."

"You're brave."

"Or stupid." Eden laughed.

"Yoo-hoo," someone called from the back door.

Eden turned to find Jess staring at them quizzically.

"Have you two lost your minds? It's freezing out here." Jess pushed out into the darkness, her brown curly hair lying soft against the wool peacoat she wore. She rubbed her arms and blew out her breath which was easily visible in the chilly air.

"It's warm by the fire," Rosemary said, her chattering teeth betraying her words.

"So I see." Jess walked halfway across the patio before stopping and shaking her head. "You know what? No. I know the chairs are new and you want to use the fire pit Sal built you, but it's too damn cold. Come inside. I brought some of Mom's spiced tea."

Eden sprang up. "Thank God. I was freezing."

"Well, you didn't say anything." Rosemary grabbed the fire screen and settled it over the pit.

"I was trying to be polite."

"You have to stop worrying about offending people. You're moving to a city," Jess said, holding the back door open as Eden ran inside into the blessed heat.

Entering the warm house felt like butter sliding off a biscuit. Delicious. "And what? People in cities aren't polite?" Eden rubbed her fingers to restore circulation.

Rosemary closed the back door and shrugged off her coat. She smelled like smoke, which wasn't unpleasant when combined with the perfume that wafted out as she hung her coat on the peg by the back door. "In New York City they weren't impolite per se, just not interested in anyone around them. In fact, New Yorkers always looked startled when you asked them a question. And then they walked away awfully fast."

"We got crap to do is all," Sal called from the recliner, his Brooklyn accent as thick as his wife's Mississippi one. The man had never had a recliner before and now wouldn't get out of it. Or so Rosemary said.

Rosemary gestured toward her husband. "Well, there you go. They got crap to do."

Jess and Eden smiled as their friend walked over to her handsome husband and dropped a quick kiss on his lips. His hand came up and cupped her butt, giving it a squeeze.

Rosemary swatted his hand, but her gray eyes danced as she said, "We're going in the kitchen. Need anything?"

"Another kiss?" he asked, tugging her toward him.

Jess stuck her finger in her mouth, mimicking gagging, and turned into the small kitchen. Eden followed because she heard more kissing and didn't need to be reminded she had no one *to* kiss. Not that Eden longed for a relationship at that moment. She had things to do first. But someday she wanted what both Rosemary and Jess had found over the past year.

"You have no room to talk," Eden said, pulling off her own coat and tossing it onto the chair in the corner of the dining nook. She still wore her Penny Pinchers polo shirt and khaki pants. Antithesis of stylish. "Where is the boy genius anyway?"

"At his parents' house. His father found a box of his comic books and Pokémon cards when he pulled down the Christmas decorations this year. Ryan was ecstatic. When I left, he was in the process of filling out a spreadsheet."

"I remember how much he loved those silly cards when he was a kid." Eden slid onto a barstool.

Jess's current boyfriend, Ryan, had attended Morning Glory High School with all of them, but he'd been much younger, advancing though high school and college at lightning speed. At thirteen, Ryan had been awkward, nerdy, and carrying a huge torch for Jess . . . along with a binder of trading cards. Back in the summer, Jess had tripped over Ryan lying naked on the beach when she went down to Pensacola to do contract work as a surgical nurse. She'd not been looking for love after a rough divorce from her high school sweetheart, but the Brain had grown into such a hottie, Jess had tumbled into love with him. They lived in Pensacola where Jess had found a full-time position and were as happy as two pigs in a patch of mud.

Jess tossed her coat on top of Eden's and swung the kettle toward the faucet. In a snowman jar sat the powdered spice-tea mix Jess's mother made every year. "Yeah, still a nerd at heart."

"But a hot one," Eden added.

"Who's good in bed," Jess purred, filling the kettle with water. "Thank God."

"TMI." Eden lifted the plastic wrap on a plate of cookies on the counter and snagged a sugar cookie with red icing. She didn't want to know the details of Jess's sex life.

"Really? Cause you've been in quite a drought, Eden. When's the last time you even went on a date?" Jess crooked an eyebrow at her.

"What does it matter? Have you looked around? Morning Glory doesn't have much in the way of choice," Eden said, biting into the cookie. Like everything Rosemary did, the cookie was spectacular. "Unless you want me to date Hooter. I mean, he just got new dentures and all, so I think that makes him the most eligible bachelor in all of Morning Glory. Or maybe Earl Vetters? I heard he won good prize money at the lawnmower races this year."

Jess gave Eden a deadpan look. "You don't have to date Earl or Hooter. There are other men here. But no worries, you're heading down to a nice big city full of eligible men."

Eden shook her head so hard her dark hair flew into her mouth. "Nuh-uh."

"What?"

She pushed the tendril from her mouth. "I'm not looking for love. Forget about it."

"Forget about what?" Rosemary said, sliding into the kitchen in her socks. She grabbed a cookie shaped like a star and took a bite.

"Eden finding a hot man to curl her toes in New Orleans." Jess cranked up the flame beneath the burner and set the kettle on it.

"I don't want to find a man. I want to get my degree. To live on my own. To sleep late . . . but not on days I have class. A man doesn't factor in." Eden pushed the rest of the cookie into her mouth and crossed her arms. She meant it. Her friends had found love and she was happy for them. Truly. But she didn't have time for love to railroad her. She had dreams, big fat dreams that involved her name in lights. Men were a dime a dozen and she had her whole life to find love, but a career on the stage had a shelf life, and she was fast approaching career spinsterhood.

"Oh, Eden, a man is the best reason to sleep late. I love the way they look in the morning light. All scruffy with bed hair and naked chests. Mmmm . . . delicious." Rosemary took another bite of cookie, her eyes glazed and dreamy.

Eden made a face because her mouth was still too full of cookie for her to snort.

Jess put both elbows on the granite counter and settled her pointed chin into her palms. "Hey, E. I gotta ask. Are you still a virgin?"

Eden sucked in a breath and swallowed at the same time. Which was not a good idea. Because as soon as she did, she choked. In spectacular fashion. She hacked up glumpy lump of sugar cookie, which landed on the counter near Jess's elbows and caused her friend to lurch backward. Then Eden dissolved into gut-wrenching coughs that made her sound like a goose being mounted by a gander. Or was the gander the girl goose? Didn't matter. She'd seen geese doing it, and it was a noisy affair.

"Oh God," Rosemary said, thumping her on the back. Hard. "Do I need to do the Heimlich?"

Eden shook her head and gasped, "Water."

Jess grabbed a nearby glass and filled it at the sink. Setting it in front of her, she stepped back, looking guilty and a bit scared. "I'm sorry, E. I didn't mean for that to happen."

Eden waved her hands, trying to cough up the last piece still hung in her throat. "I'm good. It's fine."

Rosemary patted her back, and Eden cleared her throat while wiping away the tears that coursed down her cheeks. Finally she got the last bit up. Then she drank the rest of the water.

After an uncomfortable minute ticked by, Jess said, "Well?"

"Well what?"

"Are you a virgin?"

"It's none of your business," Eden said, feeling heat bloom in her cheeks. She'd shared a lot with her friends, but they'd agreed that unless it was a medical issue, bedroom talk was off the table. Or maybe she'd agreed because she had no tales to tell. Okay, maybe some heavy petting and one near orgasm in the back of Clem Aiken's truck, but sex wasn't a topic she felt comfortable discussing, and even though they knew tons about each other, Rosemary and Jess had always respected her privacy. Lacy . . . not so much. Her former friend went to her grave being the only person who knew Eden had yet to surrender her *V* card.

Jess slid Rosemary a knowing glance, but they remained silent.

Sucking in a deep breath, Eden said, "So technically, yes."

"Oh, wow. I would have never . . . I mean, I knew you didn't . . . Wow," Rosemary said, sinking onto the stool.

Jess said, "So not even with Clem? Seriously, E?"

Eden merely shrugged and remained stone silent.

Rosemary reached out and patted her hand like she'd been diagnosed with a disease or something. "It's okay. You've not had much opportunity."

"But you dated Clem Aiken." Jess squinted her eyes like she didn't quite believe Eden.

And that's because everyone knew Clem Aiken was the town man whore. His exploits were fodder for the gossip mill all over Morning Glory and two adjoining counties. And in the Bahamas. That's what had done it for Eden. She'd ended their relationship when Delores, the other manager at the Penny Pinchers, found out from Rachel Bartlett that Clem had a ménage à trois while on vacation. Eden couldn't handle giving her virginity to a man who could handle two women at once. There was something not right about giving it up to a man like that. So she hadn't. And that was that. "Yeah. I dated him. I didn't do him though."

Rosemary slid another glance at Jess. "Well, do you have any questions?"

Eden laughed. "Why? Are you going to give me the birds-and-bees talk? Draw pictures? Lord."

Jess smiled. "Do you need pictures?"

"No. My mother was a stripper. I know how it all works. And I have, you know . . ." She left off, not wanting to say the actual word.

"Masturbated?" Jess finished.

Eden closed her eyes, opened them, and then took another cookie she didn't need. "I don't want to talk about my sex life . . . or rather lack of one. I share plenty with you girls, but I'd rather not share details of my alone time . . . or time with a dude. I'm not a freak, you know."

"We know. But so *you* know, it's perfectly natural to masturbate," Jess said, donning her clinical voice. "In fact, it's very healthy to have an awareness of your body and its needs."

"Jess," Eden said, nodding toward their friend. Rosemary was already approaching the shade of the poinsettias sitting along the stacked stone hearth behind her. Rosemary might be married to a sexy Brooklyn pizza maker and having sex every night, but she was her mother's daughter. Which meant she was a true lady who didn't talk about things like tampons, masturbation, or voting for a democrat.

Besides, it wasn't as if Eden had a hang-up about being a virgin. If she found the right guy, it would be a nonissue. But so far, she hadn't found a man she cared about enough to sleep with. Because she wasn't her mother. When Eden had sex, it would mean something. Or it would at least be more than what she'd had with Clem Aiken.

"Okay, okay," Jess said, holding up her hands.

"So when do you leave?" Rosemary asked, her color fading a bit.

"In a few weeks. Sunny should arrive in a week or so. She

spent Christmas with some friends. Dragging her feet as much as possible."

"Why?" Rosemary asked.

Jess's gaze met Eden's, acknowledging she understood. Sunny had left Morning Glory when the girls were freshmen after her longtime boyfriend knocked up a fluffy debutante at a fraternity party. Three weeks before Sunny was to graduate valedictorian of MHS, she ran away, leaving Eden and their mother behind. For almost a month, they didn't know where Sunny was or who she was with, but since Eden's older sister had already turned eighteen and left of her own volition, they couldn't report her missing. Finally, Sunny had called and told them she was married. The whole thing had been a shit storm and had everyone in the small town talking. Sunny had told Eden she'd come back when her husband got out of the Marines, that she could handle coming home with Alan. But now Alan was gone, and Sunny was coming home alone.

"It's not easy taking care of Mama. Sunny deserved to have a nice holiday with her friends. She's hurting over Alan and won't have time to do much of anything once she gets back here."

"That's true," Rosemary said.

"Hey, gals, want to go into town?" Sal said, strolling into the kitchen and rubbing his belly. "I have to go to the restaurant. One of the ovens isn't working right. I'll treat you guys to eggnog lattes at the Lazy Frog."

"We have spice tea," Rosemary said, nodding toward the cups of steaming water awaiting the spiced tea.

Jess shook her head. "No, let's take him up on it. Sassy only serves them until New Year's Eve. Plus Sal's buying."

Rosemary looked at Eden.

"Okay," Eden said not really caring one way or the other. Her aunt Ruby Jean was sitting with Eden's mother, giving Eden an evening off with her friends. A regular sitter came during the week so Eden could work. It was hell supplementing Medicare with what little Eden made, but it was worth it. As much as Eden hated Penny Pinchers, work was a much-needed break from a world of bedpans, towering bottles of medication, and her mother's acerbic complaints. Eden was thankful her aunt was good enough to spell her every now and then.

Rosemary looked at Sal. "We're all getting larges. Bring your wallet, Brooklyn."

Ten minutes later, the girls found themselves at their table. They'd sat at the four top since sixth grade year when Lacy deemed they needed a place to meet and have "drinks." Lacy had spent the summer before junior high watching episodes of *Sex and the City*—unbeknownst to her parents—and assured the other girls they must have a place to be seen even in small-town Morning Glory. Once a week they managed girl time at the local coffee/ice cream shop, and the table near the back left corner had witnessed several breakups, tales of first kisses, and more than enough hilarity to last a lifetime. Every time Eden sank down into her regular spot, her back to the ice machine, her gaze was pulled to the empty spot across from her. In fact, they all three glanced at that empty spot . . . before tucking the pain away and doing the living Lacy expected them to do.

The Lazy Frog's owner, Sassy Grigsby, looked pleased as punch they were the last customers of the day. She locked the door and flipped the sign to Closed before heading over. "It's cold as a well-digger's butt out there. Why are you girls out in this?"

"Sal had to fix something on an oven. We came here for lattes."

Sassy beamed. "Eggnog all around?"

The girls nodded.

Jess looked at the empty seat. "Still weird."

"Yeah," Rosemary said, blinking rapidly and turning toward Sassy. "Can you make mine light, Sassy?"

Sassy nodded and went to work on the lattes. For a few seconds, all three of them sat quietly, almost a moment of silence in memory of Lacy.

"So you want to have a farewell party?" Rosemary asked

Eden. "We could have something at our house. Maybe invite your aunt, Sunny, and a few of your coworkers. And if your mother can manage . . ."

"No." Eden shook her head. "That's not necessary. I'd rather just have dinner together or something. I don't want a fuss."

"That's our E. Never wanting a fuss," Jess said with a smile. "It's amazing how someone who always blends in can be such a powerhouse on stage. You're like night and day."

Eden smiled. "I'm not. I'm just me."

Rosemary reached over and gave her hand a squeeze. "I'm going to miss you."

A sudden thickness clogged Eden's throat just as doubt slithered through her belly. "Yeah, me too."

Rosemary shook her head. "Gosh, it's going to be so weird with both of you gone. I'll be in Morning Glory alone. This time last year, all four of us were here, and next week it will just be me. How did that happen?"

For a moment they let that thought sink in.

"Life changes so fast, huh?" Jess said with a slow shake of her head. "I never could have imagined Rosemary would be married and living on Hollybrook Lane. And I damned sure wouldn't have pictured me living on the beach with Ryan 'the Brain' Reyes. I would have laid down money against that."

"Wow, you were still married to Benton this time last year," Eden said, taking the steaming-hot latte from Sassy. "How weird is that?"

The other girls took their drinks, and Sassy waited for them to take a sip and mmmm in pleasure. Then she went back to scrub down the counters and balance the register.

"It's damned weird, but I'm so glad I let Benton go. Ryan hits the spot," Jess murmured.

"I bet he does," Rosemary drawled.

"Look at you making G-spot jokes," Jess said.

Like clockwork, Rosemary blushed, which seemed to amuse Jess even more. Rosemary cleared her throat. "That wasn't a . . .

sexual joke. So, I wonder what Eden will bring to the table this time next year."

"Speaking of bringing something to the table . . ." Jess reached into her purse and pulled out the familiar paisley ditty bag.

Eden stared at the bag, sadness pinging inside her. A few months back when she and Rosemary had gone to see Jess, her friend had tried to give the bag holding Lacy's charm bracelet to her. But she hadn't taken it. Eden hadn't been at a place to take on the challenge Lacy had left them. At that point Sunny still waited in North Carolina for word on Alan, and Eden had no hope of ever changing her life. She'd handed the bag back to Jess and told her to wait until it was time.

Lacy had left her best friends with a quest. Their late friend had spent most of her life in Morning Glory, but her joy had been in traveling. With a natural zest for living and a curiosity that couldn't be contained, Lacy had lived for trips to Paris and jaunts to the Caribbean islands. When she'd been diagnosed with advanced cervical cancer, she'd been planning a trip to Australia and New Zealand. Socking away ten grand was tough for the paralegal, but since Lacy lived at home with her parents, she was able to save the needed money. But she would never see someone play a didgeridoo or swim with sharks—yeah, she had that on the list—because that son of a bitch cancer took her before she could.

Lacy hadn't given up easily. She wanted the money she'd set aside to be used for living out a wish, so she'd divided it among her three dearest friends and left them with a request. Each woman would use the 3,300 dollars to carry out a wish she'd always had. After each completed something she'd always longed to do, she'd choose a charm and attach it to the travel charm bracelet Lacy had received from her grandmother when she was ten. Once the bracelet was complete, they were to choose someone who had no hope left and give the bracelet to her.

It was all very cryptic, mystic, and very Lacy-like.

So far, Rosemary had used the money to fund her trip to New York City where she met Sal and bumbled into a terrific opportunity for her vintage pillows. And Jess had used the money to rent the beach house she'd always dreamed about while she'd healed from her divorce, which led her to Ryan. And now it was Eden's turn to live out her wish. In a few weeks' time, she'd pack up the Mercury Milan—which was in bad need of new tires but would have to do—and head south toward New Orleans. There she'd enroll in the college she'd passed up eleven years ago, supplementing her student loans by working as a dance-school instructor.

Leaving Morning Glory was what she'd always wanted, but still, she felt so . . . scared. Yeah, she could admit it. She was terrified of going out into the big bad world, but even more terrified of not doing it.

Eden lifted the bracelet, admiring the tiny Empire State Building charm Rosemary had added along with the jeweled flip-flop Jess had attached in the fall. "I guess it's truly my turn."

Jess smiled. "Don't be afraid, Eden. Something good's waiting for you. Karma demands it."

Eden folded her hand around the warm metal and summoned determination. It was her turn. Lacy had helped clear a path by providing her money and a challenge. Time to walk the walk. "Guess it's time to put on my big-girl panties and get what I want."

"And that is . . . ?" Rosemary drawled.

"For now, a degree in theatre, but one day I want my name on the marquee."

Jess covered Eden's fist with her hand. Rosemary added hers atop. For a moment they looked at their joined hands. Rosemary smiled and said, "Okay, Lacy. Time to do work for Eden. Let's get her a happily-ever-after."

chapter two

two weeks later

EDEN LOOKED HARD at the sign as if the letters might suddenly rearrange themselves and spell out something other than CLOSED.

But the letters stubbornly refused to move. Damn them.

> SORRY, WE'RE CLOSED.
>
> MORE INFORMATION, ALONG WITH REQUESTS FOR REFUNDS, CAN BE MADE THROUGH OUR WEBSITE
> WWW.JILLSHANDYSCHOOLOFDANCE.COM
> QUESTIONS?
> CALL (555) 504-3256.

This can't be right. Eden ran a finger over the print and tried to peer inside the glass door. Inside, it was empty save a few inspirational posters on the wall along with empty clothes displays where leotards and dance shoes had likely hung. Eden stepped back and dug her cell phone from the depths of her oversized bag. Dialing the number on the sign, she paced toward the end of the wide porch. The dance studio was in an old house off Magazine Street, which had been a bitch to park on. Eden wasn't so good at parallel parking. Still, the charming gray studio nestled between a knitting shop and a dry cleaner looked like the perfect place to teach little ballerinas, so excitement quickly replaced aggravation at nearly hitting a Volvo that had parked over the line. But then she'd climbed the steps to find a darkened studio and the sign taped haphazardly to the door.

"Hello," a voice said on the other end of the line.

"Hi, I'm calling about the dance school?" Eden said.

"Oh, sorry, we're no longer in business."

"But I don't understand. I talked to Jill the first of December."

The woman clucked. "Oh, I'm sorry. Jill decided to close two weeks ago. Her father passed away and her circumstances changed. We can recommend a new school for your daughter."

"Uh, yeah," Eden said, glanced back through the window, "but I was supposed to start teaching there today. No one called me."

"Oh no. Is this . . . Eve?"

"No. Eden."

"That's right. Eden. Of course. Jill said she emailed you before the holidays. Did you not receive the message?" the woman asked. Her tone was one of concern, but somehow it seemed forced. Like she had to be nice but really wanted to get off the phone. Eden didn't blame her.

"No," Eden said, shaking her head, something akin to panic welling inside her stomach. She *had* to have a job. Everything depended on the three hundred dollars she'd make each week.

The grants and loans she'd obtained for school only covered so much. She had to eat.

God, what a string of bad luck.

Eden had arrived in New Orleans on Saturday. Well, if one could call breaking down on the Bonnet Carré Spillway arriving. She'd sputtered to the side of the long bridge, uttering every curse word she could think of. Then she'd spent a good five minutes using precious data on her cell phone looking up tow services, worrying about the dwindling amount in her checking account and how this snafu would impact it. While she was sitting there, flinching every time an eighteen-wheeler whooshed past her, an older man had pulled up. Together they'd lifted the hood and stared at the innards of her car. The gentleman had walked back to his rather beat-up vehicle, pulled out a gallon of water, and poured some into her radiator. Thankfully, her car started and she kicked it in to the Kenner exit. Eventually, after a few wrong turns, she found an AutoZone.

Eden suspected her water pump was failing. Big Eddie, the guy who worked on cars in her neighborhood in Morning Glory, had warned her it needed replacing, but she'd ignored it in favor of paying a plumber to fix her mother's toilet. Thankfully, replacing the water pump on her car wasn't too hard thanks to a YouTube step-by-step instructional video. The manager of the AutoZone allowed her to pull around back to change it. Took a whole hour to complete, and afterward Eden sent up a silent prayer of thanks to her neighbor Dally who had insisted on putting together a tool kit as a parting gift. The AutoZone manager seemed impressed Eden could use a socket wrench. What he didn't know was how many other things Eden could do because calling in a professional was never an option. She had changed out the heating element on the dryer, spackled drywall, and replaced PVC piping under the sink. She was a Jill-of-all-trades thanks to being near poverty level.

To top off the water pump going out, Eden received another doozy when she arrived at her new apartment. Chateau Dauphine had looked so quaint in the Internet pictures, with its shady courtyard filled with banana plants and aged-brick façade. Eden had been excited to see the apartment she'd rented.

But first she had to figure out parking. There was no lot, and the parallel parking on the street freaked her out. Not to mention daylight slipping away, leaving a filmy gray over the city. Finally she found a spot two blocks over near a dicey-looking club. Telling herself it would be fine, that her poor old car fit the run-down neighborhood, she climbed out, carrying a large duffel bag with her clothes and an inflatable air mattress. Clutching her key chain and small canister of pepper spray, she locked her car.

"Hey-ey, sugah," a woman called out, wiggling her fingers at Eden.

"Hello," Eden said, jerking her gaze away from the scantily clad woman with a bad weave . . . who looked like she was smoking a joint. Dear Lord. A man came out of the club and joined her. His goatee brushed his faded T-shirt, and his pants looked as if they'd not been washed since the George W. Bush administration. The woman passed the joint to him.

"Wanna come hear some good music, little mama?" he called out.

Eden swallowed hard. "No thank you. Maybe another time." Then she practically ran toward Chateau Dauphine.

Overall, the apartment building was a huge disappointment. The wrought iron scrollwork that had seemed so charming online was flaky, and the courtyard looked crowded with ratty patio furniture. Eden's heart sank as she climbed the outside stairs to the second floor. Her new neighbors didn't seem overly tidy. Broken umbrellas and soggy newspapers sat beside the two doors on either side of 3B, her new place. She managed to juggle her bags and pull out the key the landlord had mailed. Opening the paint-chipped door, she winced at the frigid air . . . and the smell.

"Okay, okay," she chided herself. "It's been unoccupied and closed up."

She said a prayer as she found the light switch.

"Thank you, Jesus," she said as the overhead light illuminated a postage-stamp living room. At least the landlord had turned on the electricity.

In the yellow glow, the apartment didn't look so bad. She stepped inside and locked the front door, noting the sliding bolt was loose. She'd need to have that fixed. Someone could put a boot on the door and smash it in. Setting her bags down, she went in search of the air-conditioning unit.

It rattled.

Next, she found the kitchen with its gold-flecked Formica and chipped sink.

It smelled like something had died there.

Then she found the bedroom.

It was the size of a walk-in closet.

And finally the bathroom with a walk-in shower.

It was covered in mildew.

"Great." Eden sighed, heading back toward the kitchen. First thing, she had to find the source of the smell. Opening the refrigerator, she found a carton of spoiled milk and a half-used stick of butter. She poured the milk down the sink, saying another prayer of thanks that the water had also been turned on.

And then an enormous roach crawled over the counter.

"Holy Jesus, Mother Mary," she squeaked, jumping back. With nothing to grab to smack it, she left the kitchen and went back to the living room. She needed to go to the market, but since she'd lost a good hour on changing the water pump and another half hour trying to find the apartment, darkness had descended. No way she'd venture out alone in the dark. Besides, she wasn't parallel parking again. Opening her purse, she pulled out a protein bar and a half-full bottle of water. Would have to do. She wasn't going back to her car tonight. Not even for the cheerful plants, lamp, and other odds and ends.

And please, sweet Jesus, let that cockroach stay in the kitchen. Please.

The next morning, after walking through the strange neighborhood, Eden got her next piece of bad news over eggs she splurged on at a local bistro. Her furniture wasn't coming until the following weekend.

Rosemary and Jess had rummaged through their parents' attics to find an old coffee table, end table, futon, and dresser, and Eden had used part of the money Lacy had left her to buy a new mattress and box springs. Her Aunt Ruby Jean had paid a few guys in the neighborhood to take the furniture down in their pickup truck, and Eden had planned to meet them in the morning before she reported to the dance school. But Jerry called to say his truck had thrown a rod and he'd have to fix it before he could bring her "shit"—his exact words. And not only that, but he didn't have a day off until Saturday, so she'd have to spend a week on the blow-up mattress on, to be honest, sketchy-looking carpet.

So not having a job was the icing on the cake. Or the straw that broke the camel's back. Either way, it sucked.

Turning her attention back to the phone and the woman who'd just given her the bad news, she said, "No, ma'am. I didn't receive anything from Jill or anyone associated with the studio. Which would have been appreciated because I really need this job. Now I'm in a bind." To her ears, her voice sounded whiney. Defeated. Eden straightened her shoulders. No. She was not defeated or whiney. She could handle this.

"I'm sorry, but there's nothing I can do. Even though you never technically worked for us, Jill will probably vouch for you at other dance studios."

"Yeah. Sure. Tell Jill I said thanks for being so considerate," Eden muttered into the phone.

An awkward silence ensued.

"Will that be all, dear?" the woman asked finally.

"I guess that's all there is, isn't it?" Eden pressed the End button before she said something that showed her blue-collar roots. Like maybe "go fuck yourself." But, of course, she wouldn't do that. She'd worked hard on not using the profanity that seemed to come so easily to her . . . and on using correct grammar, which did not come so easily to her. That's what happened when a gal was raised by a drug-addict stripper and a stepfather who robbed banks. She didn't excel in social graces. But she was trying.

Pocketing her phone, she looked up at the porch ceiling and took a few calming breaths. When that didn't work, she kicked the square column because it gave her some satisfaction, then trudged down the steps. She'd have to find a job. Today. Perhaps another dance studio might be hiring? It was worth a shot. Spying a cute coffeehouse across the street, Eden headed for free Wi-Fi and a cup of coffee. She'd Google surrounding dance schools to see if there was a position available. If not, she'd broaden her search.

Because she was not going back to Morning Glory defeated.

That's not how she rolled.

Nicholas Zeringue couldn't believe his bad luck was persisting. After spending all morning negotiating over a piece of land for the new restaurant, the owner had sold it out from under him. And then he'd emerged from his office to find the van he'd purchased a few months ago had been hit. Of course the culprit hadn't bothered to leave a note, so Nick had to spend an extra hour he couldn't spare filing an accident report and another twenty minutes on the phone with his insurance company. Which meant he'd been late to pick his daughter up from school. And that resulted in Sophie pitching a fit that was only soothed by reminding her they were meeting their soon-to-be ex-nanny Rhoda at the Earthy Bean. His seven-year-old's love for both Rhoda and a cocoa loco was enough to calm her. Of course Sophie would, no doubt, end up smearing whipped cream all over her face. But big deal. The kid loved the damn sticky, sweet drink.

Don't sweat the small stuff.

Rhoda waited out front, her whimsical skirt and crazy dreadlocks easily identifiable. She hurried to help him unload Sophie. Because the asshole had sideswiped the side of the van with the sliding ramp, it was hard to get the ramp out. Thankfully, the structure hadn't been too damaged and was still useable.

"Been waiting long?" He huffed, getting the bent sliding door back in place.

"Only a few minutes. What happened to the van?" Rhoda asked, making a face. Rhoda Soileau had worked for him for five years, taking care of Sophie after school, traveling with him, being his right-hand woman. He depended on her more than he'd like to admit. She understood what it was like raising a daughter who had limited mobility, who needed to go to therapy twice a week, who had to be lifted on and off the toilet. But Rhoda had fallen in love with some dude over the Internet and wanted to move out to Lake Tahoe with him, leaving Nick without a caregiver for Sophie.

Which sucked way worse than the dinged-up van or the missed opportunity on the land.

"Some asshole hit me and didn't leave a note," he said, setting his hands on his hips and taking a deep breath. He needed to start running again if slight exertion like unloading his daughter rendered him out of breath. "Already have a call in to a shop that can get it done in a day, so that's good."

"Some people," Rhoda said, bending down to drop a kiss on Sophie's cheek.

His daughter jerked away, still intent on making Rhoda pay for leaving her. Nick needed a scotch and soda, but decaf coffee would have to do since after their coffee and snack, he had a meeting with Sophie's teacher. Ever since Rhoda had announced she was moving away, his daughter had been acting out both at home and obviously at school. Sophie had refused to do her homework, PT exercises, or to bear any weight on her legs, punishing him for something so out of her control. And likely she was punishing her teacher Dayna Young too. Thus the meeting later today.

They rolled up the ramp to the coffeehouse with its bright awning and fragrant entrance. Since school had let out, the place was rocking with little girls in Catholic-school uniforms sucking down syrupy organic lattes, their thin moms in athletic gear sipping water and chatting on their phones. Nick spied an open table and left Rhoda with their order. He snagged the table and helped Sophie maneuver into a spot that kept her out of the way. After helping her reverse and inch forward a dozen times, he collapsed into the chair across from her.

His daughter had thick dark hair he braided every morning and soft white skin that reminded him of her mother. Cerebral palsy had caused many of her facial muscles to atrophy, and the periodic jerking of her limbs drew attention, but her blue eyes were bright. She liked the sparkly lip gloss he applied every morning, and the pink watch on her wrist was her current obsession. She had learned to tell time last semester.

Usually Rhoda picked Sophie up, but she'd taken part of last week and today to handle last-minute details of her move. Last year his father had retired, and with his mother focusing on the renovation of the downtown restaurant, much of the business was left to him. Which was fine. He loved being a cog in the wheel of the family restaurant dynasty. When it came to fine dining in South Louisiana, the Zeringue name was mentioned in tandem with the Brennans. Or Emeril or John Besh. Owning seven restaurants meant Nick spent much of his time putting out fires, meeting with marketing, and supervising the day-to-day operations. But his baby was the new seafood restaurant he wanted to build closer to Baton Rouge. If only he could find the right location. And not have the location sold out from under him. And if only he could stop Rhoda from—

"Dad," Sophie said, her hand jerking toward his.

He smiled at his daughter, his heart filling with love as he chastised himself for dwelling on everything wrong with his life when Sophie was sitting beside him. Afternoon coffee was special. "What, baby?"

She curled her hand over her watch. "Three thirty."

He checked his own. "So it is."

Rhoda started their way, balancing their order, and he realized he hadn't grabbed an extra chair yet. Looking up, he spied an unused chair at the table next to them. Sitting there was a tiny woman who had her face buried in her hands as if she had a headache or was in some sort of despair. She looked up as he approached.

God, she was pretty.

The first thing he noticed was her eyes. They were a gorgeous purplish blue fringed with long sooty lashes. Her jawline was square, lips pouty, and her severe black hair only served to heighten the femininity of her face. Her tight spandex top clung to breasts the size of freestone peaches, and she didn't look like anyone's mother. No dyed blond hair, Juvédermed lips, or legs tanned by tennis. She looked naturally beautiful as she ducked her chin and averted her eyes.

"Would you mind if I borrowed this chair?" he asked.

Her gaze lifted and a faint pink warmed her cheeks. "Go ahead."

"Thanks," he said, pulling the chair to him. As he turned, he noted the sheen of tears in her eyes. "You doing okay?"

She stared at him for a moment, her eyes slipping toward Sophie, who fiddled with her watch. Finally she said, "Yeah. I'm fine. Thanks."

He nodded, wondering why he'd bothered to ask. She was a stranger, and just because she was cute didn't mean he had to involve himself in the slightest way with whatever had made her sad. Still, something about her tugged at him. Vulnerability and the blush. Dangerous combination.

Rhoda set his coffee down and slid a monster of a drink toward his daughter, drawing his attention from the lone woman to the whipped cream erupting from the domed plastic lid. Yep, sticky. Sophie motioned to her iPad and dangling earbuds. His daughter loved music, rocking back and forth. He popped her earbuds on, hooking them around her ears. She knew he and Rhoda were going to talk about the upcoming weeks. His daughter obviously would rather lose herself in Justin Bieber or Taylor Swift.

Rhoda settled her ample butt in the chair he'd snagged for her and gave a heartfelt sigh. Her brown eyes found him. "Any luck?"

"You know the answer."

For the past two weeks, he'd interviewed potential nannies to replace Rhoda. He'd thought it would be simple. It was not. One candidate he wouldn't leave a rock with, much less a child, one was too elderly to lift his daughter, and the other seemed perfect but got hired before he could settle things with her. The referral agency had assured him they would do all they could, and last week they'd sent over Calli. She was in her early twenties, had no experience, but was in school working on a degree in early childhood education. He'd agreed to a trial run for a few days while Rhoda was off. Everything had gone well until Friday afternoon.

Nick had arrived home early, set his briefcase on the counter, and frowned at the mess in the kitchen. The new caregiver wasn't exactly the best at housekeeping. But then again, he hadn't listed loading the dishwasher in the job description. Rhoda had spoiled him by making sure the place was tidy before she left for the day.

"Hello?" he called, stepping into the living area. The TV blared Nickelodeon, and a bowl of popcorn sat on the end table. "Calli? Sophie?"

No one answered. Nick walked toward Sophie's room, but it too was empty.

Maybe they were outside. The day had been temperate for mid-January, as was often the case in New Orleans, so maybe Calli wanted to give Sophie some fresh air and sunshine. He'd mentioned doing that periodically because vitamin D was critical to Sophie's moods. He retraced his steps and headed for the courtyard, pushing open the double french doors.

When he looked out, he saw his daughter sitting in her wheelchair beside the urn fountain. Water gurgled and splashed on the stones below, and one of her wheels was caught in the grating. Calli, her new caregiver, was nowhere to be seen.

"Soph?" he called.

His daughter tried to look behind her. "Dad."

He pulled the chair free from the groove where it had hung up. "Where's Calli?"

"Don't know," his daughter managed.

"What do you mean, you don't know? She's supposed to be with you."

"She's smoking," Sophie said, her arms spasming more than normal. The child was upset. More so than usual. "I tried to find."

Nick felt rage flood him though he tried to mask his emotions. No need to get Sophie more upset. "Come on. Let's get you inside and I'll look for her. It's getting cold out."

He pushed Sophie into the house. His daughter was working on getting proficient at manipulating her chair, but sharp turns and small tables were her enemy. A motorized chair wasn't an option with her lack of muscle control. Seconds later, he settled her with the iPad and the newest book in her favorite series and went to find Calli.

After searching the whole house, he found the twentysomething with the nose ring and too-tight clothes standing beside her compact car in tears. His first inclination was to grab her and shake some sense into her. But Nick never went with his first inclination. He prided himself in maintaining control.

Taking a deep breath, he moved so he stood directly in front of her. "Calli, you left Sophie alone in the courtyard. How long has she been there?"

Calli wiped her nose and sniffed. "Not long. I'm sorry. Just some personal stuff, you know." Her eyes were red rimmed and her face bore evidence of effusive crying.

"No, I don't know. At the moment you're on my time, and that supersedes personal *stuff*."

Calli brushed a hand over her cheeks, smearing mascara. "I know. It's just Frank broke up with me. Three effin' years and he said he doesn't want to do this anymore. He wants to go out with this whore at his bar. I mean, she's only like eighteen years old. A child. And he ends things with me? He even told this bitch she could move in with him. Do you know how fucked up that is?"

Nick knew very well how screwed up something like that was, but that was no reason to leave a handicapped child alone. "You have a job. A child who depends on you."

Calli looked up, pain mirrored in her eyes. "Man, you're cold as shit. My boyfriend just dumped me in a text. A fucking text. And you're upset because your spoiled brat kid had to sit outside for an extra ten minutes while I dealt with this? Did you want her to hear me call him a douchebag cocksucker? 'Cause I could have parked my ass next to her and given her a lesson in how to cuss out a douchebag cocksucker."

"That's enough," Nick said, crossing his arms, fighting against his fury. His surrender to anger never gained him what he needed from those around him.

Calli shook her head. "Look, I don't need this shit. I told her I was stepping outside for a smoke and would be right back. All she was doing was sitting in the courtyard and watching the cat next door stalk bugs. I even put sunscreen on her." She pushed by him, waving a hand.

"I'm not done discussing this matter with you, Miss Brayden."

"Well, I'm done discussing it with you. This job isn't for me. Your expectations are too high."

Expectations too high? She'd left his daughter on her own. Sure, the courtyard was only a few dozen yards away, but Sophie wasn't like other kids. She was . . . different. And he was paying Calli to tend to his daughter. Not take smoke breaks out of—well, almost out of earshot—of his daughter. "My expectation is that you have your eye on her at all times. She's not like other—"

"Really? Like I didn't notice," Calli said, swinging around. Her hair stuck out in five different directions, and the smeared mascara made her overly dramatic as she gestured. "You're her problem. She's old enough to sit for a few minutes without her father freaking out. How's she supposed to grow up and gain independence with you sitting on her? But it doesn't matter, because I can't take this job."

Alarm streaked down his spine. "You can't quit."

"Actually, I never started. I need to get out of New Orleans. I can't handle the shit going down here."

Damn it. He didn't want her to quit. He needed her. "Look, you don't have to do that. Sophie and I need you."

Calli shook her head. "Nah, this isn't the job for me. It's cool. I'm not mad or anything. Just need to clear my head about my life."

She walked away, leaving Nick looking much like a fish out of water.

When Rhoda patted his hand, it jarred him back to the coffee shop and the present. Rhoda gave him a half smile. "Something will work out."

"What if nothing does?" He rubbed a hand across his eyes, shifting a glance over to his daughter, who still had earbuds in but had turned to watch a gaggle of girls near her age play games on an iPad at a nearby table. "Don't do it, Rhoda. Tell your Internet boyfriend to move here. We have nature in New Orleans. He can photograph that."

"Look," Rhoda said, cupping her hands around her coffee cup, glancing at Sophie to make sure she wasn't listening. "This is my shot at love, you know? I'm nearly forty-five and no spring chicken. Cedric's asked me to come be with him, so I can't stay here, living my life as your nanny. I need more than that. And frankly, Nick, so do you. We're in a holding pattern here. You working like a dog and me . . . Well, I want to be in a full relationship. Skyping is not the same as touching. I have to take this chance." Rhoda pressed her hands to the table. "I'm sorry."

Obviously Bieber wasn't turned up loud enough because Sophie started to cry. Crying wasn't pretty for a child with cerebral palsy. People turned to look at them. He was used to it, but he still didn't like it. He placed a firm hand on his daughter's free hand. *Don't do this, Soph. Hold it together.*

"Damn." He closed his eyes and shook his head. "You need to get her out of here."

"I know," Rhoda said, spreading her hands. "But, Nick, Sophie has to learn to deal with disappointment, to understand life is not about getting everything she wants."

Nick slammed a hand down on the table. "Really, Rho? You think she doesn't know that?"

"Nick."

"No. She's about to lose it and so am I," he said, pushing his chair back. He wanted to yell at Rhoda for doing such a stupid thing. Chasing after a man she'd known for a few months? Why? Her home was here in New Orleans. She had a good job, sold her pottery at a friend's stall in the French Market and seemed happy. Why was she rocking the boat? Because she thought she was in a rut? Hell, being in a rut was a good thing. It was called routine, and he wanted the routine they'd had for the past five years back.

"Nick, I love Cedric. I'm not trying to hurt you or Soph. I love y'all too, but this is the right thing. I know it in my bones," Rhoda said, sliding a hand over to stroke Sophie's arm.

Love? What a crock of shit. He'd been there and done that and look what it had gotten him—sole custody of his disabled daughter and a frickin' ex-wife who always had a reason she couldn't come to New Orleans to see Sophie. Love was selfish, and it sucked people dry.

Sophie screamed when he took the drink from her, and his already frazzled nerves frayed even more. A hot, panicky feeling rose inside him.

Rhoda took Sophie's chin and turned the child so she looked at her. "You can stay and finish if you calm down. Do you want to stay?"

"Yes!" Sophie said, tears still streaming down her face. "I wanna stay."

"Then you have to stop fussing, Soph."

Nicked eased back in his seat and tried to relax the hand gripping his own cup. He counted to ten, watching Sophie struggle to rein in her emotions.

"Okay," his daughter said, trying to nod. She jerked her chin from Rhoda's grasp and looked out the window, effectively dismissing her nanny. For a few seconds he saw the regret, guilt, and hurt in Rhoda's eyes, and something inside him took comfort in those emotions. Rhoda should feel bad. She was abandoning his sweet girl for a crazy photographer who ate fried bologna. Yeah, Nick had checked Cedric's profile on social media. Who used "Likes bald eagles, playing the flute, and frying bologna" as their Twitter bio?

"Well, that was fun," he said, picking up his coffee, relieved Sophie had been able to calm down quickly. She was getting better at that, which was a relief. Her tantrums rivaled any toddler's, and often they had to vacate wherever they happened to be. Who knew there was such power in the Earthy Bean's signature drink?

Rhoda shot him an apologetic glance and mouthed, "Sorry."

Nick sucked in a deep breath and then donned his fake restaurant smile. "Everything will be okay. We'll get a new nanny, a fun nanny. That will be cool, huh, Sophie?"

His daughter ripped her gaze from the window and gave him a slack-eyed look. "No."

Nick felt his phone vibrate and glanced down at where it lay on the table. It was Maude's, the uptown bistro. No doubt Chef Fredrico had quit again. Or thrown a saltcellar at a dishwasher's head. Or something equally dire. Nick couldn't go on this way. He needed help. So instead of answering the call, he clicked his contact list and dialed the only person he'd not tapped for help yet. He needed a miracle.

Yesterday.

chapter three

Two hours and three cups of coffee later, Eden tossed her phone onto the table at the Earthy Bean and dropped her face into her hands. No job opportunities at any dance schools. Tears pricked at the back of her eyes, and she contemplated letting them fall. After all, she didn't know anyone who lived in New Orleans. Okay, she knew one person who lived here, but Morgan was out working on a cruise ship for the next few months. So who cared if she broke down and sobbed at a random coffee shop on... What was the street called again? Oh, yeah, Magazine.

Eden squinched her face and tried to think about happy things. Baby duckies. Mocha ice cream. Twinkling Christmas lights. Anything to prevent boo-hooing on top of the café table.

"Would you mind if I borrowed this chair?" a man asked, interrupting the version of "My Favorite Things" running through her head, drawing her attention to the fact she was sitting in a public place. Even if the coffee shop contained no one she knew, people probably didn't want to witness ugly crying.

"Uh, sure."

"Thank you," he said, giving her a smile and pulling the bright orange chair toward the table across from her. "You doin' okay?"

He had a New Orleans accent, a rich mellowness balanced by hard vowels.

And he was good-looking. Very good-looking.

Then she noticed the little girl in the wheelchair across from the man. Suddenly she felt small for indulging in pity. She had two good legs that could twirl, pirouette, and tap-dance. She might have roaches on her counters, no job, and $950.00 in her checking account to last until her first nonexistent paycheck, but she had a body that worked. This child did not. "Yeah. I'm fine. Thanks."

The man sank down and looked over his shoulder. Eden followed his gaze to the counter where a woman balanced two coffees and a fluffy coffee creation with sprinkles. The woman didn't match the man, who had a sleek, sophisticated look. She wore a bright skirt, clogs, and had dreads. But she definitely headed toward the table with the man and child.

"I borrowed a chair for you," the man said, giving the woman a smile. He had good teeth—perfectly straight and very white. He had a thick five-o'clock shadow and a small cleft in his chin. Eyes looked light. Maybe gray like her friend Rosemary's. He wasn't super tall, but he commanded attention like a celebrity. Larger than life. Here was a man who could get what he wanted. Eden knew that at once.

"Thanks, Mr. Z. Here's your coco loco, Miss Priss," the woman said, setting the whipped-cream-topped cup in front of the girl, who looked about seven or eight years old. The arms that moved involuntarily paired with rigidity of the trunk told Eden the child likely had cerebral palsy. The woman turned and caught Eden staring and gave her the stink eye. Eden jerked her gaze away and tried not to blush again. Hastily she picked up her phone and pretended to study it. She knew how it felt to be stared at. Whenever she took her mother to the doctor, people looked.

Eden's stomach growled. She'd had a decent breakfast and planned on supplementing with a protein bar during her break, but since she had spent the past two hours desperately seeking employment, she reasoned she deserved more than a damn crumbled Quest Bar. Scooting her chair back, she left her cup to hold her table in the suddenly crowded coffee shop and headed toward the counter.

The girl behind the counter had red and orange hair, a ring in her nose, and a friendly smile. "You want more coffee?"

"Lord, no." Eden laughed. "If I have any more caffeine, you'll have to pull me off the ceiling. Better go with some food this time. Give me a turkey on ciabatta bread and a large ice tea, please."

After digging out the twenty-dollar bill Aunt Ruby Jean had tucked in her back pocket when she hugged her goodbye, Eden slid it across the counter to the girl. The thought of every single dime now mattering caused Eden to take a chance. "Hey, you don't happen to need any help, do you?"

"Doing what?" the girl asked, pulling a large cup from a stack and scooping ice into it.

"Oh, sorry. I didn't mean with my order." Eden shook her head. "I was supposed to start work at the dance school across the street today, but they closed down. I'm without a job."

"Oh, for a second I thought you didn't trust me with your sandwich," the girl said with a teasing smile. "You're not from around here, are you? I noticed the accent."

"I'm from Mississippi. Just got off the boat yesterday."

"Right," the girl laughed, grabbing a pitcher filled with tea. "That's tough luck on the job thing. One of the dance moms came in and said Jill's father died and left her millions. Guess she no longer needs to work or something. Lucky Jill. Unlucky you."

Eden sighed and slid the change off the counter, dropping a dollar into the tip jar. "Very unlucky me. I kinda need a job."

The girl turned and jabbed a long black fingernail toward the plate glass window over Eden's shoulder. "We don't have anything, but Sister Regina Marie from over at All Souls came in a few days ago and said they were looking for someone to work janitorial. She knew my brother had been looking, but he got hired at Best Buy last week. You might check over there to see if they filled the position or not."

"Oh," Eden said, peering out the window, noting the large white wall partially covered with some sort of ivy she didn't recognize. Janitorial? Not so glamorous, but a job was a job. And how different would it be from what she'd been doing for the past few years? She had cleaned the public bathrooms at Penny Pinchers many a morning before opening, and she was head housekeeper at home. Okay, only housekeeper. Either way, Eden knew her way around a mop and duster. "It's a school?"

"Yeah. For special-needs children. In fact, Sophie goes there." She nodded toward the little girl in the wheelchair. The conversation at the table seemed to have grown intense, and the child looked to be in tears. "I'm Mia, by the way."

"Hi, I'm Eden."

"I bet Nick wouldn't mind answering some questions about the school. That's Sophie's dad." Mia leaned close and lowered her voice. "And he's total hotness, right?"

Eden felt flustered at the question and immediately hated herself for being so lame. Who got worked up over a stupid comment about a guy being cute? Okay, more than cute—cornea-scalding hot. But still.

Mia didn't notice because she'd turned away to pop bread in the toaster. "The good news is that people who work there seem happy. Sister Regina Marie is like, the most awesome nun ever."

"Thanks," Eden said, taking the block with her order number on it.

"No problem. Hope it works out, and sorry about the other job. That sucks."

"Yeah, it does."

Eden headed back to her table and tried not to look at Nick, the hot dad who no longer smiled. In fact, he looked upset.

Settling back in her chair, she pulled her attention toward tapping a message to her two best friends:

> Made it to NOLA. Apartment is great but my job fell through. In process of finding another one. But I love New Orleans!!! Can't wait for y'all to visit.

There. That sounded positive and halfway truthful. Okay, maybe two-thirds true. She couldn't wait for her friends to visit, and she *was* looking for a job.

She knew Jess and Rosemary were worried about her. Hell, she was worried about her. But she knew what very few people knew—she was a fighter. She might look small, quiet, and sometimes mousy, but she was a Voorhees. That meant beneath her calm demeanor lay a scrapper, born to hold tight, weather the storm, and lift a defiant chin. The white trash in her blood gave her something her gently reared friends didn't have—a swagger that dared life to knock her down. Because Eden would always get up again. It was coded in her DNA. Never surrender.

Her phone dinged.

> Oh, crap. What will you do without a job?

Jess never minced words.

Eden tapped,

> Find another one. I've got mad skills at the cash register. Don't worry.

She smiled her thanks and pocketed her phone as Mia set the basket containing her sandwich on the table. She already knew what her friends would text. Jess would give suggestions. Rosemary would use lots of emoticons and exclamation points. Nothing either one of them could do about the lack of employment. Eden's fate lay in her own two hands.

After eating her sandwich, Eden tucked her small notebook away and pushed her chair in. Hot Dad Nick glanced over at her. So did the child who wore whipped cream on her nose, which somehow made her adorable. The child said something, but Eden couldn't understand her. So Eden gave a little pinky wave.

Exiting the coffeehouse, she headed toward the school. It was almost four o'clock and likely a good time to stop in and see if the position was still open. The block was busy with cars rolling one right after the other through the surprisingly cramped street. Branches of oaks hung low, bowing gracefully, and the stores and businesses along the street were festooned in varying colors as if refusing to be sedate. The scrolled iron gates of the school stood open with large banana plants waving a greeting, and the building bore yawning stained glass windows. Eden climbed up the stone steps to a double door that looked straight out of a European monastery. A buzzer sat to the left. She pressed it and waited.

"Yeah?" an older woman asked.

"Uh, I'm here to see . . ." Eden searched her memory. What was the nun's name? "Uh, Sister Marie Anne?"

"There isn't a Sister Marie Anne. Maybe you're wanting Saint Pius. Five blocks over." The woman's New Orleans accent was heavy and sounded kind of like Rosemary's husband Sal's.

Damn. "Uh. Sorry. I got her mixed up with a nun at my old school," Eden said, her mind tumbling over the two names Mia had spouted. "Uh, it was Sister Marie . . . uh."

"Sister Regina Marie?"

"Yes," Eden nearly shouted. "Sorry, it's been a shi—uh, bad day."

"What do you want with Sister Regina Marie?"

"Mia told me to see Sister Regina Marie?" Eden said in her sweetest voice. *Please let me in. Please let them still have the job open.* She could clean toilets. Mop floors. Sprinkle those weird pine-shavings on vomit. "My name's Eden."

The woman snorted but the buzzer sounded. Grasping the iron handle, Eden hefted the old door open and stepped into a foyer. The blue linoleum was dated, but the beautiful dark wood surrounding her was timeless.

A head poked out from a little sliding glass partition. "Hey. Over here."

"Oh, hello," Eden said, donning her best customer-service smile. "I'm Eden."

"Come on around and I'll check you in. I'll need your license."

"Oh."

Eden stepped through the open doorway to find a rotund woman in a shirtwaist dress sitting at a small desk. The secretary wore horn-rimmed readers that perched on her fat nose, and her white hair had been set in tiny pin curls. Her expression was dour, but her blue eyes were sharp and somehow kind. The name placard said Pearl Guillot.

Eden pulled her driver's license from the beat-up wallet she'd had for ten years. "Here you are."

The older woman swept Eden with an appraising look and apparently found her yoga pants and tight spandex top lacking because she frowned and harrumphed. "Sister Regina Marie is in the library, but I'll tell her you're here. Of course, I don't know who you are or why you're here, but you don't look like you're a serial killer." She glanced back at the driver's license before handing it back to Eden. "And besides, you're from Mississippi."

Did that mean people from Mississippi were harmless? Eden didn't ask. She'd learned long ago to never look a gift horse in the mouth. She'd gained entrance, and that was a first step in a direction. What direction that was, Eden could only guess. But it was better than sitting at the Earthy Bean, steeped in pity. "Uh, I'm actually here about the position."

"What position?"

"Well, Mia over at the Earthy Bean said Sister Regina Marie told her about a position on the janitorial staff. See, I was supposed to start teaching over at Jill's School of Dance, but they closed and didn't even call to tell me. I just moved here from Morning Glory and used most of my money to move here, so when I found out I didn't have a job anymore, I sort of panicked. When I said something to Mia, she pointed me here. I'm hoping the position isn't filled because I really need a job.

Like, it's vital to my being able to stay here and go to school at UNO." Eden snapped her mouth shut, horrified. The stream of words that had poured from her mouth might have been the most she'd ever said at one time.

Pearl blinked three times. "Well, that *is* a problem. Let me call Sister Regina Marie. Go sit over there." She pointed to a bench against the foyer wall.

Eden nodded and shuffled backward, wondering what in the hell had come over her. Maybe all the bad luck had snowballed and smacked her silly. Her mother would have been appalled at her telling private business to a receptionist. Betty Voorhees Smitty might have danced at Club Legz in Jackson and smoked more crack than that Detroit mayor, but she would never tell a stranger her business . . . or how much she had in her checking account (or didn't, as was the case more times than not). And Eden had come very close to telling Pearl Guillot that she had exactly $953.17 in her checking account.

Pearl slid the partition closed. Eden picked at her fingernails and thought about bolting toward the door. She could likely find a job at a fast-food joint. Maybe dunking fries in grease would be better than pushing a broom. Or perhaps one of the dance schools might call her back. Or maybe the university would have some work-study programs. Years ago she'd signed up for that. She'd not even thought about—

"Hello?" a voice said beside her.

Eden jumped at least half a foot and turned toward the impossibly tall woman with a plain, broad face, painfully short spiked hair, and the kindest smile Eden had ever seen. "Oh. Sorry. I was woolgathering."

"Do quite a bit of that, do you?" the woman asked, an Irish lilt in her soft voice.

"Only when I'm not working," Eden said.

"Good answer," the nun said, her mouth twitching.

Eden stood. "Hello. I'm Eden Voorhees."

"Sister Regina Marie O'Malley. Welcome to All Souls

Academy." She held out a weathered hand.

Eden took it. For a brief few seconds, Eden felt totally at home. Gone were the panicked thoughts of running for the door. In their place was . . . peace. Which was strange, because by all accounts she should be painfully uncomfortable. After all, she was there to beg—no, inquire—about a job. And just because the woman releasing her hand was a nun didn't mean she magically transferred well-being in a simple touch.

"Won't you follow me to my office? We'll have more privacy there," Sister Regina Marie said, turning with purpose down a hall in bad need of a coat of wax. She paused in front of a handsome wood door, waiting like a friendly gargoyle for Eden to enter the office, which was painted a virulent pink.

Eden winced at the color.

"I know. It's shocking, but Madison—whom we lost last year—won the contest to choose the new paint color. She was very fond of pink."

"I see," Eden said, turning around, noting the framed prints of childish scribbles and the very gruesome crucifix above the tall door. "It's, uh, cheerful?"

"It's hideous, but since I despise spending the school's money more than I care about the paint color, I live with it. Now, tell me how you found us." Sister Regina Marie sank down into a leather armchair, indicating Eden should sit in the one beside her.

Pressing trembling hands against her legs, Eden lowered herself onto the cold leather. "I appreciate you seeing me. Mia over at the Earthy Bean suggested I check with you about a job." Eden folded her hands into her lap and chewed at her lower lip.

"Mrs. Guillot said something about the school of dance closing."

Eden flushed. Her stupid babbling had made her look whiney. She hated being whiney. "Uh, yeah. I was supposed to start today."

"You have taught dance before?"

"Yes, ma'am. For eleven years."

"I see," the nun said, folding her hands before spreading them. "I'm afraid we're not looking for an instructor, and we've already hired someone for janitorial. What other skills might you possess?"

Eden's stomach sank, and she tried not to let her disappointment show. Getting a job here was a long shot anyway. Besides, she wasn't sure she wanted to clean toilets for less than ten dollars an hour. "That's okay. I appreciate your seeing me though."

The nun tilted her head. "Pardon my manners. Would you care for a cup of tea, dear?"

"I had three cups of coffee while searching unsuccessfully for a job. I better not."

The nun nodded. "So you're going to school?"

Time was a wasting, but Aunt Ruby Jean had taught her manners, so she answered the question. "Yes, ma'am. I'm majoring in theatre at UNO."

"I can see you're not fresh out of high school, if you don't mind my saying. What else did you do in . . . Mississippi, was it?"

Eden didn't know why it mattered, but something about the older woman comforted her. She didn't want to trudge back into the dying day and feel so alone in the big city. The office was warm and cozy even if a violent pink. "Yes, Mississippi. Morning Glory, Mississippi. I worked at a discount store and took care of my mother. Uh, she's confined to a wheelchair."

Gee, she'd almost made a habit of telling strangers her entire bio. And nothing sounded more pathetic than implying she was a martyr taking care of an invalid. Feel bad for me, please.

"Oh?" Sister Regina Marie shifted forward, her forehead crinkling as her blackbird eyes shone with . . . excitement? "Your mother's disabled?"

"Partially paralyzed by a stroke." No need to bring up the cocaine addiction or alcoholism or pole dancing. "My sister's taking care of her now. Because I'm in school. Here."

"I see," the nun said, settling back in her chair, her gaze lifting to the gruesome crucifix above the door. The older woman grew still as a puddle after a storm.

"Well, I should go. Thank you anyway." Eden started to rise.

Sister Regina Marie tented her hands but didn't reply. Eden froze, and after a few seconds she lowered herself back into the chair, not knowing if she should leave or wait for the nun to dismiss her. She didn't want to be rude when the woman had been nice enough to see her, but she needed to go to the store before it got dark outside.

Finally the nun smiled. Then she looked at Eden. "I prayed for you. Just fifteen minutes ago, I went to the chapel to pray about a specific situation. And you showed up. I believe in divine intervention. I do believe that you, my dear, are the answer to a prayer."

Eden didn't know what to say. After all, she'd never been the answer to anyone's prayers. "I'm not sure—"

"But I am. In fact, I'm certain," Sister Regina Marie said, slapping a hand on her desk. "Let me show you around the school, and then I have someone I want you to meet."

"But I—"

Sister Regina Marie held up a hand as she rose. "The Lord meets our needs, Miss Voorhees. Do you believe that?"

Did she? Eden had never been one to wax philosophical about God. Sure, she went to a nondenominational church with her aunt upon occasion, liking that she could wear her blue jeans rather than the stiff skirts and toe-pinching Mary Janes she'd worn when her Gramma Ruth took her to the Pentecostal church. Most Sundays she worked, giving the other manager Delores time to attend church with her family. In her experience, God didn't bother giving the people who lived on her street what they needed. The state of Mississippi did. And everyone on the sunny side of town with their fresh-painted picket fences complained about the food stamps and social security checks the people on her side of town received. As if people in Grover's Park enjoyed whipping out the SNAP card or going to the free clinic for Pap smears. So what should she say? Lie to make the nun feel better?

"I've never found that to be the case. I usually provide for myself. No offense, Sister Regina Marie," Eden said fearing the censure she was certain she'd see in the older woman's eyes.

"Oh, so that's the way of it," Sister Regina said, a small smile flickering at her mouth. No judgment. "Still, walk with me and talk with me."

"And tell me I am your own?" Eden joked. She had, after all, sung many a hymn.

"Ah, we'll avoid the garden. Nothing of interest there this time of year, though with your name, perhaps you feel at home there?" the nun said with a chuckle. "I like you, Eden. You are definitely unexpected."

"Thank you. I think."

Eden followed the nun from her office and toured the school, marveling at the lovely gilding of the chapel altar, impressed by the modified gym, the water therapy offered in the indoor pool, and blown away by the classrooms with their specialized desks, whiteboards, and warm décor. All Souls seemed to be a very special school.

"Well?" Sister Regina Marie said after the tour.

"It's a wonderful place."

"Indeed it is." Sister Regina Marie turned and ran a gaze over the stained glass above the bank of hallway windows. "You're perfect."

"I thought you said the job had been filled. I don't understand."

Sister Regina Marie smiled. "That job has been filled, but there is another. If you'll excuse me for a minute, I'll see if I can make this work . . . because I feel deep in my bones you are here for a reason."

The nun moved away, sliding a cell phone from the depths of her skirt. Eden stood, half of her longing to slip out before the nun came back with some crazy religious mission and half of her warmed by the thought that perhaps the universe had brought her where she was meant to be. Since Eden had arrived in New Orleans, she'd felt bereft. Misfortune had rolled in like the thick fog over the Mississippi River, but something about the nun's assurance that Eden belonged somewhere cleared out a little of the thick grayness. Belonging was what she'd always had in Morning Glory. Belonging was what she longed for even now. Preferably somewhere that wrote her a paycheck every two weeks.

So she stayed put, pacing back and forth in front of the huge stained glass window, waiting on opportunity, hoping Sister Regina Marie was right.

chapter four

Sophie's teacher Dayna Young seemed to have two reasons for asking Nick to meet with her. One was a very legitimate concern about his daughter's inability to handle Rhoda's upcoming departure. The other reason was evident in her coquettish smile, the flirty flipping of her brown hair over her shoulders, and the hungry way she looked at him. He could appreciate the efficiency of killing two birds with one stone and the fact Miss Young had put her best foot forward by wearing a wraparound dress, high-heeled boots, and good bra that displayed her very nice assets.

When Nick entered All Souls Academy for the parent-teacher conference with Dayna, he pasted his "let's do business" smile on his face. What he really wanted to do was snarl and stamp his foot. Or perhaps revert to childhood by throwing himself onto the floor and pitching a royal fit. Because life was spinning out of control, and he felt like a toddler who could not get his shoes on his feet.

But, of course, he was not a child. He was a grown man with too many burdens resting on his shoulders. But that was life. Soldier on as they say. Of course, "they" didn't have a pissy special-needs daughter, a selfish ex-wife, and an award-winning egomaniacal chef threatening to take his talents to the competition. And a parent-teacher conference at five o'clock in the afternoon. Yippee.

"Well, looky here. Mr. Nick Zeringue himself," Pearl Guillot said, setting the purse she'd been poised to tug onto her plump shoulder on her desk. "It's good to see you, darlin.'"

"Always good to see you, Miss Pearl."

"You know, my son and I went to your place down on Poydras. The crawfish au gratin was almost as good as my mama's."

And that was the highest compliment ever paid by any New Orleanian. "Glad to hear it, and don't forget I want to buy your mama's cookie recipe. Best shortbread I've ever had."

Pearl tittered. Nothing like flirting with a seventy-three-year-old school secretary to ensure his tin of Christmas cookies each year. She also slipped him some of the pastries she made for Saint Joseph's Altar each year. No one was more authentic New Orleans than native-born, Italian-descended Pearl Caruso Guillot. She could cook anyone under the table, including some of the chefs at his five-star restaurants. Okay, not exactly, but there was something about cooking old school the way Miss Pearl did that satisfied the belly and the soul.

"You know my mama would tan my hide if I gave out her secret family recipe. Well, if she were still alive, God rest her soul," Pearl said, ringing him through to the inner office.

"I would never comprise a mother-daughter relationship even beyond the grave," he said with a smile. "I'm here to see Ms. Young."

"Go on down. Dayna should be in her room. She always stays too long. I worry about her. It gets dark around five thirty, and that's no time for a woman to be running around this city alone. I gave her pepper spray for Christmas, and she looked at me like I'd sprouted horns. Young people," she said with disgust.

Nick decided not to touch that one and started down the empty hall toward his daughter's classroom. All Souls was housed in a 1920s building owned by the Archdiocese of New Orleans that had been damaged in Hurricane Katrina. Thanks to several grants and the hard work of the Dominican Order, All Souls had opened six years ago as a school for children with special needs, including developmental, emotional, and physical disabilities. With a forward-thinking, progressive model for educating those students who have special challenges, All Souls had been the perfect place for Sophie. With only six to eight students per class, there was ample space for maneuvering wheelchairs and walkers, and the modified student desks were clustered to promote communication. He'd never experienced a more caring, encompassing place. In fact, every time he entered the historic old building with its cheerful courtyard and mullioned windows casting whimsy onto the hallways, he got a lump in his throat. It was . . . a special place.

And now he sat on a straight-backed chair in the middle of the welcoming classroom, Dayna Young's perfume tickling his nose. Her dark hair was perfectly parted and pulled into a low ponytail, and her makeup was flawless. She didn't look like a teacher for special-needs children, but rather a young executive. Or a real estate agent.

Dayna opened her laptop. "I know you've been dealing with some issues. Sister Regina Marie told me as soon as she learned about Rhoda."

"Yeah, Rhoda's in love." He put air quotes around "love," which drew a smile from Dayna.

"Terrible, isn't it? A fatal disease." Her brown eyes crinkled around the edges. Leaning forward, she clasped the hand he'd rested on the edge of the desk. It was a bold move. One he could appreciate because her dress was low-cut. And since he'd been celibate for the past few months, he noticed. Really noticed. "Sophie's not doing well with this change as I'm sure you're aware."

Dayna knew how to play the attraction game well because she gave his hand a companionable squeeze before releasing it and settling back in her chair. She'd recently glossed her lips, and everything about her was open. If he suggested coffee, she'd pack up her purse. If he suggested dinner, she'd slip into some heels, and if he suggested going straight to bed, she'd unzip her dress. Whatever he wanted. That's how she made him feel.

"Nick?"

He mentally shook himself. "I know, Dayna. I know. I'm working on it."

"How can I help you, Nick?" Dayna asked, turning over the manicured hands that had cupped the chair arms. "I want to help Sophie, but I'm here for you too. Being a single parent of a special-needs child is hard. You need help and I'm willing to give that to you, but I need to better know the situation. Have you had any luck in finding a replacement? She needs a caregiver who—"

"I'm her caregiver, Dayna," he interrupted.

Dayna made an apologetic face. "You know what I mean, Nick. Rhoda's leaving in a week."

So she wanted to tell him something he didn't know? The panicky feeling in his gut intensified. "Well, you can help by giving me some candidates. Do you know someone who might need part-time work? Because I need someone who will deliver the perfect balance of love and discipline. Someone strong enough to lift my daughter from the bathtub but soft enough to plait her Barbie's hair. Someone who loves her, who doesn't mind mopping up her messes, and can deal with constant Justin Bieber and Taylor Swift music. And most importantly, someone Sophie likes enough to stop acting like a farthead. Because that would solve everything."

Dayna gave a small laugh. "Farthead? Not the most technical of terms, but an apt description of Sophie's behavior these past few weeks."

Nick smiled. "Sorry. I'm at my breaking point."

Dayna stood and walked around the desk. "I know, Nick. You're a good parent, and we'll figure this out." She set a hand on his shoulder, and her hip brushed his bicep. How easy would it be to pull her to him and find comfort in the arms of what seemed to be a very willing woman? Would it be so wrong to find a reprieve from the hard reality of his current situation? He needed to lose himself in something good, and hot sex with an attractive woman on her sturdy-looking desk qualified as something very good.

But this very attractive and seemingly willing woman was his daughter's teacher, and he couldn't go there. Much too complicated.

Nick knocked the lights out of the temptation that flared inside him. Then he stood. Dayna's hand fell away. "I appreciate it, Dayna. Can you give me an idea of what she's doing here so I can address it at home? Otherwise, I need to get going. I have to deal with something at a restaurant."

When he met her gaze, he saw the disappointment. Her touch was an invitation, and he'd tossed it aside unread.

"Of course. Let me grab her folder and we'll go over her Individualized Education Program and see what modifications might need to be made for a situation such as this."

Nick resettled himself in the chair, and for the next ten minutes tried to think about how he could help his daughter instead of how he could run from his life. He needed a vacation. A getaway. A wife. A cure for cerebral palsy.

Or just a good nanny for Sophie.

He'd settle for that.

Just as he was about to leave, Sister Regina Marie knocked on the door. "Hope you don't mind my interrupting."

Nick rose. "No, I was about to leave."

"But it's you I wish to speak to. About your earlier call," she said, her dark eyes smiling at him. He wasn't sure how eyes could smile, but this woman had that twinkle thing going. "I have someone I wish you to meet."

Nick's heart tripped. "You found someone?"

"After I ended my call with you, I went to the chapel. Our Lady particularly likes to intervene, you know. Like all women, she's not afraid to try her hand at matchmaking." Sister Regina

Marie grinned.

"I need a *nanny*. That's what you prayed for, right?"

Dayna gave a bark of laughter at the wariness in his voice.

"Well, Mr. Zeringue, our Mother Mary and the good Lord do as they wish," Sister Regina Marie said with a little shrug, her teasing smile still in place. "Now come meet the woman I prayed for. I believe she's exactly who you've been searching for."

Eden stared at the stained glass. A nearly nude man with curly golden hair carried a lamb across his shoulders. Latin words wreathed his head. She wondered what the phrase meant. Perhaps she should have taken Latin in high school rather than Spanish. Walking a few more steps, she frowned at the mop bucket with its mop propped against the plastered wall, sitting at the edge of the hallway. A bright yellow sign warned of a wet floor though it was obvious the floor had dried long ago. Eden never would have left a mop bucket full of dirty water unattended, but she didn't have to worry about what she would do or not do with a mop at All Souls. Glancing at her watch, she sighed and glanced down the hallway where the enigmatic nun had disappeared. Eden really needed to go.

"Miss Voorhees," Sister Regina Marie called as if summoned by magic. Or—Eden looked up at Jesus as a boy—divine intervention.

Eden turned to see the nun rounding the corner down the hallway, a man about the same height walking beside her. He walked with purpose, an energy radiating from him that was easy to discern even in the fading light. As they grew closer, recognition hit her. This was the man who'd been sitting with his daughter across from her in the coffee shop. Uh, Nick. Hot Dad Nick.

"My dear, thank you for waiting," Sister Regina Marie said, giving her a smile as they reached her. "I have to say this afternoon has been most providential. I always marvel at the way God works in our lives."

As Hot Dad Nick moved closer, Eden felt the full effect of his gorgeousness. His hair looked ruffled as though he'd recently pushed his hand through it. His skin tone hinted at Creole roots, and he possessed broad cheekbones, a square jaw, and shoulders that stretched for miles. His mouth seemed sensuous, whatever that meant. She'd read her fair share of erotic novels in the discount bins at Trader Jack's Antique Mall in Morning Glory, and that's how the hero's mouth was always described. Sensuous. Eden figured that meant a woman wanted to kiss it. Hot Dad Nick sooo had that going for him.

"Eden, may I introduce Nick Zeringue. He's one of our parents here at All Souls, and he's been looking for you," Sister Regina Marie said.

"I beg your pardon?" Eden said, stepping back, suddenly uneasy. She wasn't sure if it was the intimidating vibe Nick had going on or if it was what those words implied. Either way, she forgot about the stupid mop bucket someone had left in the hallway. The back of her calf hit the edge of the bucket before the realization hit her. And she lost her balance.

Nick lunged toward her, hand outstretched, right before she fell backward.

"Ahhh," she squealed, clawing at the air. His fingertips brushed hers, but nothing could stop her downward trajectory. She went back, her butt slamming into the floor, mop water spilling everywhere, soaking her yoga pants. Luckily she caught herself with her elbows before her head smashed into the floor.

"Oh, dear Lord," Sister Regina Marie squeaked, rushing toward her, holding out her hands.

Eden popped up, her face flooding with color at the horrible realization that she'd fallen on her ass in front of Hot Dad Nick.

Good Lord.

Nick instantly extended his hand. Eden grabbed it and planted her feet so she could pop up and shake it off like a trouper. But her slick-soled shoes, so perfect for teaching dance, could find no traction in the puddle. Which made her look like a complete goose flailing around.

"Here," he said, grabbing her elbow and jerking upward a little too hard.

Eden managed to rise, but just as she straightened, her foot slipped again. Down she went a second time, this time pulling Nick off-balance. Again her butt smacked the floor, but this time she managed to keep upright. Nick yelped right before he crashed on top of her. His leg hit the now-empty bucket, sending it careening across the floor toward Sister Regina Marie and the abandoned mop.

Quick as spit, Nick rolled off her, but not before his hand awkwardly grabbed a boob. Eden gasped and scooted away, refraining from chanting "oh my god, oh my god" like an immature tween experiencing her first feel-up.

"Are you okay?" he asked, rolling onto his knees before pushing himself into a standing position. He extended his hand again. Eden looked at it and then glanced toward Sister Regina Marie, who looked alarmed. He didn't mention touching her boob, obviously intent on playing it off.

Dear God. She'd just done that. Tripped over a mop bucket. Pulled a hot dude into her lap. How had that happened? She never fell. Never.

"Are you all right?" Sister Regina Marie asked, fluttering her hands again.

"I'm okay. Horrified, but okay." And though she sat in dirty mop water and had been unintentionally groped, she glanced up and reverted into customer-service mode. "It's nice to meet you, Mr. Zeringue."

He dropped his hand. "What?"

Now she felt doubly stupid for completing the introduction. Sitting on the floor in wet pants with a bruised ego probably negated the social obligation. But hell, what else could a girl do after making a fool out of herself? She had to pick up the pieces of her pride in some way. Might as well be polite.

"It's nice to meet you too, Eden," he said, no doubt lying. Because what was nice about having to wear sopping-wet pants because some loony tune ran into a mop bucket?

"I don't usually greet people that way. Falling down in spectacular fashion is reserved for special people."

"I'm honored," he said with a smile, a devastating smile that warmed her. And she needed warming because the mop water was cold.

"Good gracious, let me get you a towel or something," Sister Regina Marie said, nudging the empty bucket aside with her foot before stalking to the closet.

Not trusting a hand up again, Eden rolled to her knees and carefully stood. Her panties had totally crept into her crack, the polyester blend suctioning to her chilled flesh. She really wanted to pull them loose, but the impression she'd made on Hot Dad Nick was already in the toilet. Digging her panties out of her butt probably wouldn't be the best thing to do.

"Here we are," Sister Regina Marie said, handing both her and Nick two white towels. Eden did the best she could to blot her bottom and pant legs while the man next to her rubbed at the wet spots on his trousers. When they both were done, Sister Regina Marie clapped her hands together. "Now that you're both dried off and properly introduced, let's talk turkey."

"Turkey?" Eden echoed.

"Nick needs you, Eden."

Eden looked at the man next to her, who had stilled. His gray eyes were focused on her, seemingly measuring. "I don't understand."

"I need a nanny for my daughter," he said, shifting his gaze to the nun who looked quite pleased with herself. "But I need someone who has experience in taking care of a special-needs child."

"Well, there she is," Sister Regina Marie said, sweeping her arm toward Eden like a ringmaster introducing the next act.

Wait. Eden wasn't sure she *wanted* to take care of Nick's daughter. Why trade the care of one wheelchair-bound person for another?

Maybe because you need to eat next month?

Pesky mosquito of reason. She flicked it away. "I'm not sure this is what I'm looking for, Sister Regina Marie. After all, I don't—"

"You said you were looking for a part-time job," Sister Regina Marie interrupted, her beetle eyes reflecting confusion. "Do you not like children?"

"Of course I do. I've taught dance for years. It's just—" Eden closed her mouth, trying to figure out how to explain that she'd spent too many years taking care of a needy disabled woman, and while she didn't find caring for the disabled necessarily objectionable, she'd rather wait tables or ring up groceries. Was it shortsighted of her? She didn't know. Was it selfish? Quite possibly. The irony of escaping Morning Glory only to end up doing the same thing in New Orleans didn't escape her.

"It's fine. I prefer someone experienced in handling medical issues," Nick said.

"Actually, I'm plenty experienced. I've cared for my disabled mother for many years. That's not the issue."

"You don't want to be tied down," Nick said. A statement. Not a question.

Guilt flooded her. She needed a job and here one sat. "It's not that. Since I arrived, things have been rather . . . challenging. I'm good at rolling with the punches, but . . ." Eden looked around, wishing someone would toss out a life preserver. But that wasn't going to happen. As usual, it was up to her to make her life work. She faced a muddy, rocky row to hoe. Easy Street was far, far away.

"No worries," he said, sounding resigned.

Eden lifted her gaze. No worries. Such simple words. For most people. In Eden's experience, not worrying wasn't an option. Worry was her little friend, constantly tugging at the hem of her skirt, always there. But Nick Zeringue's eyes reflected sincerity, and something in their depths gave her pause. "Guess it wouldn't hurt to have a conversation about the position. I *do* need a job, and since I have the skills you're looking for . . . Well, it seems silly for me to look a gift horse in the mouth. Maybe this *is* a meant-to-be."

"A meant-to-be?" he repeated.

Now she sounded as silly as the nun. Perhaps all the religious imagery surrounding her had imprinted onto her brain. She could admit to the occasional romantic wobble, but mostly Eden was pragmatic. Meant to be was something misty-eyed girls sat around and dreamed about. "Or maybe I should have said coincidence. I need a job, you have a job, yada yada."

"Please use my office to discuss this further," Sister Regina Marie said, gesturing past them. "I need to go to the preschool wing to measure for the new whiteboard before I leave for the day."

Internal acceptance sighed inside Eden. If the job paid well enough and the hours worked, she'd be stupid to pass it up. Taking care of Nick's daughter didn't have to be permanent. If she found something else, she could always quit. His daughter seemed sweet, but at one point, the child had flirted with pitching a fit. Of course, dealing with her mother had given her plenty of fit-pitching experience. Betty wasn't just a disabled ex-junkie. She was bipolar.

Sister Regina Marie retreated, leaving them alone.

Nick crossed his arms. "This doesn't seem to be something you want to do. My daughter is the most important thing in the world to me, and I won't hire someone who resents her, regardless of skill."

"I would never do that," Eden said, feeling a bit prickly before realizing his response was fair. Nick didn't know her. He had no clue that when she did something she did it well or not at all. Initiative was something Aunt Ruby Jean had instilled in her growing up. How many times had Eden heard "Stop half-assing everything. Give good effort"? With those words ringing in her ears, Eden hadn't had a chance at being a slacker. "If we agree upon this job, you'll get my best effort."

His assessing eyes lightened. "Sister Regina Marie's office sometimes makes me nauseous. All that pink. Want to sit in the foyer instead?"

Eden nodded. "You'd think an office the color of Pepto-Bismol would lessen the queasiness."

"But it doesn't." Nick stepped back and let her pass, and though she really wanted to pull the panties spackled to her backside loose, she didn't. Because she was about to embark on a job interview.

Fifteen minutes after a brief game of twenty questions, Eden had a new part-time job. Caring for Sophie paid almost exactly what the dance school had offered, and the hours were flexible enough to ensure her own education at UNO was a priority. Eden would pick up Sophie after school, take her to physical therapy twice a week, and would stay until Nick arrived home, usually around six o'clock in the evening. She would also work one day on the weekend, to be determined by both Nick and her depending on his issues with the restaurant and her needs as a college student. After he checked her references and she completed a two-week trial period, she would officially go on his payroll.

"Here are the pertinent phone numbers to reach me. Since tomorrow is your first day at UNO, I'll cover Sophie. Can you start on Wednesday?" he said, handing her a business card.

"Sure. I'll be at your house." She paused, glancing at the number he'd scribbled on the back of the card. "By two o'clock. If you'll make a list of her likes and dislikes, including what she likes for meals, et cetera, that would be helpful."

"I don't expect you to cook."

Eden smiled. "I'll be taking care of your daughter. That includes all of her."

Gratification unfolded when she saw appreciation blanket his face. Poor man. Had to be hard juggling being the—she glanced down at the heavy vellum card featuring a leaping sailfish—Vice President of Operations at Parran Z Inc. and a single father.

"I need to head downtown," he said.

Eden extended her hand. "Nice meeting you."

Nick took it, causing warmth to again envelop her. For some

odd reason, she wanted to hold on a bit longer. Which was odd. And wrong. He was now her boss . . . and a huge step up from Squicky Gary at Penny Pinchers. Huge.

She pulled her hand away.

"And you. I hope this arrangement will work out. I *need* this to work out," he said, releasing her hand and rising from the bench. "If you see Sister Regina Marie, tell her I said goodbye . . . and thanks."

Eden nodded. "See you Wednesday."

Minutes later, after saying goodbye to the nun who looked a bit too pleased with herself, Eden climbed inside her car and dumped her bag on the passenger seat. Thankfully it wasn't yet dark, which meant she'd be able to pick up a few things from the store to hold her over until her furniture came. Like an electric blanket and some roach spray. As she cranked the engine, she noticed a paper flopping beneath her windshield wiper. Unrolling the window, she leaned out and snagged it.

A ticket?

Parking in a fire lane?

She spotted the fire hydrant she hadn't seen early because of a car that had parked over the line. Jumping out, she studied the street. Her front end was barely over the line. So not fair.

But then that was something Eden had known since she wore scuffed pumps from the Goodwill bin to her first prom. Life was so damned unfair.

God, what a day.

But at least she had a job.

chapter five

TWO WEEKS LATER, Eden stood in front of her psychology class and tried not to dissolve into a puddle of misery in the middle of the hallway.

Despite procuring a job, things weren't getting any better.

Over the past two weeks, she'd managed to get her belongings down to New Orleans, thanking her lucky stars Jerry and Little Ray were big and strong and able to negotiate stairs and narrow doorways. Once she'd gotten her hodgepodge furniture, she'd added a few throw pillows she'd found in the clearance section of the Walmart in Metairie and sewn some curtains from discounted shower curtains she'd brought with her from Penny Pinchers. A full-price area rug made the place somewhat livable, but she resented the amount she'd been forced to spend even while rationalizing that the better quality would hold up for years.

Working for Nick Zeringue hadn't been easy either. For one thing, Sophie didn't like her. Okay, the child was grieving the loss of her former nanny. A few days after starting the job, Eden had attended Rhoda's small going-away party at the Zeringues,' mostly so Rhoda could show Eden the ropes before the party.

Sophie had melted down when it was time for Rhoda to leave, and no amount of cajoling would placate her. Eden had managed to get Sophie to her room and tucked into bed, but not easily. The child had resisted every attempt at tugging on her jammies and, once in the bed, refused to say her prayers or read the book Eden had spent precious money on as a "let's be friends" gift. The whole episode left Eden feeling alienated. Nothing was worse than the intimacy of taking care of someone who glared at you.

And even now, though she'd put the check Nick had left on the counter for her in the bank, the raw, sucking sound of her money draining away pulled at her.

It was all so depressing.

Eden walked away from the classroom she should be entering, trying to tuck her grim thoughts away, trying to discount the fact she couldn't afford the class fee for her theatre class. But she'd lived this way her whole life. Why would living in New Orleans be any different? So much for being tough and determined. Perhaps she should go back home, beg for her old job back, and forget about this dream nonsense.

Dreams of being a modern woman in a big city. Dreams of museums, fancy cocktails, and cab rides to an apartment with a leather sofa and a sleek cat curled up on expensive bedding. Dreams of raucous applause and standing ovations. Stupid, unreachable dreams, fanciful notions given steam by her late friend. Eden's silly musings were all Lacy's fault.

"You deserve more," Lacy would say, blowing a huge bubble, letting it pop and stick to her lips before plucking the gum out and dabbing up the stickiness. Lacy was always doing that. Eden particularly remembered a lunch they'd shared a month before Lacy was diagnosed with ovarian cancer.

"That's gross," Eden said, watching her friend play with her gum. Lacy had brought Eden a pimento cheese sandwich for lunch, meeting her at the Veteran's Memorial by the old mill pond. Fat ducks waddled nearby, quacking their requests for Eden's bread crust. "And stop saying I deserve more. I'm nothing special."

Lacy flipped her blond hair over her shoulder and made a face. "Are you shitting me? You're fabulous. When I watch you on stage, I forget you're Eden. You become someone else. It's like the weirdest and yet most wonderful thing in the world. Getting out of Morning Glory and showing the world how good you are at dancing and singing and acting is something you have to do. Promise me you'll try."

"Lacy, I can't promise you that," Eden said, nibbling the last of the cheese stuck to the homemade bread Lacy's mom made every week, then tossing the honey-brown crust to a noisy mallard. She'd just finished a run at the repertoire theatre in Jackson. The reviews had been good, but it was Jackson. Not New York City.

"Yes, you can." Lacy unwrapped another piece of Dubble Bubble. "Why can't you?"

"You *know* why." Eden sighed.

"Yeah, well, it's not fair. Why should you have to stay here and take care of your mother? Sunny's totally selfish if you ask me. She didn't think about anyone but herself when she took off—"

"I don't blame Sunny," Eden said, popping a green grape into her mouth. The sweetness was a reminder of what she'd lost that day back in June. When her mother had collapsed at work. When she'd lost her future. "What happened to Mama came after Sunny left. She didn't know Mama would have a stroke. Sunny had to get out. My sister was destroyed by what Henry did. I don't blame her for running. Hell, she got out while she could."

Lacy frowned, knitting her high-arched brows together. She looked like that viral Grumpy Cat from Facebook. "But you won't get out."

"I can't leave. Not now."

"One day you will. I'll make sure you do. You'll have your chance to shine, Eden. You deserve that."

And Lacy had given her that chance. Too bad Eden was

mucking it up so badly. The whole money thing, the stupid bracelet, the actual thought of something good happening for her, was a fairy tale sold to her by someone who only saw possibility, never reality. When Lacy died, Eden's heart had broken. The bouncy blonde had been the glue in their group. Eden loved Rosemary and Jess. How could she not? But Lacy was, well, Lacy. Like the fireworks Eden watched out her window on the Fourth of July, her friend was so alive, so full of energy and dazzling color exploding in the darkness, and then . . . no more. Lacy had left a legacy behind. But Eden wasn't like Jess and Rosemary. She didn't have family money or the skills to bring home a decent paycheck. All Eden had was gumption and grit . . . and a killer high kick.

And obviously that wasn't enough.

So she was throwing herself another pity party. Bring out the confetti and light the candles on the soggy cake. She had every reason to sulk because on top of the parking ticket, the used laptop Rosemary had given her crashed last week. Eden had taken it to a local repair shop that had good reviews, but the stupid thing couldn't be fixed. Cost her a hundred bucks for the guy to tell her she should trash the thing and get a new reconditioned one. Something she couldn't afford, not to mention she still hadn't bought the expensive psychology textbook. Two days earlier, her sister had phoned with a request for help with her mother's medicine, which wasn't covered by insurance. Sunny had used her own savings to start fixing up the old house so she and Eden could put it on the market. Eden knew Sunny didn't want to stay in Morning Glory, but she wasn't sure putting their mother in a retirement home was a good idea. Sure, the old house was in disrepair, but it was home. And Eden wasn't sure they could afford a fancy adult-care facility. With all the cuts to health services, they were lucky her mother qualified for home health care.

God, everything felt so out of control.

This is what she got when she tried to spread her wings.

A total smackdown.

"Hey, Eden, isn't it?" someone said, jarring her out of her desperate thoughts.

Yeah, her pity parties were now a habit. Perhaps she should try party planning as a major. Was that an actual major? "Hi, Jordan."

Jordan Somebody or Other blinked at her with big doe eyes. "Whatcha doin' out here? We have class."

"I'm tossing streamers," Eden muttered.

Doe eyes blinked. Then blinked again. "Huh?"

"Never mind. Just trying to decide whether I should withdraw from this class or try to manage without a textbook."

Jordan had long platinum hair straight from a bottle and she was too thin, but very friendly. Like Bambi. Yeah, doe eyes, knobby knees and a wildflower innocence. "Those things cost an arm and leg, huh? I dug under couch cushions to get enough for mine."

"What's with them costing so much?"

"I don't know. People who got, got. People who don't, don't. Textbook people must live good."

So Bambi was a student of the school of hard knocks where Eden currently held a master's degree. "Yeah, I need, like, three jobs and a winning lottery ticket to afford that textbook."

Jordan laughed. "Wait, you looking for a job?" She cocked her head in an adorable manner.

"I have a part-time job as a nanny, but I think I need to find something else. Just not making enough." Eden normally wouldn't admit something like that to a stranger. She was very private. Misery might love company, but Eden had learned early on that complaining about her life or admitting she didn't have what she needed prompted a response she didn't want from others. They either pitied her or wanted to get away from her. So she kept it all in. But Jordan seemed a kindred spirit. Like knew like.

"You wouldn't be interested in a waitressing job or anything, huh? The place I work is hiring, but it's kinda a different joint, you know? They like a certain look."

Strip club probably. Or Hooters. Eden wasn't doing that. She'd scrub toilets at a rest stop before she worked in a place like the one that wrecked her mother's life or one that showcased her butt in shortie shorts. No way. "Uh, I don't think so. Thing is, I had a job lined up at a dance studio but that fell through. The one I have is good, but I'm not sure I can afford to stay in school. Unless I rob a bank."

Jordan grinned. "You'd look good in orange, but do you really want to do that whole prison thing?"

"Probably not."

"Look, I withdrew from school last year and saved up some money. Doing that worked out way better than stressing out. The tips at Gatsby's are killer good. I saved what I needed in no time. And if you have experience in dance, you definitely want to check this place out. Gatsby's is the hottest club in New Orleans right now. Hell, it's the hottest in the whole damn state. Let me know if you're interested. I happen to know Frenchie's looking for someone for the ensemble. I've pretty much got two left feet, so I'll stick to being a cocktail waitress, but you might be perfect."

"Ensemble?"

Bambi—uh, Jordan—nodded. "Like a chorus line thing. Let me know if you want more info. We gotta go." The girl jerked a thumb toward the classroom Eden had abandoned minutes ago.

"Go on ahead."

Hmm. A position in an ensemble? That didn't sound like a strip club. What the heck was Gatsby's anyway?

Pulling out her cell phone, Eden spied a bench near the double doors of the building. Sinking down, she entered the name into the search engine. Immediately the site popped up. Gatsby's, the quintessential vintage New Orleans experience. Five minutes later, she had a pretty good idea what Gatsby's was about—a sexy speakeasy with cabaret-style performances, tasteful burlesque, and designer cocktails. The ratings were insanely good and every major New Orleans publication had done a review or feature on the place. With a cigar room, New Orleans-style brass band, and elaborate costumes and stage productions, Gatsby's was *the* hot spot.

Hmm.

Eden would never consider working at a strip club or anything near that, but Gatsby's wasn't quite a strip club, and the idea of being in an ensemble stirred something in her. She missed dancing. For the past few weeks, she'd not been able to summon the energy to put together her barre and construct an area in her apartment for her daily stretching and dance repetitions. Her body begged to be challenged, her mind longed to lose itself in music. She needed that therapy. But to withdraw from school . . .

She looked around at the scuffed walls with the bulletin boards peppered with flyers, the gleaming linoleum. This was why she was here, right? She wanted a degree. To defy expectations. To be something other than a loser Voorhees in a crumbling house driving a run-down car. Okay, so she wasn't exactly a hillbilly, but she was pretty close.

Still, she couldn't quit her job with Nick and Sophie. At least not yet. Not if she wanted to eat and pay the bill for the stupid phone that had become her lifeline to everything that mattered, namely Jess and Rosemary. She could text them at any moment, check their photos online. Feel like she was still with the people who loved her unconditionally. So at this point, she had to have a place to sleep, food, and her phone. Maybe she could advertise for a roommate?

A door down the hall closed, and Eden realized it was the one to her class. The professor had closed the door.

Was that a sign?

Close the door. For now.

She looked at the phone in her hand. Then she dialed the familiar number she always dialed when she needed solid advice.

"Hey," Jess said, out of breath.

"Uh, did I interrupt something?" Even though Jess and Ryan

weren't married, they seemed to treat every day like a honeymoon. So it wasn't atypical for Jess to answer the phone out of breath.

"Tabada." Jess panted.

"Ta-what?"

"It's a high-intensity training regimen developed by some doctor in Japan back in the '90s. It kicks your ass."

"Oh. Well, I'll stay away from it," Eden said.

"Ryan's into it right now so I'm trying to be supportive. And not die while doing it. What's up?"

"Never mind. You sound busy."

Jess panted some more. "I can take a break. What do you need?"

A thousand dollars. A glass of wine. A pedicure. "Some Jess advice."

"Shoot."

"Well, I, uh . . ." God, why was it so hard to say "I'm out of money" or "I don't think I can do this"? Probably because everyone knew how long Eden had waited for something good in her life. She'd watched the world go by while she stocked shelves with cheap crap no one wanted but couldn't resist because it was only a dollar. "It has to do with an opportunity. I'm thinking about auditioning for an ensemble at a local dinner theatre, but I'm not sure—"

"You should totally do that, E. I know you miss performing. That's your zone, and you need that, right?"

"I do."

"So go for it. Unless you think it will interfere with your studies. How's that going, by the way?"

Being that she was sitting out in the hallway contemplating everything about herself while her class took their first quiz . . . uh, not so well. But she wasn't going to admit that. Not to Jess. Maybe not to herself even. "Fine. It just may take me longer than I thought to do this."

Jess sounded like she was gulping water. "That's okay. You

don't have to rush. And Lacy gave me good advice in my goodbye letter. Don't be afraid to stray down a new path. So this opportunity could be your new path. I mean, I'm sure the nanny job is okay, but your passion lies on the stage. And this could lead to something, right? Maybe it's your drugstore stool."

"What?"

"You know, like in Hollywood. Weren't some actresses discovered at a drugstore? All I'm saying is this could be an opportunity for something great."

Was it? Eden wasn't so sure. She'd never been much of a risk taker except when on stage. Sometimes when the spotlight was on her, she slid into the zone and every risk paid off. She was no longer the pathetic discount store manager. She was someone else, emoting into whichever character she needed to be. She became sultry or beaten-down or sexy or tragic. She dove in wholeheartedly and that's where she lived. Right in that moment. But could she do that in ensemble? And would her withdrawing from school sidetrack her too much? Perhaps if she took this new trail, she might never find her way back to her original destination. Like her mother, who started stripping so she could afford nursing school. Two rehab stints and two bad marriages later, Betty moved through life in a wheelchair. She never saw nursing school or anything better than *General Hospital*.

But Eden wasn't her mother.

And Gatsby's wasn't an airport strip club.

"You're right. I may have to do this. Wish I was as decisive as you, Jess. You always have direction."

"Are you joking? Ever since the divorce, I've been very flip-floppy."

"Hazard of beach life?"

Jess's bark of laughter felt like old times. Something stilled inside Eden. She had people rooting for her, people who would catch her . . . if she would only let them. "A gal should be flip-floppy at the beach. But it's more like I stopped bulldozing my way through life and looked around me at other possibilities. So far, it's working for me. Really working for me."

"I know. He's gorgeous and rich and super-smart. His shirt selection is in doubt, but—"

"No kidding. I keep trying to do his shopping, but he's addicted to perusing *GQ* for his look. That and Jimmy Buffett." Jess's voice held love and laughter. Her friend had a good thing going, and after the fiasco with her ex-husband, Jess deserved everything Ryan brought her. "Look, do what you have to do. You're out of Morning Glory, and opportunity is around you. Don't be scared, E. You can do this. I know you can. You're one tough chickadee."

"You bet your ass I am," Eden said, finally feeling convinced. Because adapting to change, to hiccups, to bumps in the road was what survivors did. They found a new way to fight their adversary. After all, her enemy was an old friend. Poverty never left her alone. So she'd regrettably withdraw from school, but she'd go back. Eden wasn't a quitter. She merely had to find a better way to achieve her goal.

So why did it feel like she was quitting on something?

"Okay, I have to get back to kettlebell swings. Thanks for giving me a break."

"I'm always good for it," Eden said. "Thanks for the advice. I miss you, Jess."

"I miss you too. But New Orleans isn't far away. I'll come visit. And you can come here. That emerald water is waiting on you."

"Love you," Eden said.

"Back at you."

Eden hung up and stared at a flyer for a band named Money Juice on the bulletin board across from her. She wasn't quitting. She was rolling the dice. Nothing ventured, nothing gained. And she needed gain. Big gain. Holding two jobs would allow her to pay her bills and save for the next semester. Rising, she headed toward her advisor's office. She dreaded telling him she'd have to withdraw. He'd been so enthusiastic about her course of study. But it had to be done.

As she pushed open the door, she clicked on the link for Gatsby's and dialed the number. She'd use Jordan as a reference. If she couldn't get ensemble, she could wait tables. She just hoped she had packed her push-up bra. Cleavage was necessary for good tips when one was a cocktail waitress, and Eden was challenged in that department.

Fake it to make it.

Nick unlocked the front door and pushed into the foyer of his Lakeview house. The air smelled like home—a combination of lemon furniture polish and chicken noodle soup. Strangely, a peaceful, easy feeling settled over him. Like an Eagles song. Like the soft quilt at Grammy's house. Like a good cup of coffee on a cold morning. Comforting.

He heard her singing before he saw her. Eden's voice was good, almost sultry, which didn't fit her at all. She should have sounded like Joni Mitchell, not Etta James.

"I'm home," he called out, glancing at his watch. He was late. Almost seven o'clock.

"Hey, we're in here," Eden called from the direction of the kitchen.

Nick set his messenger bag on the credenza along with his keys and cell phone and walked into the kitchen. Sophie sat in her chair at the breakfast table, tongue caught between her teeth as she tried to butter rolls sitting on a baking pan. Eden stood at the stove, pouring macaroni noodles into a large dutch oven. And though Nick had arrived plenty of times to Rhoda and Sophie involved in domestic activity that warmed his heart, something about the scenario playing out in front of him squiggled deep inside. Sister Regina Marie had been right. Eden fit them.

His new nanny wore a ruffled apron cinched around her tiny waist. Her ebony hair was tucked behind dainty ears and her face looked slightly flushed.

"Hey, welcome home."

Magic words after a too-long day. He could almost imagine this was how it should be. And though he wasn't a sexist pig, he could acknowledge something about a woman saying those words while she looked cute and homey and—He couldn't go there. Dumb idea.

Sophie looked up, and for the first time in weeks, his daughter smiled. "Hi, Dad."

Nick walked over and kissed her head. Her hair smelled clean and she had sparkly barrettes holding back the tangle of waves. "Hey, Soph. How was school today?"

"Good," Sophie said, redirecting her attention back to her task. Several pats of butter dotted the parchment paper, but she'd managed to cover most of the rolls with the spread.

"Hope you don't mind, but I made my maw maw's vegetable soup," Eden said, picking up a wooden spoon and giving the soup a stir. Steam wafted up to curl about her face like she was a character in a fairy tale. Snow White. She'd totally be Snow White. "I'm not a great cook, but since it's cold and rainy, I figured it would be appreciated. Can't screw up this recipe." She turned the burner to low and untied her apron.

"You don't have to cook for us. I can bring something from one of the restaurants." But he hadn't. After another showdown with the head chef at the flagship restaurant, he'd wanted nothing more than to get out, escape to something easier. Which was how home felt now. Chef Dom Rizzo had made his mark thirty years ago, but as he grew older, his temper grew meaner and Nick, who'd grown up at the man's knee, could no longer reason with him. The thought of firing Rizzo made his stomach cramp. How could he replace an institution? One who made sauces so good the governor of Louisiana had once picked his plate up and licked it clean. No joke. But complaints about Rizzo from the wine steward down to the busboy couldn't be ignored any longer. They'd already lost two prep chefs and their best waiter to Rizzo's shenanigans.

"I know," Eden said, interrupting his heavy thoughts, "but

once I told Sophie stories about Maw Maw and her silly Chihuahua Poco, I got nostalgic for the smell of her soup. It was no trouble, especially since Sophie helped me." Eden shot a smile toward his daughter.

Sophie didn't look up, but Nick felt his daughter's pleasure. Finally. The child had been a terror for the past two weeks. He wasn't sure how Eden had managed to move Sophie, but somehow she'd made progress. Perhaps it was her nature. Unlike Rhoda, she didn't push or fill the silence with idle chitchat. She gave Sophie space to grieve the loss of her former nanny and time to accept her presence. The woman was unfailingly patient in her approach.

"You should eat with us," he said, hoping Eden would agree. He liked talking to her, but often she darted out as soon as he pulled into the garage. It was as if she was afraid of him. Or maybe she respected his privacy. Still, sometimes it was nice to have a conversation with an adult. "It's raining pretty hard out there."

"No, I should go. I have some work to do." She pulled her apron overhead, making a hank of hair stick up at the crown of her head.

His hand clenched because if he touched her, it would cross a boundary he didn't want to cross. There was something about Eden that called to him, but she was his employee. And Nick didn't play those games.

"School?"

"Um, no. I'm thinking about taking a second job. I have an interview of sorts."

Guilt slapped him. Should he be paying her more? Rhoda had always been fine with the salary he paid, but of course, he'd paid Rhoda more because she had more years of service. "Do you think a second job is a good idea?"

"It won't interfere with taking care of Sophie. No worries there," Eden said, her eyes shuttering. The woman didn't reveal much about herself. She'd drawn a line with him and wasn't crossing it.

"I wasn't implying it would interfere," he said, trying to smile to set her at ease. "You've been doing a fine job with Sophie. I just worry about you. Going to school full-time while working two jobs is a tall order."

At those words, she lifted those startling violet eyes. "Why would you have to worry, Mr. Zeringue? I'm not your concern."

"Call me Nick. Please." He knew it wasn't his concern, but who did the girl have to look after her? He had a big family—cousins who managed restaurants, parents who called him daily and one overbearing, interfering sister. But Eden had admitted on her first day she knew next to no one in the Crescent City. "And of course you're right. I just—" He couldn't say he cared about her. That might be weird.

And thankfully at that moment he was saved by the bell. Doorbell, that is.

"Should I get it?" Eden asked.

"I got it." Nick walked to the door and peered out the mullioned panes on either side of the large wooden door. Looked like—

The door burst open before he could answer it.

—his sister.

"Good God, it's coming down out there," Caroline said, shaking her sleek blond coif and stepping past him. Damp, cool air followed her into the house, invading the warmth. "We have to talk about Rizzo. Mom says under no uncertain terms are you to let him go. She doesn't care how many damn prep chefs we have to replace. Rizzo is Du Parrain."

"Good evening to you too," Nick drawled, closing the door behind his sister, who brushed errant droplets from the shoulders of her raincoat.

Caroline cocked her head. "Oh. Yeah. Good evening, brother dearest." Her cat smile had feathers in it. That was Caro. Brash, opinionated . . . annoyingly smug. But she loved him. And she loved her family. So Nick tolerated her bossiness most of the time.

"Smart-ass," Nick said, walking back to the kitchen. Eden had just slid the rolls Sophie had buttered into the top oven. She spun, her eyes taking in Caroline but giving nothing away.

"Oh, hello," Caroline said, setting her no doubt overpriced purse on the granite island and studying the small woman sliding the oven mitt from her hand. "I'm Nick's sister Caro. You must be the new nanny I've heard so much about."

"You've heard a lot about *me?*" Eden said, her eyes darting to Nick, showing surprise.

"Well, I told her Soph has a new keeper," he said. No big deal. Don't scamper away like a frightened kitten.

"Oh, well, I'm Eden. It's nice to meet you." But Eden didn't offer her hand. Like she knew her place. Something about that inaction bothered him. "I'm going now, Mr. Zeringue. Have a good night."

She walked over to Sophie and leaned down, whispering something in his child's ear. Sophie nodded and said, "Yes."

Eden tugged a piece of Sophie's hair. "See you tomorrow, ladybug." Grabbing her bag and giving a brief wave, Eden slipped out the hall door.

"She's cute." Caro's gaze measured him, weighed his reactions.

"Sophie seems to like her."

"Nick seems to like her," Caro said.

He jerked his gaze from the closed door. "What do you mean by that?"

Caro gave him a sly smile. "Don't even. I can see the way you look at her."

"Are you insane?" Nick cast a frantic look at Sophie to see if she heard his big-mouth sister, but his daughter had the iPad on the table in front of her, focused on controlling her hands enough to press the oversized buttons on YouTube. Thank God. "I don't look any way at her. She's a nice girl. She's the nanny. Period."

Caro shrugged. "I don't care if you diddle the help. Apple

from the tree and all that."

"Caro," he said, a growl in his voice. "She's not the—"

"Isn't she? But I'm joking. I know you're not Dad. Just because he screwed the hostess at Du Parrain doesn't mean you're like him."

"That's a bad joke," Nick said, sliding onto a barstool as Caro shrugged out of her raincoat, walked over to the bar, and pulled out two highball glasses. He loved Caro but he hated how she dealt with their father. Yeah, George Zeringue had cheated on their mother during a low point in their marriage. But their mother Dani had forgiven her husband after a year of counseling. Their parents were still together, and that meant something. Zeringues didn't give up on one another. Not even when things got dark and twisty.

Pouring them each two fingers of Glenfiddich, she sauntered back, hiked up her beige pencil skirt, and sank down beside him. Clinking her glass to the one she set in front of him, she tossed back a healthy shot. With a sigh of contentment, she set the glass down and tented her fingers. "Sorry. I'm crappy at making jokes. I know you don't diddle. Though you should." She lifted an eyebrow and gave him a rare genuine smile. "You really should."

"No time for diddling." Nick sighed, taking a sip of the scotch. The fiery liquid shot straight to his stomach before radiating warmth.

"But diddling is such fun." Caro studied the amber liquid, running a manicured nail around the rim. "Stephen left."

"I'm sorry, Caro."

"Yeah, me too. But it was inevitable. We wanted different things. I wanted a career. He wanted two point five kids and a ranch house in Mandeville." Caro jutted her chin out even as tears glittered in her eyes. Those tears wouldn't fall. His sister wouldn't let them. That's how much control she always had. Tough Caro.

"Two point five kids? How do you do half a kid?"

She rolled her eyes. "How would I know? I swear, I'm allergic to kids. Remember when Sophie would cry every time I held her?"

"She cried every time anyone held her, Caro."

"Still." For a moment Caro fell silent. She swirled the liquor in her glass. "What's wrong with me?"

"What's wrong with me?" he countered.

"Our parents. It's all their fault. They totally screwed us up. We need therapy." Caro cracked a smile. Lifting her glass, she said, "To the best therapy ever invented. Scotch."

"That therapy will land you in rehab, nutjob. But I'll drink to that." He clinked his against hers and took another gulp. This time it didn't burn. "How about some of Maw Maw Voorhees's veggie soup?"

Caro made a face. "I'll pass. But I found a friend for you."

"Not this again."

"She's perfect—sweet, funny, and has all her teeth. You'll get along perfectly," Caro said, finishing the last of her scotch. "Stephen works with her. I'll need to set it up before he changes the lock and his cell phone number."

"Not funny."

"Which one?"

Nick lifted the lid on the soup, sniffed appreciatively, and leveled a flat look at his sister. "Neither."

"Her name is Montana," Caro said.

"Dear God."

"Come on, Nick. You're not planning on staying single forever, are you?"

Was he? "No. I'll eventually get around to finding someone. But I have more pressing issues now."

Caro shrugged. "Look, I'm coming off a busted-up marriage, but I don't want to be alone for the rest of my life and neither should you. Nothing wrong with keeping an eye out, right?"

"I guess."

"Now let me tell you about Montana. She's got so much going for her."

chapter six

EDEN PULLED HER windbreaker together at the throat and tried to ignore the drag queens calling out to people walking down Bourbon Street. The rain had stopped only to be followed by a cold wind that obviously didn't bother the scantily clad performers. Thursday didn't seem to be the busiest night in the Quarter, but Mardi Gras awaited serious playtime in a few weeks.

"Hey, baby. Come see what I got for you. I'll let you touch my—"

Eden squeaked at the flagrant description of what she—or was it he?—had under her flouncy, very, very short skirt. Bourbon Street paired raunchy with elegant well. Several doors down from Larry Flynt's Hustler Club sat a primo restaurant with a maître d' visible through the brass-trimmed door. Eden slid her hand into her jacket pocket and touched the canister of pepper spray she carried, the thought of it comforting. Surely she wouldn't need it.

Garish neon blinked, reflected in the numerous puddles taxis pushed through. A few people clumped together, casting annoyed glances at the cars nudging them aside as they sucked down potent brew from funny-looking containers. Other people gawked at the spectacle that was Bourbon Street.

As Eden sidestepped a suspicious puddle, a group of drunk fraternity boys nearly mowed her over.

"Hey, what's up?" one of them slurred, spilling his cup into the street as he leered at her.

"Excuse me," she said, pushing past.

"Hey, hey." Another frat boy, gingham bow tie hanging harmlessly over his unbuttoned collar, stepped in front of her. "You're pretty. You want something to drink? We got you."

"No, thanks," Eden said, lowering her gaze and moving to the side so she could slip past him.

He blocked her, his hot breath smelling of stale beer. "Come on. Come party with us. You're so hot."

His gaze slid down her body. She'd worn tight jeans and her black vampy boots, trying to look like someone a speakeasy should hire. Now she wished she'd not played up her looks.

"I said no thank you." Her voice was firm even as she looked over his shoulder for someone to help her. No one close enough to hear the rowdy group of oversized toddlers. On the corner an older couple stared at LIVE NUDE GIRLS through a flimsy partition. If she screamed, they might come to her aid. If Pop's hearing aid was turned up.

Frat boy moved closer, lowering his voice. "Come on. We need a hot girl like you to party with us. Cam here loves to go down on girls. When's the last time someone went down on you, baby? Come on. You know you want it. I hear Cam's the best." The group laughed. Someone slapped him on his back, nearly falling in the process.

Annoyance fled as fear quickened inside Eden. She curled her fingers around the canister. If he touched her, she'd use it. She summoned the girl who'd grown up in Grover's Park, Morning Glory's rough neighborhood. She'd handled men who took bigger dumps than the prep standing in front of her in his suede bucks and needlepoint belt. "When you have a little dick, you have to be good at that. Step aside before I introduce you to my pepper spray."

Frat boy backed up. "Hey, don't be a bitch. I was just trying to be friendly."

"Leave her alone, Jace." One of his friends tugged on his arm. Jace shook his head and mumbled something about uppity whores and lumbered off.

"Jesus," Eden whispered, relief flooding her. She checked the street sign for the block number and moved forward. From the corner of her eye, she caught the gaze of a large bouncer outside the next club where someone sang a horrendous cover of an Aerosmith hit. He shrugged. She shrugged back.

Assholes. What you gonna do?

Eden pulled a piece of paper from her pocket. The code to enter the speakeasy was 35NOLA#. When she'd called yesterday morning, the hostess had taken her name. Hours later Frenchie Pi, the stage director and choreographer, had called her. When Eden had seen the number, she'd had a huge moment of doubt. Maybe she was doing a stupid thing. She hadn't dropped out of UNO yet. She could try something else.

But she'd pressed the Answer button.

Frenchie wasn't a bullshitter. She got down to business. Yes, she needed someone for ensemble, but she wanted someone with experience. Could Eden fax her dance and acting résumé to Gatsby's? Could she make the midday rehearsal? Could she work from eight p.m. to one a.m. each night? The questions had been endless. Eden answered each one but asked that before she set up an audition she have a chance to visit the club. Frenchie Pi had given her the code, but the directions for getting into the club had been cryptic—go to the corner of Bourbon and Saint Ann. Make a right. Go into the silver phone booth with a penis spray-painted on the double doors. Pick up the phone. Dial the number given.

That was it.

Eden reached the corner, noting the street was darker than the part of Bourbon closer to Canal Street. Rainbow flags hung from several balconies, and loud laughter spilled onto the street from the bar on the corner. She glimpsed a few guys dancing together and got the picture. Eden dutifully made a right, looking cautiously around her. The phone booth sat against an aged brick wall and would have looked innocent but for the spray-painted penis adorning the front.

Just as Eden moved toward the booth, a cab stopped and three laughing women in club clothes spilled out. They looked primed for a night on the town, and as soon as one paid the driver, they all three crowded into the phone booth and pulled the door closed. Eden couldn't see what they were doing, but seconds later they disappeared.

It was serious Hogwarts stuff.

Looking left then right as if she were about to do something illegal, Eden walked to the booth. The metal edging was cold from the damp night and the glass squeaked as she pulled the door open and stepped inside.

"This is so weird," she whispered to herself, nerves jangling as she lifted the receiver. Probably should have used some hand sanitizer or something. All those people lifting and dialing. She pressed the number and held her breath. Immediately to her left, a door slid open, elevator style.

Eden stepped inside and entered another world.

The alcove was much like a foyer in a fancy home. Except there was black-and-white honeycomb tile, a crystal chandelier, and a smartly dressed woman sitting behind a high desk. She had a sexy librarian look with cat-eyed glasses and very red lipstick. Her neatly secured auburn hair reminded Eden of Rosemary.

"May I help you?" she asked, perfect eyebrows lifted in question.

"Hi, I'm Eden Voorhees. Here to see Frenchie."

The woman smiled. "One does not merely see Frenchie, but she told me you'd be stopping by tonight. A prospect for ensemble, huh?" The woman's eyes moved over Eden in an assessing way. Eden staunched her need to wipe her hands on her jeans. "Follow me. I don't have a table free, but the stools at the bar provide great viewing. You're in luck because Sista Shayla is about to go on."

Eden had no clue who Sista Shayla was, but she delivered a smile. "Awesome."

Redhead pressed a button. "I'm Marla, by the way. I'm one of the hostesses with the mostesses." A panel slid open, and a fusion of jazz and hip-hop music welcomed Eden to Gatsby's.

Eden wasn't sure what she'd expected, but it hadn't been what was revealed to her through the entrance.

Stepping through time.

The room seemed to be divided into three sections with an ornate rococo-style bar on either side of a huge warehouse space. Round tabletops with ivory tablecloths and flickering candles dominated the main part of the room, and a large dance floor stretched before the seating area all the way to a huge stage. An orchestra pit with a horn section sat on one side of the stage and a platform with a Fazioli grand piano on the adjoining. The honeycomb tile continued into the space, and a gargantuan chandelier hung from a rough-hewn wooden beam. It was as if Glenn Dorsey had a baby with a hipster. Art Deco, midcentury modern, and French Regency exploded and somehow looked . . . perfect.

"Wow," Eden breathed.

"I know, right?" Marla said with a ghost of a smile. "It's the usual reaction. I'm going to put you at Mike's bar. He'll get you something to drink and fend off the sleazy guys."

Eden followed Marla through the tables where couples and friends sat drinking and laughing. The cozy intimacy made her miss Jess and Rosemary. Her fingers itched to pull out her cell phone and snap pics for Snapchat. But she didn't have time because before she could even reach for her cell phone, Marla parked her on a red velvet barstool nestled into a corner close to the stage.

"Enjoy the show. Gotta get back. We're full tonight," Marla said, holding up a finger to catch the attention of a burly man with a dark beard who wore a vest and bow tie. When he glanced her way, Marla pointed to Eden.

Then Marla was gone.

The bar was crowded with businessmen, too-pretty women, artsy bohemian types, and one man who looked like a 1920s gangster, hat and all. They all looked as if they belonged.

One of these things is not like the others.

Eden should have worn something nicer. Something not so biker bar. She felt like a wart on the ass of an upscale lingerie model.

"What can I get you?" the man she presumed to be Mike asked. He didn't smile, but he didn't look unfriendly. "On the house."

"Uh, thank you. I'll just have . . ." She should have water. She wasn't much of a drinker, but her nerves felt shredded and the whole self-conscious, uncomfortable-in-her-skin feeling had to go. She needed to relax. " . . . a white zinfandel."

Mike would make a face. She knew that because it was such lightweight drink. Unsophisticated. Country as a turnip. But white zin was what she drank on the back patio of Rosemary's carriage house, lazy fireflies dotting the night as the girls talked about dreams, hard workdays, and the fact Ginger Hannigan wore clothes more geared to a twenty-year-old than a seventy-five-year-old librarian.

But Mike didn't make a face. He merely turned, grabbed a sparkling glass, and filled it with the sweet pink stuff. Glancing at her, he paused a moment. And then he added two ice cubes.

Laughter burbled up in Eden. "Yeah, I'm that girl."

Finally a smile cracked his face. "I've known lots of those girls. Let me know if you need anything else."

Eden took a sip and willed herself to let go of the angst. The walk down Bourbon and the whole inappropriate-dress thing had twisted her tight as a champagne cork. Sucking a deep breath through her nose, she shrugged out of her jacket. *Try to look relaxed, and for God's sake don't make eye contact with any guys. No more offers of cunnilingus.*

Just as she spun on her stool toward the stage to check out the setup again, a beautiful voice rang out, a plaintive and pure tenor.

The room quieted with an anticipatory hush as everyone's heads swiveled toward the stage.

The curtain rustled as a long leg the color of creamy café au lait and clad in a towering black stiletto teasingly emerged. A smattering of excited applause erupted as six women in sexy military uniforms trotted onto the stage. The distinctive sound of tap shoes clacked a merry rhythm. But all eyes were on that leg, a leg now being caressed by a very large, white-gloved hand. Opera gloves with a diamond bracelet winking at the wrist.

"It's that time, darlings. Sista Shayla time," someone crowed into the microphone.

This time the applause was rousing.

Eden took a sip of her wine as the curtain inched backward. The background dancers stood like mannequins, right feet pointed, hands on hips.

Silver flashed as the curtain jerked fully open to reveal a large woman—or rather man—frozen in a vogue. His gloved hand reached out as if balancing a platter, chin was up, mouth in a moue. Golden hair spilled across bared caramel shoulders, and a sparkling Andrews Sisters-style cap perched jauntily atop the smooth coif. A matching sequined gown hugged every inch of an hourglass figure.

The crowd went nuts as the band struck up.

"'Don't Sit under the Apple Tree'?" Eden whispered to herself as the dancers started a boogie-woogie dance perfectly in sync. Finally, Shayla brought the microphone up and with a quick snap of her head, the show was on.

And Shayla was good. Perfectly choreographed and with a voice smooth as satin, the big drag queen made a 1940s classic sound . . . dirty.

When the song ended, the place went crazy.

Eden couldn't help laughing and clapping along herself. And

thankfully, Shayla wasn't done. Another song, this one modern, followed. The ensemble sang, pranced, and seemed as much a part of the production as the handsome piano player whom Shayla seemed to key on a lot. The horn section swayed along and never missed a note.

"Impressive enough for you?" someone asked at her shoulder.

Eden turned to find a tiny woman wearing a corset, tutu, and combat boots. Small Benjamin Franklin glasses perched on her nose, and it was obvious she was of Asian descent. "Uh, yes. It was marvelous."

"I'm Frenchie Pi. And no worries, this is a costume. I'm doing an Ace Ventura thing later."

Eden held out her hand and tried not to laugh. Ace Ventura? There were surprises at every turn at Gatsby's. "I'm Eden, and I think I'm in love with this place."

Frenchie nodded. "Yeah, it does that."

"It's so different than I imagined."

Frenchie gave the man wearing the gangster garb a flat look. He immediately rose and pushed his stool toward her. "Butch."

The man growled, grabbed his drink, and walked off.

"He's a grump. Shoulda got his fat ass up as soon as he saw me. Bustin' my chops about hiring a new girl, but he don't get up and let me do business," she said, hopping atop the stool.

Ooookay, so Frenchie really didn't bullshit. And she was sort of rude. And offensive. And ironically cute as a button. Eden tried not to let her thoughts show, but evidently Frenchie could see the censure in her face.

She waved a hand. "Don't worry. That's Butch. He's usually not so pleasant," Frenchie said with a smirk. Humor twinkled in her eyes before they shuttered. She tapped a blood-red fingernail on the ivory marble top, and seconds later, Mike set a highball glass half-filled with what looked to be whiskey in front of Frenchie.

Lifting her glass, she waited. Eden grabbed her wineglass and winced as Frenchie clinked hers against it.

"What the hell are you drinking?" she asked before tossing back half the contents of her glass.

"Uh, wine," Eden said.

"Pink wine?"

Eden lifted her chin. "Yeah. Pink wine."

Frenchie shrugged and leveled almond eyes the exact color of brown shoe polish at her. "Be here at ten tomorrow morning. Two other girls are auditioning. Two other girls who didn't need to come interview me."

"I'm not interviewing you. I'm new to town. I don't jump in without checking the depth. I'm a performer, not stupid." So she sounded defensive. Eden didn't care. She wasn't letting Frenchie bulldoze her or draw conclusions about her motives. She'd learned the hard way about trying too hard to please the boss.

Frenchie narrowed her eyes, then gave a slow nod. "Fine. I'm hiring someone by the end of tomorrow. Michelle's leaving next week—moving to Nashville to sing country music. But she'll be back. They always come back."

Doubt gnawed inside Eden, but she chased it off. If she didn't roll the dice, she couldn't win big. Or crap out. "I'll be here. Anything I need to bring with me?"

"An impressive audition." Frenchie Pi slid off the stool and jerked her head toward Mike. "Have another drink."

Then Frenchie left.

Eden eyed the half-empty wineglass. She didn't want another drink. What she wanted was to know was how much she'd get paid or if being a cocktail waitress was more lucrative. The ones milling around in smart little suits carrying old-fashioned cigarette-box serving trays looked plenty busy, and the crowd looked happy enough to tip big. Perhaps Eden would rather flirt her way into fall tuition than deal with Frenchie Pi.

"Another?" Mike asked.

"No. Thank you for this one though." Eden grabbed her jacket and slid off the stool. Pulling out a precious five-dollar bill, she jammed it into the overflowing tip jar.

"Maybe I'll be seeing you around."

"Maybe you will," she said, shrugging into her jacket. The crowd hadn't thinned in the least, and as she gave Mike a wave goodbye, the curtains slid open and a voluptuous redhead slunk onto stage. Whistles and a smattering of applause followed.

Eden paused on the edge of the room and watched the redhead's sultry version of "My Funny Valentine." Red needed voice lessons, but the way she filled out her skintight, barely there dress seemed to make up for being off-pitch. Sista Shayla was a much better singer.

And if Eden wanted to give her best effort, she needed some sleep and some early morning run-throughs of "Le Jazz Hot" from *Victor Victoria*. She'd used it to land the Sally Bowles role in *Cabaret*, the last role she'd played at the local Jackson theatre. So much change over the past two weeks had led to little sleep, and worry played dodgeball with her attempts to count sheep. But if she could land a job at Gatsby's in the evenings and take care of Sophie in the afternoons, she'd be in high cotton. Tuition money and a new life would be right around the corner.

Thoughts of Sophie led to thoughts of Nick.

Nick Zeringue.

God, how she couldn't keep her mind off him which was so uncharacteristic. Eden wasn't the sort to moon over a guy, but some strange fascination with the dynamic man had embedded itself in her brain. Maybe it was the fact she worked in his house. She caught whiffs of his cologne and folded a pair of his silky boxer briefs when she'd folded a load of Sophie's clothes. Or maybe it was the way he treated her. He didn't treat her like Gary—one moment inappropriate, the next nagging about her not filling out reports correctly. Gary treated her like she was a nobody. But Nick treated her respectfully. Thoughtfully. And he hadn't held the whole mop-bucket incident against her. In fact, he liked to crack jokes about her slipping in puddles. Like it was an inside joke.

And he'd asked her to stay for dinner.

Oh, how she'd wanted to. For a moment when he'd called out as he came through the door, her mind had gone there—that crazy, ridiculous place where she waited for someone who loved her, warm and safe in the four-thousand-square-foot home with the travertine floors and the marbled columns.

But that was nuts. N-U-T-S.

Nick Zeringue was her boss. And he saw her as she was—a quiet, obedient employee who took care of his daughter. Nothing more.

With that thought, Eden slipped toward the foyer and a date with a Tylenol PM.

chapter seven

Montana liked to flip her hair and talk about how much she loved craft beer and sports. That she knew next to nothing about sports didn't seem to dissuade her. His blind date also talked about self-help books, film noir, and giving back to her community. Volunteering at the Irish Channel Girls Club had made her a better person. She was whole now. And she longed to buy a mini-dachshund she could use as a therapy dog.

And Nick was bored out of his mind . . . and doubtful a little weenie dog would be a good dog for touchy-feely stuff. His aunt's mini-dachshund Odie had been a grump with sharp teeth.

And he wasn't bored because Montana supported volunteerism, but because she never shut up about topics she deemed important. And she said "You know?" a lot.

"I just love watching puppies being born, you know? There's something so beautiful about new life awakening, you know? That's why I'm applying to vet school. I've spent five years doing the vet-tech thing, and I know I can make better contributions as an actual veterinarian, you know? I've finally grabbed hold of my dream."

Nick sipped his gin and tonic. "That's cool."

"I'm teaching a tightrope class at Sleek Physique on Sunday afternoon. You want to come? It's total core and balance work, you know?" She stirred her Skinnygirl vodka drink with the cocktail straw and looked plaintively across the table at him. Her enthusiasm, sleek body, and low-calorie drink choice screamed something he couldn't put his finger on. Maybe it was that she tried too hard. Either way, he felt tired just talking to her.

"You're involved in a lot of things," he said, looking desperately for the waiter so he could request the check.

"I believe an involved life is a complete life. What am I going to do? Lie around? Life doesn't happen when you're Netflixing on the couch, you know? I do a coed soccer team too. Do you play?" She smiled like the date was going swimmingly. Maybe it was for her. But Nick liked crashing on the couch and watching *House of Cards*. With a bowl of ice cream.

"Not since high school. I run. Only for exercise. I find nothing pleasurable about it anymore."

"Really? I love to go for a run. I do five every morning. Except on the weekends. I relax with yoga." She waved at someone and the waiter appeared at his elbow. Thank God.

Montana tapped her glass. "I'll have another. And so will Nick." She arched her eyebrow in question, her teeth bright against lipstick the color of a good cabernet.

"Uh, act—"

"Of course," the waiter said, disappearing like a fart in the wind. Nick snapped his mouth closed. How in all that was holy had his sister thought Montana was perfect for him? She was likely getting him back for stealing the LSU tickets at the annual family Dirty Santa Christmas party. Caro held grudges and was patient . . . a deadly combination.

"Excuse me for a moment," Nick said, pulling out his phone and waggling it. "Gotta check on this."

He pushed back from the table, slightly shamed he'd resorted to lying in order to take a break from Montana. But God help him, he needed respite.

"Sure," Montana said, smiling adorably. "I saw a sorority sister at the bar. I'm going to say hello. We're on the gala committee together, you know?"

"I didn't," he said, pushing past a group of businessmen entering the posh uptown bar right off St. Charles. He emerged onto the wide porch which, thanks to the earlier rain, was damp, cool, and empty. He sucked in a deep breath and wondered why in the hell he'd agreed to go on a blind date.

A blind date with someone who thought yoga was perfect for a relaxing weekend.

Maybe a lot of people thought yoga was relaxing on the weekend. He'd rather have pancakes himself. And read the *New York Times* from cover to cover. Not because he was pretentious but because he actually liked lounging in his pj's pants doing nothing for a good hour. At least he had enjoyed that up until his life had taken a spill. But Eden had solved some of that.

Quiet, pretty Eden with her whisper smile and calming hands had helped mop up the mess of his life.

His mind flashed to her sitting in the hall of All Souls, wet and apologetic. Even as she'd politely introduced herself while sitting in dirty mop water, she'd been like the breath he'd just taken—refreshing. Even with her pants wet and heat flooding her cheeks, she'd not seemed fazed by the whole deal, giving him a glimpse into how she would handle Sophie knocking over a bowl of soup or shattering one of those stupid figurines his mother kept buying. And Eden had proven her worth over the past few weeks. His life felt much easier.

If only he didn't have that feeling when he was with her—the itchy yearning one that a man really shouldn't have for his daughter's nanny. After all, Eden wasn't even his type. She was too quiet, too perceptive, those pretty eyes saying so much more than words. At times it came across as submissive, as if she might bob a curtsy or something. But then her eyes would flash, and he knew fire smoldered beneath the smooth calm.

No lying to himself—he was drawn to her. Her softness. Her stillness. Her vulnerability. And the fact she didn't talk about herself twenty-four seven. Instead of prattling, Eden listened, her mouth curving as he humorously reflected on his day or made inane observations about his nosy neighbor Edith Schwegman.

Had he imagined a flicker of something in her eyes when he'd told her he had a date?

Nah. Couldn't be.

Or maybe—

"Nick?" Montana touched his shoulder. "You done with your call? The waiter brought our drinks, and I'm dying to tell you about my trip to Jackson Hole. I have pictures." She waved her phone and smiled with . . . yeah, enthusiasm.

A woman like Montana would wear him out.

"Sure. One more drink, then I need to get home to my daughter."

Montana looked puzzled. "You have a kid?"

He gave an inside fist pump. Kids were deal breakers. Sophie was his ticket out of an awkward blowoff. "Yeah, Sophie's special needs. She has cerebral palsy."

"Wow, that's . . . Well, I love kids," Montana said, blinding him with her hundred-watt smile.

Of course she did.

Eden tugged on her scuffed tap shoes and tied a sad satin bow. They were her old tap shoes and she needed to replace one of the metal plates that kept detaching, but they would do for practice.

Frenchie Pi clapped her hands. "Places. We're running through the *Ziegfeld Follies* spoof. Once it's perfect, we'll have Derrick work on the Aretha Franklin number. Did everyone get the video I uploaded? I expect you to know your steps."

Eden had gotten the ensemble job. She'd never done "Le Jazz Hot" better at an audition. Desperation did that sort of thing to people. And the pay turned out to be good—$13.50 an hour for six hours work plus split tips with the band. The tips were fairly good even if they were divvied between sixteen people, though Jasmine, a slender African-American with a pierced nose, swore Freddy the trumpeter was pocketing some on the side. All in all, if Eden was thrifty, she'd make enough between her two part-time jobs to cover her expenses and save the money she'd need for tuition next fall. Not to mention, her counselor had given her some hints about financial aid and art grants that might help her cover some fees.

She wasn't giving up on getting her degree, just exploring a different path. And if that path gave her street cred or padded her résumé with stage experience, all the better.

Eden stood and took her place—right side on the end. That's what being a shrimp got you—bookend.

"Where's Sadie?" Frenchie asked, her sharp eyes narrowing.

Sadie was the principle. That's what Jasmine had told Eden Frenchie called the headliner. Like it was a ballet company. Supposedly Frenchie Pi had been a budding ballerina in San Francisco before she got mixed up with a rich guy who went to prison. Word on the street and all that.

"Are you fucking kidding me?" Frenchie muttered, slamming the water bottle she held onto the small table at the side of the stage. "This is the second time this week. I'm going to fire that—"

"I'm here. Jesus, French," the buxom redhead Eden had seen several nights before called out. The woman took a long drag on a cigarette and ground it into the palm plant flanking the opening of the club. Eden managed to hold back a frown. Poor palm tree.

"Why are you late?" Frenchie demanded, stalking around like a field general, doing knife-blade strikes with her hands. Anger obviously made her combative.

"I'm not that late. Chill." Sadie rolled her eyes. The girls in the chorus line stilled, frozen with half wariness, half excitement at seeing a showdown between the two women.

"You're not dressed for rehearsal. This gives everyone a bad attitude. Pure laziness." Frenchie set her hands on lean hips. Frenchie wore all black Lycra with soft leather ballet flats. Her gray-streaked hair had been asymmetrically cut shorter on one side. A slash of bright red lipstick was her only color.

"I'm here. Okay?" Sadie said, huffing and sliding out of baggy sweats to reveal a leotard heavily reminiscent of 1980s Olivia Newton-John. The woman had serious curves. Like every red-blooded hetero male would line up to buy a map to that roadway. It seemed evident Sadie knew that as she sashayed up the steps, tossing a sultry smile to the piano player who moved his eyes over what was on display. "And I'm ready."

Frenchie glared at Sadie for a good five seconds while the woman found her mark and set a hand on her rounded rump. Then Frenchie sniffed and clapped her hands. "From the top. And you better know the goddamn words."

Sadie rolled her eyes again. "I do."

But she didn't. She flubbed her lines, missed a cue, and generally pissed Frenchie off even more.

"Cut, cut, cut!" Frenchie yelled right in the middle of the bridge.

Eden was in the middle of a step-ball-change, flip kick when the music stopped.

Sadie crossed her arms like a childish brat and said, "Jesus H. Christ, French. Let us go through it once. I'll get it."

Frenchie stabbed a finger at Sadie. "You lazy cow. We debut this tomorrow night, and I know you didn't watch the instruction video. I sent it out for a reason. So everyone knows and we don't waste time."

Sadie dropped her hands, spreading her fingers like cat claws. "Don't call me a cow, you fuck—"

"Take five," the young piano player yelled over Sadie's explicit insult. He was the only musician there. They'd do a dress rehearsal at tomorrow's practice, which would include the orchestra. Eden needed to make sure Nick would be home by six tomorrow night if she didn't want to incur the same wrath

Sadie had. Juggling these two jobs could be harder than she thought. Nick sometimes had to go to his restaurants when there were issues. But they'd agreed upon her times, and as long as traffic or other disasters didn't crop up often, she'd be able to braid Sophie's hair and tap-dance her way into good tips.

"Thank God," Jasmine breathed next to Eden.

The chorus girls shuffled off the stage, Eden daring to chance a look over her shoulder. Frenchie looked positively glacial and Sadie more Old Faithful.

"Is it always like this?" Eden whispered to Jasmine, who'd uncapped her water bottle.

"Eh, pretty much."

Since most of the girls were tapping at their phones, reminding Eden of the chickens in her maw maw's backyard, Eden decided to do the same. She'd missed a call from Rosemary. A sweet ache bloomed in her chest, a yearning for her friends. Loneliness felt like her middle name. Oh sure, she'd made friends with Lupe Gonzales, the older woman who lived next door to her and worked in a convenience store in Bywater, a neighborhood one over from where they lived, but that didn't come close to what she'd had with Lacy, Rosemary, and Jess. Mostly because Mrs. Gonzales was sixty-four years old and, to be honest, Eden didn't understand her all that well. She often agreed with Mrs. Gonzales when she didn't know what she asked. Eden prayed she hadn't agreed to marry one of the older woman's four sons still living in Mexico City. Eden's Spanish was rustier than the pipes in her apartment, and she wasn't down with the mail-order groom thing.

Deciding she didn't have enough time to call Rosemary, Eden wandered over toward the piano player and introduced herself. "I'm Eden. The new girl."

"Yo, nice to meet ya," he said, holding out a thin hand the color of fertile soil. "I'm Curtis. People call me Fatso. I ain't much on it as a nickname, you dig, but people don't care about that."

"Oh, okay."

After a few minutes of rote, polite answers about Mississippi, New Orleans weather, and Curtis's favorite football team, ironically the Atlanta Falcons, Frenchie called out for everyone to take their places.

"Guess I better get back," she said.

"You know what? You the first girl who ever introduced herself to me. You must have a good mama," he said.

If only he knew. Betty hadn't instilled manners in her, at least none she could remember, but her aunt and grandmother had made sure she knew how to say please and thank you. And then there was Rosemary. Her good friend was a bit of a stickler on sending thank-you notes, keeping her elbows off the table, and saying exactly the right thing. And Eden was good at observing and learning. "I guess so." She gave him a small wave goodbye and took her place.

Sadie looked to be trying harder even if she missed a few words. Eden screwed up one of the steps, and of course Frenchie's blackbird eyes zeroed in on the fudged footwork. That woman seemed to miss nothing. But Eden felt good about her performance, especially since she'd learned the material in less than a day.

Derrick, she learned half an hour later, was Sista Shayla. He looked nothing like the vampy drag queen who'd seduced the audience several nights before. Instead, he wore gym shorts, a tight T-shirt, and high-tops. He looked normal.

"And who are you, Miss Thang?" he asked when they took a water break.

Eden wiped her mouth. "I'm Eden Voorhees. New girl."

"I like your moves, new girl."

"And I like yours. I've never seen 'Don't Sit under the Apple Tree' turned into vocal sex."

Derrick laughed. "Then, darling, you ain't seen me."

Which was true. "So what's next? You going to take a hymn and turn it into a song about the devil?" She grinned at him.

"I could. 'Cause down here on Bourbon, God's always busy.

The devil's always the substitute. But hey, I can't complain. The devil keeps me in business . . . and pearls."

"And here I was thinking you were a diamond kind of girl."

"Ooh, I like you. You look sweet but you ain't," he said, laughing and slapping his leg. "Just like my wife. She looks all sugar, but she can hum whatever's at hand at my head at the drop of a pin."

"You're married?"

"Eight years next month. You?"

"Nope."

Derrick laughed. He seemed to do a lot of that. "That much against it, are you?"

"No. Just not ready for it. I want to concentrate on me for once. I don't have time for love."

Derrick made a face. "Don't do that."

"Do what?"

"Jinx yourself like that. You know when you don't want it, that's when you get it. That's what happened to me. One day I was in New York City working on *Lion King*, the next month I'm here in New Orleans, married and lovin' it."

"You gave up Broadway for . . ." She didn't want to say "this" or "her."

"I'd give up my life for my lady. She had to be here. I had to be with her. Do I look unhappy? Sometimes someone comes along and there ain't no decision to be made."

Eden's mind jumped to the image of Nick standing in the kitchen, telling her a story about Mrs. Schwegman nearly falling through the oleander bush while spying on him out by the pool. Nick made her laugh. Nick made her want to touch him. Taste him. Catch a glimpse of what old Edith Schwegman was trying to get a peek at.

But that wasn't love, marriage, or anything close to anything. That was her crushing a little on her boss. Hey, it was easy to do. She wasn't blind.

Frenchie called for places, and she and Derrick moseyed back so rehearsal could resume. But this time Eden didn't mess up, and the appraising gleam in Frenchie's eyes as she watched Eden made her stomach flutter.

Could she see Eden's natural ability?

Or had she found her lacking?

Eden had no idea. What she did know was that she had two jobs, at least for now. And like every other day in her life, she would be grateful for what she did have and not what she didn't.

chapter eight

Luckily rehearsals didn't run late because Eden had to drive to Nick's house and swap out her puttering car for the shiny van. Traffic was bad on I-10, and when she tried to take a different route, she ran into construction. By the time she turned a bit too quickly into All Souls, the carpool line was nonexistent. The panicky feeling churning in her gut as she drummed her fingers against the steering wheel at backed-up traffic turned into a sinking dread when she saw Sister Regina Marie sitting outside on a bench with Sophie next to her.

Sophie was the last kid to be picked up.

Great.

But then she saw Sophie laughing as the elderly headmistress blew bubbles from a giant wand. A flash of ginger disappeared into the bushes as Eden abruptly braked.

"I'm so sorry," Eden called through the open window as she slammed the gear into Park and climbed down from the driver's seat to open the sliding door so she could load Sophie's wheelchair. "Construction by the canal slowed me down."

"No worries," said Sister Regina Marie.

Eden glanced at Sophie, searching her face for displeasure, but the child looked nonchalant. Her sparkly iPad case sat on the small tray that pulled out from the wheelchair and the ever-present earbuds dangled unused.

"Sophie and I were trying to outdo each other blowing bubbles. I blew the biggest, but she blew the most. And Ralph over there did his best to burst our bubbles."

Eden spied an orange tabby sitting beneath a cluster of banana plants that flocked the entrance to the car pool line. The cat stared intently at Sister Regina Marie, awaiting more iridescent prey. "Ralph looks like a champion bubble popper."

"He seems to think so, doesn't he?" Sister Regina Marie said, patting Sophie's arm.

Sophie kept moving her head, trying to see Ralph who lifted a paw and leisurely licked it as if he had no care in the world. Sophie had vision issues and sometimes focusing was difficult for the child.

"You ready to go, Sophie?" Eden asked.

Sophie gave a half shrug.

"Wait just a minute if you will," Sister Regina Marie said to Eden. She turned to the child. "Will you be okay here for a moment, dear? I need to talk to Eden."

Sophie shook her head. "I wanna go."

Sister Regina Marie gave another pat. "And you will. Give me a moment."

Had Sophie done something? Since Eden started, the child had seemed to settle into a routine that was, if not comfortable, acceptable. She no longer refused to talk to Eden or made routine chores overly difficult. Eden had managed through patience and, admittedly forced, cheerfulness to gain a first stirring of trust. Refusing to push and domineer had been the right approach as Sophie finally started to communicate, even going so far as to share her favorite music and television shows with Eden. They'd bonded over *The Muppets* and Taylor Swift. The weekly report from Sophie's teacher had been almost glowing in regards to her behavior and focus.

"Is everything okay?" Sophie asked Sister Regina Marie when they were out of earshot. She glanced over her shoulder, noting Sophie trying to listen to their conversation. Eden delivered a calming smile and refocused her gaze on Sister Regina Marie.

"Yes. Everything is well, Eden."

"Sophie's behaving? She's been doing so well. I hope—"

"She's fine." Sister Regina Marie looked more flustered than she normally did. "Well, I'll say it straight out—Sophie told Dayna her father's going to marry you."

"Wait, what?" Eden looked down to see if a rug had been pulled from beneath her.

"She said her aunt said her father wants to 'diddle' you."

Eden couldn't prevent her mouth from falling open. "Um, diddle?"

"Her words, dear."

"Uh, we're not diddling. Or anything close to it. Nick's not interested in . . . I mean, no. That's crazy." Eden couldn't have been more shocked if Sister Regina Marie had asked her if she wanted to buy a dime bag or join her in a bank heist. Diddling Nick? Good Lord, it sounded . . . sort of wonderful. But impossible. The man had done nothing outside of a few appreciative glances to lead her to believe he was interested in anything other than casual conversation and writing her a paycheck. "There's nothing going on, Sister Regina Marie. Nothing."

"I figured as much. I'm very familiar with Nick and know he has a strict no-dating policy with anyone who works for him. Or teaches his daughter. Believe me, the teachers have tried. But he's a good man who plays by the rules."

"Of course. Our relationship's purely business. In fact, he went on a date a few nights ago. So why would she—"

"She longs for a mother."

"She has a mother. I understand her mother lives in San Francisco and they don't see much of each other, but why would

Sophie say something so . . . absurd?" Eden grappled to wrap her mind around the preposterous claim, but at the same time she wondered why a handsome, super-rich, super-wonderful guy couldn't be hers? It's not as if she had a wart on the end of her nose. Or missing teeth. And even if she had those things, why would that make her subpar? Couldn't a guy like Nick fall for a girl like her?

Probably not. But a girl had to have hope that one day she could nab a sexy, generous, okay, straight-up perfect man. The ideal was what kept a gal plucking her eyebrows and shaving her legs.

Sister Regina Marie issued a gentle smile. "Well, she's a child. You wouldn't believe the number of fake siblings we've had around here. Sometimes when a child lacks something, he or she will create it. Sophie's conjuring what she wishes. I almost phoned Nick but then thought perhaps it would be best for you to handle. A well-placed word and whatnot."

"I'll try to bring it up in an inconspicuous way."

Sister Regina Marie patted her shoulder. "I'll say good day then. I have a meeting in a few minutes." She stepped away and called out, "Bye, Sophie. Don't forget to wear a silly hat tomorrow."

Eden made short work of getting Sophie into the van, noting the tenderness of muscles that hadn't been used in a while. But it was a good ache, one she'd missed. Gatsby's would be good for her. She hoped.

As she slid into the driver's seat, her phone buzzed.

Nick.

"Hello," she said, smiling at Sophie in the specialized mirror that allowed her to see into the back seat. She mouthed, "Your daddy" at Sophie.

The Bluetooth switched on in the van and Nick said, "Hey. You got my girl?"

"Just picked her up. We're heading home to do homework. Right, Soph?"

"No homework," Sophie complained.

Nick laughed, and the sound of his voice made a little shiver run up Eden's back. The man had a great laugh. "She sounds like a typical kid."

His statement laid there for a moment because they both knew Sophie wasn't a typical kid.

"She *is* a typical kid," Eden said in spite of the fact.

"Well, yeah. She's a typical kid who's the apple of her daddy's eye. With that in mind, y'all wanna meet for a treat? I gotta run to the Metairie restaurant, but since it's warm today I'm craving a Plum Street snoball. Thought you girls could join me."

"Soph?" Eden said, arching her eyebrows in question.

Sophie's whole body nodded in agreement. "I want purple."

"Guess we're getting whatever snoballs are," Eden said.

"It's a New Orleans thing. You'll love it," Nick said with a smile in his voice.

Eden knew she shouldn't get a flutter in her belly, especially with Sister Regina Marie's words still ringing in her ears, but Nick made her feel gooey as a warm chocolate-chip cookie.

"When in Rome," she said.

"Or New Orleans," he joked.

Fifteen minutes and two wrong turns later, Eden pulled up to the snoball stand. Finding a large parking spot, she showed off her superior parallel parking skills and expertly unloaded Sophie. Nick arrived as she was maneuvering Sophie onto the uneven pavement. New Orleans roads and sidewalks suffered from the humidity and the intrusive oak roots that strained to rise up through the concrete.

"Perfect timing," Nick said, leaning down to drop a kiss on his daughter's head.

"I'm good at that." As soon as she said it she felt silly. Sounded like flirting. She shouldn't do that. She really shouldn't do that.

"I noticed," he said, his gaze growing somehow deeper. As if he made a profound statement. Eden felt her blush deepen, so she turned away.

She couldn't be so affected by this man. He was her boss. He had a strict no-dating policy. Sister Regina Marie had said as much. Everyone knew that nuns didn't lie.

Besides, she had too much on her plate to nurse a crush on someone inaccessible.

"Come on, Soph, show me this New Orleans snoball thing," Eden said, heading toward the stand, which had cheerful blue benches and a striped umbrella in front. A small line had formed, girls in Catholic-school uniforms and guys in slouchy pants and artsy T-shirts.

Took Eden forever to decide, but she settled on buttered rum. If she was going to eat a summer treat in winter, she should at least be appropriate about it . . . even if the sunshine on her shoulders made it feel more like springtime.

She made sure Sophie's chair was secure before sinking onto the bench. Handing Sophie her snoball, which was in a Chinese take-out bucket, she fastened a plastic bib around the child's neck and placed a small towel in her lap.

Then Eden took a bite of the cold treat. And sighed.

Nick walked up just as she made an *mmm* noise and crooked an eyebrow at her. "That good?"

"Oh, wow. And with this condensed milk on top . . ." Eden took another bite and tried not to make another sound that sounded like sex. Not that she would know. Well, she kinda knew. But not in an official capacity.

Nick dug into his strawberry snoball. "Sometimes you can't wait until summertime to enjoy life's good stuff."

What would it be like to lose her *V* card with Nick? Maybe she shouldn't wait anymore. Not that he was necessarily into her, but she'd caught him looking a few times, and there was that "diddle" remark. Wasn't like Sophie even knew what that meant, so she had to have overheard it.

Eden snuck a peek at the gorgeous man who tilted his face to the sunshine.

But how did a girl go about seducing her boss? Strike that. How did a virgin go about seducing an obviously—if judging by the condoms in his bedside table—experienced, hot guy? And she'd only looked in there to find the extra remote control he said was in his bedroom. She wasn't that nosy.

She was being ridiculous.

Seducing her boss or surrendering her not-so-cherished virginity was the plot of a Lifetime movie.

Be content. Enjoy the snoball. Savor the afternoon.

After five minutes of slurping, Nick said, "I like how you don't fill the silence with conversation."

"Are you saying I'm a boring conversationalist?" Eden grinned, making a swipe at the grape syrup running down Sophie's chin.

"On the contrary. The woman my sister set me up with talked my ear off."

"She was probably nervous."

Nick made a face. "Maybe so, though I didn't do anything to make her feel uncomfortable."

"You have that way about you. Not unpleasant, but intense. It can be off-putting." Eden said the words before she could think about them. It was an intimate observation by someone who truly didn't know him well enough to make one.

"Really?" he asked, his gray eyes narrowing in concern. "I try hard to hide my temper or irritation. My father was quick to anger or speak before he thought. I fight against that."

"I don't mean it as insulting. It's how you are."

"Hmm," Nick said, taking another bite.

His mouth was nice. Very nice. His lower lip wasn't plump, but she still longed to fit her lower lip against it, feel the prickle of the small patch of whiskers centered just below. What would he taste like? Syrupy strawberry? She bit her own lip and tried to think about something not so delicious.

Lord, she had to be ovulating or something.

Refocus on the conversation.

She took another bite. "Sometimes people mistake my quietness for disinterest. I don't talk a lot, but that's who I am."

Nick nodded. "And Sophie Bug is a sunshiny chatty Cathy sometimes. That's who she is," he said, this time using his napkin to swipe at Sophie's chin. The intimacy of the action—each of them seeing to the child's needs—struck Eden. This was how it would be if Nick . . .

She slammed a roadblock in front of her thoughts.

Her mind sucked at following directions. It seemed determined to dream about being a family with Sophie and Nick. Probably the loneliness. She could admit she'd been homesick for Morning Glory lately. She missed Aunt Ruby Jean's afternoon lemonade and soda crackers. She missed Rosemary and Sal bringing her pizzas to sample. Eden even missed her mama. They'd watched *Law and Order* together, trying to outguess each other on the murderer. She didn't miss Gary, but who would miss a dweeb like him? So this obsession with her boss had to be about homesickness.

Or maybe the itch everyone had to be taken care of. Nick would do that so well. He was the kind of guy to take care of a woman.

"Tell me about Morning Glory, is it?" Nick asked, stretching out, crossing his feet. He wore khaki pants and a sport shirt featuring a tiny crawfish emblem on the pocket. The bright blue of the shirt did wonders for his eyes.

"It is. It's near Jackson."

"And?"

"Well, it's a typical small town. Sits on a square. We have an old courthouse on the historical register and businesses clustered around the square, including my friend Rosemary's fabric shop and her husband's new restaurant. Um, that's about it."

"Sophie told me she likes your stories about home."

"Tell the parade," Sophie said, her eyes lighting up.

Eden smiled. "About the clown?"

Sophie nodded her body.

"Well, Old Man Tatum had this ugly dog named Goober, and he always took Goober to the parades because he was too cheap to buy the poor boy some treats. Morning Glory National Bank throws dog treats during the parade," she explained before winking at Sophie. "So this particular time was the fair parade, and my friend Lacy was the fair princess that year. She decided it would be hilarious to dress up like a clown and wear her tiara. She painted circles on her cheeks and wore a big red nose and a silver sparkly pageant gown."

"She wore a clown nose with her gown?" Nick asked.

"That was Lacy. She liked themes," Eden said, smiling at the memory. Lacy had felt the county fair theme needed full support. Thus the nose and clown shoes.

"Well, long story short, no one had a clue that Goober got nervous around clowns. And when he's nervous, he makes a puddle. So when Lacy stopped to pet Goober, he wet all over her clown shoes. The urine ran into her shoes, and Lacy had to rinse her feet off in the church parking lot. Her car left without her, and she had to run down Main Street with her dress hiked up to catch up with the parade."

Warmth bloomed inside Eden as Sophie giggled throughout the tale.

"Sounds like something to see."

"If you think that's funny, you should have seen the goose that humped my friend Jess. Uh, I mean . . . wanted to dance with Jess. Very badly."

Nick laughed. "Sounds like you miss your friends."

A statement, not a question.

"I do. Lacy passed away last spring. She had cancer." Just saying the words hurt her. Lacy had been so alive and vibrant.

"Oh, I'm sorry," Nick said, sobering.

Sophie stopped laughing and looked concerned. "Lacy died?"

"Yeah, baby, she did. But she's alive in my memories and in my stories. That's the cool thing. She's not here, but she is." Eden swallowed the sudden rasp in the back of her throat.

"Guess we should get going. Sophie has sight words, and I want to fix dinner before I leave. I have to be somewhere by seven fifteen tonight. That shouldn't be an issue, right?"

"I told you I'd be home around six every night and that stands. If I run late, I'll take care of it. Did you get another job? That seems rather late."

Eden felt the familiar doors inside herself slam shut. She turned the lock with "Don't worry. Nothing will interfere with my care of Sophie. I can stay late on Mondays and Tuesdays if you need me to."

"Good to know," he said, standing.

The happy moment was over, dissipated by the reality of who they both were, much like the bubbles from Sister Regina Marie's wand. Reality was a ginger cat with swift paws popping the bubbles of yearning hidden deep inside herself. Even though she longed to spread her wings, tread the boards, and bask in the limelight, she still carried a natural longing for a faceless man in her future. Someone to cradle her in the bad times, hold her hand, dance with her to old standards while whispering sweet nothings in her ear. After all, everyone needed someone.

"Later, gals," Nick said, dropping a kiss on Sophie's head and pausing before giving Eden a smile. "See ya tonight."

"Okay." Eden gave a more businesslike nod. She was the nanny. That was all.

As she struggled to navigate Sophie over the uneven pavement, she broached what Sister Regina Marie had told her earlier.

"Soph?"

The child looked up as Eden nearly ran her chair over a knotty root.

"Whoops," Eden said managing to steer the child toward more secure ground. "You know I'm just your nanny, don't you? Like, your dad is my boss."

"I know," Sophie said, not looking up. "You're pretty."

"Thank you," Eden said.

"And nice. My dad likes you."

"Sure he does. He hired me, didn't he?" Eden tried to keep the conversation light.

"He told Aunt Caro he's going to find a wife. You don't have a husband."

"I don't, but that doesn't mean you can hook me together with your father like you do your Barbies. Grown-up stuff is more difficult than, well, playing Barbies." The conversation wasn't going like she planned. To a seven-year-old, dating was simple. Marriage was simple—it was cake, a pretty dress, and driving a pink convertible into a pretend world where everything was happy. Unfortunately, an abnormally tiny waist and permanent blue eyeshadow didn't ensure a happily-ever-after. "What I'm saying is your father isn't interested in me. I'm his employee."

"Oh." Sophie rocked in her chair. "You'd be a good mom though."

"Thanks, kid," Eden said, ruffling her hair.

"Don't." She jerked her head. Sophie liked a pretty ponytail.

Mission accomplished. Eden congratulated herself on her childcare skills. She had mad ones. She was born to handle even the most difficult of—

"Maybe he'll fire you," Sophie said.

Or not.

chapter nine

NICK SPRAWLED ON the uncomfortable couch his ex-wife had picked out years ago. He really should buy something he liked. After all, a designer sofa that "friends would envy" did him no good when friends rarely stopped by. Plus it was crap to watch basketball on.

His sister snagged the last pretzel from his plate.

"Hey," he complained.

"Stuff it. I need carbs. And chocolate. And liquor. All things comforting and numbing," Caro said, snapping the pretzel in two and propping her socked feet on the coffee table. On the TV, the Pelicans zipped up and down the court. "Mom saw Stephen with another woman at the Carousel bar."

"Damn."

"He's moving fast, huh?" Caro brushed back her highlighted hair and popped the pretzel in her mouth. "I thought he loved me. I mean, I know I'm difficult. I can be a total bitch, but he loved me. And now he's just . . ." She sighed and shook her head, fastening her brown eyes on the TV screen. They were enormously sad, those eyes.

"I'm sorry, sis."

"His loss. I was good in bed. Seriously good."

"Aaaaand I can never unhear that," Nick said. His sister needed support. She needed to talk to someone. But he had never been good at relationships, something quite evident since he'd not had a real relationship since his wife left five years ago. Which, come to think of it, was pathetic. He should do something about that. Rhoda had said he'd gotten too comfortable, and perhaps he had. It wasn't as if he hadn't dated or tried. There had been a few women he'd seen for a month or two, but those relationships had never grown into anything serious. Instead they'd sputtered, mostly because he hadn't been attentive enough. Women liked attention. They liked to be important. What had one said? Yes, intentional. He hadn't been intentional toward her.

In his defense, he seemed to be attracted to the same kind of woman—ambitious, competent, and busy. Women who were like him. He'd always admired a woman who had purpose and took pride in her career. He liked a woman who wouldn't make him the focus of her world . . . which was ironic, because those very attributes had led to the failure of his marriage.

Caro nodded. "I guess you didn't need to know what a hellcat your sister is between the sheets."

"Right. I don't," he said dryly, pouring some more pretzels onto his plate. He tossed the nearly empty bag onto the coffee table. Caro dropped her feet and grabbed the bag. His sister had come by right as Eden had given him a silent wave, departing quick as an alley cat. He'd stifled his disappointment. Not over his sister coming by. He was happy Caro felt she could turn to him. For many years they'd not been as close as they now were. Failed relationships and their parents' rocky split and reconciliation had united them over the past few years. No, he was disappointed that after the pleasant afternoon they'd passed at Plum Street Snoballs that Eden had reverted to being just an employee.

But, of course, that's what she was.

"So how did the date with Montana go? You liked her, right?" Caro asked, propping her feet back on the coffee table.

"Uh, sure."

"You're such a liar." Caro slid her gaze to him.

"Okay, so she wasn't my cup of tea." Or glass of scotch. Or bottle of beer. Or—

"But she puts out. Or that's what people at the office used to say. Figured that was just what you needed—a girl that gives it up on the first date."

"You're trying to get me laid?"

"How long has it been? Come on, you're good-looking and still young. Why aren't you out there?" Caro dropped her feet and turned toward him. No more teasing. His sister was getting down to brass tacks.

"I went on the date, didn't I? I'm out there."

"Bullshit. You hide behind business. Behind Sophie."

"So you'd rather me be an asshole who takes out girls so I can nail them? Or is sex going to fulfill me? Make me magically happy?"

"Maybe. Look, you don't have to see every woman you date as a potential wife. Believe it or not, there are plenty of girls who are looking for a good time. Not a ring," Caro said, looking as if he were crazy for not jumping on the "I gotta hit that" train. "Maybe if I'd had done that with Stephen . . ."

"You did."

She chuckled. "I only wore white to appease mother, good Catholic girl that I am."

"Caro, I'm not twenty years old. I've been there and done that. College was a parade of girls. I'm nearly forty," he said, feeling the old guilt creep in when he thought about his college days of random hookups. He had a daughter and, yeah, she wasn't going to have a typical college experience, but he got the whole protective-daddy thing. Which meant he saw young girls, keggers, and frat boys ready to give coeds a tour of their bedrooms in a way different light.

"You're in your mid-thirties, Nick," Caro drawled, sounding disgusted. "Stop being such a paw-paw. There's nothing wrong with enjoying the single life until you find someone you want to have a relationship with. You live like a monk, and I feel—"

"Sorry for me?"

"No, that you're punishing yourself for a failed marriage when it was totally that selfish bitch's fault. You shouldn't have pulled me back that afternoon at Mom and Dad's house. She needed her ass kicked."

"Let's not rehash, Caro." He didn't like to remember that day over five years ago. Susan had emerged from trying to change Sophie, had thrown down her napkin and declared herself done with being a wife and mother. Her blue eyes had been so cold. So finite. She was leaving New Orleans. She was leaving him. Leaving the baby girl she'd never wanted in the first place.

"What?" Caro barked, anger crackling in her eyes.

"I'm over Susan, and some of it was my fault too. There's always blame to share." And he *was* over her even if the hurt lingered like a skinny dog looking for handouts.

Because Nick had been wholly in love with Susan Shamwell Zeringue, and when she bailed on him and Sophie, he hit the pavement hard, his heart splattering onto the bystanders in his life. Of course he'd seen it coming. Susan hadn't wanted children, and he'd talked her into it. Susan *had* tried. When Sophie had been born with the cord around her neck, Susan had taken a year off from the restaurant to care for their daughter, but she'd hated being a stay-at-home mom. She'd gotten depressed, combative with him, and angry at their helpless daughter. Eventually he'd encouraged her to go back to the kitchen. To pursue the dream she'd always had.

Oddly enough, that's what first drew him to her. They'd met at a bar.

Nick had been out with friends, a little wasted after celebrating the opening of Reynard's Oyster Bar, the first restaurant his father had entrusted to his care. She'd been alone, test-tasting the cocktails, scouting for a new barkeep for Pat-

Ago, the upscale bistro on Magazine where she served as sous chef. Nick bought her a drink, danced with her to "Moby Dick," and traded a hot kiss with her before he learned they were soul mates, both foodies, obsessed with lychee sorbetto, and determined to stomp their way into culinary greatness—him knocking over conventions while she cut all other chefs off at the knee. Susan had been a dynamic, inventive chef with dreams of being the puppet master at top restaurants in New Orleans, New York, Paris, or wherever she could receive stellar reviews, big money, and international acclaim. She never apologized for being ambitious. And Nick had loved that about her. The woman had been intoxicating, the ultimate aphrodisiac.

And she wanted him.

Until she didn't.

"Who gives a shit? Susi effed you over and left her little girl. Who does that? I hope her ovaries shrivel and she never finds a man who can love her."

"Harsh."

"She deserves it." Caro sniffed. "Sorry. Just the thought of her makes me itch to punch something."

"She's coming for Sophie's birthday in April."

"Yeah. Right." Caro didn't believe it and neither did Nick. Not really. Susan lived in San Francisco and worked at Tarte, the top restaurant in the Bay City area, also listed as a top ten in the US. She'd been named Chef of the Year by Zagat last year and regularly did guest spots on nationally syndicated cooking shows. Her gorgeous body and enthusiasm for the food she prepared made her a natural for TV. And she'd been dating the tight end of the San Francisco 49ers for the past six months. That she couldn't find room to see her daughter stuck in Nick's craw.

"Let's not talk about it," Nick said, refastening his eyes on the television as the Pelicans fell behind in the last few seconds of the first half. He hated talking about Susan, about being left behind while she went after what she wanted. One sliver of himself admired the way she hadn't let anything stand in her way.

The other 99.5 percent of him hated her selfishness, hurt for their daughter, and resented the hell out of her tossing love out for a career. Susan chose fame, money, and admiration over family. Love hadn't mattered to her.

So yeah, he had a hard time trusting a woman. Silly but true. He was afraid to date and fall in love with someone who might turn out to be like Susan. He knew not all women were like his ex. But how could he be sure they wanted him and not the money and social position he could give them? What were the indicators? He didn't want a woman he had to rescue or coddle. Having a disabled daughter made him appreciate women who could stand on their own two feet. Yet he didn't want a relationship with someone who didn't need him at all.

He needed a woman to need him . . . at least a little.

"Fine. We won't talk about your evil ex-wife or my horny soon-to-be ex-husband. Or how good I am in bed. Or the fact you haven't gotten laid in ages. Should we talk about Hitler or the devil?" Caro grinned at him.

"Hitler?"

"An expression. He's really not that great of a topic."

Nick gave a bark of laugher. "You're a handful. Poor ol' Steve just didn't know what to do with you."

Caro snorted. "Now I'm free to find a virile pool boy to figure out what to do with me. But first I'll need to build a pool."

"That's an expensive way to get a guy, Caro."

"You can't give advice. You're celibate . . . and obviously okay with it."

He went back to the pretzels. "I'm not happy with it. But I don't want to jump into a lifestyle I can't keep up. I don't want a pool boy."

"You don't have a pool either."

"Good point." Maybe Caro wasn't far off the path. He'd been avoiding—what had his sister called it last week?—oh yes, diddling. He'd decided a year ago he'd look for a lasting relationship but had never gotten around to it. Perhaps he needed to stop worrying about finding the perfect woman to wake up beside for the rest of his life and have some fun. Like when people stopped trying to have a baby and then, whammo, they get pregnant. Relax, enjoy, don't create expectations. After all, he was only thirty-five years old. He still had game.

But then he thought about Sophie.

Then, oddly enough, Eden.

His nanny wasn't the kind of girl a guy took for a test drive. Not that slipping her into his car was an option. Something about her was wholesome, almost innocent. She was the kind of girl who deserved to be cherished. The kind of girl to kiss, cuddle, lick wine off her stomach. Eden was the kind a man married, and that's the kind of woman he should be investing his time in. Yes, he needed a woman who—

Wait. What in the hell was he doing? Just because he had a small thing for his daughter's nanny didn't mean he couldn't enjoy being a red-blooded man. Nothing wrong with wanting some hot, sweaty sex. And if he got laid, maybe he'd stop thinking about licking cabernet off the nanny's stomach.

As the Pelicans stormed off the court and the halftime talking heads started analyzing the game, Nick Zeringue decided he was going to climb out of his suburban single-dad world and enjoy himself a bit more. Caro's chatty coworker might not have been his cup of tea, easy as she was, but surely there was a woman out there who would tickle his fancy.

'Cause he was a man who obviously needed his fancy tickled.

And he was going to get him some.

The next night Eden chewed her bottom lip and watched Frenchie jab a finger at Butch. Something bad was going down.

When she'd scooted in with the second hand on the :58 mark, she got an uneasy feeling. Frenchie was aggravated. Very aggravated. The stage manager paced up and down the dressing room floor, muttering words under her breath that would make a whore blush and pecking on her cell phone, lifting it to her ear and growling when the result was not what she wanted.

Eden tried to concentrate on her makeup. Tonight was her first night in the ensemble. She'd stayed up extra late last night practicing the steps. The downstairs neighbor had knocked on her door at about ten forty-five to ask her to stop dancing. Eden felt terrible. She'd never given a thought to the rat-a-tat-tatting keeping the older man awake. But she was determined to be flawless. So she put on heavy socks and softened her footfalls as she practiced over and over the three numbers they'd do that night.

All day she'd fought against the butterflies—a feeling she both despised and cherished. Luckily the day had been easy. No spontaneous conferences with principals, no snoball dates with Nick, no balking when she helped Sophie with the exercises the physical therapist required the child to do each day. Nick got home on time and spent a few minutes chatting with her in a most companionable way. And even though the butterflies still flitted in her stomach when he was near, she didn't spend too much time staring as he leaned against the sink and told her about the new dessert his pastry chef had debuted at Voo Carre, the French Quarter bistro that had opened a few years ago. Not that Eden could afford to go and try it. And not that she hadn't wanted to drool a little at the way his shoulders seemed even broader when he crossed his arms. Or simper when he gave her that pretty, hot dad smile he'd first given her the day he'd hired her. The man was fine with a capital *F*. And, yeah, she had a crush on him.

Big deal.

"Sadie's not coming," Frenchie Pi roared, slamming her phone on the table. "That mother fu—"

"No time to bitch," Butch interrupted, storming into the dressing room, making half-dressed girls squeal and scatter. "You're going to have to get your ass out there."

"And do what?"

"Fix it. Sing the damn song," Butch growled.

"I don't know the effin' song. I know *my* song. Not hers," Frenchie hissed and then scowled at her phone, her eyes searching as consecutive dings sounded. "Stupid girl. I knew I should have fired her last month. Now she's running off, leaving us high and dry."

"I don't care who you have to blow, you better do something. I have investors here tonight," Butch said, turning abruptly and stomping out. The Great Oz had spoken.

Frenchie muttered more foul obscenities. After a few seconds, she looked up at the ladies surrounding her. Eden eased off the chair where she'd been trying to line her lips. The stage manager swept them with a broad glance. "Who knows the words to 'Anything You Can Do'?"

No one said anything.

Eden had played Annie Oakley in the Morning Glory High School's production of *Annie Get Your Gun*. She knew the words, but—

"Someone step up. You heard Butch. Investors," Frenchie ordered.

"I can," Eden said, frogs jumping in her belly. Frogs were way more demanding than butterflies. Sort of slimy too.

"New girl?" Frenchie said, narrowing her eyes. "You haven't even gone on the stage before. How can I trust *you*?"

Eden lifted her chin. "You asked if someone knew the words. I know the words. I can't speak for who you trust or don't trust."

Frenchie turned a stormy face to the racks of costumes lining the wall. Wire hangers hung drunkenly, sequined swaths dangling much like the upcoming number. "I can't believe this shit. I really can't believe this shit."

The other girls cast suspicious glances toward Eden. She could feel the questions, the censure, and the incredulity that an untried ensemble member who'd shown up mere days ago might be the one to get the break they'd been hoping for. Eden didn't return their regard. Instead she watched Frenchie. "I've been on the stage plenty of times. You saw my audition."

Eden didn't add that her onstage experience as Annie Oakley had come when she was a junior in high school. Hey, they'd sold out all three nights, and she'd gotten a nice write-up in the *Morning Glory Herald*. Not exactly chopped liver.

After long, countable seconds, Frenchie closed her eyes, opened them, and then snapped her fingers. "Get her the costume. Lisa, see if we have a wig. Make it red. Let's get her as close as possible to Lola."

"She's almost a foot shorter than Sadie. No one is going to think she's Lola LaRue. That's ridiculous," one of the ensemble girls said.

"Fine. She'll be Lulu. Lola's sister," Frenchie said with a shrug of one thin shoulder. It seemed obvious the woman had made her decision. "Let's make this happen. We don't have time to think too hard. Someone give Fred the intro for Lulu. We'll need to take a good six inches off the skirt, and someone find a padded bra. If I'm not mistaken, she's a thirty-two with an A cup."

Just before Frenchie left the room, she jabbed a finger at Eden and said, "Don't fuck this up."

"I'm a B cup," Eden yelled, knowing full well the bra she was currently wearing was a 32 A.

But Frenchie was gone.

A woman with frizzy brown hair jerked her toward a stool and the lighted table all the other girls had avoided earlier. "I'm Lisa. We need to be quick. Your makeup's not bad, but it's too light. Derrick, toss me your 'do me' red lipstick," she commanded, rummaging through a junky drawer. The chorus line dancers unfroze from stunned positions. In the mirror, Eden could see them straightening the line in their fishnet stockings and teasing their hair. A few sideways glances came her way, but Eden ignored them. She hadn't tried to step on anyone's toes. Fact was she knew the words. She'd answered Frenchie's question. That's all.

And hadn't Jess told her she'd have to be bold? Had to stop being so complacent. Find her path and all that crap. So she wasn't apologizing for stepping up and making her own break.

"Here," Lisa said, wagging a glitter eyelash in front of her face. "Close your eyes soft."

Eden shut her eyes, but she couldn't stop the flip-flopping of her stomach. Lulu LaRue. How should she play her? Spunky and game? Or sultry and sleek? Who was Lulu? The long-suffering sister of the temptress Lola? Maybe Lulu had been waiting far too long in the wings for her chance to shine. Eden already knew Lulu.

She *was* Lulu.

Beneath the forgotten little sister breathed a brash, bold, hungry woman who tired of hiding her lamp under a bushel. Lulu didn't want to be polite or subtle because she couldn't risk being overlooked yet again. Which meant Lulu had to leave it all on the stage. Go big or go home.

"There," Lisa said, setting the second glitter lash into place. "Open your eyes."

Eden did.

"Yowser. You got peepers, babe," Lisa said with a grin. "We'll pretty up those lips, but first let's pin your hair back and try this." She grabbed the foam head holding a wavy red wig that would just brush Eden's shoulders from Derrick. The drag queen grinned like a jack-o'-lantern at Eden's reflection in the mirror.

"Well, look at you, Miss Thang," Derrick drawled. He had all his makeup on but still wore his street clothes. Air Jordans and ragged cargo pants looked plain weird when paired with sparkly long fingernails and lacquered lip gloss.

Eden rolled her glitter-lined eyes up at him. "What?"

"I knew you'd be something special. You just had that look, you know?"

Shaking her head, Eden asked, "What look?"

"Like you hungry, baby. Like you real hungry. And now you about to eat. Just don't—"

"I know," Eden said, wincing as Lisa jabbed her with a bobby pin, "don't fuck it up."

Derrick laughed all the way out of the dressing room. The next time she saw him, he was Sista Shayla.

And she was Lulu LaRue.

Eden sucked in a deep breath and took her place. The ensemble wasn't exactly shooting daggers at her with their eyes, but there was definitely some heat.

Good.

She could handle it. Because heat meant emotion. And in the theatre, emotion was good. A performer could feed off emotion, internalize it, use it as the coals to feed her own energy. If only Eden didn't feel like she was going to barf.

It had been a while since she'd stood on an *X* in the center of a stage awaiting the curtain swishing open. She loved the feeling, hated the feeling, and prayed she wouldn't, indeed, toss her cookies. And it would literally be cookies. She and Sophie had made snickerdoodles earlier that day, and Eden hadn't had anything else to eat.

While she'd been transforming herself into Lulu, she'd quelled her nerves by reviewing all the words of the song. Luckily, she'd noted no changes in the song when they'd practiced it with Sadie the day before. She couldn't forget the words. She couldn't screw this up. Like Lacy had written in the letter she'd left Eden—you have to overcome, which means you have to play a little dirtier than Rosemary and Jess. Of course, she'd done nothing dirty. But she knew what Lacy meant. When you'd been born with nothing much, you had to be a little less ladylike to get something more.

Lulu LaRue would be no lady.

Frenchie clapped her hands, gliding onto the stage. "Places."

The chorus girls slid the covers off their tap shoes, tossing the covers toward the wings. Eden did the same, only faintly smiling when she snagged the zebra-print covers on one shoe.

Rosemary had given her the covers for her fifteenth birthday, making sure, as Rosemary always did, that they were monogrammed. Her funny friend. Always doing the Southern thing. So very ladylike.

Frenchie appeared in front of Eden, eyes sweeping her from the heeled tap shoes to the teased ginger wig. Her sharp eyes snagged on Eden's glossy lips and plumped-up breasts very much on display in the tight cowhide vest. "You don't look like you're from Mississippi."

"Good, 'cause Annie was from Ohio," Eden said.

Frenchie narrowed her eyes. "You've surprised me from the beginning. Don't stop now."

"Yes, ma'am." Eden smirked.

Frenchie nodded. "Break a leg, Lulu."

Eden didn't say anything more. It was time to take a step on the path she'd started down only a week ago. Time to get hers.

On the stage. In the spotlight. Being someone she was meant to be.

chapter ten

THE MUSIC STARTED, a quick up-tempo. Over the speaker Eden heard Fred Whoever-He-Was say, "Ladies and gents, tonight you're in for a rare treat. Lola's baby sister Lulu LaRue will make her debut here on the stage at Gatsby's. She's a real sharpshooter, so ladies, hold on to your fellas. Now for your pleasure, the fabulous, luscious little sister . . . Lulu LaRue."

The smattering of applause fell away as the curtain swooshed open and the spotlight hit her. Eden slowly sucked in a deep breath and then closed her eyes briefly.

When she opened them, she wasn't a dirt-poor Voorhees from the wrong side of Morning Glory.

She was the fabulous, luscious Lulu LaRue wearing a too-short cowgirl skirt, a Western vest that showed off her padded breasts, and a sequined holster.

The ensemble started first, the tap, tap, click, click of their shoes building the anticipation. Eden snapped her head toward the audience and waggled her eyebrows. She felt certain after being jabbed with a billion hairpins that the damn wig wasn't coming off.

She fashioned her lips into a sly smile before she glanced over at the chorus. "Oh, is that how it is, girls?"

The girls in a straight line stopped, tilted their heads in unison, their eyes going comically big as their lips formed perfect Os.

"Anything you can do, I can do better . . ." Eden started the tap she'd practiced until her toes felt bruised.

And the chorus line countered with the same tap number. Each went back and forth, bragging about what they could do better and challenging each other with more and more complicated tap sequences.

Eden fell easily into character, strutting, preening, and boasting of her skills. The number was light, silly, and comical, and though it was not milquetoast, it felt a bit plain ol' grilled cheese. Nothing spectacular. And Eden needed spectacular.

Go big or go home.

So halfway through the production, Eden leaped off the stage onto the parquet dance floor. The landing jarred her teeth, but she kept strutting. The experienced band followed her lead as she prowled toward the audience, her longer, slower strides setting the tempo. Suddenly the number wasn't silly. It was sexy, and though the whole thing was off-script and potentially disastrous, Eden didn't dare second-guess her intuition.

Own it, little sister.

An older man sat at a table with his wife and another couple. Eden plopped into his lap, and as she sang the next lyric, she twisted a strand of his silver hair. With a swish of her head, she glanced back at the chorus. They countered her claim.

Eden dropped a kiss on the man's forehead, leaving a perfect red imprint before whirling from his lap and slinking toward the next table where she undulated around a younger gentleman who had a flattop and a military bearing, briefly snuggling her padded assets right under his nose as she crooned, "I can fill it better" to the chorus's claim that they could "knit a sweater." The audience laughed and clapped as Eden hammed it up, flirting, smiling, seducing her audience. She knew she'd captivated them because the air felt static with electricity. So she sucked the energy dry right down to the last "yes, I can" when she stomped back up on the stage and did her best Bette Midler impression, arms wide, voice full, note really, really, reeeeeally long.

When the curtain closed, the applause was deafening.

"Holy shit," Frenchie screamed from the wings.

Eden dropped her arms and spun around. The girls in the ensemble looked stunned . . . and then they broke into laughter.

"Oh my god, you were, like . . . like . . ." Jasmine stammered, her brown eyes wide with shock.

The adrenaline faded and Eden began to tremble. "I don't know why . . ." She didn't know what to say. She'd taken it off course big time. She shouldn't have. It was just that she wanted to be something more than milquetoast. Frenchie was pissed. The other dancers she'd practiced with were ready to, no doubt, gloat at her being . . . Oh God, what if Frenchie fired her?

Frenchie ran toward her and Eden shrank back. "I'm sorry, Frenchie. I don't know what—"

"Shut up," Frenchie growled, grabbing Eden's arm and yanking her back around as the curtain opened once again. The crowd roared, the applause so loud Eden took a retreating step. Frenchie kneed her in the thigh, nudging her back into the spotlight that hit her.

"I told you, folks, that this little sister would wow you," Fred crowed into the system. "Give it up for the fabulous, luscious Lulu LaRue!"

"Curtsy, dumb ass," Frenchie hissed under her breath.

Eden executed the curtsy she'd perfected in fifth grade after she'd watched *My Fair Lady* umpteen times. The crowd got louder. Behind her she could hear the chorus girls clapping.

They liked it.

Frenchie stepped back, putting her own hands together. From the corner of her eye, Eden saw Butch smiling. Actually smiling.

They weren't going to fire her.

Thank God.

"You ever pull that kind of shit again, and I'll dust the floor with you," Frenchie whispered under her breath as she stepped back, executing a sweeping bow, extending her hand toward Eden like she was a gift being presented. Cheers and piercing whistles rent the air. Eden lifted the bouncy short skirt by two fingers and curtsied, then, playing Lulu to the hilt, she spun and stuck her butt out so the skirt fluffed before sashaying off the stage.

When she hit the wings, she collapsed onto a stool right beside a glittering Sista Shayla.

"Well, well, well," Derrick crooned. "We got a new diva in town, girls." He licked his finger and stuck it to her shoulder, making a hissing sound before he strolled off laughing. Eden lifted shaking fingers to her face as the chorus girls swarmed around her, patting hands, half hugs, squeezes, all accompanied by "you were awesome."

Frenchie halted right in front of her, her stony face sending the chorus to the dressing area.

Eden blinked up at her.

Frenchie's mouth curved into a full-blown smile. "I always liked a little sister. Gutsy little bitches. So come by tomorrow and we'll talk about your hours, better pay, and ideas for how Lulu can set Gatsby's on its ear. You did good, kid."

"Thanks," Eden said to the air beside her. Frenchie was gone, no doubt to prepare for her own act—a tasteful burlesque with ostrich fans. The woman wasn't much for niceties or small talk.

Something hot bloomed inside Eden as she sat on the stool. The world moved around her. A stagehand rolled out props for the next number. Girls twittered in the background, and the band played an old standard she'd danced many a time to in her bedroom, pretending to sing into her hairbrush. All normal for a Thursday night.

But nothing was normal for Eden because she'd taken hold of something and pulled it to her, claiming it for her own. And it was going to mean something. She felt that in her gut. When she'd said, "I know the words," she'd changed her path yet again. How? Only time would tell, but it was a moment to remember, to imprint on her brain.

"Eden!" someone called.

She turned her head to find Lisa motioning her toward the dressing area. "Next number."

Eden rose, realizing she couldn't sit and soak anything in. She had to do her part in the ensemble for Derrick's number. She might have made her own break, but no one would ever be able to say Eden Voorhees wasn't a team player.

The next day Nick found Eden folding laundry in his bedroom. "Hey."

She jumped a foot, dropping the Crescent City Classic T-shirt onto the floor. "Shit."

That made him laugh. "Sorry. Didn't mean to scare you. I yelled when I came in the door a few seconds ago. What're you doing?"

She scooped up the T-shirt and gave him a flat look. "Frying chicken. What does it look like I'm doing? I'm folding laundry."

"Why? That's not—"

"I know, but I'm just going to be honest with you—I started washing my clothes here a few days ago. Using my own detergent and fabric softener, of course. But I figured you'd be okay with me running a load or two if I did all your laundry." Her pretty eyes were apologetic as she picked up a pair of his underwear and folded them in half.

Something about her small, quick hands handling his unmentionables did funny things to him. Which was lame. Because they were underwear and to her it was a chore. But it made is mind wander to places where she handled his undies with him in them. Yeah, he totally needed to find a hookup. Lusting after Eden had become a habit he needed to give up. Like really soon. But for some reason, he couldn't control where his mind went when it came to Eden. "It's fine."

"Good, because I went to the laundromat near my apartment last weekend, and the white powder coming out of that place wasn't Tide, if you know what I mean."

He made a face. "Seriously? Like . . . cocaine?"

Eden shrugged and tucked his favorite soft T-shirt beneath her pixie chin before folding it. "Or something like that. And I'm pretty sure a few prostitutes wash their hot pants there too. I didn't want to get hassled by johns or anything." She gave a self-deprecating chuckle.

"Where in the hell do you live?" he asked, picking up a pair of warm sweatpants and folding them. She'd created small stacks all over his duvet. He found the stack containing his clothes and set the pants atop it.

"Lower seventh ward."

Crime and poverty went hand in hand in that particular ward, but then again crime and poverty permeated much of New Orleans. The city was complicated and awash in sin and beauty. Lots of haves but even more have-nots. Being an old port city with varying cultures, New Orleans had given birth to incredible food, music, and festivals, but it had also given birth to racial injustice, profuse gang activity, and political corruption. Like a painted woman, his city was desirable, scheming, and desperate. "But where you live is safe, right?"

'Cause if it wasn't, he was bundling her up and installing her in the spare room.

"It's tucked away on a fairly quiet street. I have good neighbors and strong locks," Eden said, rooting around in the basket for a matching sock.

"Where's Sophie?" he asked changing the subject because he could tell she was uncomfortable, maybe even embarrassed.

"She's in her room listening to an audio book. Her therapy was good today. Rick said he'd send you an email report."

"Thank you."

"Hey, it's my job," she said, folding the last shirt and setting it atop Sophie's T-shirt pile. Then she started loading all the stacks into the basket. "You're home early."

"Rarity. You want to join me for a drink?" So much for drawing boundaries, but having a drink wasn't against the rules. People who worked together often shared drinks. He used to drink all the time with his boss at Ruth's Chris in Baton Rouge when he was in college. They'd had no weirdness between them—merely a mutual appreciation of fine spirits.

"A drink?"

"Since you've nearly an hour before you leave. Plus I know not to disturb Soph when she's mid-story. Hell hath no fury like a little girl who has Harry Potter interrupted."

"She's a bit obsessed with that first book." Eden smiled.

"Let's sit out on the patio. Nice evening to hear more about you and Morning Glory."

Eden pulled out her phone to check the time. "I suppose one drink won't hurt."

Five minutes later, he sipped a nice twelve-year Balvenie while Eden took cautious sips of the Tom Collins he'd poured for her.

"Not to your liking?" he asked, secretly amused by the way she eyed her drink with suspicion. Like she thought he might slip her Rohypnol. Or maybe she didn't care for hard liquor.

"Kinda strong. I'm not much of a drinker," she said, pulling her knee to her. The chair she sat in was large and overstuffed, making her look even tinier. She tucked a hank of coal-black hair behind her ear and fingered the edge of the highball glass resting on the table.

"So tell me about your job."

"Not much to tell. It's just a gig at a place in the Quarter," she said, her gaze settling on the ragged-eared banana plant looking sad in the corner of the courtyard. "But I make decent tips. What about you?"

"I don't have a second job," he joked.

Her curving lips made him think of dirty things. Like how

she'd look naked, splayed on that soft duvet she'd just folded his undies on. Or how that mouth would taste. She'd be soft, sweet, and a little tart. Would he be able to taste the gin? Get drunk on his child's nanny? He was half-hard just thinking about touching her, peeling that tight, stretchy dancer-looking top from her torso, stopping to sample the tight nipples outlined by the forgiving fabric. Her breasts were small ripe peaches, and he yearned to feast on them.

Nick swallowed hard and took a large draw on his drink.

Get a grip, pervert.

"No, tell me about your restaurants. I read somewhere you have seven of them? Which is your favorite?" she asked.

It pleased him she'd done some research on him. He liked her curiosity. Or maybe it was the cautiousness? Something about Eden was intentional but also achingly vulnerable, as if she was unsure of her footing. The first time he'd seen her, he'd wanted to take her into his protection, erase the worry from her eyes, and give her a serving of the happiness she deserved. "They're so different, it's hard to say."

"Which was the first one?"

"Du Parrain. My grandfather opened it in 1948 on Poydras. Canal Street was the place to shop and be seen back then, but Poydras was filled with large office buildings and businessmen who needed to wine and dine their clients. He focused on traditional Creole cuisine and excellent cuts of beef. The sommelier was French and a hero from the French Resistance in the war. Very traditional, interesting, and a mainstay in the city."

"Why would you mention the sommel—What is that anyway?"

Nick eyed the bottle of scotch on the bar cart he'd wheeled out. Susan and her stupid bar cart. She'd insisted upon one, but at least it was useful for times such as this. "It's a wine steward. Most upscale restaurants with an extensive wine list employ them. And I don't know why I mentioned it. I guess as a kid his stories of thwarting the Nazis always intrigued me. You know how it is when you're a kid. You fasten upon things that seem daring and cool."

"My great-grandfather was a bootlegger. He knew Bonnie and Clyde."

"Really?"

"Yeah, he was a real character. Bit of an outlaw. But that's normal for my family."

Nick snorted. "I don't believe that. You don't seem like you'd do anything remotely illegal."

She took another sip of her drink, a secret smile hovering around her lips. "Oh, you wouldn't believe the lunatics in my family. But all families have them, right? We just got more than our fair share of them."

"I guess that's true. We have a US senator who got caught sleeping with prostitutes in DC."

"Hey, I thought that was the norm."

Nick gave a soft laugh and sipped the last watered-down bit of his drink. The sun had tiptoed to bed, leaving the city bathed in soft amethyst. The twinkle lights woven into the shrubbery framing the courtyard lent a romantic glow. He could almost imagine he and Eden were the only two people in the world. A man. A woman. A suggestion of attraction vibrating between them.

What would she do if he reached out and touched her?

Or if he folded her into his arms, breathing in her scent. He'd passed her many times, catching the clean scent of shampoo and earthy vanilla. He could start at the corner of those plump lips and nibble his way to a full-blown, wet, hot kiss. Would she push him away or issue a soft sigh and open herself to him?

"I should go. Never know what the traffic will be," she said, breaking the silence.

"Finish your drink." It wasn't an order. It was a plea. He wanted a few more minutes with her. There was something between them, wasn't there? Or not. Maybe he wanted there to be something more. She was such a mystery to him. He'd never been able to resist a challenge, and Eden had presented him one with her refusal to give him much of anything about her life. He wanted to unfold the origami that was Eden. Explore the mystery of the diminutive woman who held so much of herself apart from the world.

"I can't. Not my kind of drink, but I appreciate your fixing it for me." She rose and set the half-filled tumbler on the table near him.

Nick stood and when he did, he brushed her side. Eden moved back almost too quickly, but not before he caught her scent, before he felt how soft she was in the places that mattered most. "Sorry."

"It's okay," she said, a faint flush staining her cheeks. He looked down at her, at those sooty eyelashes and brilliant violet eyes. Her lips were slightly parted, almost an invitation. Just a few inches and he could brush them with his own. What would she taste like? He wanted to know. God help him, he wanted to know.

The moment stretched between them, heavy and somehow profound. Her eyes clouded as she watched him, still and hyperaware like a doe framed in a meadow. She sucked in her bottom lip, nipping it with her teeth, plucking the taut guitar string of desire inside him.

Nick swayed toward her, his head angling so that he could perhaps—

"Dad," Sophie said before banging into the jamb of the french doors with her chair.

Moment over. Opportunity missed. Doused by reality.

"Hey, baby girl," he said, shifting away from Eden and smiling at his daughter. "You look pretty this afternoon. Braids?"

His daughter glowed. She'd recently lost a front tooth, so she was a bit snaggly with her grin. But the happiness that tumbled from her was so . . . reassuring. Sister Regina Marie had been right—Eden was a meant-to-be for them. "Edie did it."

"Edie, huh?"

"That's what I call her," Sophie said, grinning at Eden. "Only I can call her that though."

"I see. So I can't call her Edie? How about Den? Can I call her Den?" He walked over to ruffle his daughter's hair. Sure, he was disappointed at the loss of a possible . . . something . . . with Eden, but he was pleased to see his little girl building a relationship with her. It had been touch and go for those first few weeks, leaving him to wonder if Sophie was as resilient as everyone kept telling him she'd be.

"You're silly," Sophie said.

Hardly anyone would call him silly. But he liked that he could be that man with his daughter. And he didn't mind that Eden knew it. A man didn't necessarily have to be on his game when the woman had already folded his underwear.

Eden gave Sophie knuckles. "I'm out, Soph."

"That's what she calls me." Sophie giggled. "A nickname."

"I knew that," Nick said, following Eden into the house, hyperaware of the sway of her hips, the sheer femininity on display. His libido was obviously very much out to play. Before he could think about it, he grabbed Eden's elbow.

She turned. "I'll see you—"

Her words died as he brushed her cheek with a soft kiss.

"Thank you," he said softly.

"For . . . ?"

"Making her smile again. Making me . . . smile again. You've done well."

Her hand came up to touch the cheek he'd kissed. "You don't have to thank me for doing my job, Mr. Zeringue."

"Nick. You gotta call me Nick," he said, slightly exasperated she'd pulled the Mr. Zeringue card from her back pocket. Why would she throw up that barrier? Because of the almost kiss? Maybe Eden was a whole lot smarter than he.

"Right." Eden smiled and lifted the beat-up canvas bag she hauled wherever she went. "See you later, Nick."

He watched from the front door as she made her way toward the car he suspected was on its last leg. It didn't suit her, but at the same time it did. No pretention. Pragmatic. Small. She needed something more reliable. She needed a better place to live. She needed someone to wait up for her. But what could he do about it?

He was her boss.

He was Mr. Zeringue.

Shutting the door, he sighed and pulled his phone out of his pocket. Time to do as his sister suggested. Scrolling through his contacts, he found what he was looking for. John David Mangham—college roommate, investment broker, notorious womanizer. Nick had run into John David at a Christmas party a few months back. John David berated him for not calling since the divorce and suggested they go out and relive the good old days. If Nick wanted to meet some available ladies, John David was the perfect person to call.

His friend answered after two rings. "Z Dawg, what's shakin'?"

"I need a drink and a woman," Nick said, eyeing his daughter as she struggled to close the french doors he'd left open. Of course, he'd just had a drink with a woman . . . one that was off-limits no matter how much he wanted it to be different. She'd sent him a strong reminder. Mr. Zeringue.

"Who the hell doesn't?" his friend said with a snort. "You're lucky. I have discerning taste in both. How's next week looking?"

"I'm open," Nick said, hoping that was true on several levels. He had to start looking for opportunities to get a life. So he had to be open to what the world sent his way. "When do you want to try for?"

"How about next Thursday? There's this really cool place I've been to a couple of times. You'll love it. Great drinks, hot women, and there's this drag queen named Sista Shayla. Total hoot."

"Drag queen?"

"Trust me. You're going to find something so hot at this place."

"I don't want to find something hot with a penis," Nick joked.

"Nah, trust me," John David said, amusement filling his voice.

"That's what you said when we broke into the football stadium. We ended up in the slammer."

John David laughed. "You should have run faster. I'll come to your house and we can take Uber. It will be awesome. This place is life-changing. Tr—"

"I know. Trust you."

chapter eleven

WHAT A DIFFERENCE one week made.
Eden felt like she had been at Gatsby's for much longer. Something about being back on stage and in the spotlight was like slipping into a pair of favorite jeans. Just right. For the past week she'd balanced taking care of Sophie, performing as Lola's little sister, and trying to get the paperwork done that Sunny needed to list the house back in Morning Glory. She was still on the fence about selling the house. Her sister had already invested in paint and new countertops, but the old house had too much wrong with it to be attractive in the current market. Not to mention the yard was little more than a dirt patch, something Eden had always been somewhat thankful for because it was less for her to mow. Of course, Henry Todd Delmar often came over to mow, trim, and whack, saving Eden from dying of heat stroke each summer. Still, something inside wriggled uncomfortably at the thought of the only place she'd known as home being signed away.

Lisa jerked Eden's chin and began painting her lips a bright vermillion. Each time Eden spun around and looked in the mirror when Lisa finished, she was amazed. Lisa could transform Eden into a vampy Jessica Rabbit in five minutes.

"You are such a good performer, doll," Lisa said, making an O with her lips as she lined Eden's.

"Thank you," Eden said, closing her eyes in prep for the long eyelash extensions Lisa would glue into place. The woman's cool, nicotined hands somehow felt comforting on her face. Like having Wanda Treat at Hair Teasers trimming her hair. Competent fingers taking care of her.

"Sadie wasn't nearly as good or as nice. I know the girls appreciate how professional you are. Jasmine said you never flub your stuff in rehearsals."

Only because Eden practiced at home in her apartment until her muscles screamed and her body collapsed onto the rug she'd spent $299.99 on at Lowe's. Being nearly perfect was what she demanded of herself, and it was a tried-and-true way to stay in Frenchie's good graces. The woman's eyes had glowed with appreciation when Eden had nailed all her numbers in the first rehearsal she'd done as Lulu LaRue. And Frenchie had almost smiled. Let's just say the atmosphere had been decidedly more relaxed with the ensemble and Fatso almost jovial throughout the rehearsals.

"I try," Eden said, blinking her eyes, adjusting to the heaviness of the lashes. Tonight she was wearing a slinky black strapless gown with long satin gloves. The gel-padded strapless bra plumped her boobs, and the faux band of diamonds at her wrist and long dangling chandelier earrings at her earlobes achieved a veneer of classiness perfect for crooning "Hey, Big Spender." And for the first time, she'd be flying solo—no ensemble tap-dancing or swaying behind her.

She was prepared to own the stage.

Because she had to. That's what determined, somewhat desperate women did. After all, if she envisioned herself hitting every note and bringing the audience to its knees, it had to come true, right? The power of positive visualization and all that.

Lisa leaned back and narrowed her eyes critically. "That'll work. Now go knock 'em dead, kid."

"I'll try," Eden said again, rising and nearly hitting Frenchie, who'd entered like a cat on silent paws. "Oh, Frenchie. Sorry."

"Butch wants sexy. You understand? Sexy," Frenchie said, her eyes piercing as if she could ensure Eden's compliance.

"I've been doing sexy," Eden said, wondering how in all that was holy she could be any sexier. She'd shimmied, plopped into laps, and rubbed her padded ta-tas up against enough bald pates to make her contemplate having a rabies shot.

"Yeah, yeah." Frenchie brushed away her claim with a wave of a hand. "But tonight there are more investors. Butch's grumpier than normal. That means he's nervous. Get your sexy on like JT."

"JT?"

"Justin Timberlake."

"Oh, of course," Eden said, making a face. "I'll work on bringing sexy back."

Frenchie snorted. "This is your first solo number. Don't fuck it up."

"I wouldn't think of it." Eden tugged on her black high-heeled dancing shoes and buckled them. She attached beaded shoe clips to cover the plain buckle and snaz them up a bit. Then she rubbed her scarlet lips together. Be sexy. Remember the words. And don't fuck it up. Easy peasy, lemon squeezy.

Five minutes later, she stood behind the old-fashioned microphone near the Fazioli piano. When she was introduced, the crowd erupted into rousing applause, and she wondered if word about Lola's little sister had gotten around that fast. Or perhaps it was the special they'd run on Sazeracs during the cocktail hour. Either way the enthusiasm of the audience did its job. Eden felt the buzz.

She sucked in a deep breath as the curtains opened. The band struck the first note, and she fell into that place she loved so well, into that zone in which the world faded away and there was only her, a song, and an audience to conquer.

Grabbing the mic, she took control. This number called for

her not only playing the vamp but being demanding. She wasn't asking. She was telling. So she stalked across the stage, ringed Fatso, walked her fingers over his shoulder, then sang to him. Finally, when he shook his head and pulled his pockets out comically, she bumped him with her butt and stomped down the steps, grabbing the red feather boa hanging conveniently over a brass coat stand on her way to the floor.

Once there, she gyrated, teased, propped her hip on tables, and even half-draped herself across one table, playing the ballsy temptress who needed a sugar daddy.

The audience laughed as she looped the feather boa around the shoulders of a graying gentleman, pulling his face toward her shimmying bosom. Just before his chin hit her décolleté, she spun away. She knew Butch wanted sexy, but she had to draw the line somewhere, and snuggling a seventy-year-old man between her breasts was that line. Her version of sexy would have to do, and judging by the grins on the faces of the audience, she'd say her approach was perfectly done.

She sashayed to the middle table, then propped her foot on the white pressed tablecloth, allowing the slinky material of her dress to open at the slit, revealing the length of her leg and the garter belt holding up her silky sheer hosiery. She dipped as she sang, stroking the length of leg to the top of her thigh. Then, before her fingers reached the top, she smacked her bare flesh and sang, "Hey, big spender, spend a little time . . ."

She spun away and plopped down into the next gentleman's lap, wrapping her arms around his neck, opening her mouth to deliver " . . . with me."

But then she saw devastating gray eyes filled with amusement . . . and appreciation.

Familiar gray eyes.

Eyes she saw nearly every day.

Oh, shit.

Her mouth snapped closed as shock jarred her. What in the hell was Nick doing here? At a place like Gatsby's? And who was taking care of Sophie? And . . .

Fatso repeated the verse. Everyone waited on her big finish.

Eden swallowed hard before reaching out and drawing back the professionalism she'd lost for a moment. Donning a teasing smile, she slid from Nick's lap. Part of her wanted to run like hell for the dressing room and duck into a closet or something. The other part recognized the man had no clue that his child's nanny had been undulating on his lap. Classic fight-or-flight. And when had Eden ever run from anything?

Not this side of never.

So she turned back to Nick, leaned down, and cupped his chin. Drawing him to her, she positioned her lips mere inches from his.

Whiskey and warmth came to mind at his nearness, and for a second, her little game backfired. Because all she could think about was leaning in and taking a taste of what she'd craved for the past month. What would it hurt? Nick hadn't recognized her as his shy nanny. And Butch wanted sexy. But to kiss a customer? That was another line she couldn't step over no matter how much she'd dreamed of pressing her lips to her boss's impossibly gorgeous mouth.

Decision made, she pressed a finger to his lips, praying her mic would pick up the sound of her whispering, "with me."

His lips curved against her finger, and for some crazy reason she wanted to dip her finger into the wet heat of his mouth.

Nick lifted his hand as if to catch hold of her, but before he could, Eden turned and strutted back to the stage. Climbing the steps beside Fatso, she stopped to listen to him key in the last notes of the song, propping her chin on her hands as he expertly picked out the finale. When the last chord sounded, she moved to the center of the stage and executed a bow, sweeping her hand to both the band and Fatso.

Eden didn't dare look at Nick for fear she might give herself away . . . or jump off the stage and take what she so craved. Just one little kiss.

But that was stupid-ass crazy.

The curtains swished closed, drowning out the applause.

"Nice job," Frenchie said, flipping the switch on the mic and unhooking it from behind her ear. "But no kissing the customers."

"I didn't. You said to bring the sexy. JT and all that."

"We want sexy, not a lawsuit," Frenchie snapped, jerking the mic from her ear a bit too hard.

"Ouch," Eden said.

"What a baby," Frenchie responded.

"Sadist." Eden moved off the stage, giving Jasmine a high five as the girls made their way onto the stage. Her legs felt like rubber bands, her gut like a meat grinder.

Nick was at Gatsby's.

And if she wasn't mistaken, the man had liked what had landed in his lap. The warmth of that revelation almost edged out the panic that he'd find out she was Lulu LaRue.

But what if he did?

It wasn't like she was doing something tawdry. Gatsby's was more than reputable. Sure, some of the acts were irreverent, bordering on risqué. But even though what they did there every night would be deemed adult entertainment, it wasn't "adult entertainment." The acts were always tasteful, playful, and the epitome of New Orleans, which meant drag queens, cabaret singers, and burlesque numbers—just the sort of naughty romp that kept the city jumping. So if Nick discovered she was Lulu, what did it matter?

But something inside her balked at the thought of letting him in on her secret. It wasn't like she was embarrassed that her part-time job relied on her donning skimpy costumes and shaking her groove thing for every Tom, Dick, and Harry. She liked assuming Lulu's persona. Lulu didn't take shit from anyone, and she looked everyone in the eye. Lulu wasn't poor white trash from a Mississippi ditch. No, Lulu was a naughty debutante tired of Catholic-schoolgirl skirts and her mommy and daddy's expectations. She had manicured nails, a big bank account, and too much time on her hands. Or at least that was the way Eden played her . . . and she did it so well that Nick hadn't recognized her as the woman who folded his underwear.

"Good show," Lisa said, reaching for the pins securing the wig in place. "I love the way you ended it. Always doing the unexpected. That's why Frenchie likes you. Artistry."

Eden opened her mouth to thank Lisa, but from the open doorway someone said, "Hope I'm not intruding."

Oh God.

Nick.

Eden brushed Lisa's hands away as the makeup artist said, "Who let you back here?"

His smile in the mirror made her toes curl . . . around the heart that had plunged to her dancing shoes. Yeah, a killer smile did things like that. Made you forget that your boss, the man you'd been crushing on for a month, was about to discover you had a secret life.

"Butch told me it was fine to give my regards to Ms. LaRue. We go way back. Butch and I. Not Ms. LaRue," Nick said.

Lisa shifted her gaze to meet Eden's. "No one's supposed to come back here, but if Butch said it was okay . . ." She arched a brow, asking Eden's permission. The frizzy-headed woman wasn't going to permit Nick entry if Eden didn't want him there.

Nick didn't move. His gaze remained on Eden, searching her expression before dropping lower to take in the suddenly too-tight gown. "I didn't want to intrude. Just wanted to . . . thank you."

"For?" Eden spun around, intentionally deepening her voice. Even to her own ears it sounded husky, dripping implication.

"Making me feel like a man again."

Her knees went wobbly at his admission, especially when his hue deepened as if he just realized what he'd said.

"That didn't come out right," he said, shaking his head, clearly embarrassed.

A rubber band of tight emotion broke inside Eden at the

implication of those words. Here stood a man whose wife had left him, who struggled to run an empire and take care of a special-needs daughter. He didn't date much, didn't seem to have much of a life beyond his narrow world. And the thoughtless antics of a sassy vixen in a borrowed wig had made him feel like a man again? How did a woman respond to something like that?

Lisa nudged her, breaking her study of Nick.

Play it flirty. Be a confident Lulu. "I think it came out exactly right, Mr. . . . ?"

"Nick. Nick Zeringue."

"Mr. Zeringue. My job is to make you feel however you need to feel. It's part of Gatsby's charm."

"Mission accomplished, Miss LaRue. Because you're exactly what I needed tonight."

Damn it. Eden was toast.

Nick had never met a woman who made his blood race the way Lulu LaRue had. Which was absolutely idiocy. After all, he'd fallen hard for Susan, and she'd driven him wild with desire during those early days of their romance. He distinctly remembered her failure to wear panties beneath her dresses and one steamy night in the elevator of the Superdome. But something about this woman electrified him enough to seek out Butch Mandina to find out more about his newest star. His interest in Lulu amused his friend John David who'd said, "This ain't no strip joint. You can't buy a lap dance, dude."

Nick had laughed but pushed his chair back anyway. He'd never felt such an immediate desire, a sort of lust to possess someone. It frightened him as much as it excited him. He had to meet her. Maybe ask her to have a drink with him. Something.

Now she sat before him, no longer prancing and seducing. Just a gorgeous woman with a confident air taking him in with eyes the shade of bluebells. There was something so familiar about her, yet so foreign and aloof. She was a woman who knew her value and took no pleasure in the ordinary.

At his admission—one likely too honest—her eyes had deepened. Her lips had softly parted as she considered his words that she was what he needed. Finally she peered at him through those ridiculous glittery lashes. "Then, monsieur, my work is done."

"Let me buy you a drink."

She shook her head. "I'm afraid I can't."

"Your performance is over."

Lulu slid a glance toward the woman he knew would toss him out with one word. "I have another engagement."

Disappointment pooled in his stomach. "I see."

She inclined her head as if to dismiss him, refusing to utter platitudes or appreciation for the invitation. He didn't know what to do. Obviously he'd been out of the game for much too long. Did he ask for her number? Be brutally honest and say he wanted to take her to dinner . . . to bed?

"Perhaps another time." There. An open door. She could give him her number, drop a crumb of encouragement or say "My place or yours?" Perfect lob to her side of the net.

"Maybe so," she said, rising and presenting him with a lovely view of her naked shoulders. Her red tresses brushed alabaster skin. No freckles, just smooth creaminess, begging for his touch. Or his mouth. He curled his hand before he reached for her.

She'd essentially dismissed him. No drink. No number. He should feel like a fool, but he didn't. It had been years since he'd felt such interest stir. "I'll say good night. Again, I enjoyed your performance, Miss LaRue."

She turned then, her eyes so . . . serious. It was as if she understood him better than he understood himself. "Thank you."

For a moment a connection surged. And then the frumpy woman who'd begrudgingly let him stay flipped the door shut.

Right in his face.

Nick took a step back. Then another. Anger flooded him, and he almost reopened it and gave Lulu's protector the evil eye. Or the finger. The witch had slammed the door right when he'd started making progress with Lulu.

Talk about humiliating.

Someone bumped him as he slunk back like a whipped pup.

It had been a long time since he'd been so utterly rejected. Not that he thought he was the cat's meow, but a decent-looking guy of some means could often find himself cornered by a gaggle of attractive ladies in certain social situations. Like restaurant openings. Or country-club socials. Or gala benefits his mother or sister dragged him to. Maybe he'd gotten too big for his britches with all the phone numbers gained by fetching drinks at open bars or pulling out chairs at dinner. Pretty, eligible women had practically dropped at his feet.

"Strike out?" John David asked as he skirted the people departing next to their table. Another group waited on the perimeter. Butch Mandina and his investors were sitting on a gold mine. The cocktails were superb and even the appetizers were creative. Maybe Nick shouldn't have blown off the call Butch had given him two years ago.

"Decided not to bat," Nick said, sliding into the chair, shifting his eyes so his friend couldn't see the truth in them.

"Bull to the shit. You were like a dog catching a scent, bro." John David held up two fingers and then pointed at his empty glass. Immediately a blond waitress with gamine eyes and a whip-thin figure appeared. "But I get it. She was smokin' hot. Always worth a try when one falls into your lap."

Nick managed a shrug. John David didn't seem to think anything of his being back so soon. Maybe modern-day guys threw spaghetti on the wall and saw what stuck. Maybe getting a door slammed in his face wasn't such an embarrassment.

Still, it bothered him.

"Can I help you gentlemen?" the waitress inquired, her New Orleans East accent somehow adding to her charm.

"Another round. This time on me," John David said.

"Keep your money. The women at the end of the bar bought your next round. They send their compliments." She indicated the bar lined with fancy bottles. Old leather-bound books nestled in with the booze, making the display somehow both classic and cool.

John David peered around the waitress in the direction she'd indicated. When he spotted the two women, a smile curled his lips. His friend was notoriously choosy when it came to women, so Nick could lay down a twenty on the bet they were decent-looking. "Nice. Send them our gratitude and an invitation to join us."

Nick started to protest, but the twinkle in John David's eye stopped him. That and the fact he'd been mowed down seconds earlier. His wounded ego needed a bandage, and a pair of long legs or big breasts would go a long way in easing the sting. After all, he'd been determined to get out there, hadn't he? When one door shuts . . .

"Evening, gentlemen," one of the ladies said moments later as she slid into the chair beside him. "We've been eyeing this table all night. Thanks for getting us closer to the stage."

"That's the only reason why you wanted to join us?" John David crooked an eyebrow.

The blonde, who looked straight out of a Victoria's Secret ad, smiled. "Well, the scenery ain't bad."

The woman with the blonde sat down beside John David, dangling a martini glass in one hand. Her fingernails were painted the color of a summer sky, and she had curly brown hair, dimples, and thin legs displayed nicely by a short skirt. John David mouthed, "Smokin.'"

And the women were. But still, even as Nick smiled and made small talk, drinking a bit too much and letting the blonde plaster herself against him, his mind filled with the image of a redheaded vixen with wildflower eyes. Lulu had entangled him with her invitation to spend a little time with her. Okay, so it wasn't an actual invitation, it was a song. But he'd wanted that invitation to be real. Really wanted it to be real.

The blonde, Sammie, smelled like expensive perfume and cigarettes. And she laughed a little too loud. But he went along with John David when he suggested they go to a quieter bar with dark corners. He bought Sammie a drink and smiled when he was supposed to smile, but inside he wasn't so into it. Being single had been fun when he was in his early twenties. Postdivorce with a seven-year-old daughter, it felt more like a chore. Picking up random chicks wasn't for him. He wasn't John David. And the thought of taking Sammie to a hotel room seemed . . . tawdry.

Or maybe it was like settling for a ham sandwich after smelling a sizzling filet mignon.

He knew himself. Once his mind was set on something, he became fixed on it. He didn't want Sammie. He wanted the luscious redhead who had strutted, shimmied, and seduced.

Yeah, Lulu LaRue had grabbed hold of him, and there was no shaking free from the desire.

So while John David and the brunette made out in the dark corner of the Carousel Bar, he talked to Sammie about her children's boutique and the lack of clothing for special-needs children. Sammie was a nice woman who faked interest in his take on a clothing line that had easy-to-fasten clothing, reversible capabilities, and was better suited to accommodate wheelchairs and medical equipment. Eventually, when their conversation turned more personal, he learned she was recently out of a relationship.

"You're the first guy I've actually felt an attraction for," she said, sipping the martini. Her eyes were a bit glazed, and she kept touching his forearm playfully.

What to say to that?

"I'm flattered. You're a gorgeous woman." Not a bad response.

She licked her lips and leaned in so he could see the valley between her breasts. The action was no doubt contrived to entice him. Still, even though Sammie was saying all the right things and showing off her, frankly, very nice breasts, it seemed forced. Like she'd made up her mind she was going to score tonight and, by God, she was. Birds of a feather. "Thank you. You're not so bad yourself."

She bit her lip as she slid her gaze toward Ashley and John David, who looked to be cannibalizing each other. Then she ran her hand along his thigh, giving it a squeeze. Blatant invitation.

But he wasn't accepting.

A little vee appeared between Sammie's eyes before she brushed sticky glossed lips across his. Her blue-green eyes went soft as she whispered, "I'm enjoying getting to know you better, Nick."

He caught her hand and lifted it to his lips for a gentle kiss. "Sammie, you're gorgeous, but I'm not interested in doing this."

Had he really said that? Because he'd never had a problem with a one-night stand before he was married, and the first time he'd been with a woman after his divorce, he'd had drunk sex in the powder room of the Hilton Riverside. Not even a one-night stand. Though he'd literally been standing. Or rather swaying. Too many bourbons at the Mardi Gras ball had made him brave.

Sammie's cheeks pinked. "So you're not . . ."

"You're really beautiful. Out of my league."

Sudden tears trembled on her lashes. "Right."

"I wouldn't say it if it weren't true."

Sammie gave him a flat look, tears still welling in her eyes.

"Ah, hell. I'm sorry. I'm trying to be decent here. Not treat you like . . . Damn it, I didn't want tonight to be like this," he said, shaking his head, wishing he could fall through the damn floor. He'd hurt this woman who'd been dumped by a gym owner last month. Jesus. He was *so* out of practice. He'd turned down a willing, beautiful woman . . . and made her cry.

Sammie swiped at her lower lashes. Her embarrassed expression and the fact he'd hurt her feelings made him feel like he'd stepped in dog crap and tracked it into the queen's parlor. Persona non grata. Total asshole.

Nick patted her hand. "I'm out of practice with, uh, dating. Or whatever it is we're doing."

"No shit," she said, sliding from the booth. "I need to powder my nose."

She walked away, snagging her friend's hand and pulling her along with her. John David looked dazed at the loss of his handful of hotness. His friend's gaze was accusing when he jerked his head toward Nick.

"What in the hell are you doing, bro? That girl was all over you," he said, jiggling the ice in his empty highball.

"What?" Nick tried to play dumb.

"What do you mean what? You said you wanted to get laid. Another woman's landed in your lap, asshole, and you're screwing this up. Chill, okay? Stop acting like a goddamned moralist and take the stick out of your ass."

"I'm going to grab a cab and—"

"The hell you are." John David jabbed a finger at him. "I'm about to score with this chick. She ain't leaving her friend high and dry. So chill and let me close the deal."

Close the deal?

"Listen to you, man," Nick said, lifting the glass that was still full. "You're treating this woman like she's produce or something. She's a person."

". . . who wants to get laid. Or can't you tell anymore? Who are you?" John David shook his head. "I get you're, like, a dad. And you're settled and boring, but don't cockblock a dude."

The waiter appeared with the check. "Pardon me, gentlemen. The young ladies you were with wanted me to give you these." He set a Post-it note in front of John David that had a phone number and the words "Call me tonight" written across it. Nick's had only two words. Two very dirty, disdainful words that ironically weren't going to happen that night. Well, not to Nick anyway.

John David looked at Nick's sticky note. "Exactly what I was thinking."

Nick pulled a few bills from his wallet and tossed them on the table. The crowd had thinned out, and with Sammie's parting words to him, he was beyond ready for his own bed. Alone. "I didn't want a ham sandwich," he said as he slid from the chair and stood.

"What the hell are you talking about?" John David tossed some cash atop his and stood. "Don't bother explaining. I'm out. Have fun flying solo."

chapter twelve

EDEN HELPED SOPHIE flex her toes as she stretched the child's leg in the air. What would be a piece of cake for most people often brought Sophie to tears. Her muscles, especially those on her right side, were like tightly wound elastic bands that curled her limbs inward, causing Sophie's face to screw up in pain and sweat to blanket her forehead.

"Let's count together," Eden said as she shifted on her knees, grateful for the plushness of the mat Nick kept in the formal living room for Sophie's daily stretches. "And five, four, three, two, one. Done."

She helped Sophie lower her leg and then spent a few minutes massaging the tightened calf muscle before moving up to the quad, which had atrophied more than it should have. Poor child. She should be running, twirling, dancing her heart out.

The activity was so different than the stretches she helped her mother do each day. Betty went to a physical therapist who gave her a series of exercises to do to help her withering limbs, but the woman was stubborn and hated the energy it took to do them. She had fought relentlessly with Eden each day and most days Eden gave up. Having distance from her mother had given

Eden some clarity and some much-needed room to see her previous life and her mother's frustrations with it. Funny how a daughter rarely saw her mother as a person, and for Eden, she'd spent too many years thinking of her mother as a burden rather than a person who had nothing much to look forward to in life. The tight resentment had loosened a bit, much like Sophie's muscles with the daily stretching.

"Good girl, Soph. You're getting stronger every day," Eden said, clasping the child's elbows and pulling her into a sitting position. Though her legs twitched occasionally, she was able to sit with her legs crossed so Eden could massage her hands, one of which curled badly. As Eden worked to loosen the muscles, she sang a little song and made Sophie shimmy with her. The child giggled and it made stretch time almost fun.

"Do a dance, Edie," Sophie said, her head falling back as Eden made her shimmy and shake.

"You want me to dance?"

"Yeah, like you do in the kitchen," Sophie said.

"Okay, let's see. When I was in high school I was in a production of *Annie*. Have you seen *Annie?*"

"Yeah, I liked it," Sophie said, grunting as Eden settled her in the odd plastic chair that was essentially a large foam infant sitter. It helped Sophie sit upright comfortably. Eden looped the spongy neck brace around her so her head didn't fall to the side.

"Okay," Eden said pushing off the floor. "Let's do 'You're Never Fully Dressed without a Smile.' You know that one?"

Sophie nodded, her smile big.

Eden stretched briefly because after the successful solo performance the night before, she didn't want to pull a muscle or do anything that would keep her from performing. Frenchie had raised her pay, and the tips that had come in last night alone were substantial enough to plant the thought she could eventually quit her job with the Zeringues. But when she thought back to how bereft Sophie was after Rhoda left, she couldn't imagine stepping out of the child's life.

Or Nick's.

Last night had been one of the hardest performances of her life. Not because she'd portrayed a bold siren rubbing against men while looping a feather boa around them. No. It had been her performance as the aloof Lulu LaRue in her dressing room.

How she'd pulled off fooling Nick she'd never know.

When she'd closed her eyes after slipping exhaustedly into bed that night, she couldn't erase the look on his face. Reflected there was fierce longing, the sort of heat she'd never seen before in his eyes. Not even after their near kiss the day before, sipping cocktails on the back patio. That was the thought she'd planted front and center in her mind—Nick hadn't wanted the bumpkin nanny but instead had hungered for the brash Lulu with her pouting lips and padded bra.

Of course, there had been something yesterday. An almost. But because theirs was a business relationship, neither she nor Nick would go there. Sister Regina Marie had relayed that Nick refused to entangle himself with anyone responsible for his daughter's well-being. Not to mention, it was obvious Nick and his friend weren't at Gatsby's merely for a good cocktail and a funny drag queen parody. She didn't need a decoder ring for that.

So why had she kept her identity a secret? Because if Nick didn't have a clue Eden was Lulu, why hadn't she sauntered out the door with him last night? She could have gone out with him for a drink . . . and something more.

For years she'd dreamed about the faceless man who would be her first. She'd pined for the perfect man to make her a woman in the truest sense. And because that man had never materialized, Eden shelved her sexual needs. Last night had given her the opportunity she'd been waiting on . . . with a man she hungered for.

So why hadn't she pounced?

Because it was Nick. And when she finally gave herself to a man, it wouldn't be under a ruse. She'd waited this long, she could wait a bit more.

Pressing the play button, she grabbed the remote control to use as a microphone.

"Be my backup, Sophie?"

The child nodded her body, making Eden laugh. "Okay, so you hold this."

She gave Sophie the large remote, helping the child to close her fingers around it.

For the next few minutes, Eden jazz kicked, hopped on the ottoman, and sang the fun number from Annie. Sophie did her best to join in, giggling when Eden shook her rump, and even more so when she grabbed Sophie's elbows and they swayed together. The ending called for Miss Hannigan to catch the girls goofing off, and when the last note died, Eden found Nick watching them from the doorway.

"Ack," she squeaked, hurrying to press the button to turn off the next song. "I hope you didn't see me jump on the ottoman."

"You jumped on the ottoman?" he asked, his eyes twinkling as he dropped his briefcase and eased into the room. He looked at her for a full three seconds and shook his head. "You're pretty damn good at that."

"I'm a theatre major. Or at least I will be soon." *Oh, and I sat in your lap and crooned for you to be my big spender last night.*

Hello . . .

The fact that the man still, even after observing her rousing rendition of the *Annie* number, didn't realize Eden and Lulu were one and the same proved two things—Eden had truly managed to capture the essence of Lulu and men were dumb.

Nick tossed a smile to Sophie. And even though that smile was for his daughter, it made Eden's belly flop. "I didn't know my daughter was a budding Broadway star."

"Do it again," Sophie said, clapping her hands, which was something hard for the child to do.

"Oh, no. I've already abused the furniture, which is grounds for dismissal. Let's go to the potty and then get dinner ready,"

Eden said.

Sophie made a stubborn face, but Eden tweaked her nose. "None of that, missy. We'll put together a fun routine to do for your father another day. You'll have to practice hard, but you can handle it."

The child took the bait. "Really?"

"Really." Eden rose and pulled Sophie's chair toward her.

"Let me take her. You're probably tired from jumping on furniture," Nick said with a wink.

"I'm still on the clock. You've no doubt had a long day and need a cocktail or to put your feet up or something," she said, warming at his words.

"You working tonight?"

"Yes. And I need to get a firm schedule together for weekends. We left it loose-ended, but knowing would help at . . . my other job." She nearly said Gatsby's but caught herself at the last minute.

Here was the opportunity to come clean about last night. She could reveal her second job was being a cabaret singer at Gatsby's. If she had told him weeks ago instead keeping it a secret, there wouldn't be an issue. But if she told him now, it would embarrass him. Surely he wouldn't go back to Gatsby's. She'd made it fairly clear she wasn't interested . . . even if it had been the biggest lie ever told under the sun, moon, and stars.

"You never told me where you're working," he said, lifting Sophie from her spongy chair. "Use your legs, Soph."

Sophie's face turned red as she planted her feet and strained to use her limbs. The child inched her foot forward.

"It's just a place in the Quarter." Eden moved to put the brake on the chair. "Good girl, Sophie. Soon you'll be doing kicks with me."

Just tell him.

But she couldn't. She'd landed in his lap while cooing about big spenders. He'd told Lulu she made him feel like a man again. How could Eden bring up the fact she was the woman from last night without making him feel like a fool? Maybe say, "You know how you asked Lulu for drinks last night? The answer is yes. I'll have a drink with you and whatever else you had in mind."

Yeah, that would so work.

'Cause that wouldn't be awkward at all.

Sophie took dragging steps—three of them—to reach her chair. Nick helped her get settled and then spun the chair toward the back of the house.

"Nick, I can—"

"I got this," he said, thankfully not probing any more into her second job.

Eden went to the kitchen and started making a light dinner for Sophie. The laughter down the hall warmed her heart, and once again she was struck by how good it felt to be part of their world. A few minutes later, Sophie and Nick returned. Nick's shirt was soaking wet and droplets of water hung in his hair.

"You gals, always getting me wet." He laughed, unbuttoning the light blue dress shirt and shrugging out of it. He wore a soft white undershirt that was plastered to his chest. That came off too. And . . . wow.

His torso wasn't ripped like an underwear model, but he was muscled in all the right places. Flat belly, broad chest, and droolworthy shoulders. Dark hair peppered his pecs and trailed down to disappear in the waistband of his pants. The words Rosemary had uttered months ago about a bed-rumpled man came roaring back. Nick would look incredible against white bedsheets. All that tanned skin and masculine yumminess.

Eden stared. She couldn't help it.

And Nick caught her.

For a moment their gazes hung up and held.

A barely perceptible quirk of his lips transmitted the awareness. Eden turned away before she could turn the color of the oven mitt on her hand and before he could see the hunger in her eyes. She wanted to touch him. She curled her hand in the mitt. God, she wanted to touch him. Just once. Maybe even accidently.

No. Stop.

"Goodness, what happened?" she asked, diverting her attention to the vegetarian bean-burger patty she heated for Sophie's dinner.

He strolled toward her, both shirts balled in his fist. "This little devil got me when she was washing her hands."

Sophie giggled and used her strong leg to maneuver her chair toward the huge granite-topped island where Eden stood lining a jelly-roll pan with foil. Carefully Eden placed a serving of sweet potato slivers on the pan. "She got me yesterday. Seems someone thinks it's funny to splash around like a fish. She should be careful someone doesn't catch her and fry her up for dinner."

Another giggle.

Eden caught Nick watching her. Again she was punched in the gut by his sheer masculinity as he leaned against the counter. The achy feel she got when she read a spicy book or watched a racy movie bloomed in her pelvis. Nothing like wanting to jump your boss in the presence of his child . . . while wearing a bright red crawfish oven mitt. Why couldn't he be fat and bald? Or short with a bad complexion? Or married. Why did her new boss have to be Hot Dad Nick?

"Anything to report before you go?" he asked, looking totally comfortable sans shirt. His naked chest wasn't bothering him in the least.

"Uh, no. Everything went well. Sophie doesn't have homework other than working on her Mardi Gras mask. We can do that tomorrow. We'll need some things from a craft store. I can run by tomorrow after reh—Um, after I finish some things."

"Sure," Nick said, pulling his wallet out of his pants, drawing her attention to the flex of his biceps. Eden swallowed hard again. She probably needed some water. Her mouth was awfully dry. "Hey, you live and work in the Quarter. Ever heard of a place called Gatsby's?"

Oh, crap.

"Uh, sure. Everyone's heard of it," she said, averting her eyes.

"I went there last night. You ever been?"

"Actually I have." No need to elaborate. Or relate the fact she knew he'd been there last night.

"It's pretty cool. Good talent and the food's decent." Nick shifted and crossed his arms across his chest.

Eden ducked her head and started moving the potato wedges into perfect lines. "Yeah. The crab dip's good."

Eden had never felt more uncomfortable, which was silly because this was the kind of small talk they made all the time. Except normally they were, you know, fully clothed, and Eden wasn't trying to hide a stupid secret.

"I better get going. Have to be at work by seven." Eden slid the pan into the oven. That's one way to avoid awkward conversations with your sexy boss. Just leave.

"You okay?" he asked, lifting himself from where he leaned.

"Of course." She tossed the mitt back into the drawer and set the timer on the oven. "Why?"

"You're acting weird. Is it the courtyard yesterday? There was this funny vibe, and I don't want you to think I was coming on to you or something. I'm not that kind of guy. You're safe around me."

The achy want disappeared at those words. Exactly. He hadn't been coming on to her. All her imagination because Nick Zeringue wasn't into the nanny. Yes, exactly. "I know. I'm distracted. That's all," she said, jerking her head toward Sophie who watched them with curious eyes.

"You sure?" he asked, before catching on to her unspoken warning about his daughter.

"Sure," she said, tugging Sophie's ponytail. "Bye, Soph."

"Bye, Edie," Sophie said, pulling out her iPad and flipping down the small tray on the chair arm.

Nick moved behind her as she walked toward the back door near the laundry room. "Sorry. I shouldn't have said something about coming on to you. Poor choice of words, but I meant it. You're safe with me, Eden."

Even though on one hand his words had destroyed her ego, she warmed at the thought of his protectiveness. Safety. So taken for granted by many people. So craved by others. "I know."

For a moment they stared at each other.

Then Eden reached out and gave his bare forearm a squeeze. "You're a good guy, Nick."

He didn't say anything. Just watched her as she slipped out the door into the darkening evening. Raising his hand, he waved goodbye before turning around and disappearing back into his palatial house. Eden's heart squeezed and she started to backtrack. But what would she say? What could she do? He was her boss, and he'd made a point to draw a line he wouldn't cross. Besides, she had bigger fish to fry than her crush on her hot boss.

Like the fact that *The Weekender* wanted to do an interview with Lulu LaRue.

And Jess and Ryan were coming for the weekend.

And Sunny needed another three hundred dollars to help cover the co-pay for the fall their mother had last week. The fall hadn't been serious, but the bill was. Not to mention her sister was refinishing the floors and found more repairs than anticipated.

Eden said the short prayer she said every time she cranked up her old car and pulled out of Nick's driveway, her head full of troubles, her heart yearning for something she couldn't have.

When she made it to the speakeasy, using the nondramatic back entrance, she found another surprise—a short, neatly dressed man with small round glasses and a clipboard.

Frenchie frowned as she jerked her thumb toward the well-dressed man. "Fredric wants to talk to you. Don't freaking sign anything."

The man laughed. "You she-devil. You know you'd drop your panties right now if I offered you representation."

"Bah," Frenchie said, wrinkling her nose and shoving past them both. Several members of the ensemble popped their heads out, eyes going wide before disappearing again. A few more heads popped out seconds later.

Eden didn't know who the man was or why he was there, but he certainly drew a crowd.

"You wish you could sniff my panties, old man," Frenchie said before lifting her nose in the air. "Be smart, Lulu."

Eden turned to the older man, who extended his hand. "Hello, Miss LaRue. I'm Fredric Stall from Harmony Talent Agency."

"Hello," Eden said taking his hand, trying not to look confused. Talent agency? "I'm Eden Voorhees. Not Lulu LaRue."

"I beg to differ, my dear. You *are* Lulu, and you're terrific at being her." He released her hand and turned to the women peering at them. "If there's a place we may speak privately?"

"Uh, sure," Eden said, trying to think where they could go. Her mind had already started chasing the bunny of hope that had hopped onto the scene. An agent? Who wanted to talk to her? "Maybe Butch's office?"

"No. I'm not helping him," Frenchie cried from the open door of the office sitting adjacent to the dressing room. "Go outside, you thieving bastard."

Fredric's mouth twitched. "She's still mad because I never called."

"Hah. In your dreams, you old fool," Frenchie called.

"Let's do go outside," Fredric said, gesturing toward the long narrow cobbled walkway that led back out onto the street.

The ancient brick was damp, but it was as private as one could get at Gatsby's. Because it was dark, it was hard to see Fredric well. Eden pulled her hoodie up against the chill. "So what's this about, Mr. Stall? I need to get into makeup and wardrobe."

"Fredric, if you please," he said, pulling a clipboard from beneath his arm. "Now, this is my card." He unclipped a business card and handed it to her.

Eden gave it a cursory glance before looking back at him. "Thank you . . . I think."

Fredric gave her a mysterious smile. "Ah, you've not heard of me."

"Sorry, but no."

"Not to borrow lines from bad movies, but 'I'm kind of a big deal.'" Though the words were as egocentric as they come, his demeanor was anything but. "I'm a talent agent. The best in New Orleans. Eh, probably the entire South."

"Oh," Eden said, looking back at the card. "An agent?"

"You don't have representation, do you?" he asked, his warm eyes suddenly like razor wire in the flicker of the lanterns guarding the back entrance.

"I wasn't aware I needed representation. I've only been headlining here at Gatsby's for a few weeks. And I'm not acting at present. I mean, I will. Or I have. I did theatre in Jackson and will be going back to school in performing arts, but—"

"You need an agent, my dear." His statement brooked no argument.

"I do?"

"Most assuredly. That's why Frenchie Pi wasn't so welcoming. She knows they're going to have to put out if I represent you."

"You want to represent me? And wait, they already raised my pay," Eden said, feeling oddly defensive of the crass Asian woman who'd imagined Lulu in the first place and given Eden a shot.

Fredric made a face. "I'm fairly certain they did. What? A dollar or two more?"

Eden frowned. She wasn't about to admit that they'd raised her only a dollar and a half more. Frenchie had said it was for now. That they'd evaluate her performances and talk about another increase later. There had been no clear date for "later."

"You think they're not paying me what I'm worth?"

Fredric held up a copy of the Living section of *The Times-Picayune*. The bottom quadrant showed Lulu LaRue draped on the piano, microphone in hand. The headline read GATSBY'S BRINGS THE WOW FACTOR WITH THEIR NEWEST SENSATION. Eden hadn't seen the article before. She reached for it, and Fredric handed it over as if he'd planned to do so all along. The man had come prepared. "You don't seem to comprehend that Lulu's the hottest act in the hottest club in the city. Gatsby's reservation waiting list stretches down Bourbon Street, my dear. Getting a table is a veritable coup. I caught your show last night. I think you are superb, and"—he tapped the paper she held—"someone at *The Times* agrees with me."

Eden glanced down at the paper where she splayed sexily in print. Her first inclination was mortification. What would her aunt Ruby Jean think about her sprawled out, wearing a come-hither expression in the middle of the newspaper? What would Reverend Al at the Church of Christ think? She looked . . . not herself. But the next feeling was euphoria. She was a "new sensation." That had to be a good thing. "Uh, thank you."

"I represent top-notch performers in the city—film and theatre mostly—and I have contacts in LA and New York. You want to stay in New Orleans and be Lulu LaRue, I'll get you better money, better press, and make you a living legend. You want to go somewhere else, I'll get you auditions. There's no one else who can do what I do. You understand?"

Eden nodded, understanding that Fredric's words rang with truth. Otherwise, Frenchie wouldn't have let him backstage. The sharp-tongued stage manager wasn't warm and fuzzy, but she wasn't going to prevent anyone from Gatsby's getting a break. "I'm not prepared to sign right now, Mr. Stall. In fact, I'm late for makeup. Can we talk at a later time?"

"Of course. Tonight I wanted to meet you. We can do great things together. And I think, even if you don't sign with me, you should ask for more money. My dear, they're now coming to see you. Don't tell Derrick though. Drag queens can pitch a helluva hissy fit."

With a tip of his hat, Fredric Stall headed toward the street. Eden tucked the business card into her pocket and stood a few minutes in the shadows of the small alley, marveling that an agent had approached her. She looked down at the folded newspaper in her hand. Maybe she should ask for more from Gatsby's. After all, she wasn't making very much for all the work she put into her numbers.

Maybe an agent was exactly what she needed.

And maybe she should get her behind inside and into her costume for the next number.

chapter thirteen

"OH MY GOSH, you were fabulous," Jess said, wrapping Eden into a bone-crushing hug that smelled like mojito and clean apple shampoo. "I mean seriously, sister, you were great."

Eden blew Jess's apple-scented curls out of her mouth and managed a breathless "thanks."

Jess released her and stepped back, giving Ryan a meaningful look and a slight jerk of her head.

The man glanced at Jess and then reached over to awkwardly pat Eden's back. "You were good, Eden."

His discomfort made Eden smile. "The Brain" was like a supersexy Sheldon Cooper. Not so good with social situations or . . . touching. Unless it was Jess, of course. He couldn't seem to keep his hands off her friend.

They stood outside Gatsby's, midnight closing in on them, yet Bourbon Street was jumping. Drunken revelry at its finest. And oddly enough, the exuberant crowd suited Eden just fine. Tipsy people were loose with their money, which meant good tips. Of course, it also meant the bouncers at Gatsby's had to be very aware, especially when a slurring shrew grew incensed over Eden or another performer rubbing against her equally intoxicated man. The night before last, one such woman couldn't comprehend it was all in fun and tried to attack Eden when she shimmied a bit too close to her boyfriend. Ah, drunkenness, a double-edged sword.

"I'm starving," Eden said, drawing her friends down the street, away from the bustle of the Quarter. Toward Esplanade sat her new favorite tourist trap—Port of Call. The place kept late hours and had the best burgers. She swerved around Corky, a homeless man, and his dog Elmo. Corky shamelessly used the beagle mix to get change dropped into his worn top hat. The man spent every night there, raking in plenty. Eden had bought him a sandwich the first night she'd encountered him . . . and then she realized he was a fixture and not so hard on his luck. The city was full of down-on-their-luck scammers.

Ryan stared at the man and fished into his pocket. Eden winked at Corky as Ryan dropped a ten-dollar bill into the hat.

"And God bless you, sir," Corky cried.

Before Ryan could blink, he was accosted by Sandra, a thong-and-pasty-wearing photo opportunity carrying a lacy parasol. Two seconds later, a man coated in metallic paint showed up to con his few dollars from Jess's softhearted boyfriend.

"Come on," Eden said, pulling Ryan from the grasp of Bourbon Street's "performers" and maneuvering them toward the outer French Quarter, which was quieter if not any less pungent. "You'll give away every dime if you stay much longer."

Jess put her arm around her big nerd's waist. "I love how bighearted you are, babe."

Ryan beamed and dropped a kiss atop Jess's head. "And I love how you—"

"Good Lord, stop it already," Eden said, faking a shudder.

Both Ryan and Jess dropped their arms and looked sheepish.

"I'm just kidding. Y'all being happy makes me happy." Eden quickened her step. Usually she went to Port of Call with some of the other performers. Never alone . . . though she sometimes walked home by herself since parking her car close to Gatsby's was too difficult. A couple of times she'd had Jimmy, the guy who drove a pedicab, peddle her to her apartment, but only on decent tip nights. She still had to watch her nickels and dimes. But after signing on with Fredric Stall the day before, she was hoping for a slight reprieve. Hailing from a naturally suspicious family meant she'd hemmed and hawed (and slightly panicked) over the terms of the agent/talent agreement. As she read through the complicated jargon, she'd wished for Lacy's counsel. As a paralegal, Lacy had been familiar with all sorts of contracts and had helped Eden file medical forms and any other confusing documents that came her way. Eden thought Lacy would have approved of Fredric. He'd actually rolled up his sleeves before entering a meeting with Butch and Frenchie to renegotiate her salary.

Less than ten minutes later, the three of them were seated in the busy late-night restaurant with two orders of Port of Call's infamous grog and a light beer on the way.

Jess put her paper napkin in her lap and shot the stink eye to the women ogling Ryan. Eden couldn't fault the women surrounding them. The former physics state rally winner looked like a movie star with his shaggy locks, tanned skin, and bright smile. Eden knew what kind of body lay beneath the khaki pants and ice-blue polo shirt thanks to a long weekend in Pensacola last fall. If being a boat captain didn't work out for the man, he could always model.

Jess gave up with a shrug and fastened her brown eyes on Eden. "You're juggling a lot, E."

Eden raised one shoulder. "I'm used to multitasking. It's one of my many talents."

"True," Jess said, accepting the globed drink the waitress passed to her. "But what about school? Are you able to keep up?"

Eden's face must have given her away.

"E, you didn't," Jess said.

"I had to," Eden said, taking two chugs of the potent brew the waitress had set in front of her. Her empty stomach begged her to slow down even as her mind screamed, "Escape!"

"That's why you came down here. For school. And to act and stuff. Why would you give up school and not the job as the nanny? Haven't you had enough of changing diapers and wiping drool?"

Jess had a point, but she couldn't understand the way things had fallen into place. And she wouldn't understand the loyalty Eden now felt to Nick and Sophie. "I know. But I can't leave them. Sophie had such a hard time when her other nanny left. She's just started to trust me, so I can't—"

"Will you listen to yourself? You spent the past eleven years sacrificing yourself, and now when you have an opportunity to . . . to . . . be a little selfish and claim a life, you revert back to being a doormat."

"Jess," Ryan chided, tapping her hand. "Back off a little."

Jess clamped her mouth closed and took a deep breath. "I'm sorry. I just love you and want you to—"

"Live my own life?" Eden finished. Jess's words had hit their target, but Eden knew her own mind. She always had. "That's what I'm doing. I get what you're saying and understand the irony of escaping my mother only to find myself doing the same thing three hundred miles south, but I own my decision. The timing isn't right for school. Things weren't working, and I couldn't devote myself like I needed to do. And, truthfully, I couldn't afford it."

"But you had Lacy's money," Jess fired back.

"Do you know how little that stretches when you live in a city and have to pay for a new water pump, computer repairs, and your mother's very expensive medications? It doesn't go far, Jess. I don't make what a surgical nurse makes. I don't have parents who paid for my college or my car. Don't you dare lecture me about the choices I had to make . . . or the ones I want to make. Like being there for Nick and Sophie." Eden's voice had risen, attracting the attention of the next table.

Jess released a sigh. "You're right."

"I know I am," Eden said, lowering her voice. "I'm not giving up, Jess. I'm just saving some money. You don't understand, but—"

"I do. I understand, and therefore, I shouldn't have put you through the third degree. You're a big girl, E."

Eden quirked her brow.

Jess smiled. "Okay, so you're a tiny thing but a grown woman. I'm protective of you, but I'd be the same with anyone I love. Sometimes I speak before I think."

"Yeah, you do," Eden said.

Jess slid a glance over to Ryan. "But I hope you really thought this out. You don't—"

Eden gave Jess the look, the same one she'd given her when she'd tried to set her up with Moose for homecoming their senior year. It was the look exchanged between countless girlfriends since the dawn of time. *I know what you're doing and it's not going to work on me.*

Jess got the message and clamped her mouth shut before she could do more damage.

"Thank you, Jess," Eden said using the tone she used on Sophie when she capitulated. Jess wasn't buying what she was selling, but her friend would let it go for now. Jess Culpepper had a lot of good attributes, but accepting she was wrong wasn't one of them. Jess always thought she knew best. She wasn't quite as managing as Rosemary's mother, but she could have been Patsy Reynold's padawan.

"So tell us about your charge. What's her name?" Ryan asked, sipping his beer, doing the good-boyfriend thing by changing the subject.

"Oh, huh, I've never thought about her as a charge. That sounds so Jane Eyre."

"Well then, what do you call her?" Ryan asked.

"Sophie?" Eden smiled, thinking about the exuberant girl who bore the disease pulling at her body so well. "She'll turn eight in a few weeks. She's a pretty little thing in spite of the cerebral palsy. Her cheeks are always pink, her eyes always sparkling. Except when she's being bullheaded, which isn't all that often. She's a sweet child who needs me."

Jess looked at her this time, her eyes dawning with understanding. Eden knew it was weak to want someone to need her, but she couldn't help it. Both Nick and Sophie had needed her, making it doubly hard to step away.

"What about the dad? You said he's a chef or something?" Jess asked.

"His family owns several prominent restaurants around the area. Du Parrain and Maude's Uptown. He's like a vice president of marketing or something. He's pretty busy but good about being home when he says he will be."

"Home?" Jess quirked an eyebrow.

"You know what I mean," Eden said, trying not to color at the implied intimacy.

"You like him?" Jess continued.

"He's a nice man."

Jess delivered a cat smile. "E, do you like him like him?"

Damn it. How could Jess sniff out the attraction she held for Nick so easily? Was she that obvious? Was it in the way she said his name? Or the spark in her eyes when she thought about him? Or perhaps something else? "He's my boss, Jess."

"So?"

"So, I can't be into him in that way. It's too complicated."

"Why?" Ryan asked.

"Because."

Ryan regarded her with a thoughtful expression. "Do you have a company policy that guides your behavior in regards to your employer?"

"I don't have a company policy. I'm the company."

"Perhaps you should." Ryan shrugged and hungrily eyed the burgers and fries on a tray as a waitress passed their table.

"She doesn't need a policy, Ry," Jess said, focusing her

intense gaze on Eden. "Eden needs some good lovin.' Or as my dumb-butt ex-husband would say, she needs some experiences."

Eden drew back. "I do not."

"Sure you do. You never had a chance to be irresponsible. Ryan didn't either. You both skipped the keg parties, the walks of shame, the really bad decision to let your roommate cut your bangs. Ry tried to make up for it, and from what I understand enjoyed himself a little too much," Jess said, shooting her boyfriend a look of censure.

Ryan lifted his beer bottle. "Amen."

"That doesn't mean I'm making up for lost time. With all due respect, I'm not Ryan," Eden said.

"She's not," Ryan said with a grin that made him look nothing like the brainiac he was.

"I'm not interested in jumping my boss because I have an attraction for him. I—"

"Aha! I was right." Jess jabbed a finger at her.

"Well, yeah, he's extraordinarily good-looking and single. But our relationship is a working one." Other than the fact she'd sat in his lap and flirted outrageously with him as Lulu LaRue. And that he'd liked it. A lot.

"Whatever," Jess said, accepting her cheeseburger with extra pickles from the waitress who finally stopped with their food. "It's not like you're going to stay Sophie's nanny forever. You're going back to school. What's the harm?"

Eden didn't answer immediately because she wasn't sure. She'd known many people who'd carried around regret from indulging in affairs they shouldn't have. She'd seen it firsthand with her mother and her sister. Yeah, the Voorhees women weren't exactly great at making good decisions. Eden might not be experienced when it came to sleeping around, but she knew jumping into something haphazardly could set her back. Being with Nick could be very good, but it would also be messy at a time where she didn't want the hassle of a relationship. Eden wasn't tossing aside her goals for a man. After all, she and Nick would never work. They were too different. One day, she'd have time for matters of the heart, but Broadway had always been her ultimate destination. Fame and fortune were still far off, but at least she'd set her feet in that direction.

"Guess what? Fredric has contacts in New York City. I may go up in the summer or fall and do some auditions," Eden said, feeling convinced about where her future lay.

Jess frowned as if she was quite aware Eden had intentionally changed the subject. Her friend didn't speak for a few seconds, and Eden could almost see her mind whirring. Press? Or let go? Finally, Jess said, "That's exciting."

Relief bloomed inside Eden. Jess could be like a terrier. That her friend had given up the juicy bone of Eden chasing her boss was a small victory. "That doesn't mean I won't go back to school. If I go to NYC this summer and nothing happens, I'll head back to UNO in September, but if something does . . ." She didn't have to say what that would mean to her. Jess knew.

"Cool," Ryan said, scooping up some ketchup and shoving three fries into his mouth. "Maybe you'll get the hookup and we can score some *Hamilton* tickets."

"*You* going to New York City?" Jess asked her eyes wide. "You hate crowded cities."

"Sal made it sound kinda cool," Ryan said.

"Kinda cool? Who *are* you?" Jess joked as they launched into a boisterous discussion of Broadway musicals and celebrities Sal had seen in his once-upon-a-time city.

Eden dug into her food, glad the conversation had shifted to something less controversial. She vowed she would enjoy having her friend with her for the next two days. Nick had told her to not worry with coming in Saturday or Sunday, and because she'd been so busy working, she'd not had time to explore the city. It was Ryan's first true experience in the Crescent City . . . because going for an international robotic competition didn't really count. So they had plans to go to the Mardi Gras museum and visit the music clubs on Frenchman Street. Not to mention Sunday brunch at Brennan's. Frenchie had fussed about moving

Eden's performance to earlier in the evening, but she'd relented when Eden promised to learn a burlesque-style fan dance for a new number. Frenchie drove a hard bargain. Eden was allergic to chicken feathers, but the sneezing would be worth doing something decadent like taking a few days for herself.

"Let's order dessert," Ryan said, polishing off his cheeseburger.

"Yeah, let's." Eden grinned at the handsome bottomless pit who sat across from her. She had weekend liberty, and she was going to enjoy it.

With chocolate sauce.

Gatsby's was busy on Saturdays. Extremely busy. But Nick had managed to score a table for two by using his family name. Kinda squirrely, but he'd only stooped so low because he had to see Lulu again.

Had to.

As he entered the establishment and gave the snooty hostess his name, he wondered why he felt this ungodly need to show up alone to a nightclub to watch a saucy redhead trot around the stage. Dime a dozen in this town, right?

He'd argued with himself right up until the moment he called Gatsby's. And then after making the reservation, he told himself it was only because he'd been slightly inebriated. That was the reason her sultry voice and smooth moves had haunted his dreams for the past week. She couldn't be that good. The scotch had been responsible for the huge buildup in his mind.

"And will someone be joining you?" the hostess inquired.

He hoped so.

"Not at the moment," he said, nodding when she led him to a table situated on the right side of the room. It wasn't the closest table, but it had a good view and some semblance of privacy. "Thank you."

The hostess nodded and slipped away. Nick unfolded his

napkin and smiled a hello at the gangly waitress who'd served him and John David several nights ago.

"Oh, you're back. Where's your friend?" she said with a friendly smile, setting two glasses of water on the table.

"He may join me later." A little white lie, but it made him feel less stalkerish. "I was impressed and thought I would come back and check it out again."

"Yeah?" she said, smiling even bigger. "Don't tell anyone, but I'm the person who found Lulu LaRue. Totally told her about this place."

He looked at her name tag. Jordan. "Did you?"

"I should get a finder's fee, right?" she joked. "Now, what can I get you to drink?"

He'd rather talk about Lulu, but that might look, again, stalkerish. And was he being stalkerish? Or merely determined? He wasn't sure. All he knew was that he'd felt so drawn to her in a way that hadn't existed for him in a while. Sure, he'd been with other women, but he'd never felt such an immediate attraction. Or maybe it was fascination. Or something he couldn't place his finger on.

He totally blamed it on his sister. In not so many words, she'd planted the idea that he should pay attention to the simplicity of his body's needs rather than focusing on compatibility, sparkling conversation, and potential for relationship. His body wanted Lulu. His desire was like a small child hungrily eyeing the decadent sweet behind the storefront glass. Which was why currently he had his nose pressed against the glass. And was paying a top-notch babysitting firm a small fortune to watch Sophie tonight because Eden had friends in town and hadn't been available. "Single malt scotch. Let's go with the fifteen-year Glenlivet."

She gave him one last smile—good tip insurance—and disappeared.

Maybe scotch was a bad idea. After all, it was responsible for fueling the flames of his libido.

Nick glanced around, feeling somewhat conspicuous about sitting alone. Every table held a boisterous party or at least a couple clinking wineglasses. The dance floor was semicrowded with people showing off the ballroom dancing lessons they'd taken as the ten-piece brass band performed a toned-down rendition of "Jambalaya."

Jordan delivered his drink, and he put in an order for Creole crab cakes with a tangy remoulade sauce. Then he tried to put out the cool and mysterious vibe rather than the "I'm here to drool over Lulu" pathetic vibe.

Ten minutes later the curtains swept open and there she was.

Tonight she wore a simple blue dress that swished around her toned thighs and clung to her small breasts. She swung a jaunty yellow umbrella that she snapped open to frame her shimmering red locks. Lulu's lips were painted in what seemed to be her signature—a red so deep it made his salivary glands kick into overdrive. Just the thought of brushing his lips across hers caused interest to stir beneath his belt, which was crazy and sophomoric. But very much a reality. Once again he was reminded of being that child pressed against the smudged glass. *I want some.*

He'd gone over the edge.

Jesus. He wanted.

Wanted.

The band struck up, and before he could take another sip, Lulu was off. He didn't know much about dancing, but she was good. And she got the crowd into it. Tonight she tapped, no sultry siren, but rather a wisecracking, sassy firecracker of a gal doing an old Gene Kelly number. Singing in the rain. Laughing, tapping, loving in the rain. And true to form, she moved out to the audience, inviting them to go on the splashy, fun romp with her.

He knew the moment she saw him. Her eyes blinked once, then twice, but she never missed a beat. She didn't move toward him, but her reaction told him something—she remembered him. Now whether that was a bad thing or a good thing, he wasn't sure. Still, he felt pleased that she'd reacted in some way.

Midway into the song, the lights lowered and the music changed into "Purple Rain." Lulu was joined by a handsome black man who moved as smoothly as she did. They linked hands and Fred and Gingered across the dance floor. Together they were mesmerizing, flowing like water, turning like newly greased cogs in perfect unison. Eventually, the song changed back to the lively "Singing in the Rain" and both did a spectacular tap that ended with a small explosion of blue confetti. It was campy, silly, and perfect in every way. The audience went nuts, several giving a standing ovation.

Lulu laughed and then turned and kissed the man.

Nick stopped clapping and tried to stifle the urge to leap across the dance floor and rip the man's throat out.

While everyone was distracted, Nick moved over to the piano player who had pushed back from the fancy piano and looked to be heading for a break.

"Hey," he called, hoping like heck he wasn't being too creepy. "Excuse me."

The thin man turned. "Yeah?"

"Ms. LaRue . . . can you give her a message for me?"

"I ain't no errand boy, man," he said, looking annoyed.

"I wasn't treating you like one. I just figured you were heading to the back and wouldn't mind. I can make it worth your while," Nick said reaching inside his jacket.

The piano player gave him a look of disdain. "Shit, man. I can give a message without being paid for it."

"Sorry. That came out wrong," Nick said, noting that Lulu and her partner were leaving the stage, heading back to the dressing area on the other side. He'd screwed things up trying to go through the piano player. "Never mind."

"Nah, what's the message? No use in me being a dick. Help a guy out and all that."

"Just tell her Nick wants to buy her that drink." Sounded lame when he said it out loud. So much for the cool James Bond vibe he wanted to put out. Sophistication flew out the window to be replaced by Goober from Andy Griffith. Or that weird snowman in that cartoon his daughter liked to watch. Whichever, he sounded slightly desperate and kooky.

"Aight, man," the guy said, jerking his head in a universal cool nod. The piano player was so not a goober. He had the cool vibe down.

Nick walked back to his table and jiggled the ice cubes in his glass. He shouldn't have come. It was a dumb idea. Lulu had essentially dismissed him a few nights ago, and because he couldn't get her out of his mind, he'd traipsed down here like a pathetic schmuck. *Please have a drink with me. Throw me a crumb of attention. I'm pathetic.*

A swoosh of perfumed air tickled his nose and interrupted his self-bashing.

"You rang?" Lulu said breathlessly as she sat down next to him.

Her lips were extra glossy, and a fine sheen of perspiration covered the plunging vee of the dancing costume. He felt oddly compelled to lick her chest . . . which was very unsettling and also kind of erotic.

She narrowed her eyes at him expectantly. "You wanted to buy me a drink? 'Cause I *could* use one."

"Yeah. Thanks," he said, sounding like the dork he'd imagined himself to be.

Jordan appeared with a tall glass of ice water. "Here ya go, Lulu. The usual." She set the glass with the floating slice of lemon in front of Lulu.

So she did this quite often, huh? Of course she did. How many guys had she blessed with her presence after a performance? Nothing special about Nick.

Lulu picked up the glass and downed about half. "Thanks for the drink."

"You're a cheap date," Nick said with a wry smile.

"Aw, that's what all the guys say," she said, batting her

gorgeous blue eyes. At that moment there was something so familiar about Lulu. Like they'd done this a hundred times. Maybe she looked like an actress he'd seen on TV, or maybe she reminded him of an old college girlfriend. Either way, something about her worked.

"You want something stronger than water?" he asked, wiggling his glass so Jordan would know he wanted another.

"Sure," the waitress said with a nod. "You want something else, Lulu?"

Lulu shook her head. "I don't usually have drinks with patrons, but I didn't want you showing up backstage when I'm trying to wiggle out of my girdle."

"You don't wear a girdle," he said, sliding his eyes down to her trim stomach.

Lulu smiled. "That you know of."

The image of Lulu in a girdle was also kind of erotic. Nick was losing his mind right there in the middle of Gatsby's. Sexy girdles. Jeez.

"So what's a good boy like you want with a bad girl like me?"

Nick snorted. "How do you know I'm a good boy?"

She gave him a flat stare, and again he was struck by her familiarity.

"Okay, so I'm a bit of a Boy Scout. But a bad girl like you surely knows what to do with a Boy Scout?" He was rusty on his flirting skills, but he thought that was a good comeback. How long had it been since he'd had to try so hard to be charming?

Years . . .

"Ha," Lulu said, taking another sip of water, giving him a sultry stare over the rim of her glass. "I don't play with Boy Scouts."

Nick smiled. "But you could tie me up with my kerchief. That could be . . . fun."

Her too-blue eyes widened. "That does sound fun. Would I earn a patch or something?"

"Is there a patch for tying up a Boy Scout and having your

wicked way with him?"

Lulu shrugged. "I was never a Boy Scout. I was a Brownie for about a week. Couldn't do the knee socks."

"You'd look great in knee socks," he said. And nothing else.

"Oh, yeah?" she said, suddenly sobering as if she'd crossed a line. She inched her chair back. "I have to go. Thanks for the drink."

"Don't go," he said, clasping her hand.

She pulled it loose. "Sorry. I have someone waiting for me."

She moved away, giving a little flirtatious wave to the table next to his. As she passed his chair, she trailed a finger across the nape of his neck. Chill bumps rose on his flesh, and that infernal need that had hooked itself inside him flared.

Nick stood and followed her, catching her elbow just as she passed through the open doorway. "Lulu, wait."

She turned back to him. "I'm not available. You're a nice guy and all, but—"

"A Boy Scout," he finished her sentence, releasing her elbow. Did she have a boyfriend? Or was she playing hard to get? Some girls knew how to play games.

Her mouth twitched. "Yeah, total Boy Scout."

Nick wasn't a man who took something not freely given, but at Lulu's words, something inside him snapped. He wasn't a goddamned Boy Scout. He was a man. With a man's wants and needs.

Her teasing smile disappeared as something else took its place. Nick read awareness in her eyes as easily as he could read the exit sign above her head. Her tongue darted out to lick her lower lip before she caught hold of it between her teeth. Those bluebell eyes reflected the desire he knew pooled in his own eyes.

Boy Scout, his ass.

Nick cupped her jaw and took what he wanted.

chapter fourteen

E DEN WAS IN trouble.
She'd known this could happen when she'd thrown out every lick of sense she'd been given and pranced her silly ass out to Nick.

She couldn't say why she'd turned away from the dressing room when Fatso told her Nick wanted to buy her a drink. Maybe it was the high from nailing the rain routine. Maybe it was the idea Jess had planted in her mind the night before—that being with Nick wasn't such a big deal. Or maybe she was tired of every damned decision in her life being so damned critical.

So she'd spun on the ball of her shoe and tapped out to the man she yearned for like an addict wanting one last hit. Just like her mama.

But Eden convinced herself on the way it would fine. After all, she played a part. Having a drink with Nick was a prime opportunity for her to nip the crazy attraction in the bud.

She'd tried. Lord, she'd tried. She'd had every intention of telling him she had a boyfriend or was gay or something. But the lie hadn't come. She didn't know why she couldn't cut that tenuous cord, but something in her wouldn't allow it. Maybe it was those words he'd uttered—*you make me feel like a man again.* Or maybe she couldn't take away the only chance she had to be with him.

So instead of staying in character as Lulu and doing the dirty deed, she'd muttered something about someone waiting and dragged her finger over his nape. God, why had she done that? But she knew why. She wanted to leave the door open.

What would it hurt?

After all, Nick thought she was—what had the article in the magazine called her?—the "Vixen of the Vieux Carré." He didn't know that beneath the paint and glitz lay his nanny.

One kiss. Then she'd make him disappear.

Nick cupped her jaw and lowered his head. Those half-lidded eyes, that gorgeous mouth, his very essence stole her breath. She couldn't stop herself from lifting on her toes and meeting him halfway.

Her move startled him, and for a moment he drew back, his gaze widening before his lips twitched. Then he hauled her against his body and kissed the hell out of her.

Heaven.

That's what kissing Nick was.

Eden's hands rose to tangle in the thick hair at the nape of his neck as his arms wound round her body, one hand finding her hip, the other curving around her back, pinning her to his hardness.

His lips were greedy, and she let him take what he wanted, angling her head, opening her mouth to him. He tasted like scotch, and man, and other things she didn't know existed. Things intangible but good. Oh so good.

"Mmm," she groaned as his hand dropped to her butt, tugging her even closer. She could feel his arousal, and that fueled the warmth creeping through her stomach. She felt boneless, weightless, transported to another place where there was only her, Nick, and this between them.

He shifted his head, deepening the kiss, his hands moving

over her back.

"God, Lulu, I want you," he whispered, dotting tiny kisses at the corners of her mouth.

Lulu.

Someone who didn't exist.

His words were sleet pelting her heated body. She pushed against his chest. "Stop. I have to go."

"No," he said, reaching for her as she stepped away.

"I can't be with you, Nick."

"Why?" His gaze searched hers.

"Because I—"

"Hey, you ready?" someone called from behind her.

She turned to find Ryan on the edge of the steps leading up to the dressing room. He held a bouquet of flowers, no doubt rectifying Jess's guilt in not bringing Eden her favorite flowers after the show last night. The three of them had a dinner reservation at nine o'clock, and no doubt Jess had sent Ryan to fetch Eden. Having the too-good-looking Ryan standing there holding flowers and looking concerned couldn't have been better staged than if it had been, well, staged. The opportunity to shut Nick down sat right in front of her.

"Ryan," she said, stepping even farther away from Nick. "I'll be right there."

"Everything okay?" Ryan asked, his brow crinkling.

"Fine. I'll change and be right out."

He waggled the bouquet of white daisies. "These are for you. Your favorite, right?"

"My absolute favorite, babe. Uh, wait for me out back?"

Ryan blinked, obviously taken aback by the endearment. But since the man was a genius, it didn't take but a millisecond before he caught on. Delivering a deadly smile, he drawled, "I can help you if you need it. I'm good with . . . zippers."

Good Lord, the Brain looked positively wicked. "Uh, no. I'm good."

"Rain check then. I'll be waiting," Ryan said before walking back toward the outer door where she'd told them to wait for her. Jess was likely on the phone. Or something. Who knew? But it had worked out.

Eden turned to Nick who looked one part guilty two parts junkyard dog. "I have to go."

The possessiveness in his expression didn't fade. "Is that—"

"Look." She lifted up a hand. "I can't do this with you. No more drinks. No more . . . whatever. Don't ask for me again."

"Lulu, there's something between us. I may be out of practice, but not stupid. If this guy is your guy, okay, I'll back off. But if not, why not explore this thing we got?"

"I can't." Eden turned and bolted to her dressing room, firmly shutting the door against the temptation. Her legs trembled and her stomach fluttered, but she'd done the right thing. Let Nick think what he would about Ryan or the reason why she couldn't be with him, but he had to have received the message loud and clear.

They weren't going to happen.

A knock on the door caused her to jump.

Surely Nick would respect her wishes. He was an ambitious guy, but he wasn't a douche. She cautiously opened the door and then jumped aside when Jess strode in.

"Oh my god. That was him. Nick. Your boss," Jess said, whirling on her like a defense attorney with conclusive proof. Aha! Got you now! "And he doesn't know, does he?"

"Good evening to you too, Jess." Eden closed the door and checked behind the dressing screen to make sure no one was lurking in the adjacent costume room. With all the dancers on stage, the coast was clear. Because she really didn't want to have this conversation out in the open.

"You little minx. He doesn't know you're Lulu. Ryan overheard the whole thing. And bless him, for a smart man he couldn't put all that together. He thought it was some random guy, but then I saw the guy when I came around the corner and—"

"You can put things together and have mad Google skills." Eden snorted.

"Of course. Oh my gosh, you were too scared to tell your 'boss' you're Lulu," Jess said hooking air quotes with her fingers. "This is crazy. You know that, right?"

Eden didn't know whether to be pleased she could talk about the predicament she'd landed herself in or whether she was annoyed at Jess for finding such glee in the weird situation. "Okay, yeah, he doesn't know Lulu LaRue is his nanny."

"How does he not know, and how did this even happen? Jeez, it's like a soap opera," Jess said, plopping onto the chair Eden used when Lisa did her makeup. "And hurry up. We have reservations."

"Heil, Hitler," Eden breathed as she unbuckled her tap shoes.

Jess ignored the insult. "So spill already."

"Nick came to Gatsby's a few nights ago with a friend. He's trying to date more. Or that's what he told me. I didn't know he was here until I plopped into his lap. I was doing the 'Big Spender' number, and I go out in the audience a lot," she explained while she tugged off her shoes. "When I realized it was him, I knew I was sunk."

"Why? What would he care you're a performer?"

"He wouldn't. I don't think. It's just I was vague about my second job."

"Why?"

Eden wriggled out of the tight costume. "I don't know."

"E, why would you be ashamed of this? They're doing articles on you. You're packing them in. You have an agent, for God's sake."

"I know." But still there was the viscous shame that twisted inside her. Her mother had been a stripper. She didn't even know who her father was. White trash. Voorhees trash. Using her body to make a buck.

"Is this about your mother?"

"It's always about my mother, isn't it? And the fact I lived in a falling-down house, used food stamps, and took odd jobs so I could pay for my prom dress. This world isn't far from that, Jess. Right? I'm still shaking my ass to pay my bills."

Jess stood. "Okay, last year you gave me a good talking-to when I wasn't thinking straight, remember? So let me do the same."

Eden shook her head. "You don't have to. Look, deep down I know I'm not my mother, but I carry my past with me. I can't seem to let go of the stupid thought that I'm somehow less. It's pathetic and maddening. Maybe one day when I have enough, when I'm not rubbing nickels together to pay the light bill, I'll feel different. If I could afford a therapist, I'd have one."

Jess took her by the shoulders. "Eden."

"What?" Eden tried to stop the tears forming in her eyes. She hated tears. "We're going to be late for dinner."

"Stop. Just stop. You're one of the most incredible women I know. There's nothing trashy or low class about you. Not even when you're shaking your hind end. So suck it up, buttercup, and stop being down on yourself."

"I'm not having a pity party. You're just one of the people I can be real with, okay?"

Jess wrapped Eden in her arms. Eden's first inclination was to stiffen, but then she relaxed into her friend's embrace. "Your hair smells like apples."

Jess laughed. "Eden, you're like that dog that wandered up on my pop-pop's farm. Took almost a year before we could pet her. She was tough, cautious, and the best dog he ever had. You're a tough cookie, but—"

"—the best dog you ever had?" Eden joked pulling away from her friend because it was a little awkward to be hugging her while standing in a strapless bra and a pair of Spanx knockoffs.

"You're avoiding the original topic of conversation. And, by the way, Nick is yowser! Hottie, hot, hot. But clueless, am I right?"

Eden blinked back tears and gave a laugh. "Yeah, I don't quite understand how he doesn't see through this." She pointed to her wig before she started pulling out the pins. "Or the glitter and red paint."

"Men are obtuse. I guess he wasn't looking for you, so he didn't see you."

"No, just the sexy redhead I play."

"Well, to be honest, I forget you're Eden when you're out there. You're good, hon."

Eden set the wig on the form head, pulling off her hairnet and shaking her hair out. Taking a makeup wipe, she started the process of stripping away Lulu. "You know, I'm not going to protest that statement. It's something I promised Lacy I'd stop doing."

"What?"

"Stop saying I'm not good enough to make it. And since she made me promise in the letter she left me, I couldn't really get out of it."

Eden glanced over at her bag where the letter Lacy had left her sat tucked away. On the day of Lacy's funeral when she, Jess, and Rosemary had retreated to their table at the Lazy Frog Coffee and Ice Cream Shoppe, they'd each received a letter. All three had kept the contents of their individual letters private, as Lacy had intended. Eden carried hers with her because the words therein were ones she wanted to live by.

Stop apologizing for who you are, Eden. You've got more talent in your pinky toe than most have in their entire bodies, and it will take you places. I know this. Don't doubt me. So when someone says, "You were so good," you are NOT allowed to say you weren't or to pooh-pooh their compliment by trying to be humble. You've lived humble, sugar. Enough of that. So stop ducking that beautiful head. Chin up. Smile on. Accept your fate. You will be great. And, E, I really don't want to do the whole haunting thing, but I will if I see you running from your meant-to-be. I can totally do the ghost thing. With style, baby, with style. Boo!

"Yeah, Lacy, always liked to have the last word. And she got it." Jess chased the sadness away with a smile. "But I agree with her on this one."

Eden picked up her favorite sweater and tugged it on. "Actually, Ryan showing up with flowers probably did what I couldn't do."

"What couldn't you do?"

"Destroy Nick's chances with Lulu. But I'm pretty sure Nick jumped to the conclusion Ryan was, like, my date. Your boy wonder played along nicely, so now I don't have to worry about Nick finding out I'm Lulu. Pretty sure he won't be back."

"Glad Ryan could help," Jess said, brushing a hand over the various makeup brushes lying on the dressing table. "You sure you don't want to tell Nick that you're Lulu? It might get you what you want."

"It will get me what I don't need and with a man who doesn't want the real me but a fantasy."

Jess opened her mouth, but Eden held up a hand. "Look, I know you and Rosemary have found happily-ever-afters, but not everyone wants love. I want a career, and if I allow myself to fall in love with my boss, that would be messy. I don't need messy right now. I need security."

"There can be security in love, Eden."

Eden pulled on her jeans and slipped into the clogs she'd bought on sale at T.J. Maxx last week—a little bonus for herself on payday. "Maybe, but I'm not ready for that kind of security. I need financial security and a career. Love can wait."

"Ha, you think love waits. Uh-uh, sister, it will sneak up on you and punch you in the face when you least expect it," Jess said with a snort. "Just don't let something pass you by because you're stubborn."

"I'm not."

Jess cocked her head. "Wait, maybe it's not stubbornness. Are you afraid to be in a relationship?"

Eden jerked her head up as she shouldered her bag. "Afraid? No. But you know my past. I don't sleep around for a reason. I don't bounce on a happy cloud of daydreams for a reason. I also don't step on cracks, walk under ladders, or break mirrors. My life is just that fragile. I'm on the path I need to be on. Stop trying to turn me into you or Rosemary."

Jess stared at her for a moment, making her feel a bit like an asshole, but Eden meant what she said. She wasn't going to slip up, not when she barely balanced on the tightrope she currently walked. She didn't have room for error or she'd lose every bit of momentum she'd caught hold of.

"Guess that was another comment I should have kept to myself," Jess said with a sigh. She donned a smile. "I'm really hungry."

"I could eat a moose. Or a small child."

"Eating children is illegal. Not sure about the moose." Jess tapped something on her phone while she waited on Eden to put on lip gloss. "Ryan's outside. He said the thong chick won't leave him alone, so he wants us to hurry before he has to take Pasties to dinner too."

Eden laughed. "They'd make a nice couple."

Jess made a face. "I'd hate to rip her hair out, but I can."

"Meow," Eden said, opening the door.

But her laughter died when she found Nick standing against the wall.

His eyes went wide. "Eden?"

Nick couldn't believe his eyes. Eden stood dressed in jeans and a cable sweater, laughing with a tall brunette. For a moment his mind couldn't process what was taking place. How was Eden here? And where was Lulu?

But then like a stack of cards falling into place during a shuffle, everything lined up. Eden was Lulu. Lulu was his nanny.

Holy shit.

"Nick," she said, staggering back and hitting the doorjamb.

"What the hell is going on?" he shouted. He hadn't meant to shout, but the betrayal, embarrassment, and confusion tangled into something that demanded shouting.

"Uh, what are you doing here?" she said half-heartedly, her gaze shifting to the right and left, looking for escape.

"Don't even think about it."

Eden glanced at the woman beside her and then back at him. "Uh . . . okay then. Surprise?" She held out her hands and wiggled them. Jazz style.

He didn't say anything because he couldn't find the words. His mind grappled with what had been revealed. He had a crush on Eden. No. Lulu. Both? He wasn't sure. He didn't know what to think or feel at the moment. Part of him was incensed. She'd lied. Made a fool out of him. But at the same time, part of him rejoiced because this woman wasn't aloof or unattainable. At the top of his pile of emotions was the thought that this explained so much. How had he not known? Why hadn't she told him?

The brunette with the curly hair and amber eyes looked somewhat amused. She stuck out her hand. "Hi, I'm Jess. Eden's friend."

Nick looked at her hand before remembering he should take it. "Nick Zeringue."

"Nice to meet you, Nick. Should I leave you two?" Jess withdrew her hand, glancing at a silent Eden.

Eden swallowed. "We have reservations."

"I'll call and let the restaurant know we're running late," Jess countered.

Eden slid too-familiar blue eyes back to Nick. "No. I'll see Nick on Monday. He and I can talk then."

How had he not realized the eyes were the same? There was so much he now saw. But wait, was she blowing him off, trying to slink off without explaining why she'd lied to him? "You're seriously running from this?"

"I just think you need—"

"No. You don't get to decide. I want the truth. What you should have told me a long time ago. Like when I asked you about your job. Like when I asked you if you'd ever been to Gatsby's. How could you lie? And why?" Anger reared and pawed at him. What a fool she'd made of him. He'd sniffed after her like a stray waiting for a scrap. She'd played him. Why? For amusement? Had she enjoyed his humiliation?

"Nick, my friends are waiting."

"They can wait." His voice was hard. "You *kissed* me."

Eden's eyes flashed. "No, *you* kissed me."

"This is all so interesting," Jess said, sounding embarrassed yet somehow intrigued.

Eden looked at her friend. "Go save Ryan from Shelia. I'll be out in a minute."

"That's her name? Hmm. She doesn't look like a Shelia," Jess said, still looking interested . . . and obviously unconcerned about whoever Shelia was.

"Jess." Eden wasn't asking.

"All right. Nice to meet you, Nick. Good luck." Jess gave a little wave and then shot Eden a pointed look before heading toward the back door.

Just as Jess disappeared from sight, a gaggle of women descended from the wings of the stage. They were breathing hard and were as noisy as a herd of water buffalo. He squeezed his shoulders together as they brushed by.

"Good show, Eden. You and Derrick were awesome!" one called out.

"Thanks," Eden called back.

The women looked at him questioningly but disappeared into the room behind Eden, not quite slamming the door behind them. The click was ominous.

"How could you not say anything, Eden?"

"I don't know," she said, her voice quiet, full of regret. "I . . ." She wouldn't look at him. No explanation. Seemed obvious she didn't have one.

"You made a fool of me." His gut burned with shame.

Her gaze jerked up. "No. That's not true. I didn't know how to tell you. I . . . have issues sometimes. It's hard for me to be—"

"Honest? 'Cause it would have been easy when I first asked you about taking the second job. I thought you were waitressing. You let me believe that."

"I know. It's hard for me to be forthcoming. I didn't tell you I was Lulu because I wasn't sure you would accept me taking care of your daughter. And I wanted to stay with you and Sophie." Her words sounded truthful. Sincere. His anger took a blow with those words. *I wanted to stay with you and Sophie.*

"You thought I would judge you?"

She directed her stare just over his shoulder and gave a shrug. "Maybe."

"Because you're a dancer?"

"Because I dance, sing, and shake my caboose. For money." She paused for a moment. "I know what kind of man you are. I was shocked to see you here at all."

"I'm a dude. I'm pretty sure I established I'm no Boy Scout."

"But you're a good guy, and you have a certain reputation. You're just beyond all this," she said, finally looking at him. "I wanted to keep my worlds separate. I didn't want you to see me . . . this way."

He tried to wrap his mind around the idea that she'd tried to protect his delicate sensibilities. Which was absurd. Gatsby's wasn't a dive, and she wasn't stripping. She headlined at a reputable nightclub. And she was doing it with panache, pizazz, and all the theatre verbiage he could think of. "I don't understand you."

At those words she sighed. "You wouldn't be the first to say that."

He watched her silently.

"You're right. I should have told you," she said finally.

"It would have saved me from looking like a fool."

"You're not a fool." Eden sounded adamant. "Look, I tried blowing you off. I figured if you thought Lulu was unavailable, you wouldn't come back. That you'd never know. That was stupid though. You'd eventually find out. I don't know why I hid this."

"Why did you kiss me? Why did you let it go that far? You could have stopped me."

As he said the words, he knew. She wanted him. He'd seen it in her every move when they'd stood in his courtyard sharing a cocktail. When the strung lights paired with moonlight caught her just right, he'd seen the hunger. He had almost kissed her then. Tonight Eden hadn't been able to help herself any more than he could have stopped himself from kissing Lulu LaRue.

For a moment they stood, two people so unsure about everything. But knowing the truth. He knew it was reflected in his eyes.

Reprieve. They both needed it.

"You have to go," he said, giving her an out.

She nodded. "I do."

"We'll talk later. We both need time to process this."

"Okay." She looked at the door her friend had disappeared through moments ago.

A frantic-looking Asian woman nearly mowed them down, brushing past and carrying a bag of ice. She spared a scathing look for him before saying to Eden. "You missed three steps. You want top money, don't miss steps."

Eden's face colored, and Nick almost snatched the woman by the hair and dragged her back to apologize to his nanny. Christ, his nanny.

"I didn't miss a single step, and you know it," Eden called out.

The woman flipped Eden off. Eden merely smiled, the pink fading from her cheeks. "She loves me."

There was so much he didn't know about the woman who sometimes washed his clothes and bathed his daughter. So small and so complicated. Now things were even more complicated. No longer was this just about sex. There was more at stake. He needed to think. "We'll talk Monday."

Eden nodded. "Bye, Mr. Zer—Um, Nick."

He shook his head. "Yeah, after what just happened, you *cannot* call me Mr. Zeringue."

chapter fifteen

Sophie splashed in the tub and shrieked when Barbie fell out of the boat into the bubbles. "Help! Help!"

The child's hands jerked when she grabbed the doll, but she was successful. Sophie wasn't a normal kid, but she managed to lose herself in her own magical world of make-believe.

"What made Barbs fall?" Eden asked, resting on her knees beside the soaker tub in Nick's master-bath suite. The modern bathroom was as big as Eden's living room and kitchen put together. One day she'd have a bathroom like this—big, unlimited hot water, and lots and lots of scented bath salts.

"A big storm," Sophie said, making the accompanying noises. The child's face was screwed up in concentration as Ken dove off the side and swam to Barbie's rescue.

"Needs Ken to save her, huh?"

"No," Sophie said, making Ken sink beneath the foam. "He's a bad swimmer."

Eden laughed, cocking her ear toward the open door. Nick would be home soon. The dread she'd carried around with her all day fluttered against her heart. Rehearsals had gone smoothly, though Frenchie hadn't let her forget she'd promised to learn a fan dance. Fredric had called to tell her he had negotiated a higher salary, and she'd hugged Jess and Ryan goodbye that morning with a promise to visit the beach soon. All in all, a good day . . . except for the horrible knot in her stomach.

Nick was angry.

And he had cause to be. She'd lifted onto her toes and met him halfway in that kiss, wanting the memory of his lips more than peace in her life. Just one kiss to keep her company on cold nights when she huddled beneath her cheap comforter and prayed the roach spray was working . . . along with the new lock she installed. When she was lonely, she could look back and recall the feel of his body against hers along with the taste of whiskey and warm male. She could remember how good he smelled—clean and expensive—and how he'd devoured her mouth like a man tasting water after a drought. That kiss had legs and would stay with her a long time.

But that kiss was to be a secret. Nick wasn't supposed to discover she was Lulu.

She felt the garage door vibrate.

No more secrets.

"I'm home," Nick called to them.

"We're in your bathroom," she called back, the knot sinking lower as she picked up the baby shampoo. "Let's get you clean, sugar britches."

"I ain't no sugar britches," Sophie said, her own response making her laugh as she tried to make Barbie kiss Ken.

Yep. Couldn't get away from the kissing.

"Hey, gals," Nick said, popping his head into the bathroom. "Oh, bubbles today, huh?"

"Daddy," Sophie cried, splashing around and nearly coming out of her safety seat, "I'm a mermaid. Edie's gonna make me a tail."

Nick's gaze met hers. Eden lowered her eyes and flipped the top of the shampoo. "My aunt sews."

"That's awfully nice of her," Nick said.

"I'll finish up and get Soph into her jammies," Eden said.

"And then we'll talk," he said, softly closing the door.

"Is Daddy mad?" Sophie asked.

"No," Eden said, knowing she was telling a fib. Nick was angry with her because she'd made a fool out of him. But he had to see it her way. She hadn't been trying to deceive him. Heck, she hadn't thought he'd ever come to Gatsby's anyway. How was she to know that they'd do an article on her and that suddenly she'd become the toast of Bourbon Street?

Because I told you so, dork.

She could hear Lacy's voice in her head. Her dear friend had been so certain Eden was destined for greatness. Any daydream Eden had through the years regarding fame and fortune hadn't sounded ridiculous to Lacy. Her friend had called them attainable goals. Even the limo and cabana boys. Lacy believed Eden deserved good things in life, and that belief had bled into Eden. She didn't have confidence in much, but she had confidence in her God-given talent to become whoever she needed to be on that stage.

"Grown-ups like to talk. My mama talked to my dad. She don't want to see me."

"Who doesn't?"

"My mama. She lives in California. You been there?"

"No, but I've seen it on the map," Eden said, squirting some shampoo into her palm and lathering it into Sophie's thick brown hair.

"Disneyland's got Sleeping Beauty's castle. I want to go see Cinderella's castle."

"Of course." Eden scrubbed Sophie's scalp, inhaling the scent of the shampoo. She'd gleaned through conversations with Sophie and a few remarks by Nick that his ex-wife wasn't overly concerned with her role as Sophie's mother. She knew how Sophie felt firsthand.

"That's in Disney World. You want to go?" Sophie had

moved on from her mother to the things that preoccupied little girls—princesses, castles, and fantasies. Eden knew that too. She'd been a little girl. Once.

"Sure I do," Eden said, picking up a plastic Mardi Gras cup on the side of the tub. "Let's rinse."

Ten minutes later, Sophie was in bed watching a video. Eden had tidied up the bathroom, rinsed the tub, braided Sophie's damp hair, and done everything she could to postpone the inevitable. Eden trudged down the hall, wondering if she could make some kind of excuse to get the hell out. She hated uncomfortable conversations. And this would definitely be one.

Nick sat on the couch sipping a drink and staring into the flames of the fire he'd ignited in the hearth room. He didn't look up when she entered the room. One glance at the kitchen clock told her she had thirty minutes before she had to depart for Gatsby's.

"Sophie had an early supper. She wanted to put on her new Tinker Bell jammies. That's why I went ahead and gave her a bath." Keep it neutral. Maybe he'd drop everything and do the ostrich thing. Pretend nothing had happened. That's what they did in Eden's family. Pretend all the bad stuff away. Or fight about it until someone called the police. Toss-up.

"Thank you. You want a drink?"

"No thanks."

He glanced over his shoulder at her. "You sure? I find alcohol makes hard stuff easier."

"I find alcohol leads to things like pregnancy, bar fights, and/or rehab. It does not make things easier. Just hazier."

"Touché," he said with a ghost of a smile.

She sank onto the edge of the couch, knowing it looked tentative, but it wasn't as though she could sprawl casually. Tension thickened the air.

"I'm not going to fire you . . . or beat you," he said, amusement lining his voice.

"I'm not scared of you. I just like this spot."

Nick shrugged. "I've been thinking about this situation for the past forty-eight hours, but I've got nothing. Well, not nothing. I'm disappointed, embarrassed, and pissed."

Eden bit her lip.

"Still, I've tried to put myself in your tap shoes, so to speak. Harder than I thought. I personally would have told my boss and friend I had a second job performing at Gatsby's. But I've never worn tap shoes."

Her lips twitched at his last comment.

"I'm not you."

"No," she said, allowing her body to relax at his words. His tone and demeanor portrayed an understanding man, a man who knew others weren't always comfortable being who they were. "You're right. Telling someone I work at Gatsby's would have been the practical thing to do. Most people wouldn't hide the fact they worked there. It's not like the place is low-rent. Maybe titillating at times. Slightly bawdy. But not classless."

"It's a nice place."

"My only excuse is that sometimes my past colors my present."

"We all have baggage, Eden."

"But some people's baggage is heavier than others . . . and some of us make ours heavier by our own insecurities." She knew that was true. The way she'd been brought up had made her cautious, less likely to misstep. Not to mention she shouldered a huge chip of inferiority.

"But none of that solves this matter. None of it explains the attraction I have for you," he said, setting his glass on the coffee table and turning toward her. "That's not so easy."

"Maybe I'll have that drink now." She laughed.

"Even if it leads to a bar fight?"

"I'll take that over getting pregnant," she said, finally allowing herself to smile before realizing what that implied.

"I can forgive you for not telling me about the Lulu role, but this thing between us"—he waved his hand in the space between them—"is still here."

Relief sank inside her only to bypass the rising anxiety. She *was* attracted to him. But he was attracted to Lulu. So should they pretend the toe-curling, earth-shattering kiss hadn't happened?

"I'm good at ignoring things," Eden said.

"But I'm not," he said, clasping his hands between his knees staring at the coffee table with eyes the color of stainless steel. "This isn't going to go away."

"But I work for you."

"You want to ignore any potential . . ." He didn't seem to know where the glimmer of possibility could take them.

"Exactly." Eden stared at her fingers. She'd been biting the skin around her thumb, and it was raw and red. "You don't know what to call it because where can we really go with this attraction? We're so different from one another. I'm not looking for love. And you, well, you have a daughter, an established career."

"Why's that an issue?"

"Maybe it's not. But you went to Gatsby's looking for a hookup. It's not the sort of place you look for something serious, right?"

Nick made a face. "I don't know. Maybe. I thought I'd look for something to help me forget my world for a little while. I don't know if that makes sense."

"No, you want more. And I understand that when things get hard, you just want something easy."

Nick paused. "Guess that's spot-on. I have a bit of a hole in my life. When my sister suggested I stop worrying about a future and instead look for something fun, it sounded like something I should want. When I saw Lulu, she seemed like the perfect escape. I won't lie—there was insta-lust. But something about the joie de vivre Lulu displayed hit me where I needed it."

"But you're talking about Lulu. Not me."

He studied her a few seconds. "What do you mean?"

"Lulu's a creation. I designed her to be flamboyant, bold, yet have this 'little girl lost' vibe that works on men. Lulu knows how to work the stage and get what she wants. She's not me." At that moment Eden wished she *were* Lulu. She wanted to be the woman Nick wanted. So desperately. "The good news here is you're attracted to Lulu. Not me. That makes things easier."

Those words were hard to speak. Deep inside a voice cried out, asking why she wasn't good enough to draw the attention of someone like Nick. Like the fontanel on a baby's head where the bones hadn't grown together, Eden possessed a vulnerable spot, a crippling insecurity of being poor, insignificant trash not worthy of the country-club life Nick led. She'd seen his membership card, ridden in his leather-drenched Mercedes, glimpsed the extensive cellar of expensive wines. She wasn't the kind of girl Nick Zeringue dated. Not even close.

"You would think, huh?" He shifted, draping his arm on the back of the couch. "But thing is, I've been attracted to you way before Lulu was in the picture."

Her heart hit the pit of her stomach.

"It all clicked into place when I saw you come out of that dressing room. The reason I was so obsessed with Lulu is because I had suppressed the attraction I felt for you," Nick said, pausing for a moment. "I thought about it all night. The instant closeness, the intrigue, the desire, was all because I was already attracted to . . . you."

His words were like a three-point shot. Swoosh. "You're confused."

"I don't think so." He picked up his glass and shook the ice. Lifting it to his mouth, he sucked in one of the ice cubes. It wasn't meant to be a sexy move, but it brought all of her attention to his mouth . . . and allowed his words to chip at her resolve. What if this had nothing to do with Lulu? What if her brazen antics were merely the vehicle to lead them to where they were supposed to be? Dare she hope he wanted both of them? Or rather saw through Lulu to the woman beneath the feathers and glue?

Nick crunched the ice between his molars, his gaze hot on

her. "How about we find out?"

"Find out what?"

"If this thing is . . . real. How about Friday night? Go out with me. We'll do a genuine date with white tablecloths, wine, and hopefully not-so-awkward conversation."

"You're asking *me* out? Or Lulu?"

He narrowed his eyes. "You are Lulu."

Eden frowned.

"You. I want to go out with the woman beneath both the yoga pants and the sequins. What do you say?"

Eden hesitated. If they went there, it could be wonderful. She could experience a world she'd never allowed herself to experience before—a handsome man taking her out to somewhere other than Dean's Diner. On the other hand, she could be plunging herself into something that could not only end badly for her but for the sweet child watching a movie in her very purple bedroom down the hall. "Are you sure? We can't go back. Or maybe we can. I don't know."

"If we don't see what this is, we'll regret it. We can ignore it, but we might miss out on something fantastic. I've been living a life of okay. I need a little fantastic in there somewhere."

She wanted fantastic too. Her life to this point had been anything but. Was it wrong to want to hold something good in her hands for a little while? "Okay. We'll try a date. I have to work Friday night, but we could do a late supper."

"Perfect. It's Mardi Gras weekend, so lots of places are open late."

"I better go," she said, rising. Would he kiss her again? Because she wanted him to kiss her. Once. Twice. A thousand times.

"No more running."

"I'm not. I'm going to my other job."

"I want you to stay," he said, his gaze a caress. He reached up and snagged her hand, tugging her slightly, teasingly.

"I can't." She pulled him up from the sofa.

"If you must. But Friday night, you're all mine." He brought her to him, tucking an errant strand of hair behind her ear. The tender gesture caused a prickling of tears in her eyes.

Damn, this man had destroyed her resolve to remain platonic with his careful blend of masculinity and generosity. She longed to tuck herself into his arms and pretend the hard stuff away. Everyone needed that sometimes . . . needed someone to shoulder her burdens for her if only for a little while.

"You realize I'll be here tomorrow for work. And the next day. And the next." Her voice was a near whisper.

His answer was a smile.

"Bye, Nick." She resisted the urge to rise on her tiptoes and kiss him silly.

"Bye, Eden," he said before gently setting his lips against her forehead.

Her heart gave a sigh.

Yeah, this man could do real damage to her heart.

He hadn't brought Eden flowers because it seemed too gauche. Instead, he'd called his daddy and asked if he could use Johnny T and the company limo for the evening. In the backseat of the limo, a magnum of champagne chilled. If he had only one chance to test the theory that he and Eden should be together, he was going to do it right.

He'd called in a favor, and they had a nine forty-five reservation at the chef's table at Commander's Palace. Normally it was reserved for a party of four, no more, no less, but the manager Dan had once worked for Nick and owed him a favor. After dinner, he'd planned a midnight sail on Lake Pontchartrain. The marina was a skip and a hop from his house, and since he'd sweet-talked his parents into taking Sophie to the country house outside Abita Springs for the weekend, he could serve Eden breakfast in bed tomorrow morning . . . if she wanted.

Because he so wanted to feel her body against his.

Was he moving too fast?

Probably.

But he wanted her so much he'd tossed out his unspoken rule of not dating anyone who worked for him. And he'd tossed it out quick, without a second thought. Since the moment he'd seen her distraught at the coffeehouse over a month ago, he'd known something was there. Her vulnerability paired with the saucy showgirl had dragged any reservations he had and tossed them out the door. His Creole grandmother had always believed in signs. She'd said nothing was coincidence, only meant to be. A person could resist, but fate would bend him as it wished. When he'd first hired Eden, she'd said as much herself. A meant-to-be. Something had brought her to him, and he was tired of ignoring the signs.

"You here again?" The Asian woman sighed, brushing by him, jarring him from his thoughts. Tonight the stage director wore a schoolgirl costume with Buddy Holly glasses. "I'm going to start charging you. You take up too much space."

"I'm Nick Zeringue." He held out his hand.

"And I'm not impressed. I didn't ask your name," she said, ignoring his hand and giving him the once-over twice. She pushed at her glasses, mouth still flatlined. "But since you feel the need to do so, I'll bite. I'm Frenchie Pi, and this is my house." She made a tornado with her index finger to indicate the backstage area.

"I'd say nice to meet you but . . ."

She reached out and patted his cheek. "Hurt my Lulu and I break your pretty face. I know stuff that will make you shiver in your bed at night." Then she smiled and blew him a kiss as she sidled off.

"She doesn't mean that," Eden said, appearing at his elbow as he watched the fierce woman snap her fingers at a chorus girl.

"I think she does," he said, finally turning his gaze on Eden.

She was wearing the wig and a tight, pale blue dress that

floated out at her knees. Her lashes were long and curled, and the ruby lipstick on her lips made her look like a pinup model. Her blatant sexuality punched him in the gut but it was all . . . wrong.

"Are you ready?" she asked.

"Not yet," he said, trying to figure out how a person took a wig off a gal. Pins. Bobby pins if he remembered correctly. He lifted her hair on one side and started rooting for them.

"What're you doing?" she asked, swatting his hand.

"Finding Eden under this. I like redheads, but I don't want Lulu. I want Eden."

"You do?" She sounded surprised as she caught his hands in hers. She crooked her head adorably. "I thought maybe you'd want the fantasy? See how it played out?"

"You thought wrong. I wanted Lulu. Sure. You know that. But I want Eden more."

Her smile could have lit all the candles at the Saint Louis Cathedral altar. She started pulling pins out. "I'll be right back."

Five minutes later she emerged from the dressing area wearing the same dress. Only this time she'd traded her stilettos for a lower pair of pumps, and her shiny black hair framed a face devoid of heavy makeup. A ladylike pink lipstick had replaced the riveting red. A heart locket nestled at the swell of her breasts. She looked perfect.

"Better?" She crooked an eyebrow.

"Much," he said, wrapping his arm around her and giving her a squeeze. "Your chariot awaits, madam."

They made their way through the back to a passage he'd never seen before. Thankfully, the limo sat shining in the low lantern light across the street.

Johnny T had shed his normal jeans and Bob Marley concert T-shirt for the uniform he wore when the family needed to put their best foot forward. He doffed his cap and opened the door for Eden. "Ma'am."

She turned to Nick. "You're kidding? A limo?"

"Too much?"

Shaking her head, she slid inside. "No, but the only one I've ever ridden in was at a funeral, and that was just around a block. Is this champagne? Someone pinch me."

Johnny T gave a genuine smile. "I like this one."

Nick clasped the shoulder of the man who'd taught him to tie his shoes. "I do too."

Eden hadn't heard the exchange because she was too busy checking out the bar and marveling at the open sky roof. The vision of an exuberant Tom Hanks in *Big* popped into his head. Maybe they'd act like fools and stand on the seats with their head out of the sunroof.

"Better give y'all some privacy then." Johnny laughed, closing the door and walking to the driver's side.

"We have reservations for nine forty-five, but I think we have time to take it slow, right?" he asked Johnny before hitting the button that would raise the glass divider. Johnny's answer was a grin. The glass slid up, and Nick pulled the champagne from the silver bucket. "Champagne?"

"Is it like pink champagne? I had that once." Eden fiddled with the hem of her skirt, suddenly looking embarrassed.

"Not pink champagne, but let's give it a try." He popped the cork and suds erupted, making Eden squeak. Something about her very girlish response to the fizzy outburst made her all the more desirable. Eden never acted girly. On the contrary, she was competent and methodical . . . almost too cautious.

She wriggled her nose on the first sip. "Oh, it's, uh, different."

"You're probably not used to dry," he said, filling his own glass, then lifting it. The stars winked through the sunroof and the full moon peeked into the limo. "A toast?"

Eden lifted her glass. "To?"

"To Sister Regina Marie for seeing that you belong with me."

Her lips parted slightly. "That's a powerful statement, Nick Zeringue. And a Taylor Swift song."

"It *is* a Taylor Swift song. But I mean it. Every word. I think this was in the . . ." He looked up through the roof before clinking his glass to hers. " . . . stars."

They each took a sip before Nick took her glass and pulled her into his arms.

"Wow, you really know how to sweep a nanny off her feet," Eden said, sounding almost breathless.

"Can't say I've had much practice." He smiled, then kissed her.

Eden tasted like champagne and something he could never put into words—a rightness? A fierce desire to possess and protect this woman he held vibrated inside him. Her life had been hard, and he wanted to make it easy. If only for a little while.

She drew back, her eyes soft. "You are lethal, mister."

Nick kissed the tip of her nose. "The feeling is mutual."

By the time Johnny pulled up to the front of Commander's Palace, they'd drank most the champagne and had successfully worked themselves into a mutual state of breathlessness.

"Nick Zeringue, I can't believe you are darkening my doorstep," Dan Finn said, holding open the door as Nick escorted Eden through the canopied entrance. Dan had worked for Parran Z for a decade before being seduced over to Commander's by his wife and head pastry chef, Twyla Leonard. Nick couldn't fault him as Twyla created delicious combinations that rivaled the traditional menu items. And she had a killer pair of legs.

"Gotta check out the competition every now and then," he said, tamping down the residual resentment he still felt at Dan's jumping ship. They'd paid the man a small fortune to bring Maude's into prominence. Nick supposed loyalty deflated when a flamboyant, sexy chef crooked her finger. Glancing at Eden taking in the storied landmark restaurant, he could understand how that could happen. Beautiful women had always been man's eternal downfall.

"You know we only have competition from you. No one

else." Dan grinned, gesturing toward the inner sanctum of the grand old dame that had sat on Washington Avenue since the late nineteenth century. The key to Commander's wasn't merely the quality of the food, it was Southern dining at its best with gloved attendants pulling back chairs and draping napkins. Live jazz music filtered through the various genteel rooms over the sound of the polite clinking of glasses. Dining at Commander's was like walking down Bourbon Street or taking a streetcar. It was all part of the New Orleans experience.

"Wow," Eden breathed as they passed the other diners and headed for the kitchen.

Sitting near the line in the center of all the action was a pristine table set for two.

"Chef's table," Nick said as Dan pulled out the chair for Eden.

Dan tipped his head toward the slender young man standing to one side. "This is Luke. He's the sous chef and will be taking care of you. Bon appétit."

"It's so quiet in here," Eden whispered as Luke ducked a quick bow and set a watermelon gazpacho with tomato caviar at each of their places.

"A well-run kitchen is never noisy. Creativity and perfection takes a certain amount of gravity," Nick said.

For the next two hours, Luke kept them entertained with tales from the kitchen as the dishes to sample flew by. They dined on escargot, duck confit, flavorful soft-shell crab with caviar, pork belly boudin, all cut occasionally by a coupe de milieu to give them reprieve from the richness. And, of course, they finished with an array of desserts, including the popular and to-die-for bread pudding soufflé.

"Oh, my Lord," Eden said, sipping the sparkling water and surveying the remains of their desserts. "I've never had something so decadent in my life. This has been incredible."

Luke glowed, and Nick gleaned the young sous chef had fallen a little bit in love with Eden. Her genuine appreciation and marveling at the food was the ultimate in attraction for a chef.

And that Eden was gorgeous wasn't so bad either.

"Whoa, it's midnight already," Eden said with a yawn.

"You ready to cash it in or are you up for more adventure?"

She blinked, and he realized what his words sounded like. "No, not that. Though I could be talked into it." He gave her a teasing smile. "But I was thinking more along the lines of a midnight sail."

"On a boat?" she asked.

"Uh, unless you know another way to do it," he said with a laugh. "So are you game or do you want to hit the sack?"

"A midnight sail sounds incredible. I've never done that either, but I'm pretty tired. Long day."

Guilt walloped him when he realized she'd been up early for rehearsals, had a full afternoon with Sophie, and then ran across town to do an early performance so she could go on a date with him. Eden never complained about what she had to do each day. Total trouper—another thing he liked about her. "Of course."

"You're not disappointed? You planned this incredible date for me, and I'm pooping out."

He took her hand as she rose. "How could I be disappointed in this night? The food was excellent, the wine fantastic, and the girl beautiful. Add in that story about Joe Dale and the night he caught the gazebo on fire in the Morning Glory town square, and a guy can't have a better time."

"It really was an accident. But of course, if the man hadn't had brought the moonshine to the gig, it wouldn't have happened."

They walked out into the balmy-for-February night where Johnny T waited in the car, the blue glow of his phone illuminating his features.

Nick held up his hand in an "I got it" gesture as Johnny clued in and tried to climb out to get the door for them. Nick opened the door for Eden. Settling in next to her, he lowered the glass. "It was a great dinner, Johnny."

"No leftovers?" the man cracked.

"Did you want some?"

"No, but I thought I would remind you I'm always hungry." Johnny's gold tooth winked as he cackled. "Where to? The marina?"

"No. Eden's tired. Head to—" He turned to Eden, who bit the corner of her lip, looking suddenly serious. "Where do you live again?"

She pulled her gaze from the softly lit bar in the limo. "Did you say Soph was with your mom?"

He nodded as hope stirred inside him. Was she suggesting . . .

"How about we go to your place? Mine is, well, to be honest, I have a bit of an insect problem and I set off a bomb earlier today. Gross, I know. Those dang roaches really could survive a nuclear holocaust. I hoped for a"—she swallowed—"uh, sleepover?"

Johnny cackled again and started the car. "I guess I know where we're headin.'"

The glass slid up as Johnny pulled the car from the curb, passing huge houses from days of old that were nestled in lush foliage beneath the spread of the ancient oaks. Nick turned to Eden, who was the color of the tomato gazpacho. So endearing. "We don't have to rush this, Eden. I didn't expect you . . . to go home with me. I'm not the sort of guy who—"

"Hush," she said, grabbing his hand and curling hers around it. "I know what sort of man you are. In fact, I've been waiting a very long time for a man like you. You have no idea how long."

Nick pulled her into his arms and dropped an almost chaste kiss on her mouth. With her face upturned to his, he felt his heart slam against his ribs. It was like a jolt, and he remembered he'd felt that way before. With Susan. He'd tumbled head over heels in an obvious, foolish, I'll-do-anything-for-you way almost ten years before. Did he want to go there again? And wasn't it way too fast to feel the way he did about Eden?

Of course, they'd been dancing around this for almost a month and a half now. Wasn't necessarily dating, but on some level it was much more intimate. He'd had friends who'd been friends with their wives before they'd started going out, and he always wondered about it. Where was the passion? Where was the smack of desire that slammed into you and turned you in a raving lunatic? But perhaps there was something to knowing someone before falling in . . .

Love?

No. He wasn't there, but he knew he was close to the edge. For once, it didn't feel dangerous. He felt like he could dive off, arms flung wide, embracing something good for the first time in years. Eden made him feel again, and he reveled in it. It had been so long . . .

"You're pretty special, you know that?" he said, staring into those soft eyes.

"I'd disagree, but you're a guy who gets things right." She smiled, and a small dimple creased her cheek. She looked so lovely ensconced in his arms.

"Good girl," he said, pressing his mouth against hers. She tasted better than anything he'd had at Commander's that night. In .009 seconds. the kiss grew hot . . . hotter . . . on fire.

"Mmm," Eden said, her hands plunging into his hair as she pulled him tighter to her. "You taste good. You make me want to be a little bad tonight."

He groaned, letting his hands caress the length of her back. Snagging the hem of her dress, he stroked the firm dancer legs he'd admired before he even knew she was a dancer. Supple flesh, smooth as a baby's bottom. He slid around to the back of her thigh, brushing the curve of her ass.

Eden ripped her mouth from his, her breathing erratic. She started unbuttoning his shirt, dropping kisses at the base of his throat. "And you smell so good. How can you smell so good?"

"Bathing regularly." He grinned as he fingered the fabric snug against her chest. "Where's the zipper on this thing?"

"No zipper." She nuzzled his neck, making him want to toss her on the seat, hike up her skirt, and plunge into her right then and there. She made him crazy and he loved it.

"No zipper? Buttons?"

Her hands slid down his side, moving toward his belt. "I just pull it over my head."

He found her panties, sliding his hand beneath the elastic, clasping the full lobe of her ass. Just as he dipped his head to kiss the wild pulse at the base of her throat, the car ground to a halt.

"We made it," she panted, loosening her hold.

Nick blinked. "Not quite, darling. But we'll get there."

chapter sixteen

EDEN HAD SET the roach bomb off that morning in her apartment so she wouldn't chicken out on going home with Nick. It wasn't as if she didn't want to be with him, she did. But having sex was a big step for her. A huge step for her. Though she knew deep down in her bones Nick was the right man to . . . make her a woman, she still felt jittery. Make her a woman. That sounded really archaic. Like the Gary Puckett records her old neighbor used to blare. This girl is a woman now.

Jeez.

In the moonlight, Nick's house didn't look the same. Somehow it seemed magical . . . Or perhaps she'd had too much to drink.

Nick opened the car door before the chauffer could come around. Before he stepped out, he straightened his pants and pulled loose his shirttail to disguise his arousal. A nervous giggle at the teenager action threatened, but she quelled it as he extended his hand.

"Thank you," she said in a surprisingly husky Marilyn Monroe voice as she stepped out.

His answer was a fast, hard kiss.

Turning, he settled whatever he needed to settle with Johnny. Eden stood in the drive, looking up at the moon, trying to coast on the desire that had swamped her in the limo and not let nerves overtake her.

The night had been absolutely perfect. When she'd seen Nick standing in the hallway outside the dressing room, wearing a light blue button-down beneath a perfectly tailored jacket, her heart had dropped to her toes. That gorgeous man was her date. And what a date it was. From the champagne kisses in the back of the limo to the luxurious treat of sitting at the chef's table at Commander's Palace to more champagne kisses on the way to Nick's house, it was a perfectly scripted night to remember.

And it wasn't over.

Nick slapped the end of the car as Johnny drove off, then turned. "You sure about this?"

"You trying to talk me out of a sleepover at your house?"

"Define sleepover. Are we going to paint our nails and braid each other's hair?" Nick said, looping his arms around her waist and pulling her to him.

"Is that your idea of foreplay?" Eden said with a smile.

Nick grinned down at her. "Do you think it *should* be my idea of foreplay? That could explain a lot. I mean, if that's what you girls have been expecting all this time . . ."

For some reason Eden didn't want to admit she didn't know what girls expected in foreplay. She'd dated Clem Aiken, who had seemed to be knowledgeable in the art of seduction. He'd almost reached home plate with her, so it wasn't like she didn't know what was about to go down. She might be a virgin, but she wasn't stupid. Still, something held her back from admitting she hadn't technically had sex before.

"If you want to braid my hair, you're out of luck." She tugged on a hank that framed her face. "Too short."

"You're perfect in every way," he said, starting up the stone walkway.

Those words nestled into her heart, convincing her for the

umpteenth time that Nick Zeringue was the right man. And that he'd refused to have any part of Lulu present on this night made him even more attractive. He wanted Eden . . . just the way she was.

Nick punched in the security code and pushed into the kitchen. He relocked the door and then strolled to the refrigerator, pulling out a bottle of wine and wagging it. "Want a glass?"

She shook her head. "I'm too full to have anything else . . . but you."

Those words were as bold as she could do, but they worked. He set the bottle down with a clunk and walked the short distance separating them.

He lowered his head and whispered, "Let's skip the hair braiding."

Eden answered with a kiss. Nick lifted her so her feet left the floor. It was both literal and figurative. She felt like she was flying and never wanted the moment to end.

His mouth was hungry, so she parted her lips, letting him have what he wanted. All his hard parts lined up perfectly with her soft parts, making her heady. Heat suffused her body, turning her into liquid want.

"Hurry," she whispered.

Nick didn't set her down. He just started walking.

Ten seconds later, they were in his bedroom. She'd smoothed her hand over the thick down duvet on his bed plenty of times when she was putting away laundry or setting out Sophie's change of clothes, but she'd never sat on his bed. He set her down on the plush rug and walked to the bedside table. One click of a button and a fire appeared in the marbled grate, illuminating the room with a flickering intimacy that mimicked the desire licking at her.

"You're so amazing," he said, his voice thick with wanting as he turned to look at her. "But we have to deal with this dress. I needed it off yesterday, baby."

Eden jerked the hem upward and pulled the stretchy fabric over her head, revealing the ivory strapless bra and matching panties she'd bought at Victoria's Secret that morning.

Nick gave a soft laugh. "Shit, you're gorgeous."

His words covered her like Mississippi River fog, coating her with pleasure, preventing her from feeling awkward standing half-naked. "Your turn," she said, the Marilyn Monroe voice back.

Nick shrugged out of his jacket and tossed it toward the chair in the corner. Then he unbuttoned his oxford shirt, slowly revealing the flesh she'd seen before but only fantasized about touching. His hand went to his belt, and her gaze dropped to the erection pressing against the fly of his trousers. Anxiety fluttered in her tummy at the thought of him inside her. He wasn't a skinny, little guy, and she was small, barely five foot. What if it didn't . . .

She stamped on the thought as Nick, presumably sensing her sudden nervousness, paused. He abandoned his task but instead walked the three short steps to reach her.

"Don't get shy on me." His hand brushed her ribs as he looked down at her. "So pretty."

Her stomach contracted when he reached the sensitive flesh below her belly button. But as he ringed the elastic of her waistband, she felt need release and flood her. She'd never felt so hot, almost feverish. Or so determined to have this experience with a man.

He lifted her onto his bed, never letting his hands leave her body. He stroked her sides, glanced over her hip bones, and trailed his fingers down her legs. Reaching her foot, he slipped one shoe off and tossed it over his shoulder. Same treatment with the other. Then his lips were back on hers, devouring her. Eden wrapped her arms around his gorgeous bare shoulders and fell into crazed desire.

The groans and the touching increased. Somehow her bra came off, and he feasted on her small breasts, teasing her nipples with love bites before licking them, drawing them into the heat of his mouth. She squirmed with the need to have him inside her, lifting her butt, rubbing her silk-clad crotch against the hardness nestled between her thighs. She put her hands all over him, reveling in his hardness, in the smooth skin of his broad shoulders, the springy softness of his chest hair, and the firm abs that did their own contracting when she slid her hand between their bodies.

She wanted him now. The wait was over.

He lifted himself up and dropped his trousers. Then he slid the panties from her body, tossing them somewhere on the floor, leaving Eden sprawled before him wearing only the locket her aunt Ruby Jean had given her on her sixteenth birthday. For a microsecond, she had the sudden inclination to cross her legs and clasp her hands to her breasts. How could she feel so turned on yet so vulnerable?

But that was making love, wasn't it? Opening oneself up to splendid intimacy, baring not just one's body but one's soul. She forced herself to remain still, open to this man she trusted.

Nick brushed his hand over the heart of her, his fingers feathering, sliding briefly into the slick heat. She couldn't stop the moan that escaped her lips.

"Nick," she panted.

"What do you want, Eden?" he asked, still clad in tight boxer briefs that showed the outline of his admirable erection. His fingers stroked her inner thighs, teasing, avoiding the place he knew begged to be touched.

"Please." Her body was on autopilot. She would do whatever he wanted as long as he touched her.

"Do you want me to touch you here?" he asked, sliding his index finger against the small nub nestled within her sex.

Eden jackknifed off the bed. "Nick."

He gave a small laugh and pressed her back to the bed. "Or would you rather have this?"

Dropping to his knees, he dragged her hips so that she lay on the edge of the bed, an offering to him. Parting her folds with his fingers, he lowered his mouth.

Eden screamed.

She'd never felt anything like the heat of his mouth moving against her intimate flesh, stroking her in a firm, knowledgeable way. She wriggled against the assault, not knowing if she wanted him to continue but afraid he might stop. Nick held her still, making that decision for her.

"Shh, sweet Eden. Let me have you. I want this more than you know," he said, pushing her back and lowering his head once again. Eden allowed her legs to relax, to accept what Nick offered. Which was so damn good there were no words for it.

It didn't take long before she curled her toes and shattered against his mouth. He didn't stop torturing her. Instead, he held her hips tight with one hand, sliding a finger inside her, mimicking what would come next. Eden felt like she was being carried on a huge wave up to the vast sky. She stretched, every muscle in her body tight, and then she shattered again. And it was even better the second time.

And then it was all too much. She wriggled away from Nick and sat up, panting, her body still humming with pleasure. "What are you doing to me?"

He grinned. "Only what I've thought about doing for the past week."

She swallowed as he walked to the bedside table, pulled out a box of condoms, and ripped off a foil packet. He tugged his black briefs down, his thick erection springing forth. Eden's eyes must have widened slightly because he looked down at himself and smiled, a sort of male preening that was almost heartwarming. "It's been a while for me. I'll try to go slow, baby, but I don't know how long I can last."

He tossed the condom on the bed and settled between her knees. Lowering his head, he caught her mouth and plundered it once again. She should have been repulsed considering he'd just had his mouth on her in the most intimate way possible, but she wasn't. The thrust of his tongue paired with the way he pulled her to him, sliding her slickness against his hardness, vaulted her into a new hunger. She needed to feel him inside her, and the delicious friction he created between their bodies had her clutching his shoulders, trying to lift herself so he would slide inside.

"Wait a sec," he panted, reaching for the condom. He had it open and rolled over his erection in seconds.

She'd never seen a real-life penis clad in a condom. The latex stretched so thin it didn't look the same as the one on the banana Coach Armstead had used to demonstrate in eighth grade PE. It looked normal.

Nudging her knees apart and scooting her back on the bed, Nick dipped his hips and probed her entrance as he dropped small kisses on her breasts. Eden felt her body stretch to accommodate him. It was a strange feeling. She looked up at him, at the way his face had screwed into something akin to pain.

"You're so tight," Nick said, inching inside her.

She'd read lots of romance books and knew there was always a hymen and pain. And blood. Eden felt none of that, only a unique stretching as he filled her. She pressed her inner thighs to his hips just as if she were riding her cousin's old mare.

He paused and looked down at her. "This is so good. So . . ." He dropped a kiss on her nipple. " . . . so . . ." He dropped a kiss on the other. "Good," he concluded, catching her mouth with his. His hands went to her hips, lifting her as he withdrew and plunged inside her, establishing a rhythm.

The last thought Eden had before she allowed her body to relax and enjoy the delicious feeling of a man inside her was that she was no longer a virgin.

Nick moved inside her, slow then fast. His lips traveled over the sensitive column of her throat, nuzzling her ears, occasionally raiding her mouth once again. He pressed her knees back, causing her butt to lift off the bed. Nestling his face into the crook of her neck, he increased the tempo. The pressure was intense, and once again Eden felt an orgasm ebbing and abating. She flexed her pelvic muscles, something she'd read about in *Cosmopolitan*, and marveled at how much more intense she felt him inside her. It was a weird but wonderful feeling.

"You're good," Nick panted in her ear. "So fucking good, Eden."

She could feel the tension build in him. Saw the way his muscles tightened, the sheen of perspiration covering shoulders that offered salty kisses.

"Come with me, baby," he commanded. "Come for me again."

And those words did their job. She felt the pressure rise again as he plunged inside her.

"Oh," she said, stretching once again to catch the explosive pleasure that teased her body. "Oh, oh, oh."

Nick's cry vaulted her over the edge. He pumped steadily inside her, his drawn-out moan of release in her ear as she pulsated on a wave of sheer, extraordinary wonderfulness.

"Shit, that was good," he breathed, his hips finally stilling. Sweat covered both of them, and a languid heaviness settled over her. She dropped her feet and let loose a huge sigh. She'd had sex for the first time and an orgasm to boot. She'd not expected that. So many articles and books had warned that the first time she shouldn't plan on an orgasm. That took time. And intimacy. But maybe they hadn't banked on Nick Zeringue.

He lifted his head. "Sorry I couldn't go longer. You were amazing."

"Was I?" she asked, twisting her fingers in his hair.

"Well, you came . . . how many times?" he asked as he lifted onto his elbows, tweaking one of her breasts.

"Three times."

"I love a multiorgasmic woman. It's so hot," he said, dropping a kiss on her lips.

"I never knew I was," Eden said, kissing him back.

He crooked a brow. "Seriously? Or are you stoking my ego?"

"I don't see how I could do that. That was my first time." As those words escaped and Nick grew deathly still, she wondered if perhaps admitting she'd been a virgin had been a good idea.

Probably not. So why had she done it?

"Wait, what?" Nick asked, his brow lowering and his gaze growing serious in the flickering light. "What do you mean? Like an orgasm?"

"Um, no. Actual sex. That was my first time. Well, technically my first time. With, uh, actual penetration and all. Oh, and having a guy go down on me." She tried to play it cool. Be like Jess. It's all natural. No big deal here.

Nick pushed off, his eyes going wide. "You're joking. Tell me you're joking, Eden."

Eden struggled to raise herself up on her elbows, effectively disengaging Nick from her body. "What? It's not that—"

"You were a virgin?" he interrupted, his voice going up an octave.

"You say *virgin* like I had a disease," she said, the hazy, romantic afterglow dissolving. "I mean, it's not that big of deal."

He made a face. "It's absolutely a big deal. Eden . . ." Nick looked stunned and something else she couldn't decipher. She thought it might be regret, and there was nothing worse than a man regretting he'd slept with a woman.

"It's not. Really. I'm not a freak or anything," she said, averting her gaze to just beyond his shoulder. She glued her thighs together and covered her breasts with her palms.

"Give me a sec, okay?" Nick slid off the bed and walked to the bathroom.

Eden sat there feeling embarrassed and angry she felt that way after her first very amazing experience. A few seconds later and Nick padded back into the bedroom, but she didn't rip her gaze from the leaping flames in the fireplace. Nick set a hand towel she'd folded last week on her knee. "Here."

She looked at it and then up at him. "What?"

"In case you need it," he said.

"Oh," Eden said, looking at the towel.

Nick sat on the bed. Eden didn't move. He took the towel and set it on the bedside table before pulling her into his lap. His arms comforted her, and she relaxed against him as he said, "Eden, I wasn't trying to make you feel embarrassed. It merely caught me off guard. Your virginity, well, it's sort of precious."

"Why? We're not living in the middle ages. If the opportunity had presented itself before now, I would have done it. I worked a lot and then took care of my mother. I didn't have much time for socialization. Years passed me by, and . . . well, I never actually punched my *V* card."

"*V* card?" he asked, his breath feathering her cheek.

"That's what my friend Lacy called it. She watched a lot of reality television. I think she got the term there."

After a few minutes of stroking her back, Nick said. "So tell me about this friend."

So she told him about Lacy. Right there, naked in his arms after having multiple orgasms, she told him how Lacy loved horses and her old orange truck. How she and her friends met every week for coffee at the Lazy Frog. About Lacy getting sick, the 5K event they helped organize, the crazy blue wig Lacy liked to wear to irk her mama. And the last few days where she, Rosemary, and Jess cried too many tears and clung to each other as they watched their friend slip away. Eden cried a little bit but then smiled when she told him about the charm bracelet and the money her friend left her.

"So Lacy brought you to me?"

Eden looked up. His words were possessive and hinted at something unexpected. "I guess. I had always planned to go to college, major in theatre, and work my way into a future that included performing on the stage. That was my dream, and Lacy wanted me to have it. She was the most selfless of friends even if other people thought she was a bit too pushy. And too much of a dreamer."

"She sounds like an amazing friend. I think you were lucky to have her."

"But not lucky enough to keep her," Eden said, trying to chase away the sadness that shadowed her when she talked about her friend. Would the hurt ever abate? Would she ever feel more happy than sad when she thought about Lacy? She hoped one day she would.

Nick caught her yawn with a kiss. "I know this sounds silly, but thank you for trusting me with—"

"Don't say the gift of my virginity." Eden groaned.

"I won't, but still, you chose me." And with those words he moved her so he could pull back the soft sheets. Eden had never washed his sheets—he had a housekeeper who came once a week—but she'd imagined what it would feel like to be cradled in Nick's arms.

And her daydream didn't come close to how amazing it was curled against him, watching the dancing flames, feeling his heartbeat beneath her cheek.

She could have never planned a better date, a better night, a better first lover.

Her last thought before she drifted off into the soundest slumber she'd had since moving to New Orleans was how much Lacy would have approved.

Nick woke with a start, blinking against the bright morning light streaming through the plantation shutters and realizing someone was in bed with him.

But then everything came roaring back to him—Commander's Palace, champagne, and making love to Eden.

He shifted, but she didn't move a muscle. The quiet rise and fall of her deep slumber reminded him it was Sunday morning, his sister was on restaurant call, and he had the recipe for his grandmere's famous waffles waiting beneath the magnet on his fridge.

Part of him wanted to wake Eden and introduce her to sleepy morning sex, but the other part of him recognized she was tired out. Taking care of a disabled seven-year-old, performing nearly every night at Gatsby's, and staying out late and making love until the wee hours had to have taken its toll on her.

Carefully he eased out of bed, pausing only when she rolled over and issued a deep sigh, snuggling into his feather pillows. Slipping into a pair of flannel pajama pants and a pair of worn sheepskin moccasins, he made his way into the kitchen and the blessedness of the coffeepot. He pulled out his favorite chicory blend, eschewing the fancy roasts people liked to gift him. Less than five minutes later, he had a fragrant cup in hand. Then he started on making breakfast for Eden.

His concentration on measuring the flour and the baking powder was broken every time he thought about the sweet moment he'd shared with Eden after the very rewarding, very satisfying sex. He'd had no clue she'd been a virgin. Sure, when he thought back to when they'd first entered the bedroom, there was some awkwardness, but that wasn't necessarily atypical. Getting naked with someone for the first time took a measure of trust, and sometimes the intimacy felt too much. He'd sensed that, gone slow, and let her determine the pace. What followed had been good. Really good.

Still, had he known she was a virgin, he would have taken more time, made sure to be extra gentle.

"Morning," Eden croaked from the doorway.

He looked up from whisking the eggs into the batter to find her wearing his button-down shirt. The look was always good on a woman, but on Eden it was both sexy and endearing. The bare feet with bright blue toenails sealed the deal on her being the absolute cutest woman he'd ever seen.

"Hey," he said waving her into the kitchen. "Coffee?"

"No thanks."

"I'm making waffles. My grandmere's infamous bananas Foster waffles. Oh, and bacon." He turned to the fridge and pulled out the rasher of bacon he'd bought at the meat market a few days ago.

Eden padded toward him. "You shouldn't have gone to such trouble. I have to leave soon. Rehearsals are at eleven."

Disappointment sank inside him. "Do you have to go?"

She glanced up at the kitchen clock. "I have about forty-five minutes. That will have to be enough."

"Okay then," he said, speeding up the process by dumping the flour in and not sifting. His grandmere likely groaned and rolled over in her grave at the offense. "I'll make it happen."

She slid onto a stool and hooked her feet on the rungs. "So how's this going to work? We can't undo things now."

"What do you mean?"

"We slept together and I'm your employee. I don't know what to expect. As you learned last night, this is something I've never had to handle before. Trust me, I wasn't even close to sleeping with Gary the Creep." Her eyes looked somehow bigger this morning, clouded a bit by uncertainty.

"Gary the Creep?"

"My last boss." She sighed. "It's just that things have been good. I don't want them to change because we"—she waved a hand—"did this."

"What do you want?"

"I don't know."

Nick laughed. "Honest answer. So how about we don't overthink things. You stay on as Sophie's nanny for as long as you can . . . or as long as this works. She loves you, and I need you. You're good at taking care of her and making her feel important, cared for, and safe. As for me and you, we enjoy the minutes we have together. There might not be as many as we'd like, but every moment you can spare, I want you with me."

"I want that too." Her gaze was direct. "So we'll be flexible. Day to day, week to week. But what will we tell Sophie?"

"Nothing. We don't have to declare anything. She's a smart cookie and she'll figure it out."

"But if I stay over . . ."

"Not if, when." He poured the batter in to the ancient waffle iron he'd bought at a restaurant supply store when he was in college, then walked around the island to Eden. Pulling her into his arms, he kissed her. Hard. "I'm not giving up you in my bed, sweetheart. You have to make up for lost time, and I'm just the man to pick up that challenge."

Eden kissed his chin. "Oh, you are, are you?"

He slid his hands under the shirt to find her naked beneath. He hadn't imagined how soft her skin was last night or how terrific she felt in his arms. "Mm-hmm."

Her breath caught as he captured her breast and thumbed the hardening nipple. "A confident man who can walk the walk, huh?" she asked, moving her leg so he stood between her thighs. She hooked her heels onto his calves and moved closer.

"I'm going to burn the waffles," he said, dropping his head to nuzzle her neck and draw in the sweet scent that was Eden's alone.

Her hand caught his rising erection. "Do you care?"

Nick unplugged the waffle iron and lifted Eden off the stool. She laughed, wrapping her legs around him again. He, in return, grasped the bare lobes of her ass. "Not one lick."

She kissed him once, twice, three times before they reached his tousled bed, and any thoughts of Grandmere Charlene's waffles flew away. There was Eden, a soft bed, and forty-five minutes to introduce her to slow, sleepy morning sex.

And as she drew him down onto the bed with her, he scrapped the "slow, sleepy" part. He burned for her, and if he didn't get inside her soon . . .

"This is better than waffles." Eden wrenched his shirt over her head.

"Damn straight," he said, putting the world on hold because loving Eden was a habit he could get used to.

chapter seventeen

EDEN WIPED THE sweat from her brow and stifled a sneeze. The chicken-feathered fans were killing her. Her eyes were red and itchy in spite of nearly OD'ing on Benadryl that morning.

"Again from the top," Frenchie commanded, snapping her fingers at Fatso who looked to be checking his phone. They'd been working on the same number for the past hour, and still it wasn't ready for debut.

"Can I have a break?" Eden asked, unable to stop the huge sneeze that snuck up on her.

"You're going to get nastiness on the feathers," Frenchie said, eyeing the white feathered fans critically before sighing. "Okay, okay, I'll get you the ostrich ones. You allergic to ostriches?"

Eden shrugged. "I don't know."

Frenchie stalked off, presumably to raid the wardrobe she kept in her private office. The cheap plumed fans Eden had been using were a combination of turkey feathers and synthetic material. While Frenchie procured the longer, more legitimate version, Eden took a moment to check her own phone, smiling at the text from Nick.

It had been a month since their first real date, and Eden had been happier than she'd ever been in her life. Exhausted, but happy. She and Nick had established a sometimes complicated but satisfying schedule that allowed them to spend time together but still manage to get successfully through their many obligations. Being with Nick was like having Christmas morning every day. Of course, some of her Christmas mornings as a child were entirely forgettable, so that wasn't a great comparison, but it was the best she had. He made her laugh, made her sigh, and made her feel like she was worthy of every drop of affection he lavished on her.

Sophie hadn't asked specifically if Eden and her father were together, but she'd gleaned enough to plan their trip to Walt Disney World that summer. She'd also started doing things like asking both Eden and Nick to tuck her in at night, sharing the reading of the stories, giggling with glee when they did the character's voices. The child's eyes gleamed with happiness, and her performance in school had strengthened. Her teacher had even sent home a lovely note complimenting Sophie on being a good friend and learning skills faster than she'd ever learned them before.

Everything was perfect.

Eden scanned her other messages. Rosemary wanted her to call her back when she could, Fredric was requesting a meeting, and her sister had a lead on a potential buyer for their house in Morning Glory. While Eden existed in her own fairy tale, the real world still turned.

Eden pressed the Home button on her phone and tucked it back into the pocket of her tight studio pants, refusing to deal with the minutia of her life. Yeah, she'd encapsulated herself into a bubble, refusing to think about what-ifs in favor of savoring the sweet nights after performances when she took a cab to Nick's and he met her with a glass of white zinfandel and a kiss. She preferred to think about bubble baths, pizza-roll snacks and story time with Sophie. And then the quick, fulfilling lovemaking with Nick before she had to leave for Gatsby's.

As far as Eden was concerned, real life could wait.

Frenchie came back with the huge fans she kept squirreled away for her own burlesque performances and shoved them at Eden. "Here. No more sneezing."

"Thank you," Eden said, handing the inferior fans off to Lisa.

"By the way, your boyfriend called me. Wants a weekend with you. Surprise and all that. I don't want you to take it."

Eden's heart leaped and she tried not to look annoyed by the fact Frenchie didn't care enough to keep a surprise a surprise. "Nick called you?"

"That's his name?" Frenchie arched a brow. Eden knew Frenchie dang well knew Nick's name, but that was one of the many head games she liked to play. "Yeah, yeah. Nick. He wants you to miss work."

"Well, it's not been as busy during Lent."

"Yeah, all the good Catholics stay home." Sarcasm was a given with Frenchie. "But, fine. Whatever. I'll call Sadie. Your big sister wants to come back."

"Big sister? You mean Lola?"

Frenchie snapped her fingers. "Smart cookie."

A trickle of fear wriggled inside Eden. If Sadie was back from California, would that mean they'd share the spotlight? Eden wasn't greedy, and having Sadie split some time with her would free her up for more time with Nick and Sophie, but she liked sharing top billing with only Sista Shayla. "I'm the smart cookie who stepped in when you needed her most. Don't forget that, French."

"Huh." Frenchie sniffed, gesturing to everyone. "Back to work. Back to work. We're on the clock, peoples."

Fatso rolled his eyes.

Eden shook out the new fans, praying the ostrich feathers wouldn't cause her to chain sneeze and rub at her watery eyes. As she took her place, she wondered what Nick had up his sleeve. Calling Frenchie Pi meant he was determined to surprise her . . . and get her some time off. The man was persuasive, something she knew firsthand. He'd talked her into things she'd never thought she'd do both in the bedroom and out. Eden wasn't sure if she'd ever told the man no when he applied his charming smile and whispered sweet words. Even the stalwart Frenchie would be putty in that man's hands.

After rehearsals, with far less sneezing and watery eyes, praise Jesus, Eden picked up Sophie, who wore her lunch on her new romper and a grin big as the Crescent City Connection bridge. "I have a boyfriend."

"A boyfriend?" Eden repeated, strapping the child into the van and tossing Sister Regina Marie a wave. "What the heck?"

"You have one. My daddy."

"But I'm not seven. You can't have a boyfriend at seven. It's against the law." Eden grinned, shutting the door and jogging around to the driver's side, flashing a smile at the person next in the carpool line. Everyone was patient at All Souls. No honking horns or exasperated, dirty looks. Parents and caregivers for the children at the special school were used to everything taking longer than normal.

"No, it's not. I'm almost eight." Sophie giggled as they pulled through the horseshoe drive and turned out onto the busy uptown street. "Don't tell Daddy. His name is Charlie. He's nine."

"An older man? This will not go over well."

Sophie sobered. "Daddy'll be mad? He's mad at mommy."

Eden glanced at the child in the rearview mirror. She hadn't stayed over the night before since the rehearsal was earlier than normal and she'd wanted to sleep in. "Your daddy was mad?"

"Yeah. My mama's not coming to my party." Sophie pressed her lips together and jerked her head to look out the window at the passing oaks.

"Did your father tell you that?"

"I heard. He called her a bad name. She's a bad mommy." Sophie's face was still turned toward the window. Something in the child's demeanor broke Eden's heart.

"I'm sure your father didn't mean that. Sometimes when we're hurt, we say things we don't mean."

"She don't love me." The sadness in Sophie's words made Eden literally clutch her chest.

"That's not true. Sometimes mommies don't do the right things, but that doesn't mean they don't love their babies. Your mama loves you even if she can't always be with you." Eden wasn't so sure that wasn't an out-and-out lie. Some mothers loved only themselves. Some mothers were so damaged, so weak, so selfish, that they couldn't see beyond the end of their own nose. Kids be damned. Eden knew that firsthand and she accepted that her own mother had a demon on her back and, perhaps, some undiagnosed mental conditions. But a seven-year-old shouldn't have to grasp the concept.

"My body don't work," Sophie said, her words even more slurred than normal.

"No, baby. That's not true. I know you don't understand adults sometimes. I don't understand them myself, and I'm one of them."

"You be my mommy."

Oh crap. Not what Eden wanted to deal with today. Or any day. "We've had this conversation, Soph. Remember?"

"You and Dad kiss." Sophie was the smart cookie.

"Oh, honey. Your daddy and I like each other. A lot. But that's a bit of a . . . uh, jump. Um, how was school today? Other than getting a boyfriend?" Eden knew she was avoiding the question that had been nagging her. She'd tried to live in the moment and not think about where her relationship with Nick was going. Maybe they wouldn't go anywhere but where they were now. Would that be so bad? They were happy. Sophie was happy. What they had totally worked for both of them. But what would happen when Eden enrolled in UNO at the end of the summer? Could she give up dancing at Gatsby's for being a full-time student and part-time nanny for Sophie? And how could she afford that? The money she made a Gatsby's was significantly more than what she made being a nanny.

And there was her dream of stage and stardom.

She'd not planned on Nick or Sophie. Her eyes needed to remain on the prize, and if she took them off to settle for being... She wasn't even sure what she'd be settling for. Everything was as clear as the muddy river that flowed through New Orleans.

"Okay," Sophie said, finally answering the question Eden had asked about school. The child sounded troubled, so Eden found Taylor Swift on the radio and turned it up. Rolling down the windows to let some cool air in, she started doing the snake, trying to get Sophie to laugh.

The phone rang. Nick.

"It's your daddy," Eden sang.

"Hey, girls," Nick said, when she answered. "I got a surprise for you."

Sophie finally turned her face from the window. "A surprise?"

"Yep. I'm bringing home dinner. Chef Serina made shrimp empanadas. Your fave, Soph."

"That's all?" Sophie asked.

"Nope, but I'll tell you more over delicious shrimp empanadas."

"A hint," Sophie begged.

"What did she say?" Nick asked.

"She wants a hint," Eden clarified.

"Okay. You'll have to pack your bags for this one."

Eden widened her eyes as she looked back at Sophie. The child's eyes danced and her crooked smile was back.

They hung up with Nick and spent the last ten minutes of the drive home trying to guess the surprise. Eden thought they were going to Paris to the opera. Sophie swore they were going to Disney World. Or Lake Tahoe to see Rhoda.

They were both wrong. Way wrong...

As they finished an early dinner, Nick finally let them in on his surprise. "Okay, okay. Stop with the guesses. Here's your final clue. It's only four hours away. There's a town square and a big Easter egg hunt this weekend."

Oh. No.

Sophie shrieked, "Morning Glory! Morning Glory!"

Eden gripped the edge of the table, looking at Nick like he had grown horns out the side of his head. And the thing was, he looked so pleased with himself. He had no clue.

"I know how much Sophie loves your stories about your hometown, and since I have a business meeting in Jackson, I thought it would be fun to go see this huge Easter egg hunt and spring picnic firsthand. I got us a room at Polk House thanks to a last-minute cancellation." When he lifted his gaze to look at Eden, the pleasure in his eyes ebbed. "Eden?"

"You booked a room at Polk House?" she said weakly, scrambling to gather up the panic, the shock, and the horror leaking from every pore of her body.

His brow lowered. "It was either that or the Morning Glory Motor Lodge. The pictures of the B&B looked nicer."

Eden swallowed. "Uh, I'm not sure—"

"Yay!" Sophie clapped her hands, which was a hard feat for the child. "I'm gonna find pink ones! Or the gold one. I'll win a hundred bucks!"

"You're not happy," Nick said to Eden.

"I'm just surprised is all." Eden was usually good at shuttering her emotions. She'd had lots of experience, but Nick could read her as easily as she'd read the same three nicked-up Little Golden Books as a child. She didn't want Nick and Sophie in Morning Glory. In her hometown, she was silent Eden who stood behind a register at Penny Pinchers ringing up ramen noodles, or the beleaguered daughter who changed her fractious mother's diapers in a falling-down house in the bad part of town. In Morning Glory she'd been nothing special. A no-good Voorhees . . . even if she'd been deemed better, deserving of the charity people handed out with sympathy in their eyes.

No, she didn't want a surprise trip to Morning Glory.

"I can cancel it. I thought you'd be happy to see your friends. Rosemary and Sal, right?" Nick said, his face plaintive.

"Right." She managed a small smile. "I do want to see them."

"I wanna go," Sophie whined, shoving her plate too hard away from her. A saltshaker fell, spilling white specks all over the gleaming oak table.

Eden's gaze met Nick's. He'd been trying to please her, but he didn't know that she didn't want to be that Eden anymore. He couldn't understand being ashamed of a past. Nick was handsome, accomplished, rich, and adored.

"Eden?" Nick prodded.

"Sure. Let's go. I need to settle some things with my sister anyway, and Sophie will love the Easter egg hunt and picnic." She could keep him away from her mama. The town *was* charming, and people were usually friendly. It would be fine.

She hoped.

"You sure?" he asked, ignoring Sophie who looked to be on the verge of tears.

Eden nodded. "Sure. It'll be fun." She might or might not have choked on the last word.

Nick smiled. "Great. I can't wait to see where our Edie grew up."

"Yay," Sophie said, concentrating hard on her clapping.

"Yay," Eden echoed with no clap at all.

Two weeks later, the overcast sky couldn't dampen Sophie's enthusiasm as they passed the Morning Glory city-limit sign, but it reflected Eden's mood perfectly.

And that worried Nick.

He'd first hatched the idea of taking Eden and Sophie to Morning Glory when he'd talked to some investors in Jackson about a restaurant deal they wanted to make with Parran Z. Since

Morning Glory wasn't far from the city and he'd already heard the story about the Easter egg hunt three times that week, he'd thought it would be the perfect treat for his daughter. Susan had called to say she couldn't make it to town for Sophie's eighth birthday next week, something that had nearly destroyed his daughter . . . and the half cup of leftover fondness he had for his ex. Susan had a job interview in New York City at a premier restaurant with a recurring guest spot on *Good Morning America*. It was a once-in-a-lifetime opportunity, she'd said. And though he got that, she'd hemmed and hawed on whether she could fly down after the interview to spend time with Sophie. She'd get back to him on the possibility. Those were her exact words. Like it was a business transaction and not her daughter's birthday.

Thing was, Susan wasn't a bad person. She was just a shitty mother.

"Look," Sophie said, trying to point at a big blow-up Easter egg sitting on a used-car lot.

"That's the Crabtrees' place. They have two daughters—Gracie and Camille." Eden looked back at Sophie.

"Gracie?" Sophie asked, and Nick chanced a glance back to see his daughter craning her neck to look out the window. "I like that name."

"She's about your age," Eden said before jabbing a finger. "Turn here."

The town was a typical small town. He'd sort of expected butterflies to be flitting about as bluebirds draped a welcome sign across the shady town square, but it looked perfectly normal if not a little dressed up with daffodils and tulips dotting the landscape around the square. An old courthouse anchored the spring-green square, and small businesses huddled close around, sporting big whiskey-barrel planters full of spring cheer and signs advertising Easter-hunt specials. A few small white tents sat hodgepodge on the grass, marking territory for the big hunt the next day.

"Well, this is it," Eden said, spreading a hand in a ta-da motion. "Not much to see, but it's home I guess."

"I love it," Sophie declared earnestly.

Eden finally smiled. "Look, there's Sal's pizza place, and that's my friend Rosemary's fabric store."

"Should we stop?" Nick asked.

Eden gave a little shrug. "I could eat."

He found a handicap parking place near the pizzeria and helped unload his daughter while Eden stood on the sidewalk still looking haunted. He didn't understand what was wrong with her. The stories about her hometown had always brought smiles and laughter. Her blue eyes had sparkled when she told them about her friends and the old high school with the brick pavers bearing graduates' names. Wistfulness and pride had seemed to shadow her words. So why was she shutting down?

When they neared a shop called Parsley and Sage, the glass doors burst open. "Eden!"

He jumped back as a lady with reddish hair and a fluffy skirt attacked the woman next to him.

"What are you doing here? Oh my gosh, I'm so happy to see you," the woman shrieked, hugging Eden, then hugging her again. "And who have you brought? Is this Sophie?"

His daughter's eyes were wide. "I *am* Sophie."

"Of course you are," the woman said, bending down and giving his daughter a huge smile. Her reddish-brown hair fell into a perfect part, and she wore a headband and a strand of looped pearls. She looked like something out of a movie. "And I'm Rosemary."

"Hi," Sophie said shyly while Eden combed down her hair and straightened her collar. She looked a bit mauled by the jubilant ambush.

"And you must be Nick Zeringue," Rosemary said, straightening and giving him a once-over. He responded to the inspection by stiffening his spine and holding out a hand. The woman ignored his hand and instead reached up to give him a hug. "No need for formalities around here. You're with Eden, which means you're family."

Nick hugged her back because he didn't have an option. "Nice to meet you, Rosemary. We've heard a lot about you."

"All good, of course," Rosemary said with a snappy grin. "So what in the name of all that's holy are y'all doing here? And why didn't you call me?"

"We're here for the Easter egg hunt and picnic. Nick surprised me and Soph by bringing us up for it." Her words held a hidden edge.

Rosemary's gaze widened slightly, and that made him wonder if there was something he didn't know about Eden. She certainly was acting strangely. Maybe she had some kind of secret. Was that why she didn't want him here? Maybe a criminal record? A boyfriend she forgot to tell him about?

No. The very idea was crazy. He knew Eden. The woman wasn't a liar.

But she might have left something out. She'd done that before—being Lulu, being a virgin. She wasn't exactly the forthcoming sort.

"We were about to have a late lunch at your husband's place. Care to join us?" he asked Rosemary, shelving the irrational thoughts.

"I'd love to. Let me tell Lorriane I'll be back in an hour." Rosemary hugged Eden again and chucked Sophie on the chin, not even wiping her hand when he knew his daughter's chin was perpetually damp. Speaking was hard for Sophie and required a frequent mopping of her face. His stock of Eden's friend went way up.

Sal's new pizza place had been done in classic Italian style with a side of funky warehouse—red-checked tablecloths, an open kitchen, and exposed brick arches. It was both chic and homey at the same time. Tangy marinara and fresh-baked bread hit his nose, and his stomach responded with a growl.

"Oh, good. You're hungry," Rosemary said, waving away the server bustling toward them and seating them in a back corner booth. Two other tables were taken. "We had a huge lunch crowd, but the only people who come in this late are looking for dessert."

"So you're stealing Sassy's business?" Eden asked, helping settle Sophie at the end of the booth. She secured the funny ballerina bib around her neck, brushing away Sophie's annoyed comment with "No one's here to think you're uncool. Spare the shirt, sister."

"Nah, the Lazy Frog gets all the ice cream and fancy-latte business. Sal does one gelato a week. This week there's pistachio, and it will make you slap yo' mama it's so good."

"Better not. Betty's a fighter," Eden said, a reluctant smile emerging. This was only the second time Eden had mentioned her family, though she'd shared tons about her friends.

The server arrived, casting a nervous eye at Rosemary, and took their orders. Then Rosemary launched into a listing of events for the weekend. That night there would be a country-western band playing on a stage in the square. Tomorrow morning there was a huge pancake breakfast at the American Legion, a 5K run to raise money for a pet rescue, and finally the Easter egg hunt. A charity bachelor/bachelorette auction would follow, leading into the big town picnic. It sounded like something out of *Little House on the Prairie*. Not that he watched that show, but Caro had a thing for it growing up so sometimes she sat on him until he yielded the remote control.

"Wait, a bachelor auction?" Nick repeated. He was not going to be hoodwinked into—

"No worries. You had to have signed up weeks ago," Rosemary said with a laugh. "And your reaction is much the reaction of all the single guys in town, but the committee refuses to do away with it. The town's been hosting the auction since founding. Supposedly it's how the first mayor scored a wife."

"Seriously?" Nick asked.

"Back in the day, it was the way you snagged a bride, I guess."

Nick watched Eden as her friend talked and could feel the strange tension leak out of her minute by minute. Something about Rosemary relaxed her. The anxiety Eden had cloaked herself in the closer they got to Morning Glory started to evaporate, the guarded smiles and terse responses put away in favor of a sparkle in her eye.

"Your sister's heading up the 5K. She and Henry," Rosemary said.

"Henry? You're joking." Eden looked alarmed.

Rosemary shrugged one shoulder. "They've been spotted together a couple of times. You think . . . ?"

Eden shook her head. "No. Surely not."

"Stranger things have happened. They were in love once," Rosemary said.

"What's the deal?" Nick asked as the waitress set down his salad.

"Old news," Eden said, turning her attention back to Rosemary. "Sunny wants out of Morning Glory as soon as possible. That's why she's fixing up Mom's house. Wants to sell it and vamoose."

Rosemary didn't respond. Just took a bite of the warm bread on the table and chewed thoughtfully. "Sometimes what we want most isn't what we truly need. Maybe Sunny's finding something she's needed all along. She's not had much peace in her life."

Eden focused on the exposed brick wall behind them, pausing for several seconds. Finally she said, "She won't get back with Henry. Sunny's not the same girl she was."

Nick wasn't sure what they were talking about. Again, Eden had only mentioned her sister in passing. Eden's gaze flickered to him, and she gave him an apologetic smile. "Let's talk about something else. How's Sal? How's the restaurant doing?"

"Great and great," Rosemary said, licking crumbs from her fingers with an *mmm*. "The man can cook. I've gained seven pounds since the wedding. At this rate I won't be able to fit into my clothes."

"Which has been my plan all along," a man called from across the restaurant.

Sal Genovese wore a stained apron and a mischievous smile.

He ambled over and introduced himself to Nick. After that, he and Sal talked restaurant business while Eden and Rosemary told Sophie funny stories about when they were small. Nick would have loved to hear about Eden as a girl, but he indulged Sal, who said he had been dying to run some things by him ever since he learned Eden worked for a New Orleans Zeringue.

He'd have to give high marks to his introduction to Morning Glory . . . That was until they made their way to the exit to find it blocked by someone entering.

An aide of some sort pushed a wheelchair-bound woman wearing a sparkly tracksuit jacket into the restaurant. The woman in the wheelchair was thin as a willow branch with thinning bleached hair and red lipstick that had smeared onto her cheek, making her look on edge if not outright off-kilter. She held a cigarette in one gnarled hand, the other dangling uselessly against the side of the wheelchair.

Eden went stiff beside him when she caught sight of the women.

The older woman glared at Eden. "Your bitch sister's trying to put me out of my own damn house."

Eden briefly closed her eyes before opening them and sighing. "Hello, Mama."

chapter eighteen

EVERYTHING HAD BEEN fine until Vienna had rolled her mama into Sal's. Eden had been miserable all the way to Morning Glory, trying to figure out how she could keep who she was from Nick. Okay, so it wasn't like she was an undercover spy or had a trailer full of kids she'd ditched for dreams in New Orleans. Her secret wasn't really a secret. She merely didn't want him to see the pathetic woman she'd been. Not when he saw her as her current self... even if she wasn't quite sure who she was. But it was way better than wearing a cheap T-shirt and ringing up clearance Fruit Roll-Ups at Penny Pinchers.

So when Betty barreled into Sal's, smoking a cigarette no less, Eden's whole carefully controlled plan of keeping Nick away from anyone who could reveal how poor, downtrodden, and unimportant Eden was had been blown to itty-bitty smithereens.

Because of course her mother would find her.

Betty wasn't always sane, but when she got a bee in her bonnet, she'd squash it.

"Why'd you leave me with Sunny anyway? She won't let me have any E.L. Fudge cookies. You know those are my favorite." Eden's mother took a drag on her cigarette, blowing a cloud of smoke directly toward them.

Eden pulled the cigarette from her mother's hand. "You're not allowed to smoke in here, Mama."

"Well, shit," Betty said, sinking back into her chair, resigned. "Ain't allowed to do nothin' fun it seems."

Eden didn't look at Nick. She knew he'd be appalled at the faded woman shriveled in the ancient wheelchair. Her mother had once been lovely—long blond hair, pretty blue eyes, and a smart mouth that made people both love and hate her. But after the drug use, two stints in rehab, and the stroke, she'd withered into a dried strip of jerky with wispy hair bleached platinum, Tammy Faye Bakker eyelashes, and whore-red lipstick. To be honest, with the paralysis in her face, Betty looked a little like Heath Ledger playing the Joker.

"Watch your language, Mama," Eden said, jerking her head toward Sophie, whose eyes were big as the bread plates sitting on the table beside her wheelchair. "How'd you know I was here?"

"Lorraine, but Fred told me you were coming. Reservation at the bed-and-breakfast place." Betty huffed, her eyes following Eden as she opened the door and snuffed the cigarette out in the planter, intending to retrieve it later. "It's just I'm scared. Your sister is crazy. Brought a dog home, and I got allergies."

Her mother's speech was slurred from the stroke, but the curse words and the sour disposition were easily understood. *Welcome to my world . . . or what was my world.*

"Hello, Mrs. Batten," Rosemary said as Eden trudged back to where her friends gathered around her mother.

"I ain't Mrs. Batten. Divorced the son of a bitch and went back to Voorhees. At least that means something in this town. Or used to. Plus I'll be dead and buried before Roddy gets outta the joint, so ain't no use waiting. How's your mama? Surprised she ain't drowned yet she's got that nose pointed so far in the air."

Eden shot Rosemary an apologetic look, but her friend just grinned.

"She's still kickin,' Ms. Voorhees. Thankfully it's been a dry spring."

Betty laughed. "You've got a bit more fire than I remembered. Eden, help me home. Vienna don't know how to load me in the van. She nearly closed my leg up in the damn door last time. We gotta talk. You gotta stop Sunny from selling the house."

Vienna, the aide provided by the state, merely did a slow blink but said nothing. She was accustomed to Betty's many complaints and crazed conspiracy theories. Though this time, Betty wasn't so far off. Her sister intended on getting Betty into a senior living center.

"Where's Sunny?" Eden asked.

"I dunno. Running around like she always did. She's supposed to come home and take care of me like you did, but all she's been doing is fixing up the house. Wants to put me in a home. I ain't doing it. Done told her I ain't signing no papers. And now she's trying to open some stupid rescue. Feeding stray mutts. I told her strays are county business, but you think she'll listen? Only smart thing she's done is letting ol' Delmar's boy sniff around her. That's the hound dog she should be focusing on. Got money for miles."

"She's seeing Henry?" Eden asked, wishing she could extract herself from the conversation, the restaurant, and the whole town. Why had she agreed to this? She should have talked Nick into Disney World. Dear Lord . . .

Betty flinched as the door to the restaurant opened and Sunny charged in. "Mama, I told you not to leave the house. You're taking a new medicine, and until it's in your system good, the doctor told you to rest. Why did you bring her out, Vienna?"

The aide shrugged. "She told me you was meeting her here. I called you."

"Thankfully." Sunny then noticed the rest of them, eyes widening when she noticed Eden standing there. "What are you doing here?"

"We brought Sophie to the Easter egg hunt."

Sunny took in Nick and Sophie. "Why would . . . They came with you? Here?"

Her tone said all that needed to be said. Why in the hell did you bring them to this shit show?

"Yeah, Nick surprised us with a trip." Eden finally looked at the man she'd been sharing her life with for the past few months. His gaze was half-amused, half-alarmed. "Nick, this is my mother, Betty Ba—uh, Voorhees. And my sister, Sunny David."

Nick extended a hand, first to her mother, who stared at it for a moment as if she didn't quite know what to do with it. Betty eventually gave it a wag, and Nick moved on to Sunny. Sunny gave him an empty smile and a businesslike shake.

"And this is Sophie," Eden said, giving the girl an encouraging smile.

The child looked embarrassed, her cheeks heating.

Betty cackled. "You're taking care of another cripple? That's rich. Ain't moved too far up in the world, have you, Edie?" Betty said, her snake eyes going flat.

Eden flinched, knowing that Betty was about to show her ass in a very mean way, so she spun her mother's chair toward the door. "Enough. Sophie's a disabled child who has more gumption in her pinky than you have in your entire body. You should be ashamed."

"Ha. Left me to—"

Eden turned to her sister. "Take her home, Sunny."

Unaccustomed to Eden barking orders, Sunny blinked. Then she jumped to attention. "I'm so sorry. Vienna wasn't supposed to drive her anywhere." Sunny shot a stink eye at the aide.

"She said she'd call my supervisor and get me fired," the aide said, looking upset.

"How's she going to do that?" Sunny asked, opening the glass doors for Eden.

"Wait," Betty whined, slamming her good hand on the armrest. "We might as well get some ice cream since we're here. Why y'all so mad? A cripple's a cripple. No sense in babyin' the girl."

Nick's face grew thunderous.

Eden walked around, grabbed her mother's face, and forced her to look at her. "There have been many times you've embarrassed me, but I've never been more ashamed that you're my mother."

Betty didn't flinch but managed to jerk away. "Like I care. I don't cover up the ugly with pretty words. I'm a cripple, wasting away in this goddamned chair."

"Dance and you pay the fiddler, old woman," Eden said, closing the restaurant door.

"At least I danced. But maybe you're dancing too. I got eyes, Edie." Her mother's crooked smile was sly as she looked at Nick through the glass.

"Sorry," Sunny mouthed, pushing her mother toward the ancient van that sometimes ran and sometimes didn't. Betty continued to mutter ugly words beneath her breath.

Eden slumped, feeling like she'd gone twelve rounds with a heavyweight. She wanted to run. Anywhere. Just escape the embarrassment the viper-tongued woman had caused. *This* was exactly why she'd panicked when Nick had surprised them with the trip.

Betty was a wounded beast with a perpetual thorn in her paw. When Eden was growing up, her mother had good days mixed in with the bad. Of course, Eden never knew which mother would greet her each day. Some days she'd find a woman wearing an apron, baking chocolate-chip cookies. Some days a drunk lying in her own urine. Betty had never hurt Eden or Sunny physically, but her mother's razor-tongued insults carried a wallop. After the stroke and the partial paralysis, she'd grown half-morose, half-angry. Some days she didn't speak at all. Some days she never stopped complaining, bitching, and throwing tantrums. Eden had never realized how much her mother had worn her down. It had been her normal.

But hearing how her mother sounded in the last few minutes made her want to slap the woman silly. Eden rarely lost her patience to such a degree, but she'd been dangerously close to violence.

"Eden?" Nick stuck his head out the door.

She closed her eyes so she wouldn't cry.

"Hey, it's okay," he said, sliding out and letting the door shut behind him.

"No, it's not. She's horrible." She opened her eyes when he took her by the shoulders. "I'm so sorry, Nick. I wanted to keep you away from her. She's . . . difficult. That's about the best word I can come up with after that horrifying display."

His smile was gentle. "I'm sort of getting why you weren't jumping up and down to come to the Easter egg hunt."

A bark of laugher escaped her. "You think?"

"Sophie's fine. We talked about those words while you were rolling your mother out. She understands your mother was mad at you. Mad at everyone. If anyone understands the frustrations of not being able to make her body do what she wants it to do, it's Soph."

"God, Nick, that poor baby," Eden said, resting her head briefly against his chest, so glad to have someone to lean on. For once.

"She's fine. She's heard a lot of unkind things in her short life. She knows her value to me. To you."

Eden nodded. "I want to forget this happened."

"Already forgotten. Let's go check into the Polk House. I'm dying to see the gazebo with the clematis. It was featured in one of the pictures and seems to be a big selling point."

Eden managed a laugh against his shirt. She inhaled his scent and realized there was nothing left to hide from him. He'd seen the worst. Envisioning her in a Penny Pincher's vest was a piece of cake compared to the crazed rant her mother had just had in the middle of Sal's. "There's a rice bed from a plantation. And a koi pond . . . though Miss Edna calls them big ol' goldfish. She'll probably let Sophie feed them."

"Score," he said with a twinkle in his eye.

She could see he was trying to make her feel better, and that made her heart contract. This man was like a dream. The perfect man for her . . . at least for right now.

But what about forever?

Forever was a long time, and she still had so much left to do before she traveled down the flower-strewn path of love toward a faceless man and a happily-ever-after. She wasn't succumbing to L-O-V-E no matter how much her heart tugged her in that direction. No matter how perfect a man seemed for her. Nick was a right-now. Not a future. She'd known that when she'd agreed to go on the first date. It was getting harder and harder to remind herself though.

"Let's go," he said, kissing her forehead.

Rosemary peeped through the glass, her face showing her thoughts. Eden hadn't told Rosemary or Jessie about her relationship with Nick.

"I'm assuming you booked me a room at Polk House? If not, Rosemary can put me up."

"You and Soph are sharing. Maybe you'll get lucky and get the rice bed, whatever the hell that is. And maybe I'll get lucky and you'll lose your way and accidently wander into the wrong guest room later tonight," he said, making air quotes with his fingers around "accidently."

"I've always had a bad sense of direction," she said with a slow smile.

chapter nineteen

EDEN STARED AT her cell phone. Seconds ago she'd pressed End on the call she'd been waiting on her entire life.

Why now?

She felt as if she were split down the middle. Part of her wanted to scream in jubilation. The other part melted into a puddle of despair.

Fredric had been so pleased with himself, his reserved nature cast aside for uninhibited enthusiasm. The friend who'd owed him a favor had come through, and Eden had two auditions in New York City next week. For shows being developed for Broadway. Not off. But on Broadway.

Not only was Fredric pleased as punch about the auditions, but he'd called another agent he'd been friends with since his own acting days and found her a place to live, sharing an apartment with two other women who were single and her age— one a Rockette, the other a runway model. To top it off, he sent her a list of available waitressing jobs around Times Square, putting her close to most theatres. He'd delivered her dream to her on a silver platter, any concerns she could possibly bring up nixed. She didn't even have to worry about leaving Gatsby's hanging. Lola was back, and Fredric had intentionally inserted a clause in her new contract allowing her to pursue a Broadway position without penalty.

But the problem was she had to be in NYC in one week.

One week.

Nick waved at her from across the square, smiling over his daughter's head, and Eden headed his way. Minutes before they'd watched the crazy bachelor auction, making side bets on how much someone would go for. Then they'd spread out their borrowed picnic blanket. Sophie sat in her spongy chair, her basket of plastic Easter eggs beside her. A box of takeout from Sal's containing deli sandwiches and a jug of iced mint tea awaited them. Around them families frolicked, laughing and fussing and doing what families did on a pretty spring day. Her sister Sunny sat across the square collecting donations and volunteers for the rescue she and Peggy Lattier had started to help homeless animals. Eden's mother was at home with a properly chastised aide. Rosemary and Sal held court outside Sal's Pizza, serving lemonade and iced tea. Eden should be wearing a smile and enjoying having her boyfriend and an excited Sophie with her.

But she couldn't.

What she'd learned now dangled over her like a grand piano on a fraying rope. Everything was about to change and she wasn't ready. Not yet.

"What's wrong?" Nick asked picking up a stack of paper plates he'd bought that morning at, irony of ironies, Penny Pinchers.

"Nothing," she said, donning a smile.

His brow rumpled. "You sure?"

"Yeah," she said, deciding she'd tell him later. She sank down onto the quilt and opened the box. "Soph, you can't eat anymore candy until you have something for lunch."

Sophie looked up from opening the plastic eggs, chocolate smeared on her chin. "I don't want a sandwich."

"I'll take the lettuce off." Eden tugged the basket from the child.

Sophie pouted for a moment, her eyes darting to her father as if he would intervene.

Nick shrugged. "Edie's right."

"And if you eat your sandwich, we'll have ice cream. The Lazy Frog has a tent, and Sassy Grigsby makes the best ice cream in the county. Maybe the state," Eden said, trying to stow away the whole career issue in favor of making the picnic pleasant. But she couldn't chase it away. Because it sat there like a fat bullfrog staring at her.

Of course there wasn't a decision to be made. She had to go to NYC.

This was the opportunity she'd been dreaming about for so long, and Fredric had put himself out there in order to procure it for her. He'd assured her that one or two auditions could lead to others. The theatre community was smaller than most thought. So if a performer was wrong for a particular part but good enough to impress, she was often sent to other casting directors for other shows. Fredric said if Eden wanted to do musical theatre, she had to get to NYC. No ifs, ands, or buts about it.

Dancing and singing on Broadway had been her dream, but the timing was . . . not ideal. Because of Nick and Sophie. The thought of leaving them behind in New Orleans made her heart break. Though she'd begged her heart not to buy in, she knew deep down she'd fallen in love with Hot Dad Nick and his sweet girl. How could she leave them?

And how could she not?

"Hey, chickadee," Rosemary said, feathering her fingers through Eden's hair, pulling her thoughts from the dilemma twisting her into knots. "How are the sandwiches? Sal's working on his barbeque skills. You know you gotta serve some kind of barbeque if you're going to make it in Mississippi."

"It's good. I like the slaw on it. Has an Italian kick I didn't expect," Eden said.

"The man's a genius. What can I say?" Rosemary sank down and rooted through Sophie's Easter basket. "You did good, Sophie."

For the next few minutes, they talked about the auction. About Sal's sister who showed up to bid on Clem Aiken, which knocked the socks off everyone. Mostly because everyone thought Clem would never be caught . . . and definitely not by an opinionated city slicker like Frances Anne. Morning Glory's stud extraordinaire picked up the woman who won him and carried her away, a la *An Officer and a Gentleman*. It was all very romantic and made everyone a bit happier . . . except Eden, who couldn't escape her future decision.

After they finished eating, Nick helped Sophie get settled back into her wheelchair. They headed off to the Lazy Frog tent to grab ice creams for everyone.

"I like Nick, Eden. He's not only handsome as the devil, but he's a good guy," Rosemary said, watching as Nick wove through the blankets, thanking the townspeople who were quick to make an easy path for Sophie.

"He's pretty great."

"So . . ."

"So?" Eden responded, knowing what her good friend was asking. Where did Eden stand with Nick?

"Is this, like, a real thing?" Her friend ditched her chamber-of-commerce-ambassador vibe for the managing woman she hid behind all that sunshine.

"Do you mean have I fallen for Nick?" Eden asked, knowing she had indeed fallen for her boss but not ready to admit it aloud. Because then it would be too real, and with changes brewing, it could make things even more difficult. A woman in love didn't leave to chase after a what-if career.

Did she?

Rosemary gave her a flat look.

"I don't know," Eden said. "I mean, I think so but it's much more complicated than it is for you and Jess. Y'all are ready to settle down, and I'm not there yet."

"Settle down?"

"I want more than love, Rose."

Rosemary frowned. "You make it sound like it's an either or. I have a career too."

"I know. Being in love is a good thing, but—"

At that particular moment, Jess plopped down on the blanket. "What's up, buttercups?"

"Jess!" they both cried in unison.

Jess laughed and dove in for a group hug.

"You didn't tell me you were coming to the Easter egg hunt!" Rosemary shrieked in Eden's ear.

Laughter burbled up in all three women, and any thoughts of love, career, and hard choices got shelved in favor of enjoying the surprise of them all being together.

"I decided to come at the last minute. Mama needed me to help with Bitsy Timwell's baby shower. I sent my money to be a hostess but then felt guilty because I was going to bail on the shower tomorrow. Then I saw on Facebook that Eden was here, so I drove up this morning."

"Yay," Rosemary said, clapping her hands. "We're all here together. I'm so happy."

Eden grinned. "We haven't been together since I left in January. Lacy would be thrilled to know we all came to the Easter egg hunt."

"She so would," Rosemary agreed, grabbing their hands and giving them a squeeze. "She'd be ecstatic to know Eden is the hottest act in New Orleans! And has a boyfriend."

Jess pushed back her curly hair and studied Eden. "So it's official, huh?"

Eden shrugged, a smile curling her lips even as her heart echoed the dread of what was to come between them. Was Nick her boyfriend? Would they stay that way? Or would NYC be a deal breaker? "I guess so."

For now.

"So have you bought a charm yet? We might actually complete Lacy's bracelet in under a year," Jess said.

Eden shook her head. "I'm not sure I'm at that point. My dream wasn't about a boyfriend."

Rosemary tugged the hem of her shorts and looped her arms around her knees. "But you're famous in New Orleans. And you're in love."

Eden opened her mouth to deny she was in love but then closed it. Maybe she was in love. Maybe she'd fulfilled all that Lacy wanted for her.

"So you've done it, E. Now we have to do the last part," Rosemary continued.

Jess snorted. "Give it to someone with no hope? That's silly. Lacy—"

"—knew something we didn't," Rosemary finished. "You can't attach the charms and not do the last part. We have to finish it."

"I haven't attached a charm," Eden repeated.

"Let's go look at Baker's Jewelers. It's open now." Rosemary pointed at the third-generation jewelry shop that had supplied Morning Glory with silver baby cups, high school graduation rings, and engagement diamonds for more years than they could count on their collective fingers and toes.

"Rose," Jess said, warning in her voice. "If Eden's not ready . . ."

"But we're here together. It's the perfect time. Right, E?"

They both looked at her.

"Do you have the bracelet with you?" Rosemary asked.

"Yeah, I brought it." Eden didn't know why she had, but it felt right. As she packed her overnight bag, she'd tossed the paisley bag inside. It felt wrong to leave it behind in New Orleans, especially since she would be in the place the four girls had found each other.

"Then we can do it," Rosemary said, tugging on Eden's arm.

"Come on. We'll help you."

"Rosemary, stop," Jess said, leveling her best no-nonsense glare at Rosemary. "Eden gets to decide when she's ready. Stop rushing her."

"But I know who we're supposed to give the bracelet to. Just a few nights ago I had a dream about it. When Jess showed up today, I knew it was time. In the dream we were all here in Morning Glory together."

"It was a dream, Rose," Eden said, knowing her friend was a bit too romantic. Not to mention superstitious.

Rosemary shook her head, her gaze serious and weirdly convinced "No. It was a premonition. At first I thought yeah, it's just dream, but then Jess came and you came and . . . I think Lacy's trying to tell us something."

Eden and Jess looked at each other. Eden could see the doubt in Jess's eyes, but she knew Rosemary believed what she'd said. Rosemary was like that. She believed in signs and funny feelings. It was the Scottish roots her father proudly told everyone about.

"So who are we supposed to give the bracelet to?" Jess asked.

Rosemary looked at Eden. "Sunny."

"Sunny?" Rosemary repeated. "My sister?"

Rosemary slowly nodded. "Lacy said we had to give it to someone with no hope. Remember?"

Eden shook her head. "Sunny has . . ." But did her sister have hope? Sunny had closed herself off, but it was understandable. She'd suffered betrayal, grief, and disillusion in her short life. But was she truly without hope? "I don't know, Rosemary. That's—"

"Right," Rosemary finished for her. "In the dream she's sitting by a lake crying and we sit down beside her. She tries to leave, but then Eden puts the bracelet on her arm. I saw it. The sun hit the bracelet. Sunny rips it off and throws it into the lake. I'm not sure why, but it was definitely your sister."

Jess's eyes widened. "That's weird."

Eden glanced at her sister sitting across the square. Sunny's dyed red hair flashed in the sun, and she looked noticeably thin. When Eden pictured Sunny, the perfect golden girl always came to mind. Once upon a time, Sunny'd had a smile that matched the brilliance of her future, but now she was an empty shell of herself. Sunny's future was uncertain and currently she seemed to merely exist. Perhaps Rosemary was right. Maybe Eden's sister was the perfect person to fulfill Lacy's last wish.

But was Eden ready to attach a charm to the bracelet? When Rosemary and Jess had done so, they'd been certain they'd fulfilled their part. Eden wasn't. She'd fallen into a good relationship and found some success in her career. But in a week she'd leave for NYC, and everything she had now could unravel. Was what she had now enough to say she'd lived her dream? Lacy hadn't said anything about a happily-ever-after. Maybe the months of hazy, precious goodness in New Orleans was enough.

Eden redirected her gaze, finding Rosemary's. "All right. Let's find a charm. Maybe Sunny needs that bracelet."

Jess crinkled her eyes. "You think?"

They all looked at Sunny. Eden's sister stood and tugged down her shirt, staring off into some world they couldn't see. Even at this distance, she looked lost.

"Yeah, maybe so. I hope Baker's has something that works. What are you thinking, E?" Jess asked, pushing off the ground.

"Maybe a music note. Or a songbird. Or maybe a dancing slipper?" She turned to Rosemary, who'd already risen. "What was my charm in your dream?"

"I couldn't tell. Just pick what you want."

"Oh good, you're letting me do something." Eden grinned, standing and looking around for Nick. She spied him in the long line at the Lazy Frog. Sassy was busy scooping as her husband Duane ran the register. Eden texted Nick that she had to run an errand and to not let her ice cream melt.

He sent a smiley face emoji back. Sophie had insisted on teaching her father to use them. She'd even made him a Bitmoji that he swore looked nothing like him but sometimes used just to please Sophie. Another reason to love Nick.

"Let's do this," Eden said, pushing away any thoughts of love. After all, she'd have to tell her generous, loving Nick that she was leaving for NYC. He was so supportive, such a good guy, but he'd been abandoned before. Eden knew he harbored resentment against his ex-wife for leaving him. For leaving Sophie.

Would he understand that she had to go to New York?

"Come on, slowpoke," Rosemary called, grabbing Jess's hand. Jess looked back at Eden and rolled her eyes. But they both smiled. Because this was Rosemary. And this was fulfilling Lacy's last wish. For a brief moment Lacy was part of them still . . . in cahoots on another crazy Lacy plan. Who knew? Maybe Lacy had a whole team of angels on her side, already doing her bidding. She probably had a heavenly megaphone, giving orders. *Deliver that crazy dream sequence to Rosemary. Make sure the right charm for Eden is at Baker's. Let's do this. Move. Move. Move.*

The thought made Eden smile as she hurried after her two friends, waving at townspeople who called out to them, teasing them about never being apart, asking questions about Ryan, about school, about when they were going to reprise their Christmas karaoke Supremes number at the Hacienda's Mexican restaurant. Eden wanted to tell them it wasn't going to happen—that the karaoke number had only occurred because they had drank too many Coronas and a too-sick Lacy had begged them to do it. No matter how tangled Eden's gut was over her future, her heart was happy to be with her friends again.

Okay, Lacy. I'm not sure I have my happily-ever-after, but maybe you can help Sunny find something to believe in. Something that will make her smile again.

Because if anyone up there can make things happen, it's you, sister.

Nick lay beside Eden, watching her stare at the ceiling. They'd made love—slow, non-bed-squeaking love—mere minutes before, and even though it had been good, he knew something bothered her.

"What's wrong, E?" he asked, brushing back the wispy bangs that stuck to her forehead.

Her gaze jerked to his as her throat convulsed. Was it his imagination, or was there a sheen of tears in her eyes? "Just some stuff I'm trying to figure out."

"Still regretting I brought you to Morning Glory? Or have you finally gotten tired of me?" he asked, something heavy pressing against his heart at the thought. Something was definitely wrong. She'd seemed okay after the incident with her mother, but after the picnic, she'd been unusually quiet. Not at all like the woman he'd grown to lo—

No. Wait. Not love. Wasn't ready to go there. Yet.

Love was serious business, and nothing so romantic as it was often portrayed—a happy couple strolling through a hazy field of flowers, heads tilted in, smiling lovingly at one another. No, love threw punches. Real love meant ferociously hanging on to commitment when you wanted to choke the person across from you. It was biting one's tongue, pulling on shoes and doing something you'd never thought you would do just because she wanted it. Love was skipping the football game for her best friend's dinner party, dealing with menstrual cramps, and fighting over the credit card bill. And the worst thing about love was the opening up of one's self only to get absolutely, positively destroyed when it didn't work out.

But even after the catastrophe of marriage with Susan, he wouldn't have changed loving his ex-wife. Because on the days it had been good, it was fantastic. On the days it was bad, he had the memories. Not to mention, he'd gotten Sophie in the bargain.

Eden threaded her fingers in his. "I will never regret you. Never."

He gave her a kiss filled with the things he was afraid to say. "But . . . something's wrong."

Her eyes apologized before she said the words. "Fredric called me this afternoon."

Nick didn't speak. Because he knew. Eden had been waiting

for that call her whole life. She'd told him as much when they discussed her going back to school in the fall. She'd mentioned her agent had suggested going to auditions outside New Orleans as a possibility.

"He got me a few auditions in New York City. One's a new show being developed. The other is replacing a cast member. If I want to pursue Broadway, I need to move to New York City."

"Move there? Can't you just go for the auditions and fly back?"

"If I had a big bank account," she said, pushing onto her elbows. "I don't have the money or time to fly back and forth. Often there's not much time between callbacks."

"But what about Gatsby's?" What he'd meant to say was "What about us?" but he clamped down on that thought.

Because even though this was a good opportunity, Eden would be reasonable. She had two jobs in New Orleans. Two good jobs. She'd talked about looking for an apartment in Metairie, one closer to his house with fewer insects and corner prostitutes. He'd been thinking about asking her to move in with him. Most would think it too fast, but Eden fit him and Sophie. She'd be safe with him, and it would save her time and money.

"Fredric negotiated a clause that allows me to break my contract for certain opportunities. He also gave me a list of places hiring waitresses, and he's found me an apartment with a couple of other roommates," Eden said, tucking the sheet tight against her small breasts.

God, he loved her breasts. So small but so perfect with large, dusky nipples. But he couldn't think about how soft and magical her body was at the moment. There was something bigger afoot. And that was no pun. "That sounds . . . less than ideal. You want to live with strangers? Bus tables for tourists?"

Eden pushed her hair back. "No. But Broadway has always been my destination, and this is a chance—even if it's a slim chance—to make it there. I'm getting older, and there won't be many more opportunities like this. In fact, this is probably my only shot."

"So you're going?" Even as he asked, he knew the answer. Hurt pulsed inside him, a Ninja blender pureeing any chance for a future with Eden into glop.

"I have to." Her gaze fastened on the antique dresser sitting next to the old iron bedstead. The light from the streetlamp outside bathed the room in a gloomy blue, but he could see the determination in Eden's eyes. He couldn't stop her.

The thought of love leaving him once again became a hurricane inside him, whirling him around and around, pinning him against desolation. Self-doubt, old hurts and rejection pricked him. *You're not important enough.* Same as Susan. Different verse, same as the first.

Those bitter thoughts drove him to climb out of bed and slide into his pajama pants. Because he couldn't stay there beside her, not when she'd thrown him aside to go wait tables in Times Square. After tugging on the pants, he stood, still feeling naked.

"Nick?" Her voice was soft as a lullaby. "What are you doing?"

"Getting out of bed."

"Why?"

"Because." He couldn't say what he wanted to. He wanted to yell, accuse her of being something she wasn't, wake up everyone in the whole goddamned place so everyone could shoulder his pain. He wanted to throw something . . . or collapse onto the floor like a toddler, surrendering to the anguish.

Because without a doubt, he and Eden were over. Oh, sure, they'd talk about seeing each other every other weekend. They'd vow to chat every night. He'd plan a trip up to NYC. But it wouldn't work. Their worlds would be too different, and eventually they'd trickle down to a used-to-be.

The call from Fredric, as good as it was for her, had put the first nail in the coffin of their relationship.

"Are you mad at me?" she asked.

Furious. He was a wounded beast, dangerous, unthinking.

Yet he knew he couldn't give in to the pain. Because he wasn't an immature asshole. This was Eden's dream. How could he be so selfish as to stand there and ask her to give it up? "I'm . . . thinking. Just surprised."

"I get it. This happening isn't the best timing. You and I are . . ." She waved a hand in the space between them.

"We're fine," he said, finding paper-thin enthusiasm beneath the despair. "When will you leave?"

She leaked out a breath. "I have to be there next week."

"Wow." That sent him reeling. "Next week?"

"Yeah, I know. That's what I've been thinking about. So much to do. Like we have to find someone for Soph. Luckily spring break's next week. Gives us an extra week to find a replacement for me."

"Sophie's my daughter and my concern. Don't worry about her," he said, moving away from Eden. He'd hurt for himself, but the child sleeping next door wouldn't take this well. The thought of telling his daughter that Eden was leaving, right after learning her mother wouldn't make her birthday party next weekend, would be like hand sanitizer in a paper cut. Serious ouchie on the way.

"I want to help," Eden insisted.

"Sure," he said, propping an arm against the window pane. "You tell her you're leaving. I'm tired of disappointing her."

"Nick, I know you're upset. I am too. I didn't know how to tell you, but that's fair. I'll talk to Sophie when we get back to New Orleans."

Nick didn't reply. What could he say besides "Don't go"?

A little voice inside taunted him. *This is why you don't get involved with employees, dumb ass. Back to square one. No nanny. No relationship. Bim. Bap. Bam.*

"Come back to bed," she said.

"In a minute." He stared out the window at the shadows dancing on the lawn. The outline of the gazebo hunched ogre-like against the lawn as the wind played with the treetops. The night matched his mood. Finally he turned. "Why don't you go back to your room? The wind is fierce. Sophie might wake up."

Eden's face wore her emotions. "If that's what you want."

"Might be best." He knew he behaved immaturely, but he couldn't pretend she hadn't dropped something destructive between them. A scratchy ache sat in his throat, telling him he couldn't fake tenderness or enthusiasm. Maybe tomorrow he could pretend happiness. But not tonight.

"Okay," she said, reaching for her billowing nightgown. It covered her from neck to toe, and he'd made a joke about her looking like someone from a Brontë novel. She'd said Rosemary had made them for all the friends as a gift. She now shimmied into it so she didn't have to crawl naked from the bed. She wasn't the only one who felt too vulnerable. After she stood, she came to him, wrapped her arms around his waist, and laid her head against his chest. "I'm so sorry, Nick. I wasn't trying to hurt you."

He looped his arms around her and set his chin atop her head. "I know. I know."

And then she slipped away from him, literally and figuratively.

chapter twenty

TWO MONTHS LATER Eden found herself wiping down a table before seating a family in the Bayou Brewery and Bistro situated in the heart of Times Square. "I hope y'all enjoy your lunch. Ainsley will be your server. Let me know if you need anything."

The mother, who wore capri pants and a fuzzy yellow cardigan said, "Well, darlin,' I can tell you're not from New York City. Where you from?"

Eden smiled because she got this four to five times a day. "Mississippi. Small town near Jackson."

"I knew it," the woman said, settling her girth into the chair. "I'm from Louisiana. Small town outside Lake Charles called DeRidder."

"Oh, I lived in New Orleans for a while," Eden said, hoping her voice wouldn't break. She sort of got weepy every time she thought about Louisiana and the man she'd left behind.

"The best food in the world's down there. Of course, where I live it's not bad either. The whole dang state knows what matters in life—livin,' lovin,' and eatin.'" She laughed and picked up her menu. "Something my thighs can attest to, and something this here man can attest to too."

The older gentleman smiled. "You can cook a mean pot of red beans and rice. I hope y'all can too. I been missing good cooking. We been up here for a week and it feels like a month."

The two teenagers with them tapped on their phones. One rolled her eyes at her father's comment.

Eden smiled. "The food's pretty good. We'll see what you authentic Cajuns think about it when you're done. Y'all enjoy."

Eden headed back to the hostess stand where another party of four waited. Valerie, the other hostess, said, "I got 'em. Take your break."

Finally. She'd been working for almost five hours without a minute to breathe. She headed to the back to clock out for her twenty-minute "lunch" and pulled her phone from the regulation black hostess pants she wore, stepping outside where frantic traffic zipped through the crowded streets. To her right she could see Spider-Man and SpongeBob prowling down the center of 7th Avenue looking for tourists to take pictures with. To her left was the bustle of 6th with rollicking taxicabs and really, really busy people talking on their phones as they hurried to meetings or wherever. It was exhausting and exhilarating at the same time.

And Eden hated it.

She checked her phone, praying for a message from Fredric. Or Nick. Just something better than the spam that popped up or the Facebook notifications that dinged, showing her the world she'd left behind.

The world she'd left behind.

Sighing, she shouldered her way over to the Starbucks in the Marriott Marquis hotel and found a table. It was still busy but not as noisy as out on the street. The barista recognized her with a nod of her head and made Eden her usual hot herbal tea. It was the best Eden could do to soothe her frazzled nerves.

Pulling out her phone, she checked her messages again.

Nothing.

She'd had only two callbacks since she'd arrived a little under two months ago, and they'd netted her a big fat zero. So far she'd spent most her time wiping off sticky menus and juggling the demanding theatre crowd that showed up in force every night. Disappointment gnawed at her. She'd left so much behind only to have little success.

New York City was not what she expected. The image she'd held in her head was much different than the reality of living there. It was big. It was bright. It was busy. And it was somehow very lonely.

Oh, sure. She had two roommates who were perfectly nice if still too busy to try on the bonds of friendship. Katie hailed from Illinois and was a Rockette. When she wasn't practicing, she was performing, sometimes three shows a day. Clair had come to NYC from California and was busy working the New York Resort show which had something to do with fashion. Eden wasn't quite up to date with Fashion Week or anything haute couture, so she had no clue. She hadn't seen either of her two roommates in two days, though there was evidence they'd come home to shower and change clothes. Clair had a boyfriend, some basketball player, and Katie was too tired to date much. Neither one of them ate very much of anything, but they seemed to like Skinnygirl vodka a lot.

Eden hadn't been able to bring any of her furniture with her. She'd put it in storage in New Orleans and had to buy a mattress, chest of drawers, and a microwave when she arrived in Manhattan. She'd nearly swallowed her tongue at the price of the cheapest furniture and had to take one of Aunt Ruby Jean's nerve pills the day the delivery guys showed up and attempted to get it up the narrow stairway. She'd tried to make her postage-stamp bedroom cozy with a pretty floral bedspread and one of Rosemary's coveted quilted pillows, but the apartment still didn't feel like it was hers. She supposed this was what it felt like living in a dorm room at college. Her old roachy New Orleans apartment felt plush compared to the tiny place she shared in

Washington Heights.

That she missed her apartment outside Tremé said all that needed to be said about her frame of mind.

"Excuse me. Would you mind if I borrowed this chair?" a man in a gray business suit asked.

The same words Nick had used those many months ago. Another fracture in her heart. "No. You go ahead," she said, gesturing toward the empty chair.

He dragged it away, no concern for the sadness that leaked out of her.

This was her life now. Just another struggling actress with no one to care whether she had a bad day or not.

Lord, this was the same kind of pity party she'd indulged in when she first got to New Orleans. She'd become the queen of the New York pity party circuit, leaving soggy tissues and long shadows wherever she went. She longed to pack her bags and head south, but her damned pride and Fredric's faith in her wouldn't let her. Eden wasn't a quitter. Wasn't in her DNA, right? She couldn't slink back to Morning Glory or New Orleans with her tail between her legs just because fortune and fame didn't happen right away. This was New York City, not a Vieux Carré dinner theatre. This was her Everest, and she couldn't back down, shivering because her dream perched among the clouds.

Her phone rang, drawing her thoughts back to where she sat. Rosemary.

"Hey," Eden said, finally feeling some warmth.

"Hey, you," Rosemary said. "I've got good news."

"You're pregnant," Eden said.

"No. Why does everyone ask that?" Rosemary sounded exasperated. Her mother Patsy had started the whole nudging-her-daughter-to-have-a-baby thing. And when Patsy Reynolds nudged, it was more like a bashing over the head. "I'm in Manhattan."

"What?" Eden's heart skipped a beat. Rosemary was here?

"We had to come up because Sal's grandmother Sophia had a cardiac episode. It's not as bad as the family thought. She's actually doing okay, thankfully. But we're here until tomorrow evening."

"I forgot Sal's grandmother is named Sophia." A small pang at the thought of her sweet girl Sophie. Eden missed the silliness they made together. She was homesick for snoballs, blowing bubbles in the courtyard, and painting Sophie's fingernails turquoise.

"Yeah. Old Italian name. I think. So you want to get together?"

"Does a bear crap in the woods? Of course I do. I've been dying I'm so lonely. Come see me right now. I'll get you a discount on the jambalaya." Eden squirmed in her chair with sudden happiness. She felt like she'd been given a present with a giant bow. Rosemary was here. Thank God. Someone familiar. Someone who ate chocolate and pasta. Someone who knew her and loved her.

"I can't right now. We're at Sal's mother's house, and if I leave in the middle of them making Italian pastry, I'll move even farther down on her list," Rosemary said with laughter in her voice. Sal's mother, Natalie Genovese, had shoved a good Italian girl (who turned out to be not so good) down his throat. She'd been disappointed when Sal ran off to God only knew where with a girl as country as a turnip but had since come to accept Rosemary, especially when she saw how happy she made her youngest son.

"Okay, when?"

"Tonight? Sal's going to hang with his brothers. I'll take you to SoHo and we'll eat there. When do you get off?"

Eden sighed. "Not soon enough. My shift is over at five o'clock. Give me a couple of hours to go home, shower, and change. Meet at seven o'clock?"

"Sure. At the corner of Broome and Broadway?"

"Perfect." Eden hung up and hugged herself. She didn't care that several people stared and one gentleman moved away from her table. She felt like a new person, and it had been almost two months since she'd felt a smidgeon of joy.

Losing Nick and Sophie had been hard. Much harder than she'd thought.

The week after she told Nick she was going to New York had been busy. At first, she'd thought he was over the funk he'd sunk into when she told him she'd be moving to Manhattan. Traveling from Morning Glory to New Orleans had been fine. Nick had made jokes, avoiding any mention of her leaving, and it had felt normal. Except he'd dropped her off at her apartment and not said anything about her coming over that evening. And when Monday rolled around, he told her he couldn't see her that night because he had to meet with some investors about the seafood restaurant the company wanted to open on the Northshore.

She knew he was hurt. Heck, she was hurting too. She didn't want to actually leave New Orleans, but she couldn't brush away the opportunity of a lifetime. It was the classic story of right man, wrong time. But that didn't mean they had to call it quits. Or at least she didn't think so. She decided to give him another day or two and then she'd show up on his doorstep.

But he'd shown up on hers.

She answered the door, thinking it was Mrs. Gonzales, her next-door neighbor, bringing her another icon to protect her on her journey. The woman had already given her three statues and a rosary . . . along with a bottle of tequila. Eden wasn't sure which she would need most during her last week in New Orleans.

"Nick," Eden breathed, stepping back.

"You shouldn't answer the door without checking who it is first, especially in a neighborhood like this." He wore a pair of worn jeans, a short-sleeved polo, and running shoes. He looked really good aside from the slight circles beneath his eyes and the serious expression on his face.

She gestured for him to enter, wishing he could have seen her place when it was clean and not covered in packing material and empty boxes. It was amazing what a person collected in such a short time. She had twice as much stuff as she'd come to New

Orleans with. "That's true. I thought it was my neighbor. She's the only person who's ever knocked on my door. Come on in."

He stepped in and looked around. "This isn't as bad as I thought."

"It took a little work. Cleaning the carpet and scrubbing the tile helped."

Silence descended. Not the comfortable silence they'd enjoyed many times before but the kind that stretched infinitely. The kind of silence when words were needed but they played hide-and-seek.

"Sorry I couldn't see you last night," he said finally, turning toward her, his face steeled into something she'd never seen before. Of course, she'd seen the expression many times reflected in the mirror. Nick was protecting himself.

"I understand." Though she didn't. Precious hours and minutes had expired.

"Do you?" he asked, plunging his hand into his hair. Like the day she first met him, the pieces stuck up. "Because I don't think you do."

A fist squeezed her heart. She'd been dreading this moment, sensed it would come for her. Nick wasn't a man who bent easily. "Nick, I don't know what to—"

"I know you don't. Part of me understands what you're doing. This is something you've wanted for a long time, and I can't ask you to give it up. That's your decision. It's just . . ." Nick paused and then shook his head. "The thing is, Eden, I love you."

Boom.

"Nick."

"I know. But it's the truth. And I know this isn't fair, but I'm asking you to stay. Stay with me, Eden." His words piled up, each syllable weighing her down. She didn't want him to love her. Because if he loved her, how could she leave? How could she do what had to be done?

Eden slid her hands against her thighs, pressing her

fingernails into her flesh. "Don't, Nick. You can't play that. It's not a game."

His gaze lasered hers. "I'm not saying it to manipulate you. I've wrestled with my emotions—with what was right and wrong to say—for the past two days. In the end, the truth is the best policy, right?"

"Don't do this," Eden said, putting her hand up. "You're not in love with me. That's not something you decide in two days so I don't leave."

"You're telling me how to feel?" His words were dropped coins plinking against cold stone, round with anger, frustration, and something she couldn't quite put her finger on.

"I'm not. You're feeling panicky. It's change once again for you and Sophie, but it's not impossible. Don't mistake love for control." Eden clutched the chipped Formica separating the miniscule kitchen from the teacup living room. She needed something to keep her standing as Nick's words sank down into those deep places she ignored, those places that wept to be loved and needed, those places that nurtured happily-ever-afters coming on a white steed.

"I'm not using my feelings to control you." He sank onto her futon couch and clasped his head. "This isn't about Sophie. I talked to the agency I used in the past and, miracle of miracles, they have one of their most experienced aides coming next week. You don't have to stay Sophie's nanny if you stay. You can go to school. Have your life at Gatsby's. Be with me."

Relief he'd found someone flooded her. She'd been worried about the stress she'd placed on him and Sophie. "I'm glad you found someone. I've been so worried about Soph."

"This isn't about Sophie. It's about what we have. A rightness has been there from the very beginning. You said it. A meant-to-be." Nick lifted his face to her, anguish etched in every new crevice. "Look, I've done heartache before, and my biggest regret is that I wasn't honest. I told Susan what she wanted to hear. I told her to go, that we'd be okay. We'd commute. We'd make it work . . . even as I knew it wouldn't. I never asked her to stay with me."

"I'm not her, Nick."

"I know. I'm just saying I didn't ask for what I wanted." He said it like it should make a difference. Like what he wanted was more important than what Eden wanted.

"But you're asking *me?*" Eden said, something edging out the sadness inside her. Of course he'd make this about him. And that he'd compared her to a woman who left her daughter and tossed aside her vows irked her. Eden had made no vows. "I'm not your wife. In fact, I'm not sure I'm officially your girlfriend. We've been together for a month."

"You know what you are to me. We're heading somewhere, somewhere permanent."

"So you're saying it's your way or . . . you're done with me? I either stay and give you what you want or it won't work?"

"Don't put words in my mouth."

"Okaaaay, so if I go to New York, what?"

"If you go, things will be hard. I don't see how we can make it." He looked resigned.

"Do you even consider me a person?"

"Of course I do. I understand having aspirations, but you're doing well here. Give it a few years and you'll be Chris Owens."

"I don't know who Chris Owens is, but I don't want to be him."

"Her."

Eden felt anger bubble up. What an ass. "Whatever. I'm not asking you to give up anything. I'm not making you choose between love or career. I didn't suggest you leave your home, your job, your family, to take a chance. But you're asking me to do that. You're asking me to give up part of myself so you can be comfortable."

"Wow," he breathed, shaking his head, his expression betraying disbelief. "I'm not discounting your dreams. I'm trying to be honest about me. That's it."

"But you are. Why can't you be happy for me instead of sad

for yourself? My going to New York City doesn't mean I'm abandoning what I feel for you. You're thinking of how this affects you . . . and how inconvenient it would be to not have me in your bed or in your life."

Nick stood up. The tic in his clenched jaw clued her in—no more Mr. Sad Nick. Instead, this was Pissed Nick. "First, I don't value you as a lay, Eden. And I don't have you around because it's convenient. I care about you. I love you. How can a woman hear a man say those words, lay his soul bare, and then fling them back at him?"

Eden jabbed a finger at him. "You know I'm not throwing anything back at you. I'm merely questioning why now? And why do I have to make this choice? Why is this black or white?"

"Because I've done gray, Eden," he said, frustration increasing in his voice. "No matter what anyone says, it doesn't work. You can't go to Manhattan and still have a life with me. I can't come there every other weekend. I have a disabled child and a business. Eventually, it will get too hard and we'll end ugly."

"So in order for me to be with you, I have to forget my dream of being on Broadway? That's the relationship you want to have?"

"No. I'm being honest. It won't work. I'm not telling you what to do. I'm telling you what I know will happen. And, yeah, I'm telling you I want you in my life. But I want you to . . ." He squeezed his eyes shut.

"Pick you," she finished.

He opened his eyes, and within the steely depths she could see the truth. That's what he wanted. He wanted Eden to choose him over what she wanted.

And there was the crux she'd always faced—everyone wanted her to give up herself for what they wanted. Her mother. Her sister. And now Nick.

As much as she cherished the thought that Nick loved her, she wasn't erasing who she was. Going to New York wasn't capricious. It was a goal. And now the dream she'd held on to when times were so hard she couldn't bear to think on them was in her hand. If she crumpled it, she'd never truly belong with Nick. Regret was a seed that grew into bitterness. Eden didn't want that rooted inside her, poisoning the love she had with Nick.

"I can't stay," she said finally, wrapping her arms around herself so she could hold herself together. "I want to be with you, Nick, but not like this. Not as an ultimatum."

"I wasn't trying to make this an ultimatum. I just wanted you to know where I stand, but I can see you're not interested." He walked toward the door.

"That's a lie," she said, anger once again edging out the pain hovering nearby. "You don't even realize what you're asking me to do. It's grossly unfair to lay down this choice. You're not even trying to make this work . . . based on what happened with your ex-wife. I'm not her."

He turned to her, his face so disappointed. "I know you're not. But you're leaving me anyway."

Eden didn't say anything. She watched him put his hand on the doorknob. Watched him turn it. Watched him open the door. Her heart crumbled as he stepped over the threshold onto the flaking balcony.

But she didn't stop him.

Because she couldn't start a future with him by cutting away part of herself.

Before he walked away, he turned and pulled an envelope from his shirt pocket. "Your last check. Don't worry about finishing out. Caro's handling business so I can take Sophie to Disney World. Probably the only thing that will make this easier is Minnie Mouse ears and Cinderella's castle."

Eden swallowed her tears. "I'm sorry."

Then she remembered. Sophie's birthday party on Saturday. Oh God. "My flight leaves Friday night. I have a gift for Sophie. Will you take it to her?"

He didn't say anything. Just waited.

Eden hurried to her room, praying she could keep it together for a few more seconds. A minute at most. Then she could sink down on the now-clean carpet and bawl her eyes out. She retrieved the package wrapped in purple with bright pink stripes and bow. She'd bought Sophie a vintage Mystery Date game. She'd told her stories about her, Lacy, Jess, and Rosemary playing it at their sleepovers, and Sophie had been intrigued by the game. Eden had planned on teaching her how to play, but now . . .

She walked back into the living room where Nick waited. He looked so hard, so resigned. She wanted to throw her arms around him and beg him not to leave it this way between them. Why did she have to choose? Why couldn't she have it all? He was being stupid. Obtuse. Arrogant. And fifty other adjectives she couldn't think of at the moment.

Nick took the gift. "Bye, Eden."

She didn't say goodbye. Instead, she stood there and watched the question appear in his eyes. Would she stop him from walking out of her life?

Eden couldn't.

So she watched him walk away.

And then she left New Orleans without ever having spoken to Nick again.

Eden rose from her table in the Marriott Starbucks and smiled at the woman carrying a briefcase, eyeing her table. Dropping her empty cup into the trash, Eden gave the barista a wave before pushing out into the madness that was Times Square. Then she went to her crappy job much happier than she'd been to leave it. Rosemary meeting her for dinner was almost as good as going home.

Rosemary picked at her halibut and eyed Eden across the table of the SoHo restaurant featured in *The New Yorker* that past weekend. "So you've told me all about this equity and nonequity stuff and about the casting director who propositioned you, but you haven't mentioned Nick at all."

"I don't want to mention Nick. Let's talk about you. When are you going to have a baby?" Eden asked, sipping her watermelon margarita.

Rosemary made a face. "Okay, point made."

Eden laughed. She didn't want to talk about how much her heart ached over Nick. It was bad enough to recount her failures as a nonequity actress whose agent had pulled strings and it still hadn't worked. She needed more experience the casting directors all said. They all said to "Do summer stock. Take some classes. Jackson, Mississippi? Um, where's that exactly?"

"What have you done in the city so far?" Rosemary asked.

"Let's see. I took the ferry over to Staten Island and saw the Statue of Liberty. Took a few walks in Central Park. Went to Top of the Rock. And the M&M's store."

"The M&M's store?"

"I like M&M's," Eden said with a half shrug. The entire time she'd been in the multilevel Times Square tourist trap, she kept imagining how much Sophie would like to make her own mix with the pink, teal, and seafoam candies. She started to send the child some but was afraid they'd melt in the mail. June was already hot. "Tell me about home. Have you seen Sunny?"

"No. She's been keeping a low profile, but she raised a lot for the animal rescue. Now Sunny and her volunteers are looking for property so they can build a kennel."

"Sunny won't stay," Eden said.

Rosemary paused mid-bite. "Maybe she will, and if she doesn't, she'll have left something good in her wake."

"True."

"So what's next for you?" Rosemary waved at the waitress and pointed to her empty water glass.

"Same thing as yesterday. Work. Audition."

Rosemary nodded. "And that's enough?"

Eden stared at the couples sitting at the bar, smiling, drinking, involved in conversations that drew smiles or smoldering looks. "Sure. This is what I've always wanted. It's not easy, but it's the only shot I'm going to get to be more than what I am."

Rosemary didn't respond. Instead she studied Eden, sipping her glass of merlot. Rosemary had grown to love red wine thanks to her husband. In fact, Eden's friend had changed a lot since marrying Sal. Rosemary was more confident, less ruffled when things went wrong, more willing to try new experiences. Maybe it wasn't Sal who had changed Rosemary. Maybe it was coming here. Or selling her pillow line to Trevor Lindley, HGTV designer extraordinaire, who would sell them in his exclusive East and West Coast boutiques.

Finally Rosemary lifted a shoulder. "There was nothing wrong with who you were, E, but I'm glad you're getting this opportunity."

"I never thought it could happen. Maybe Lacy did have something to do with it. She always told me I had to get out of Morning Glory. She believed I could make it here."

Rosemary released a deep breath. "I don't want to speak ill of Lacy because she was my oldest friend, but *Lacy* wanted out. Traveling, leaving Morning Glory, chasing rainbows—that was what *she* wanted. She thought you were as trapped as she was."

"She wasn't trapped."

"Yeah, she was. She came home from college after spending six years there to study for the LSAT, but she never made it into law school. Then she thought she would marry Jonathan, but he dumped her. Then she got cancer and she thought she would beat it, but she didn't." Rosemary swallowed the obvious emotion.

"So she didn't do what she said she would do. Lots of people take detours . . . and lots of people have bad things happen they can't control. But you're wrong about one thing—I was trapped too, Rose," Eden said, wondering where her friend was going with the conversation. "You know how trapped I was."

"Yeah, you were. But then you weren't. You went to New Orleans and you were happy. When I saw you in Morning Glory, after you got over the embarrassment of Betty showing her ass, you looked like a woman in love. Not to mention Jess said she'd never seen you more fulfilled as when you were performing at Gatsby's."

Eden started to see the picture a bit more clearly. Rosemary liked a neatly wrapped happily-ever-after with a fluffy coordinating bow atop. "I *was* happy there, but this is New York City. This is Broadway. You can't turn that down for being a nanny or for dancing with ostrich fans at a Bourbon Street speakeasy."

"Why can't you?"

"Because. Just because," Eden said, her voice rising. She couldn't believe Rosemary questioned what she was doing. So she wasn't happy in Manhattan. Yet. Things would get better. She'd get a gig and she'd get to know Clair and Lauren better. Paying her dues. That's what she was doing. That's what everyone had to do to make it.

"I'm not saying what you're doing is wrong. You're your own woman, and you have to make your own mistakes, but if you're staying here because you think you *have* to, then you need to seriously consider what you *want*." Rosemary imparted the advice easily. Yet there was nothing easy about what she'd said. In one breath, Rosemary questioned everything Eden was . . . or thought she was.

"This *is* what I want." Eden set her fork down and stared at the half-eaten shrimp taco. "I'm doing this for me. It's the career I've always wanted."

And it was. Rosemary's words weren't going to change her determination to make it in this business. Eden would make it on Broadway. Even if it took years.

Years.

Of course, it might take longer. She'd met women in the cattle call auditions—standing in line since four a.m. just to read for a part—who'd been auditioning for ten years without ever being listed in a playbill. The thought of being nearly forty years old without any measureable success sounded depressing. At that age, Eden would almost be out of childbearing years. Not that she was set on having children. Okay, maybe in the fuzzy distant future with a faceless man and a neatly painted white house. Of course now she couldn't even imagine that without that face being Nick's and her house being on the lake in New Orleans.

"Well, you know what you want. I thought maybe you were making yourself do this. Like perhaps you had to do it because you always said you would. Like my dad and the Corvette. You remember?" Rosemary lifted her eyebrows.

Eden narrowed her eyes.

"That's all he talked about, and when Mama finally surprised him with one for his birthday, Lord, he whooped and carried on. Even bought a fedora to wear when he drove it. Had it one month before he told me he secretly hated it. Couldn't swallow his pride and admit he was happier with his old truck. Remember when he 'accidently' ran over a stump with it?"

"Kinda."

"The stubborn man drove that Vette for a year before he figured out how to get rid of it."

"This isn't a Corvette, Rose. It's my life."

"I know. That was just an example. Look, I want you to be happy. When I first saw you this evening—beyond being happy to see me—you seemed . . . kind of sad. But if you're truly good with things, then I won't bug you about your decision. Just don't think you have to do this because people expect it. Dreams change. And that's okay." Rosemary took her hand, gave it a squeeze, and picked up the leather jacket containing the bill. "My treat. Got my first check from Trevor."

"In that case, I'll let you," Eden said, trying not to be defensive. She wanted to yell at Rosemary for putting doubt in her head. She'd clung so long to the notion she'd live in New York and work on Broadway, maybe do a movie if the money or part was right. She'd have things—a car, a nice apartment with a view. She'd date handsome ad execs and have loads of friends with which to spend Saturdays shopping at Barneys and having dinner at the Polo Bar. As a child she'd known it was far-fetched, but a kid had to have dreams, whether it was curing cancer, accepting the Heisman Trophy or becoming president. So how could this opportunity not feel right?

Because you fell in love.

The whispered voice she couldn't silence. Rosemary's words had only allowed the whisper to grow louder. But Eden wasn't a crybaby or a quitter. She'd only been in Manhattan a short time. How could she know anything for sure?

But you do know.

There would be time for love, relationships, and happiness . . . after she did what she'd set out to do. If she didn't give it a go, she'd be disappointed in herself for the rest of her life. How could she go back to New Orleans defeated? What would everyone think about a woman who has her dream within reach but passes it up because she had feelings for the first guy she'd ever been with? That would be stupid.

Or it could lead to . . . happiness.

"Is Sal happy?" Eden asked.

Rosemary looked up. "We're both happy. I never knew it could be like this. I mean, we fight sometimes. I nag him too much and he hates that. But yeah, we're doing exactly what we want to be doing. Nothing's passing either one of us up. Is this about he-who-must-not-be-named?"

"He asked me to stay. He told me he loved me."

"Wow," Rosemary said, her face softening in the low light. "That's heavy stuff."

"Yeah." Eden gave a flashbulb smile to the waiter who took the ticket and stalked away. "I didn't know what to say. It felt like he said it to keep me there. Because I made life easier for him."

Rosemary paused for a moment. "I make life easier for Sal."

"That's not what I meant. I'm talking about Sophie and stuff."

"You think Nick told you he loved you to keep you as his

nanny? That doesn't sound like a man you would fall for, E."

"Who says I fell for him?" Eden snapped a little too quickly.

"No one. And when I said I make life easier for Sal, I meant that I'm there for him. He has someone to go through life with, to support him and love him no matter what. It's not about the material things or even the attributes I bring to the relationship. It's about loving him. By doing that, his life is better, more meaningful . . . easier."

"So I'm supposed to give up what I want?"

Rosemary shook her head and stood. "No, sugar. I didn't suggest you have to give up what makes you happy. I'm suggesting you don't *look* happy."

"Well, I'm definitely not happy now," Eden grumbled, pushing back her chair and standing.

"Hey, I bought you dinner." Rosemary grinned.

"And made me doubt everything I thought I was," Eden said.

Rosemary gave her a soft smile as her eyes filled with a mixture of sympathy and love. "Eden, that's what friends are for."

Nick climbed aboard the Learjet and sank down next to his sister. His parents shared the cost of the plane with a few other businesspeople. Made for travel with fewer restrictions and hassles at short notice. He and Caro were flying to Destin for a few days to consider a partnership with a former chef who wanted to open a restaurant along 30A. With Sophie off at camp and, for once, everything going well at all the restaurants, Nick was pleased to have a few days to stare at the emerald waters and read a Tom Clancy novel.

"You barely made it," Caro said, handing him a fishing magazine.

"Traffic."

"Can I get you a drink, Mr. Zeringue?" a pretty flight attendant asked. She wore a smart navy skirt, white blouse, and a bright smile.

"He'll have the Pappy on the rocks, splash of water," Caro answered for him.

"Any particular year?" the woman whose name tag read Kelsey asked, her eyes dropping to take him in. He'd grown a beard and lost a little weight. He blamed his moroseness and lack of appetite directly on Eden.

"The twelve is fine."

"I'll see what I can do for you," she said as she moved to the back of the plane, disappearing behind a retractable door.

"I bet she will," Caro quipped. "And maybe you should take her up on it. I'm tired of this mopey-recluse thing you've got going on. Like the beard. What's with the beard?"

"I like the beard, and I'm not interested in joining the mile-high club with Kelsey."

"Maybe I'll join the mile-high club with Kelsey. I'm thinking about going gay. It's gotta be easier."

Nick snorted. "I'm thinking it's not easier and not really a choice. But if you think it will work for you . . ."

"Probably not. I don't want to fight over hair spray, tampons, and who ate the last of the Dove chocolate. Better stick to stupid men."

"Yes, stupid men." He'd said it like it was a joke, but the thing was, he *had* been stupid. Like an idiot, he'd tumbled into love with the same kind of woman who'd stomped all over his heart years before—a woman who picked ambition over love. Sure, it had been two and a half months since he walked out Eden's apartment door, but it didn't hurt any less. He really sucked at getting over a broken heart.

"You're all stupid. Easily led by your dicks but really useful when it comes to getting things off a high shelf or killing mice."

He gave her a flat look, took the whiskey glass Kelsey brought him, and opened the saltwater fishing magazine in his lap. He hadn't thought about going fishing, but maybe he would. Dining on fresh fish sounded perfect. Or maybe he'd lie on the beach and exist on beer and potato chips. "I'm actually scared of mice."

Caro smiled as she killed her own drink. "I'm going to take a nap. I'm a heavy sleeper, so if you want to wash the taste of that nanny from your mouth with the hot flight attendant, I won't wake up. Just don't fall in love with her, okay?"

Nick rolled his eyes as his sister pulled out a satin sleep mask. "I'll try."

The pilot came on the speaker, told him about aeronautical things he didn't care about, and then they rolled down the runway. Seconds later, they were in the air heading southeast . . . and Nick was left with that last thought.

Washing the taste of Eden from his mouth.

How could he? She seemed to surround him even now. He'd find a note she'd made about Sophie's doctor's appointment pinned to the corkboard by the garage or discover a barrette she'd left in the bedside drawer. Sometimes he thought he caught her smell on the air. All of it hurt like a bitch. If he'd been able to wash the taste out, it would have been done by now.

She'd taken the gift he'd given her and tossed it out the window . . . all so she could go wait tables, audition for crappy off-Broadway plays, and pursue something that seemed lonely and . . . just wrong for her. Or maybe he thought that because he wanted to be so right for her. Maybe he really didn't know her like he thought he did.

Obviously.

She'd called several times that first week. But he'd not bothered answering the phone. He didn't trust himself not to call her selfish or say he hoped she failed. Very, very immature and douchey of him to feel that way, but he did. He wanted to hurt her the way he was hurting. So he didn't call her back. Then she started texting. Simple texts like wanting to know if Sophie had liked the cake made to look like a stack of her favorite books. Did she like the game Eden had given her? Was Sophie mad at her? How was Disney World? When he didn't respond to those either, she'd stopped texting.

He'd been a jerk, and he didn't know how to undo his

embarrassing snit fit. Okay, he hadn't pitched a fit, but his petulant silence was just as bad. Did it matter if he apologized for taking his toys and staying home? What would it change? Eden would still be in New York, and he'd still be butt-hurt in New Orleans. Saying he was sorry wasn't going to change her mind any more than asking her to stay had stopped her from climbing onto the 747 at Louis Armstrong International and flying away from him.

To tell the truth, maybe he'd never get over her. Eden had fit him so well, and he'd loved being with her. He craved her company, the soft touch of her hands, the way she smiled when Sophie got too excited and tripped over her words. So much about her complemented him, and he'd wondered for weeks after they'd gotten together why it had taken him so long to see it. They would have made beautiful babies together.

His mind put on the brakes.

Babies?

Jesus, he'd jumped there really fast. Eden had essentially said the same thing, reminding him they'd made no promises, had delineated their relationship in no way other than to "be in the moment."

"Still stewing over your nanny?" Caro said with a slurred voice. She lifted the edge of her satin sleeping mask. "I swear I can feel you doing it. I didn't think it was that serious. I mean, I knew you liked her, but you're acting like you did over Susan."

"What?"

"The stewing." Caro pushed the mask up, making her blond hair stick up crazily. "You gotta stop. She was the nanny. I mean, come on, Nick. She wasn't the right woman for you."

"I guess," he said, staring morosely out the window. It was easier not to get Caro started. As an older sister, she was plenty protective and a bit jaded. "Except she was. Eden was the perfect woman for me."

"Come on, baby bro. The nanny?" Caro asked sarcastically.

"What's wrong with being a nanny? It's an honest living, and

Sophie adored her. Besides, she wasn't just a nanny. She was a performer too."

"A performer?" Caro arched a brow.

Nick hadn't stopped Caro from learning he was dating Eden, but he'd not told anyone she was also the glamorous Vixen of the Vieux Carré, Lulu LaRue. Not that his father or mother would even know who Lulu was. But Caro would. She'd mentioned Gatsby's several times and had even suggested meeting him there one evening to see what all the fuss was about. Eden seemed to appreciate not crossing her two lives . . . not that she was living a double life like a secret agent or anything. She wasn't. But Nick had seen no reason to reveal Eden was Lulu. "Eden was Lulu LaRue."

"Wait, what?" Caro dashed the sleep mask from her head and tossed it onto an empty seat. Her golden eyes went wide. "You mean the dancer at Gatsby's? That was your nanny? I don't understand."

"Eden came to New Orleans to go to school in theatre. She enrolled back in the winter but ran into some bad luck money-wise. So she took a second job and dropped out of school for a while. She landed a gig in the ensemble at Gatsby's. When one of the lead people failed to show up or something, she filled in. One time was all it took. They saw how good she was and replaced the other girl with Eden. End of story."

"And you didn't tell me this why?"

"I don't know. We were new. I wasn't ready to go public and neither was she. Doesn't matter now though."

Caro drank the watered-down remains of her whiskey and soda. "That's bizarre. Like seriously bizarre. She was so quiet. Like a rabbit. I don't see it."

Nick managed a smile. "She's an actress. And when she became Lulu, she was incredible. It was like a switch got flipped and she ignited, vibrating with life. Not that she didn't do that every day, but when she wasn't acting, she was more like still water. Deep, full, and calming. That's what she brought to my life. This gravity that pulled me to the center. I can't really explain it. Can you ever really explain how love feels?"

His sister studied him for a moment like she'd never seen him before. Then she started a slow nod before stopping and saying, "No, I don't think you explain it. How could I ever explain why I was head over heels for a skinny bald man with, quite frankly, a slight overbite? Love is like shit. It happens."

For a moment they were both silent, listening to the hum of the engines.

Caro finally looked at him. "Still, that's crazy. You know that, right? It's like some Lindsey Lohan teen movie crazy."

"It was crazy, but it was good. For a while."

"I miss that feeling too," Caro said, squeezing his hand. Normally he would pull away, but this time he let his sister hold his hand.

"Do you miss Stephen?" he asked.

"I miss the feeling of being part of something more."

The plane touched down thirty minutes later, and when Nick turned his phone off airplane mode, he learned he had three messages. All of them urgent.

Sophie was in the hospital, they'd been trying to reach him for an hour, and they finally got in touch with his emergency contact.

Just as he was about to call them back, his phone rang.

It was Eden.

chapter twenty one

EDEN HADN'T BEEN in New Orleans for one hour when the hospital called.

"Hello?" she asked, paying the cab driver, thankful that for once in her life she'd done the smart thing and kept her apartment. It had been expensive, but she'd have lost two months' rent as a penalty for breaking her lease, so she decided to finish out the yearlong contract, subletting it to one of Jordan's friends in September.

"Hi, Ms. Voorhees?"

She waved for the driver to keep the change and rolled her beat-up suitcase with the small travel bag toward the dilapidated courtyard that looked only slightly nicer because the banana plants had grown taller. "Yes?"

"We have Sophie Zeringue here at Southeast Louisiana Regional and you're on her list of emergency contacts."

"Sophie? You have Soph at the hospital? What's wrong? Where's Nick?" Eden's heart dropped to her toes as she froze in place on the dingy sidewalk outside the apartment complex.

"First she's stable. Sophie's having some trouble breathing, and the doctors are running some tests. We tried to reach her father but couldn't get in touch with him. You were one of the contacts on Camp Unique's forms, so we called you," the woman said.

Eden had registered Sophie for Camp Unique four months ago. Situated outside Baton Rouge, the camp catered to children with disabilities. Sophie had been one time before and couldn't wait to go back and stay in the Chickamauga cabin. Go Chicka Chipmunks! But Nick should have been able to be reached. He was vigilant about having his phone on him at all times, if not because of Sophie then because of the restaurants.

"Okay, let me see what I can do. Where is Southeast Regional?"

"In Gonzales."

"Okay, I'll be there," Eden said. "Tell Sophie not to worry."

"Yes, ma'am. And if you could locate her father, that would be good. I left several messages but to no avail."

Eden hung up and hurried up to her apartment, pulling the key from the bottom of her purse. When she opened the door, the place smelled stale but nothing like the first time she'd pushed through the flimsy door. Rolling her suitcase to her room and dropping her purse, she grabbed her phone and dialed the number she'd sworn she wouldn't dial again.

Of course she'd lied when she'd told herself that. Obviously.

Because three days ago, she'd quit her job at Bayou Brewery, called Fredric to tell him she couldn't hack it in NYC, and left Clair and Lauren with a check for next month's rent. Then she hauled her cookies out to JFK and boarded a very expensive flight back to New Orleans. Currently she had no job, a teeny tiny bank balance, and no plan how to get her job or her man back.

But she would.

Because yeah, Eden Voorhees didn't give up easily.

Or maybe she should rephrase her old motto—Eden Voorhees didn't give up when it came to the people she loved.

She'd sorta given up on her dream, but as Rosemary so annoyingly and correctly pointed out, dreams change.

It had started with dinner with her friend. Rosemary's questioning her happiness and her determination to hold fast to her goal of making it on Broadway had stirred doubt in her. Of course, doubt had been there all along, but she'd hidden it beneath bravado, stubbornness, and the resignation because she'd made the choice and had to live with it. After dinner, she'd gone back to an empty apartment, no note about when Clair or Lauren would be home. Outside the apartment, horns honked, people shouted, and the world went about its business. Inside in the tiny apartment in Washington Heights, Eden finally cried.

Giving herself over to emotion wasn't easy for her. After her "loving" stepfather had corrected her once for being a "fucking crybaby," she'd learned to become stoic on the outside while inside she bawled like a lost lamb.

But this time she couldn't hold back the tears. They came like a hurricane, blowing into her, toppling her onto her bed, shaking her with their intensity. For several moments, she cried it out. Then she sat up and wiped the wetness from her cheeks.

What was she doing?

She didn't know.

For so long she'd headed in this direction, convincing herself being on the stage was the only way she could feel alive. She'd been so set on it that she'd stayed on the path even when there were good things worth stopping for. Eden had convinced herself nothing was more important than her dream. Nothing.

Except there were more important things. There were friends, there was community, and there was love. How could any of those three be less important than starving herself in NYC for a chance to play "girl in back row wearing red scarf"?

As a soft summer rain began to fall outside the tenth-floor window, Eden sank onto her twin bed and pulled out the letter Lacy had given her. She no longer had the charm bracelet. She'd bought a small high-heeled shoe, attached it to the bracelet, and given it to a sister who didn't want it. Curling her hand around the letter, she marveled a piece of paper could hold such warmth.

"I don't know what to do, Lacy," Eden said to the darkness.

No one answered back.

Of course not. 'Cause that would have been weird.

So she unfolded the letter, hoping somewhere the words would deliver needed advice. The first two paragraphs were full of things so precious they made her heart squeeze and tears fall faster. Lacy was in fine cheerleader form—encouraging, barking out orders, and overflowing with enthusiasm for what Eden would accomplish in her life. Here in those first two paragraphs were the embers that started the fire, making Eden believe she could set the world ablaze. Then there was the third paragraph, the one Eden often overlooked in favor of the first two.

> *Your life hasn't been easy, E. You know that. I know that. Hell, the whole dang town knows that. But one day things will be good. You'll be happy and have someone to cherish you. Maybe it will be your pool boy – I hope he's really hot too, btw. But someone will love you the way you are meant to be loved. Don't be afraid of that. Or of getting it on with him ;) I'll be watching over you, and I'll make sure that all the good things find you, Eden. I love you. Be happy.*

Eden refolded the letter and pressed it to her heart.

Be happy.

What if the good things Lacy had promised had already been found? What if Eden had been too stubborn to let go of what she thought she wanted? What if everything she'd wanted had slid through her fingers the way Lacy's bracelet had when she handed it to her sister?

She could see the charm bracelet as she'd handed it to Sunny. It was so familiar with the tiny silver cross and the tiara Eden had given Lacy when she won fair queen. The Empire State

Building and flip-flop charm had caught in the light of Sunny's bedroom, reminding Eden that Rosemary and Jess had found their future.

So was Eden bold enough to go get hers?

Could she give up Broadway for Nick, Sophie, and being constantly berated by Frenchie Pi?

She pushed off the bed and grabbed her phone. Fifteen very long minutes and several page refreshes later, she'd procured her ticket back to New Orleans.

Now Eden stood back in the world she'd once belonged in but without a clue as to how she would get Nick to talk to her. He'd ignored her messages and texts. That had bothered her— that he could shut her out of his life so definitively. She'd wondered if he was indeed in love with her or had in fact used those words to keep her here. Deep down she knew he wasn't the sort of man to say those words easily. Nick had been hurt by a woman choosing her career over him before, so she suspected his silence was a form of protection. People did weird things to stop the hurt. Eden had learned that through her mother. Betty's sharp tongue and bitterness deflected the sadness that surrounded her like a cloud of biting gnats.

Eden looked at the phone, then pressed the Call button.

Nick answered on the second ring and the sound of his voice, frantic as it was, made her close her eyes and give an inward sigh.

"Eden," he said.

"Did they call you about Sophie?"

"I just got the voice mail. I called the hospital and asked for the woman who called, but she wasn't available. I left a message."

"I talked to the nurse—I guess it was a nurse. She said Sophie was having trouble breathing and they were doing tests. They couldn't reach you or Caroline."

"Caro's with me. We're in Florida for a meeting and mini-vacation. Did they give you the doctor's name? Any clue what they think it is? I'm trying to get a flight out of here in the next hour."

Eden inhaled. "I'll try to—"

"This is them calling. Thanks, Eden," he said before the line went dead.

"Crap." Eden checked on her list of contacts. She found Derrick's name and called him. No answer, but as soon as she hung up, the phone rang.

"Hey, D. I need your help," Eden said, flipping on the dinged lamp near the futon, allowing watery yellow light to illuminate the dust on the coffee table.

"How's NYC? Get anything yet?"

"I'm not in New York. I'm in New Orleans." She rifled through her purse, looking for her phone charger. "But I don't have time to explain. I have to get to Gonzales. Sophie's in the hospital."

"What's wrong with her?"

"They don't know. But Nick and his sister are out of town, and I don't know who her new nanny is. I need to get there . . . but I sold my car."

"You want me to drive you? It's after five o'clock, sug. I gotta show at nine thirty."

"Derrick, please. You can get back by eight thirty tonight. I don't have anyone else. I don't know anyone else who has a car. Maybe Jordan if she's not working, but . . ." She left off with a sigh, feeling desperate.

"I'll do it, but I'm doing my makeup before I go. You gonna have to deal with Sista Shayla driving you. Not Derrick. Can you meet me at Gatsby's?"

"I'll be there and ready to go in ten minutes as long as Sandra doesn't hold me up outside the door with pictures of her nieces. It's really hard to concentrate on the pics with those tassels hanging from her nipples."

"She do love her nieces." Derrick laughed. "Ain't it funny how we're one big family? We the craziest family, but we family."

"Yeah, we are," Eden said, a sudden hot rush of tears

gathering in her eyes. "I hope Frenchie Pi will let me come back. She was pretty pissed at me."

"Aw, she'll get over it. You brought the big bucks. Besides, she and Sadie have already gotten into it. Frenchie said she's fed up and going to get married and retire to a golf course. Those were her exact words."

"See you soon," Eden said, unzipping her suitcase, finding a clean shirt and something more sturdy than the flip-flops she'd worn through airport security. She'd get to the hospital and stay with Sophie until Nick could get there. The child was likely scared to death being in a hospital all alone.

Hold on, Soph. I may not have been there for you like I should have been, but I'm coming, baby. I'm coming back to you and your daddy.

If he'll have me.

Nick ran through the Southeast Louisiana Regional Medical Center like a man with demons on his heels. He'd finally gotten in touch with someone who told him they thought Sophie had double pneumonia. They'd done a CT scan and were working to get her fever down. Nick had spent much of the flight to Baton Rouge ignoring the suggestion he not use his cell phone so he could call his parents (who were in Houston for a golf tournament), Susan (who was at dinner with a producer or some other shithead), and Sophie's doctor (who was in Bermuda).

His girl was all alone except for some camp counselor who'd stayed with her.

Thank goodness for Camp Unique.

He rounded a corner and nearly knocked over a man on a walker.

"Jeez, slow down," the old man croaked at him.

Nick slowed to a fast walk. "Sorry. My daughter."

"Eh," the old man called, but Nick didn't bother acknowledging him. He had to get to the step-down unit. They'd put Sophie in intensive care at first because of the cerebral palsy, but since they'd managed to lower her fever in the past hour and her vitals were stable, they'd moved her to step-down.

He came to the nurses' station, rushing upon them so quickly one clasped her chest. "Sophie Zeringue?"

A rotund man stood. "You must be the papa."

Nick stood there, panting with his shirttail hanging out. He probably looked like he'd busted out of the psych unit. "I'm her father."

"First, take a deep breath. She's doing good. Fever's down to a manageable state. We have her on strong antibiotics, and she's sipping apple juice. Come with me," he said, heading toward an open doorway adjacent to the nurses' station, squeaking in his plastic clog shoes. Nick stood for a moment and the nurse turned. "You coming?"

Nick followed him.

"Here we are." The man entered one of several small bays that lined the floor. Before Nick could step over the threshold, he heard a man reading *Pinkalicious,* Sophie's favorite book when she was in kindergarten.

When he stepped in and saw who was reading to his daughter, he laughed, partly relieved, partly amused.

Sitting in a chair next to a wan Sophie was a drag queen. And not just any drag queen, but the infamous Sista Shayla replete in sequins, long red fingernails, and glittery red lipstick.

And next to Sista Shayla, aka Derrick, was a sleeping Eden.

Derrick glanced up and said in a soft voice, "Sophie girl, look who's here."

"Daddy," Sophie shouted, holding her arms up to him.

"Hey, baby," he said, pulling her into a hug, noting her hair smelled sour and her words were more slurred than usual. His gut tightened as he squeezed her tight.

"I got sick," Sophie said, moving her legs beneath the thin white sheet.

Eden opened her eyes. "You're here. You have a beard."

"Yeah, and you're here. Why are you . . . Wait, you couldn't have gotten from New York to . . . I don't understand."

"I moved back," she said, rubbing her face and casting a glance at Derrick. "Sorry I fell asleep. You need to go."

Derrick closed the book and set it on the rolling cart next to the hospital bed. "What about you? You want to come back with me now that Sophie's dad is here? I need to leave in"—Derrick looked at the clock hanging above the bed—"ten minutes."

Eden brushed her hair back. "Uh, sure. I mean, Nick's here and Soph's better." She looked at his daughter and gave Sophie the most gorgeous of smiles.

The nurse stood in the doorway, staring at Derrick in his short silver-sequined cocktail dress.

Derrick scowled. "What? You wanna go in the supply closet and see if it's all real or something?"

The male nurse blinked. "Uh, no. Sorry."

Derrick showed his large white veneers. "Good, 'cause I don't swing that way, handsome."

The nurse disappeared. Derrick stood, all six foot three inches of him shimmering beneath the fluorescent lights. "I love being me. Now, I'm gonna step out and give you some time with Soph. Bye, baby girl."

"Bye," Sophie said, craning her head to watch him sashay out the door.

Nick turned to Eden. "What do you mean you've moved back?"

"I moved back. Today." Eden tucked her dark hair behind her ears. She looked tired and like she'd lost some weight. She wore a Gatsby's T-shirt with jeans that sagged a bit too much and tennis shoes that had seen better days. In other words, she looked fantastic . . . if only because she was there.

"Today?" he repeated, smoothing Sophie's hair down and adjusting the tie on the back of her gown. "Why?"

"Because," she said.

He waited for her to say more, but she didn't. She just sat there looking . . . uncertain.

"What kind of answer is that?"

Eden spread her hands. "The only one I have right now. I mean, there are reasons I left New York City. I guess the best one is because I wanted to."

"Soph, I know I just got here, baby, but I need to talk to Eden alone. Is that okay?"

"Mm-hmm," Sophie said, her blue eyes somewhat more vacant than normal. The fever worried him, but she seemed better than he'd expected.

Eden wiped her hands on her jeans. "Where?"

"We'll find a place close by," he said, walking out of the room.

The nurse who had scurried away from Derrick and now sat in a chair across from the station lifted his brows.

"We're walking down the hall for a moment." Nick didn't know how to feel. He was caught between worried as hell and joyous as hell. Sophie was okay. Eden was back in New Orleans.

Why hadn't she told him?

They came to a small alcove containing a few chairs, a prayer box, and a picture of a sunrise over a bayou. Nick sank down, not trusting his legs much longer. He felt the same way as when he'd run a marathon. Sort of exhausted and euphoric. "Why didn't you call me?"

"I did."

"No, not over Sophie. When you came back."

"I flew into New Orleans at three this afternoon. The cab had just pulled up to the apartment when the hospital called. I phoned you and came here."

"Which you also didn't let me know." He knew he sounded like her mother. Or rather not like her mother. Like *his* mother.

"You hung up before I could," she said, sinking down next to him.

Her wildflower scent wafted to his nose. Nick wanted to touch her. He wanted to turn her over his lap and spank her ass for hurting him . . . and not telling him she was coming home.

Coming home.

Was that what this was . . . and why was he giving her such a hard time?

"And I didn't text you because I was in such a hurry I left my phone on the charger in my apartment. I just came. Sophie needed me . . . or someone. You know?" She stared at the wall.

There were scuffs left from gurneys being pushed by. Her small face was so serious . . . so anxious. She hadn't been prepared to see him. Or maybe she'd not wanted to see him at all. He'd behaved badly.

"Thank you for coming," he said.

"Of course." She still didn't look at him. Silence stretched, a long shadow between them.

"Why'd you really come back, Eden?" His words fell like drips from a rusted faucet.

"Because I . . . I figured out dreams sometimes change," she said, chewing her lower lip before hitting him with her gaze. In the blue depths shimmered apology . . . regret . . . yearning. And hope.

This was the moment he'd imagined those dark nights when regret shook him with snaggled teeth. He'd fucked up. Made an irrational demand. Walked out the door.

He'd thrown away loving Eden.

But now maybe he'd get a second chance to undo what he'd done.

"Broadway was your dream."

"I thought so," she said, studying her hands, chewing her lip again as if she tried to figure out how to say what needed to be said. "Maybe it wasn't. I wasn't happy there."

His heart leaped. "But you're happy here?"

Eden nodded. "I am."

"But you left. You were done with New Orleans. Done with me."

She made a face. "No. You made me be done with you. What

could I say? You shut me out."

Point made. He'd done exactly that, refusing to give her an opportunity to change things. He'd taken away any chance to make something work between them with his insecurity. "That's fair. I avoided some things."

"I texted you twelve times. That's avoiding a lot of things."

He *had* avoided a lot of things. "I admit I was hurt. I didn't answer because I was afraid of the things I'd say. And then when I realized what an ass I had been, my pride got in the way. You know men and their stupid pride."

"That's an excuse. Saying that's just what men do doesn't pardon you from hurting people," Eden said, a little more heat in her voice. "I was in NYC by myself, trying to do something really big . . . and not having you to talk to was hard. I needed you."

"You're right. I'm sorry. I thought if I shut you out, it would be easier. But that didn't work. Obviously." He studied his hands, waiting for her to respond.

"How's that obvious?"

He lifted his gaze to hers. Couldn't she see how much he wanted her? How much he loved her? How scared he was she'd tell him he couldn't undo what he'd done? "Can't you see?"

Eden studied him. "Maybe I should explain why I came back."

He stilled and waited.

"You know enough about my past in Morning Glory to know life hasn't been a cake walk for me. My family was poor . . . *is* poor. You've met my charming mother, but thing is, she doesn't even know who my father is. I worked at Penny Pinchers as a manager for ten years, and my only salvation outside of my friends was doing theatre and teaching dance. When I'm on stage, I'm comfortable, alive, and meaningful. The way the audience responds gives me validation. When the nights were bad, and they were, I would hold fast to the thought that one day the gift God gave me would change my life. So when Fredric called and handed me this opportunity, I had to go."

"I know. I was there," he said, unable to keep the pain from his voice.

Her head snapped up. "Don't make this about you. Hear me out."

Suitably smacked down, Nick nodded.

"I had to go because this was the path I'd set for myself. In my mind, it was the solution to all my problems. So though I loved you and Sophie, I wouldn't let myself think of staying. I couldn't."

She said she loved him. Hope unfurled inside him, but he gathered it close, unable to give it free rein inside him. He needed to listen to her. Not make what happened about himself.

"My first week in New York was okay. I was too busy moving in, finalizing things here, and prepping for auditions. I filled my days with learning my way around, getting to know my seldom-there roommates and working at the restaurant until my feet ached. At night I fell asleep before my head hit the pillow. But once I settled in, loneliness and pain were my true companions. I missed you, and you wouldn't call or text me back. Nothing was how it was supposed to be."

He understood that feeling. When he'd first gone to college at LSU, his plans for all-night beer busts and hot chicks gave way to being confused about his major and missing his bedroom at home. But he'd not been alone. He'd had friends, and his parents were an hour away. Eden had been alone. "If you hadn't gone, it would have always been a regret. You had to experience it."

"Yeah, I did. It was a life I wanted . . . for a long time. I went to tons of auditions, and instead of feeling like that was what I should be doing, I started to doubt myself. I forced myself to be cheerful and feel encouraged, but it didn't work. When Rosemary came to town, she asked me if I was happy." Eden gave a wry smile. "And I wasn't. Not that I was going to admit to being lonely, sad, and full of regret. She implied I was making myself stay in New York City because I was too stubborn to admit I had been wrong."

"I understand that too. I just regret not being happy you had that opportunity. I didn't support your dream. Instead, I thought only of myself, about how much it hurt to have you choose your career over me."

"I didn't have to choose."

"I was wrong. If I had supported you, it might have made a difference. You might have stayed if I had put your dreams ahead of my own crippling fears."

Eden tucked her hair back and issued a sigh. "Maybe so, but the thing is, I was fulfilled here. I loved working at Gatsby's because I was part of something good there. I wasn't making tons of money, but for the first time in my life, I was making it on my own. Then there was Sophie. Honestly, at first I didn't want to take care of her. I had spent too many years caring for my mother, and she was a cranky, bitter thing, but as I grew to love Sophie, I realized caring for someone like her wasn't a chore. I got to live her small triumphs. I had purpose."

Her words bathed him in warmth. He loved her even more for loving his girl.

"Then there was you," she said with another sigh.

The exasperation in her voice made him smile. "The sand in your gears?"

She laughed. "You were. You are. You were my boss and totally out of my league."

"I'm not out of your league, Eden."

"We had nothing in common, and our worlds were so far apart we needed binoculars to see each other. Still, I couldn't help myself."

"Against better judgment, we were meant to be." He reached over and took her hand. She curled hers around his, and though her hand was small, it fit him. His Eden. Such a fighter. She was like that Corelle his grandmother used to serve him pancakes on at the camp. Looked delicate but bounced when you dropped it. "I took an unwritten vow to never mess around with anyone who worked for me, but you came along. Meant to be."

"That's what Sister Regina Marie called it."

"Nuns must know."

Eden finally smiled, then sobered when she looked up at him. "So now what?"

"What do you want, Eden?" he asked, wishing he'd asked her that in the first place. If he'd asked her what she wanted instead of asking her to choose between him and her dreams, he would have saved them both a lot of time and heartache.

"I want you," she said, squeezing his hand. "If you're still . . . I mean, if you still . . . want me."

He didn't think. Instead, he did what he'd wanted to do ever since he laid eyes on her sleeping beside his daughter's bed. He kissed her.

Eden's mouth softened and she kissed him back, putting her other hand over his and pulling herself to him. He'd had a lot of kisses in his life, had shared many with Eden, but he'd never experienced one as sweet and wonderful as this one. In the kiss there was sorrow, joy and promise. It said "I'm sorry" and "This is worth everything." In essence, kissing Eden in the hospital alcove became the most monumental kiss of his life. In that exact moment, his future started.

Breaking the kiss, he stared into her blue eyes, remembering the despair in them the first time he saw her. There was no despair today.

"I don't have a job," Eden said with a whisper of a smile.

"You don't need a job," he said, meaning it. He wasn't letting her go back to that shitty apartment in a suspect part of town.

"I do. But I also want to go to school this time. Hopefully Fredric will get me back in with Gatsby's. He said Frenchie Pi likes to play hard to get but always gives it up in the end. His words, not mine," she said, rising. "I'll be there for Sophie, but I don't think I can be her nanny."

"You don't have to be her nanny. The one we have now is good. You'll like her."

"Good. Don't worry. I'll do the things girlfriends do with

their guy's kids. I'll take her for pedicures and watch goofy movies with her. I'll help her with her homework and listen to her talk about boys."

"Boys?" he repeated, making a face. Then he asked the question he'd wanted to know all along. "So you said girlfriend. Is that all you want to be?"

Eden's mouth twitched. "For now. But I'm not opposed to a more permanent arrangement in the future. Uh, if that's where we're headed."

Nick gathered her against him, wrapping her tight. "I love you more than I thought possible, Eden. I love you to the moon and back as trite as that sounds. I love you more than dutch double chocolate ice cream. More than LSU football. More than Christmas, Halloween, and Easter combined. I love you more than my life."

"That's sounds promising. More than promising. Damn good." Eden lifted onto her toes and kissed him. "Now, I got a drag queen who needs to get to his gig in less than two hours, and you have a daughter who needs some daddy time."

"I want you with me. Don't leave me, Eden. Uh, I mean unless you want to."

"I'll stay with you and Soph," she said, linking her hand in his and walking toward the room where his daughter lay sleeping.

Derrick looked up from a magazine and grinned. "Well, well, look at y'all. I'm guessing this means Lulu ain't catching a ride back with me?"

Eden looked up at Nick with eyes so full of love, and his heart grew ten sizes. He'd finally found the woman who would stand beside him. And he would stand beside her . . . no matter where her career took her in the future.

Grinning at Derrick, Eden said, "Wild drag queens couldn't drag me away."

"Well, not in these shoes, darling," Derrick said, waggling a size-thirteen silver-spangled pump. "Can't get no traction in these puppies. Ciao, dah-lings."

"Thank you, Derrick," Eden said. "I owe you."

Nick and Eden stood in the threshold of Sophie's curtained room, listening to Derrick flirt with the nurses, their laughter so right because joy had triumphed today.

"Edie, are you staying?" Sophie managed to say sleepily.

"Yeah, baby, I'm staying. For good this time."

Sophie smiled as she fell back into sleep.

Eden looped her arms around his waist and laid her head against his chest. "I can hear your heart beating. It's saying E-den, E-den."

And a heart never lies . . .

chapter twenty two

three months later

"WAIT A SEC, I have something for you girls," Rosemary said, rising from the new sofa in Eden's apartment and hurrying back to Eden's bedroom.

Eden grabbed the half-filled bottle of white zinfandel from the coffee table and refilled her glass. She'd taken some of the bonus her agent had negotiated with Gatsby's and bought a few nicer pieces of furniture for her apartment. Nick had insisted she move to a safer location, like his house, but Eden liked her apartment and wasn't ready to take such a big step yet. So she'd put a fresh coat of paint on the walls of her bedroom and repaired the chipped Formica in the kitchen. Last week, she'd rallied the neighbors and started a petition to present to the owner of the complex for needed repairs.

Jess took the bottle from her hand and refilled her own glass. "God save us from Rosemary's gifts. I just hope whatever it is, it's not monogrammed. Ryan always teases me about how Southern girls need to have their name on everything. He asked when I was monogramming him."

Eden laughed. "I think that's called a tattoo."

"Here we go," Rosemary trilled, hurrying back into the living room. "Since we have dinner reservations at one of your boyfriend's primo dining establishments, I wanted us to have something fancy to wear." She handed both Jess and Eden a small wrapped box.

"You're always doing this sort of thing, Rose. It's too much." Eden studied the orange polka-dotted paper covering the small box. It looked just like the paper that had covered the box Lacy had left them after she'd died. After the funeral, Sassy had brought the wrapped box from behind the counter of the Lazy Frog and placed it on their table. Inside had been the personalized letters, the charm bracelet, and the challenge that had led all three girls to new lives . . . and new loves.

"I like to buy things for the people I love," Rosemary said as she plopped back onto the small linen-covered chair and curled her feet beneath her. "Go ahead and open them."

"This is the paper Lacy wrapped our present in," Jess said, still holding the gift.

"I know. I went by her parents' house and asked if they still had it. They did."

"Why?" Eden asked.

Rosemary gave a half smile, her gaze growing misty. "It's been over a year since Lacy died. Our lives are so different. I'm married and living in Morning Glory, thinking about babies, and doing this whole pillow thing. And Jess is living at the beach with Hunk of the Month. And now Eden is not only living her dream on the stage, but she's found someone who adores her as she should be. Everything Lacy wanted for us has happened. In fact, more than what she wanted for us has happened. I guess I just wanted to conclude her business here with a gesture."

"But it's not done," Eden said, thrusting her pinky into the orange ribbon atop the gift and twisting. She'd been lucky that Frenchie had been fed up with Sadie's antics and wanted Eden back. Not that the diminutive Asian woman would admit she needed anyone. Everyone at Gatsby's, outside of Sadie, had been thrilled Eden had decided to return. And even Sadie was coming around to the thought of sharing the stage with her little sister. "Or at least the last part isn't done."

Rosemary smiled. "Soon it will be. I've made sure of that."

"What have you done?" Jess asked.

"Nothing." Rosemary pressed her lips together and shifted her gaze between them. They would get nothing more from their friend. Rosemary could be a pushover, but when she got that secretive look, good luck getting her to reveal anything.

Eden's heart squeezed when she thought about her older sister. Sunny had been so unhappy, but the last time Eden had seen her, her sister had been focused on something else besides her tragic loss and empty future. Raising funds for a pet rescue had brought purpose to Sunny. Not to mention, Henry Todd Delmar seemed to have a new focus himself. Maybe, just maybe, Lacy was at work and would bring Eden's sister the same kind of hope Eden now had. Eden didn't believe in all that woo-woo stuff, but she couldn't deny Rosemary's earlier words. All three of them *had* found happiness.

Maybe that charm bracelet was . . . charmed.

"She's not going to tell us anything," Jess said to Eden before ripping open the paper.

Eden followed Jess's lead, tearing at the paper and crumpling it into a ball. She ran her finger under the lid of the box, breaking the tape, and pulled the top off. Inside, nestled on a square of Poly-Fil, was a pearl bracelet with a small silver flower charm.

Eden looked up. "A morning glory?"

Rosemary grinned. "Well, we had to give Lacy's bracelet away, so I thought I would replace it."

"Pearls, of course," Jess said with a laugh.

"Of course, dahlings." Rosemary pulled her own matching bracelet from the pocket of her pants. "We don't live close anymore, but I thought having a reminder of who we are would be . . . cool."

"It's beautiful," Eden said, opening the clasp and fastening the bracelet. The small silver flower dangled at her wrist.

"Well, we *are* the girls of Morning Glory no matter where we live, right?" Jess asked, holding her hand aloft and smiling softly at her bracelet.

"Damn right we are," Rosemary said.

Tears glossed Eden's eyes, but she blinked them away because she didn't want to get maudlin when they had reservations at Du Parrain in twenty minutes. Nick was meeting them at the restaurant to celebrate the deal he'd brokered for a new version of Du Parrain outside Jackson . . . and the fact Eden's best friends had come to spend the weekend with her. "Is everyone ready?"

Jess looked at her bare feet. "Let me grab my new booties."

"I got the cutest ones from Nordstrom last week," Rosemary said, pulling Jess up from the couch but not before Jess could down her wine. It felt the way it should when they were together. Comfortable. Like home.

"Nick's sending the car." Eden glanced at the time on her cell phone. "Hurry."

Jess disappeared and came back holding a seriously cute pair of shoes. "I'm ready."

Minutes later, the three women stepped out onto the still-shabby balcony and into the dying New Orleans evening. Gold light fell against the worn building next to the apartment complex, and the still-green banana plants swayed in a faint breeze that smelled of the river.

A somewhat intoxicating and slightly nauseous scent that was New Orleans settled around them as Rosemary linked her fingers through Eden's. "Happy now, Eden?"

Eden squeezed Rosemary's hand and lifted Jess's in her other. "Supremely happy."

"Lacy did good, didn't she?" Jess said, staring out into the courtyard, which had taken on a magical softness.

"She did," Rosemary agreed.

At that moment a gust of wind blew past them and made the

bamboo wind chimes someone had hung in the scraggly tree on the edge of the aged brick walkway clink merrily. The chimes were only a few feet away, close enough to reach out and touch.

Eden laughed. "Of course."

The three of them exchanged bemused looks.

"She always liked having the last word," Jess said.

Rosemary gave a light laugh. "Let her have it. She gave us each other, and she gave us love. Lacy gets the last word."

As they turned and made their way down the wrought iron steps, the bamboo chimes clanked again, a reminder that love did indeed win . . . at least for the girls of Morning Glory.

want more?

To find more information on Liz Talley and the Morning Glory series, visit www.bit.ly/LizTalleyAmazon. Also, don't forget to visit her website to sign up for the newsletter at www.liztalleybooks.com, and as always, reviews of the book are much appreciated.

Other books in the series:
Charmingly Yours
Perfectly Charming
Prince Not Quite Charming
All That Charm
Third Time's the Charm (coming 2018)
A Charming Little Christmas (coming late 2017)

about the author

A finalist in both RWA's prestigious Golden Heart and RITA contests, **Liz Talley** loves staying home in her jammies and writing emotional contemporary romance. Her first book starred a spinster librarian – *Vegas Two Step* – and debuted in June 2010. Since that time, Liz has published twenty-one books with Harlequin, Berkeley and Montlake, reaching number one in kindle romance with her latest series. Her stories are set in the South where the tea is sweet, the summers are hot, and the men are hotter. Liz lives in Louisiana with her childhood sweetheart, two handsome children, three dogs and a temperamental kitty. You can visit Liz at www.liztalleybooks.com or follow her on twitter or Facebook to learn more about her upcoming books.

Made in the USA
Coppell, TX
15 March 2021